D0524003

We're Tickled Pink. We want to ensure all breast cancer is diagnosed early and help improve people's many different experiences of the disease.

Working with our charity partners, **Breast Cancer Now** and **CoppaFeel!,** we're on a mission to make checking your boobs, pecs and chests, whoever you are, as normal as your Asda shop. And with your help, we're raising funds for new treatments, vital education and life-changing support, for anyone who needs it.

Together, we're putting breast cancer awareness on everyone's list.

55p from the sale of this product will be donated to Breast Cancer Now (Reg. Charity Nos. 1160558 & SC045584). **24p from the sale of this product will be donated to CoppaFeel!** (Reg. Charity Nos. 1132366 & SC045970).

Breast Cancer is the most common cancer in women in the UK, with one in seven women facing it in their lifetime. Around 55,000 women and 370 men are diagnosed with breast cancer every year in the UK and nearly 1,000 people still lose their life to the disease each month. This is one person every 45 minutes, and this is why your support and the support from Asda Tickled Pink is so important.

TOUCH, LOOK, KNOW YOUR NORMAL, REPEAT REGULARLY

Make sure you stay breast aware

- Get to know what's normal for you
- Look and feel to notice any unusual changes early
- Check your boobs regularly and see a GP if you notice a change
- Checking your boobs, pecs or chest could help save your life

To find out more about the Asda Tickled Pink partnership visit www.asda.com/tickled-pink

Readers have fallen for the Cornish Girls

'A fascinating story, beautifully written, with interesting characters I really liked. A most enjoyable read!'
Kitty Neale

'A warm-hearted story – at times I laughed and at others I held my breath'
Pam Weaver

'Much loved characters that will stay with you, due to their courage, determination and patriotic spirit'
***** **Reader Review**

'Beautifully written and totally draws you in from the beginning'
***** **Reader Review**

'A poignant and all-round heart-warming saga'
***** **Reader Review**

'Truly beautiful historical fiction. What a wonderful cast of characters to meet!'
***** **Reader Review**

Betty Walker lives in Cornwall with her large family, where she enjoys gardening and coastal walks. She loves discovering curious historical facts, and devotes much time to investigating her family tree. She also writes bestselling contemporary thrillers as Jane Holland.

A Mother's Hope for the Cornish Girls is the fourth novel in Betty Walker's heart-warming series.

The Cornish Girls series:

BETTY WALKER

A Mother's Hope
FOR THE
Cornish
Girls

avon.

Published by AVON
A division of HarperCollins*Publishers* Ltd
1 London Bridge Street
London SE1 9GF

www.harpercollins.co.uk

HarperCollins*Publishers*
Macken House
39/40 Mayor Street Upper
Dublin 1
D01 C9W8
Ireland

A Paperback Original 2023

1

First published in Great Britain by HarperCollins*Publishers* 2023

ISBN: 978-0-00-852517-0

Typeset in Minion Pro by Palimpsest Book Production Limited,
Falkirk, Stirlingshire

Printed and Bound in the UK using 100% Renewable Electricity
at CPI Group (UK) Ltd

In loving memory of my mother, Sheila Ann Mary

CHAPTER ONE

Symmonds Hall, St Ives, Cornwall, January 1943

Sonya stared at her old friend, her heart thudding erratically, sure the whole world was about to crumble to dust beneath her feet.

Summoned by the bell, she had come toiling up the steep stairs to Lady Symmonds' top-floor rooms, in the stately but ramshackle apartments next door to the orphanage, the windows overlooking green fields and the wild blue expanse of Carbis Bay, St Ives. She had half expected to be sent on some errand of mercy for one of the orphans or maybe asked for her help with an embroidery project, since needlework was her forte.

Instead, she had been told, after nearly twenty-five years as Babs' live-in companion, that she was surplus to requirements.

'Donald has asked me to marry him, and I've accepted,' Lady Symmonds had told her, clearly bursting with excitement. 'He wants us to live together in Scotland, which isn't exactly how I'd planned to see out my twilight years. But I've agreed to give it a try.'

Sonya had not known what to say.

'He has a fine old castle on the shores of a loch,' Babs had continued merrily. 'Well, you know, I showed you the photographs. Oh, I can't wait to see it again. It must be years since I was there with my dear Christopher. How much fun we all had together.' She was referring to her late husband, who had passed away many years before but whose large, silver-framed photograph still took pride of place on the mantelpiece.

Sonya put a hand to her mouth, struggling not to let her distress show. Truly, she was happy for her long-term friend and employer. But what would all this mean for her?

Everything was about to change and she didn't have a clue what lay ahead or how to order her bewildered thoughts. She groped for the correct response, for words of congratulations, but all that came into her head sounded idiotic and empty.

Meanwhile, Lady Barbara Symmonds was waiting for a response, staring at her with bright, twinkling eyes that seemed at least fifty years younger than her wrinkled skin and long, silver tresses of hair. 'Well?' she asked, a touch impatiently. 'What do you think, Sonya? Aren't you going to wish me happy?'

'Congratulations, I hope you'll be very happy indeed,' Sonya blurted out, her voice unsteady, wishing she could be alone so she could sob her heart out.

Babs looked into her eyes and then dropped the old lace gown she'd been examining for rips. She hurried forward, pressing Sonya's hands between her own cooler fingers. 'Oh, my dear, please don't look so scared. I wouldn't be so cruel as to drag you all the way to Scotland, not with your unfortunate tendency to catch cold in the winter months. Besides, you'd be very much in the way if you came with us.' She gave the infectious laugh that always turned heads. 'I shall miss you terribly, but a honeymoon would be a bit crowded with three people.'

'Of-of course,' Sonya stammered, shaking her head, 'I didn't mean—'

'I hope you'll stay here and hold the fort for me. If you'd like to, that is.' Babs shot her a sympathetic look. 'I'll need someone to keep an eye on the orphanage and the convalescent home, and I shall expect regular reports so I'm not behind on any of the gossip.'

She paused, and Sonya knew Babs was tacitly saying she wasn't to be cast out into the streets now that marriage had rendered her position as companion redundant.

'His castle is very grand, you know. It's near Loch Ness,' her ladyship added, changing the subject, 'and Queen Victoria stayed there once in his grandfather's day. How could I say no?'

'It does sound romantic,' Sonya admitted, choosing her words with care.

Babs peered into her face again and then nodded slowly. 'I see what it is. You're concerned I can't trust him. That he's after my money.'

'It is rather sudden.'

'But I've known Donald forever, darling. He was a pal of Christopher's for donkeys' years. There's nobody I trust more.'

Lady Symmonds had often mentioned Donald with a

twinkle in her eye – the dashing Scottish gentleman with a grand baronial castle built above a loch, the waters wreathed in mist in the early mornings. He had even dropped into Symmonds Hall once or twice on flying visits before, whisking her ladyship out for dinner or a trip to the theatre. But in December, he had made a lengthy stay with them, remaining through Christmas into the New Year, and Sonya had watched in surprise as Babs and Donald had grown closer and closer…

'He and Christopher served together in the Navy.' Babs was reminiscing again, gazing away into a distant past. 'And while Donald's wife Judith was still alive, we often took our holidays together, just the four of us. We were quite wild at times. But people often were, you know, in the last years of the century. Everyone complains about how stuffy Victorians were, but in fact, us younger ones could be quite wicked at times. Rebelling against our elders, you know…' She drew a long breath. 'To be honest, my dearest Sonya, I don't want to end my days alone.'

'But you're not alone,' Sonya pointed out. 'You've got me.'

'I know, my darling,' Babs exclaimed, hugging her impulsively. 'And you've been a good and faithful companion to me these past two decades. We've had some marvellous times together. But a friend isn't the same as a husband, and I've been a widow for too long.' She gave her a wistful look. 'Donald and I are planning a spring wedding and I hope you'll be my maid of honour.'

'Oh, of course.' Sonya blinked, still bewildered by the speed of events. 'But to marry so suddenly and leave everything behind like this… I can't help but worry.'

'Christopher trusted Donald implicitly, and so do I. Please don't fret for me. I couldn't wish for a lovelier, more caring husband. And as long as Scotland isn't too damp for my old bones...' Babs laughed, shrugging. 'Donald and I are both in our seventies. We don't have much time left to waste. And it does feel as though he and I have been *waiting* for each other all these years.' Her ladyship smiled, dimpling. 'Frankly, I believe our love is a reward for a life well lived.'

Gently, Sonya reached for her friend's hands, her heart filling with emotion. 'Then I wish you both a very happy life together,' she whispered, and fumbled up her sleeve for a hanky as the tears began to flow. 'And I'd be delighted to be your maid of honour. Thank you.'

She meant it too. Lovely Babs deserved as much happiness as she could get. Always a generous local benefactor, Lady Barbara had donated part of her estate and personal fortune decades ago to care for orphans from St Ives and the surrounding areas. Having subsequently lost her husband, son and beloved grandson too, she had nonetheless rallied to the war effort, bravely volunteering her home as a military convalescent home and retiring to the modest apartment she and Sonya had shared ever since. Now her ladyship had a chance of a happier future. Why should she not take it?

The path ahead for Sonya looked bleak and uncertain, though. She had been Babs' live-in companion for what felt like forever and had no idea how she would face each day without her friend and employer.

Whatever was she going to do?

* * *

That afternoon, since Donald had taken Lady Symmonds out for a drive in his swish Bentley, Sonya wrapped up well against the elements and walked across the cliffs above St Ives. Although a pleasant place in summer, in January the sea winds whipped across Carbis Bay, cutting to the bone, and spray blew white across the coarse grasses while a few hardy seabirds screamed and wheeled overhead.

Brooding over the changes ahead, she stared down at the wintry sea as it lashed the rocks below and tried to imagine life once Lady Symmonds had married her beloved Donald and disappeared off to Scotland. At the moment, her day was mostly taken up with running around after Babs: fetching and serving meals, tidying the large apartments, helping with embroidery and crochet projects, heading out with her employer to visit members of the small, close-knit community in St Ives, and listening to the wireless with her before bedtime. For over two decades now, since coming to Babs in her late teenage years, her life had revolved around whatever her ladyship wanted or needed. Soon she would be alone and need something to fill the long, empty hours.

At least Lady Symmonds had not instructed her to move out of the apartment once she'd gone to Scotland. That would have been too awful, forced by a lack of income to move back to her elderly parents' home near Truro. She and her mother and father had never seen eye-to-eye, not since her fateful mistake as a very young and inexperienced woman…

Sonya pushed that memory away with an inner shudder. This was a time to look ahead to the future, not dwell on past errors.

She was already volunteering at the orphanage and sometimes the hospital too, making bandages and mending bedlinen, as part of her commitment to the war effort, which was the duty of every man and woman not engaged in active service. But perhaps she should take on some proper war work now that her services would no longer be required by Lady Symmonds.

Being a lady's companion was rarely a paid position, although Babs, a wealthy widow, had always given her a handsome monthly allowance. Along with bed-and-board, she had also accompanied Lady Symmonds everywhere before the war, to swanky London or Parisian hotels, or on cruise ships around the world, thrilled to see far-flung corners of the globe, all expenses paid. She certainly had no complaints about her lifestyle, which had been exciting compared to her quiet, parochial existence before she came to St Ives.

Once war had broken out, life had become a little less glamorous. But it was more satisfying for Sonya as she'd helped with plans to convert Symmonds Hall into a convalescent home for wounded servicemen, and sorted out the day-to-day organisation of the adjacent orphanage after Babs had been forced to sack the directors, Mr and Mrs Treverrick, who'd been caught ill-treating the children. She had enjoyed the challenge of administrative work, itching for even greater responsibility while not quite bold enough to ask for it outright.

Now though, Mrs Rose Lanyon, the doctor's new wife, had taken over the role of orphanage director, leaving Sonya redundant and at a loss.

She'd been told by Babs that she could remain at the

hall rent-free and her monthly allowance would continue in exchange for sending her ladyship regular updates on the orphanage and hospital, which was hugely generous of the old lady. But was that all life held for her now?

Surely there was some better reason, other than pottering about and writing gossipy letters, that she had been put on this earth?

The next morning, when she fetched Babs her usual morning pot of tea with a newspaper, she found her ladyship already up and dressed.

'Dear Sonya,' Lady Symmonds said, leaning on the ornate, silver-topped cane she often used when her rheumatism was playing up. 'I know this news of my engagement to Donald has come as a severe shock to you. No, don't try to pretend. I've known you since you were only just out of school, remember? And I want you to promise me something.'

Sonya set down the tea tray, her heart thudding, unsure what to say. How could she promise something before knowing what it was?

'When I've gone to Scotland,' Babs continued, watching her intently, 'I think you should visit your mother and father in Truro. They're family, and you don't see them often enough.'

'You know how I feel about my parents,' Sonya said stiffly.

'I do,' Babs agreed, 'and I know why.'

Sonya couldn't seem to breathe. Her face grew hot with shame and embarrassment, and she hugged herself, arms tightly folded at her waist. She stared at her ladyship, too horrified to say anything except, 'I beg your pardon?'

'I know about the child,' Babs told her quietly, and when Sonya staggered backwards, shocked to her core by this admission, her ladyship sat on the sofa and nodded for Sonya to sit beside her. 'That was why I agreed to take you on here in the first place, my dear.'

Sonya knitted her hands together in her lap, horrified to know that the 'secret' she'd nursed all these years had in fact never been a secret at all. Or at least, not to her employer.

'I didn't really need a companion, not back in those days,' Babs continued. 'But your mother's family had connections with my own and she pleaded your case. She explained your predicament and said you needed to find a position with a good family somewhere in the country.' Babs looked at her sympathetically, adding, 'She also told me you would never be able to marry, so your only hope was to find employment.'

'Oh no,' Sonya cried, dropping her head into her hands.

'Nowadays, that kind of thing might simply have been glossed over or forgotten. But you know what people were like back then. And with your father being a vicar... Well, it was all rather awkward. There'd been some gossip in Truro, as I recall, and your parents wanted to get you settled somewhere far away as soon as possible.'

'I know,' Sonya said bitterly. 'I remember.'

'Of course you do.' Babs waited a moment, and then patted Sonya's shoulder, her voice softening. 'I thought I was helping by taking you on as my companion. And we've made a good team over the years. But, you know, it might be time for you to face your past and do something about it.'

Slowly, Sonya forced herself to sit up straight and not give in to the hysterical tears she felt pricking at her eyes. She was too old for such antics, anyway.

'It's a bit late for me to face my past, as you put it. Besides, if you're suggesting I should get married,' she added, with a cracked laugh, 'I doubt anyone would be interested in me. I'm forty-two, for goodness' sake.'

It was the first time she had spoken so frankly to her ladyship, and she sat in shocked silence for a moment afterwards, half expecting the sky to fall. But Babs did not remonstrate with her or become offended. To her surprise, the old lady smiled.

'And how old am I? More than my allotted three-score years and ten. Yet here I am, throwing caution to the wind and remarrying an old sea-captain.' Babs winked. 'Not merely that, but moving to Scotland to live in a remote, windy castle, of all places.'

'Yes, but you're a lady,' Sonya pointed out. 'You're wealthy and respectable. I've barely two farthings to rub together, and when I was far too young to know any better, I did something reprehensible and will never be good enough for any respectable man to marry,' she ended bitterly.

Those had been her father's words – almost word for word – when he insisted she must choose between being thrown onto the streets in disgrace or giving up her illegitimate baby for adoption.

Mere days away from her seventeenth birthday, she had not felt strong or experienced enough to stand up to her vicar father, whom she had always regarded with awe and love. But he had spoken as though she were the worst sinner of all and Sonya had crumbled, tearfully allowing the nurse to take her newborn baby from her arms.

Babs was studying her. 'Must you admit to your past, though?'

'I couldn't marry under false pretences,' Sonya cried passionately. 'Of course I would have to tell any man who proposed to me.'

'I see.' Babs nodded, looking at her with wise eyes. 'Then might I suggest you find yourself a man who isn't *respectable*? Or perhaps one who will overlook the actions of youthful folly and see instead the clever, kind and eminently sensible woman sitting beside me.'

Sonya blushed at such praise, though 'clever, kind and eminently sensible' were hardly going to attract a man who *wasn't* respectable, were they?

'Also,' her ladyship continued with a thoughtful expression, 'I'm sure you must have wondered, from time to time, how your baby – a daughter, I believe – turned out.'

Sonya nodded mutely. Of course she had wondered. More than that, as the years had passed, she had sought her long-lost child first in the face of every girl and then of every young woman in the street, burning to know what her daughter must look like, whether she had been blessed with a kind mother and father, and most importantly, if she was *happy*.

'How old would the girl be now?' Babs asked, peering at her averted face.

'Twenty-five.'

'My goodness. She might well be married by now. Or a

mother herself.' Her ladyship frowned at her silence. 'Would you not like to find out?'

'Of course.' Sonya folded her hands in her lap, her insides twisting with grief. 'But she would hate me. The unmarried mother who gave her up as a baby, who left her an orphan, with nothing and nobody in the world.' She shook her head vehemently. 'I couldn't bear that, to introduce myself and see hatred and contempt in her face.'

'Oh, my dear.' Babs smiled sadly, patting her hand. 'That would be terrible indeed, though I'm sure you would bear it with your usual fortitude. On the other hand, she may be delighted to meet her birth mother and to hear your story.' She paused. 'I'm taking a leap of faith with Donald and trusting in love to see me through… And perhaps you should too, only with your daughter.'

'But it's all useless,' Sonya cried, tears blurring her vision. 'I'm sorry to argue with you, my lady, but I have absolutely no idea what happened to my baby after she was taken from me, and that was decades ago. I … I don't even know what name she was given,' she finished with a sob, rubbing damp eyes. 'How could I possibly find her now?'

'Start with visiting your parents in Truro.' Babs handed her a clean white handkerchief, her smile encouraging as Sonya turned a wondering face in her direction. 'You may find the trail is not so cold as you fear.'

CHAPTER TWO

St Ives, Cornwall, early March 1943

With a breathless cry, Lily Fisher stuffed a damp, crumpled hanky against her mouth as joy welled up inside her again. 'Oh, Gran, don't Lady Symmonds make the most beautiful bride?' she whispered, squeezed up beside her grandmother in one of the pews of the pretty harbourside church at St Ives.

Her own tears had surprised her. From a hard-headed, working-class family in Dagenham, to the east of London, Lily had spent the past couple of years as a wartime nurse. She wasn't ordinarily sentimental, especially about marriage, which seemed to her more like a trap than a blessing. But lately, her friend Tristan's letters, arriving from an unknown location while he served as a squaddie, had become increasingly romantic, and she had even started to wonder what it would feel like to walk down the aisle with him.

Perhaps when they'd parted last summer – Tristan

Minear heading off for his basic training while she stayed in Penzance – she ought to have refused to write to him. She and Tris only been out for one proper date, after all, and that had been a crashing disaster. But she knew her letters might be a lifeline for him, so she had continued to write, despite her misgivings.

Smart in her best blue frock and matching pillbox hat, Gran pulled a face. 'How old is the bridegroom, would you say?' she whispered.

'I'm not sure.' Discreetly, Lily studied Lady Symmonds' betrothed. He was dignified and imposing in a gold-trimmed naval uniform, chest bristling with medals as he led his blushing bride down the aisle. 'Seventy? Seventy-five?'

Glancing at each other, they burst into barely suppressed, shoulder-shaking snorts of laughter.

Lily had come down to Cornwall with her Aunt Violet and younger sister Alice two years before, escaping the bombs that had been laying waste to the capital. Her grandmother had followed later, settling with them in the tiny seaside village of Porthcurno. It had all been very cosy for a while, and Cornwall's green fields were a far cry from London and its surrounding built-up suburbs. But Lily, on reaching eighteen, had decided on nursing as a career. She'd begun training on the job here in St Ives at the Symmonds Hall Convalescent Home for Wounded Servicemen, before moving to the larger hospital in Penzance, and then recently choosing to retrain as a midwife, returning to St Ives to take up a new position here.

She'd loved her work in bustling Penzance and had made some good friends there whom she would badly miss. But it was good to be with her family again for the day, here on the quiet western coast of Cornwall, and to see the lovely, widowed Lady Symmonds remarry.

On Lily's other side, her posh friend Eva dug her in the ribs. 'Hush, you two. Have a little respect for her ladyship. Without her endowment of the hall as a convalescent home, none of us would have had a job.' As a married woman herself now, she winked, adding with an irreverent grin, 'I agree though, Babs looks absolutely resplendent in her bridal togs. And to have found love again at her age… First rate!'

'Hmm.' Gran pursed her lips, muttering, 'Chance would be a fine thing for some of us "older ladies".'

Lily suppressed a grin. It was well known that Gran had been walking out for some months with white-haired Arnold Newton, a man who ran the village shop in Porthcurno. It had to be serious, as Aunt Violet claimed to have caught them kissing after church one Sunday, reporting this back to her astonished, giggling nieces with a look of horror. 'At their age too!' Violet had exclaimed, shaking her head. 'They ought to be ashamed of themselves. All I can say is, I hope Arnold's planning to marry her. Otherwise, he's making a fool of my mother, and I won't stand for it.' So far though, the old gent had not popped the question.

Lady Symmonds – or rather, Mrs Golightly, as she now was – did look marvellous, sailing down the aisle in silk and lace, her new husband on her arm.

The old lady paused as she came level with their pew, her face beaming. 'Ah, Eva, I'm so glad you and Max made it. How lovely to see you both!'

Captain Golightly tugged on her arm, clearing his throat. 'Come along now, Babs. Wedding photographs first,' his deep Scottish voice rumbled. 'Chinwag later.'

'Quite right, Donald,' his bride agreed demurely, and gave them all a gracious nod before continuing out of the church, followed by three pretty bridesmaids, all giggling girls from the orphanage, and one maid of honour in a swish dark green frock.

Eva slipped out of the pew with her husband, Max Carmichael, after the entourage had passed, no doubt hoping to pitch a little rice over the happy couple. Gran also wriggled out past Lily, too impatient to wait for Alice, Lily's sister, who had her nose in a book.

On Alice's other side, squashed in at the end of the pew, sat Aunty Violet and her husband, Joe, both smartly dressed in their Sunday best. None of them knew Babs particularly well but they had come to see how Lily was settling back in at St Ives, and a posh wedding like this always meant extra grub.

Aunty Violet blew her nose and pushed her hanky up her sleeve. 'Aw, that were smashin', weren't it, Joe? Lovely service, all the bells and smells.'

Joe tucked his hand into Violet's, and the couple smiled shyly at each other. They had not even been married a year yet.

'It was a good service,' he agreed, glancing down at Lily's sister, who had not yet taken her nose out of her book. 'Time to go, Alice. You don't want to miss the wedding reception.'

Reluctantly, Alice checked her page number and closed the library book. 'Will there be sandwiches?'

'I'd say so,' Lily told her sister cheerfully, linking arms with Alice as they exited the church. 'I spent yesterday evening up at Symmonds Hall.' The hall buildings still belonged to Lady Symmonds, along with the adjacent orphanage, though were mostly given over now for convalescent servicemen. 'I saw Rose and Harriet, and Mary Stannard… All my old friends there. Spoke to Cook too. Mrs Penhallow said Captain Golightly slipped a few bob to the butcher for extra meat. There's a spread laid on for wedding guests up at the hall, and we're all welcome.'

Alice perked up at the mention of extra rations.

Gran was already on the harbourside outside the church, watching with a grin as the happy couple were pelted with rice – though only meagre handfuls in this time of rationing – on their way to the stately, beribboned Bentley that belonged to the retired Scottish sea-captain.

She turned to Lily as they emerged into chill March sunshine, a stiff breeze blowing off the sea to ruffle frocks and lift hair.

'So sad,' Gran said, 'to think how that poor lady lost her husband, her son *and* her grandson to war, both this time and in the last show.' She dabbed at her cheeks with a hanky. 'It's not right, it just ain't.'

'But this is a happy day for her now, Mum.' Aunt Violet reassured Gran with a quick squeeze of her arm. 'And look, the rest of her family has come to wish her well.'

It was true, Lily realised, looking along the breezy harbourside. The old lady and her silver-haired and whiskered husband were surrounded by friends and relatives as they climbed into the waiting car. It also looked as though half the small Cornish town of St Ives had turned out to see their best-loved benefactor wed again, the townsfolk cheering and calling out best wishes as Babs waved back at them, a big smile on her face, her eyes sparkling with joy and humour.

'Oh, how romantic.' Mary Stannard sighed, turning to Lily with a face stained with tears. 'I hope I'm as fun and bubbly as Babs when I get to her age.'

Mary, now one of the senior nurses at Symmonds Hall, had lost weight since last year when she and Lily had worked together. But her curly dark hair was dressed prettily with flowers for today's wedding, and she managed a smile through her tears.

Putting an arm about her shoulders, Lily said bracingly, 'I'm sure you will be.' She hesitated. 'Look, how about we grab a cuppa together sometime? Maybe at that nice little teashop we used to visit.'

Mary's eyes widened but she nodded. 'I'd like that.' A dimple showed in her cheek as she grinned. 'Though good luck getting our days off to collide. I seem to be working all the hours God sends right now, we're so short-staffed.'

'It's the same for us midwives. My feet hardly touched the ground my first week on the job. But we'll manage to get together for a cup of tea and a natter one day, I promise… Oh look, there's Rose and Dr Lewis.'

Lily couldn't help smiling at the sight of tiny, red-haired Rose, who used to cause her so much trouble on the wards at Symmonds Hall. Although terrifying as a Ward Sister, she had retired from nursing after marrying handsome young Dr Lewis last summer and now ran the orphanage next door to the convalescent home.

Rose and Lewis came up, laughing and greeting all Lily's family, whom they hadn't see in ages.

'Shall we walk up to the wedding reception together?' Rose asked. Lily thought she seemed ecstatic with her life as a married woman, a pretty flush in her cheeks as Lewis put his arm about her waist. 'It's going to be a lovely party.'

Over his wife's shoulder, Dr Lewis gave Lily a curious look. 'Hello, stranger. Rose tells me you're back for good. I thought you were happy at Penzance Hospital?'

'I was,' Lily agreed, biting her lip as she recalled how hard the decision to give up nursing had been. Perhaps the hardest decision of her life. 'But I've always wanted to be a midwife too, and now I've finished my initial training, I've accepted a position here in St Ives. I'll be attached to the maternity team at the cottage hospital and might even be allowed to attend some home births too,' she added with a flash of enthusiasm, 'under supervision from Bertha, the senior midwife.'

'You'll make a smashin' midwife,' Aunt Violet said at once. 'Look how well you coped when Hazel had her baby during an air raid and you were all alone with her.'

'Ah yes, I remember that,' Dr Lewis said with a grin, and nodded his approval. 'I wish you were rejoining the staff at Symmonds Hall, Lily. But I work four days a week at St Ives Hospital now, so I daresay we'll keep bumping into each other all the same.'

Eva appeared then with her husband in tow. Max Carmichael had been a dashing pilot with the RAF until he'd been left with a damaged spine after surviving a bomb strike in London. For a long time, everyone had thought he would never walk again. All except for Eva, of course, who was determined to help him back to his feet, even when Max himself had given up hope. Sure enough, Eva's efforts had paid off and now the former pilot could walk with a stick.

Violet and Joe were also waiting to leave. Joe eyed Max's stick with a glint of interest, walking with a cane of his own, having lost his leg in a naval action early in the war.

'How do?' Joe said in a thick Cornish accent.

'Very well, thank you.' Max, who was American by birth, had a smooth, pleasing transatlantic accent. He looked Joe up and down. 'Postbridge, isn't it?' He glanced at his stick and winked. 'Up for a battle of the canes later?'

Joe's mouth quirked in a rare smile. 'I daresay.'

The Bentley had drawn away, rattling with cans dragged along behind, ribbons flapping in the sea winds, and now the townsfolk were beginning to drift away, back to their workplaces and homes.

Watching the car depart, a woman stood with her back to everyone else, a lonely, despondent slant to her shoulders.

'Rose, who's that?' Lily asked in a low voice, nodding to the woman.

Her friend turned to look, and grimaced. 'That's Sonya Thorpe,' Rose whispered. 'You remember her, don't you?'

'Lady Symmonds' companion?'

'That's right. They've been together almost twenty-five years, Cook told me. Only now Babs is heading off to Scotland with her new husband, and she's leaving Sonya behind. I expect she's feeling a bit lost at the moment.' Rose pulled a face. 'Though she does keep wandering around the orphanage, on the pretext of "helping out", and

20

getting underfoot. I don't have the heart to point out her services there are no longer really necessary. Not now that I'm in charge.'

Lily knew all about feeling 'lost'. Although she knew plenty of people in St Ives, it had not been easy moving back here from Penzance, where she had made so many friends. And despite feeling sure she'd made a wise decision in refusing an offer of marriage from Tristan Minear, the son of a Penzance farmer, she did sometimes wonder what it would have been like to be a housewife, and possibly a mother too eventually. Especially now she was constantly confronted with pregnant women her own age…

'Miss Thorpe?' Lily called out, and smiled when the tall, dark-haired woman turned to look at their noisy group. 'Care to walk up to the hall with us?'

'Oh, thank you, yes,' Sonya said, rather breathlessly, and headed their way. She too was clutching a hanky, her eyes red with weeping. A tall, broad-hipped woman, Sonya was in her early forties; close up, Lily spotted a few silvery strands in her hair peeping out under the smart hat she was wearing. 'It's Nurse Fisher, isn't it?'

'I'm a midwife now but you're right, yes, I'm Lily Fisher. We met a few times at Symmonds Hall.'

'I remember,' Sonya said, nodding in an absentminded way.

Rose excused herself politely and caught up with the others, but Lily hung back so she could keep pace with Sonya. The poor woman looked a little upset and it would have been mean to abandon her.

'It must be all change for you.' Lily gave Sonya an encouraging smile. 'What do you have planned now Lady

Symmonds is off to Scotland? Of course she's Mrs Golightly now, but I can't see anyone round here remembering to call her that. She's been Lady Symmonds forever.'

'Yes, I feel the same.' But Sonya's face had dropped. 'It's all been a bit sudden, to be honest.' They began the long trudge up through the town, heading for Symmonds Hall and the orphanage. 'And a shock too. With Babs gone, I won't know what to do with myself.'

'But a little bird told me you're a volunteer at the orphanage. That sounds like hard work.'

Sonya looked surprised. 'Oh, it's not too bad. Especially now Rose is in charge – Mrs Lanyon, I should say. She rarely lets me do anything to do with administration, which was my old job after the Treverricks left. Though I've been trying to make myself useful by teaching French to some of the older children.'

'That's a lovely idea.'

'It's the least I can do,' Sonya said, but her smile was bleak. 'Everything's utterly changed though and it's all a little unnerving. Do you know what I mean?'

'Funnily enough,' Lily said frankly, pulling her jacket tighter as the sea winds tore through the streets, 'I do.'

CHAPTER THREE

As soon as the air raid was over, Nurse Mary Stannard helped the most vulnerable patients out of the convalescent home shelter first, exchanging a few cheery words with Sergeant Timms on the way up the steep steps, who might be missing an arm but always had a grin on his face, wonderful man that he was.

'Feeling better today, Sergeant?' she asked, supporting him out of the cellar that served as a shelter during air raids.

'Can't complain,' Sergeant Timms agreed with a lively nod. 'There's many in worse shape than myself. But how about you, Nurse Stannard? Last time we spoke, you were telling me you had a … a … *dilemma*,' he finished, stumbling over the word.

'Was I?' She stared, momentarily thrown.

'Something about your mum's sixtieth birthday and how you didn't know what to fetch her for a present.'

'Oh yes, of course.' Mary grinned and handed him over to one of the orderlies at the hall door. 'Still haven't solved that one, alas! Proper Cornish, my mother, and a tough woman to please. But I'll keep you posted.'

Sergeant Timms sketched a brief salute with his remaining arm and ambled into the hall under the orderly's supervision.

Watching his progress, her heart hurt for him, and for all the brave men under her charge on the wards, wounded in defence of King and country. But, with the help of the doctors and nurses at Symmonds Hall Convalescent Home for Wounded Servicemen, most of them would recover from their injuries and go home at last to their families. Some might even be well enough to rejoin their regiments.

'Nurse Stannard?'

She turned with a quick smile as Dr Lewis Lanyon bore down on her, belatedly seeing that he had stiff-backed Matron in tow. She had a lot of admiration for Dr Lewis, always so generous with his time, but not much for Matron. In fact, terrified might be a better word for her feelings there.

'Your shift's nearly up, isn't it?' Dr Lewis asked her.

'On the hour, Doctor.'

Dr Lewis smoothed down his thatch of dark hair as it was caught and lifted by the strong March wind, and glanced round at Matron. 'What do you think, Matron? Won't she be too tired?'

'Tired? A strapping young girl like Nurse Stannard? I should think not.'

Mary was confused. 'I beg your pardon, why would I be tired?'

'We need a few volunteers to work a few extra hours today. I know, I know,' Dr Lewis said with a grimace, 'it's not ideal. But we've had a new batch of patients come in by ambulance from the train station. They were caught in the air raid and had to wait it out at the side of the road. Now they're here and we simply don't have enough personnel to handle getting them processed. The new Sister is busy with a troublesome patient in Atlantic Ward, so this task must fall to you. Each new patient will need to have his details taken, treatment needs assessed, and to be allocated a bed on one of the wards.' He raised his brows at her pleadingly. 'What do you say?'

'On any other day, Doctor, willingly. But I've requested the weekend off and I'm going to see—' Mary began, meaning to mention her two-day visit home to see her parents, but she was interrupted.

'Nurse Stannard, we must all make sacrifices in time of war,' Matron said in an arctic tone, pursing her lips and directing a grim look at Mary. A tall, angular woman in her fifties, she had thinly pencilled eyebrows, silvering dark hair scraped back off her forehead in a severe, old-fashioned chignon, and wore her matron's cap high as a tiara. 'It's still Friday, is it not? The weekend doesn't begin until tomorrow. I'm sure you can spare a few more hours today to help those less fortunate than yourself. If you didn't want a life of service, why did you become a nurse?'

Since that was exactly what she herself had been wondering, Mary was at a loss to know how to answer that.

'Well, I...' Mary looked from Matron to the doctor's hopeful face, and then swallowed, giving up in despair 'Of course I can work a few more hours, Dr Lewis, if you're desperate.'

Folding her arms at her waist, Mary pinned a bright smile to her lips. It was something she had seen her old nursing friend Eva do a thousand times and had often wondered how she could do it, looking so outwardly cheerful when she felt miserable or irritated inside. Now it was her turn to put on a show.

'Where are the new patients, Matron?' she asked.

'They've been conveyed to the side room by Carbis Ward and are waiting to be processed.' Matron was looking satisfied. 'Some of the patients are in quite bad shape. You'd better get there on the double, Nurse Stannard.'

Mary had little choice but to head into the convalescent home, barely able to suppress her annoyance.

'Thank you,' Dr Lewis called after her cheerily.

So much for her plans for the afternoon, Mary thought with an inward groan, having been looking forward to a lovely long soak in the tub before setting off to visit her mum and dad for the weekend. Now, she'd have to skip the bath and dash straight out after work to catch the last bus into town. She used to love being a nurse, but increasingly found all the rules and regulations rather restricting. Still, it was nice to know what she did made a difference in people's lives. That was the main thing.

Outside Carbis Ward, she found two of the younger nurses standing about, armed with clipboards and looking unsure of themselves. As Matron had suggested would be the case, there was no sign of Sister Buckley, whose first name was Mathilda, an experienced nurse from Bristol who had come to replace Rose when she got married. She was a pleasant

26

woman, but not particularly chatty, so Mary hadn't got to know her well yet.

'Come along,' Mary told them briskly, assuming command. 'Where are these new patients, then?'

She peered through the door at a motley gang of patients seated on chairs in the waiting room, one already in a wheelchair.

'Nurse Thrupp,' she said to Esther, 'you take the two lads to the left. Nurse Carrington,' she said, nodding to Hilary, 'you have the other two, and I'll deal with the gentleman in the wheelchair. Take their details as usual, check their pulses and any injury history, and report back to me for a ward allocation.'

'Yes, Nurse Stannard,' the two new girls chorused, and headed into the waiting room with carefully prepared smiles.

Following them, Mary pulled out a chair next to the man in the wheelchair. His face and much of his right side were swathed in bandages, and he was slumped in the chair, apparently staring at the wall.

'Hello,' she said, studying him with instinctive pity. 'I'm sorry to have kept you waiting. I'm Nurse Stannard and I'll be processing your details and finding you a bed.'

The man didn't respond, though his one visible eye blinked. Not unconscious, then. Just tired, perhaps, after the long ambulance journey.

Mary picked up the document pouch hanging from the wheelchair and flicked through several pages of notes. He'd been badly burnt, it seemed. The receiving hospital had treated his burns, and now he was required to conva-lesce for at least one month, while he continued to receive treatment and rehabilitation. It was likely there would be extensive scarring across all burn sites, she read with an inner ouch of sympathy, and potential loss of vision to his right eye, which could be permanent.

His vocal cords had also been damaged in the fire, she discovered, though only temporarily. Hence his silence, no doubt.

'Gosh, that's an awfully large amount of morphine,' she said under her breath, studying his patient notes. 'No wonder you're so sleepy.'

Quickly, she began transcribing his notes. If he couldn't speak, there wasn't much point asking the unfortunate man questions about his identity and treatment to date.

'You've come to the right place,' she went on, hoping to cheer him up. 'Here at Symmonds Hall we have some of the best doctors and nurses in Cornwall.'

The patient turned his head then, finally looking at her, and she saw his red-rimmed, uncovered eye glitter as though with tears. His left hand had clenched compulsively on the arm of the wheelchair and she heard a sharp intake of breath, followed by what sounded like a grunt of pain.

Poor man, she thought, he must be in agony with all those burns. Finishing his sheet, she said bracingly, 'Don't worry, we'll soon have you fixed up and back home with your family, see if we don't,' and glancing down at his details, added, 'Private Minear.'

Mary's parents still lived in the whitewashed mid-terrace house in St Ives she'd been born in twenty-four years ago. Her dad, Harold, had recently retired from his job with the local dairy, where he'd worked on the floats as a milkman most of his life, known to almost everyone in the small seaside town as Harry. Her mum, Rita, was a housewife and as proud of that role as any woman could be. Her doorstep was kept scrubbed and the kitchen floor so sparkling clean she often swore the family could eat their dinner off it. Thankfully she'd never insisted on them trying to prove it.

'I'm home, Mum,' Mary called out cheerfully, letting herself into the house and hanging up her coat and hat on the hall stand. She left her weekend bag beside the stairs to take up later and made her way through to the poky kitchen at the back, where she found her mother bent over the stove, a pinny wrapped about her waist. 'Sorry I'm late.' She kissed her mother's cheek and peered into the bubbling pot. 'What's for dinner?'

'Bangers and mash,' her mum said shortly. 'Though these sausages have never even been near a pig if you ask me.' She looked round at her daughter. 'Of course, if I were twenty years younger, I could get around the butcher the way Mrs Appleby opposite does. All that scarlet lipstick and her cleavage on show whenever she bends over to look at his chops...'

'Mum!' Mary stifled a giggle.

'It's not right. She always gets a big roll of sausage meat while us older ladies...' She pulled a face. 'Well, just drown the blighters in gravy and make believe you're dining at The Savoy.'

'I'm sure they'll go down a treat,' Mary assured her mother, and sat at the kitchen table, jumping up again with a cry as her bottom met something hard and cylindrical. 'What on earth...?'

'So that's where it got to.' Her mum scooped up the object and popped it into her apron pocket. 'Pip's yo-yo.'

'I should have guessed.'

Her mother returned to her pan of bubbling potatoes, pricking them with a long-handled fork to check for consistency. 'Your brother Stephen had a yo-yo at the same age, bless him.'

Mary's older brother, Stephen, had joined the Navy years ago to 'see the world' as he'd put it, and was now away, serving his country.

Then, last month, Rita had unexpectedly offered to house an evacuee, a ten-year-old boy from London called Pip. His previous host family in St Ives had suffered bomb damage to their home, and the placement officer had put up a notice asking if someone else with a spare room could take him in, and Rita had offered.

'Well, why not?' she'd said when Harold began to protest. It had been an evening when Mary was visiting and Rita had made a special point of explaining to her that the boy would be allotted Stephen's room, not her own. 'You're up at the hall most weeks now, Mary,' she'd said, 'and who knows when Stephen will be home next? Might as well pull our weight for the war effort and give the lad a roof over his head and a hot dinner every night.'

'What do we know about raising a schoolboy?' Harold had scratched his head. 'I'm past sixty now. It's twenty years since our Stephen was a young lad. Times have changed.'

'Don't fuss, Harold,' Rita had said briskly. 'Times may have changed but a boy's still a boy. I'll do what's necessary for the lad. You leave all that to me.'

So, Harold had shrugged and lit his pipe, and a few days later, young Pip had appeared on the doorstep with a battered suitcase and a mop of untidy fair hair.

The truth was, Mary secretly thought her mum had been at a loss to know what to do with all of her spare time, now her two children had grown up and flown the nest, and Harold no longer needed his milkman's uniform cleaned and pressed every week, or a cooked breakfast produced for him at five in the morning, regular as clockwork. Rita had needed a new purpose in life, and an orphaned evacuee who had lost his parents in the Blitz fitted the bill perfectly.

Mary helped her mother by laying the table in the dining room and then carrying through the cutlery. As she hurried back for the gravy jug, Pip came sloping in through the front door, looking rather the worse for wear. The boy's shoes were scuffed and his trousers were dusty, and he kept his face turned away when Mary greeted him.

'Is that Pip?' her mother called. 'Tell him to come through and wash his hands. Supper's nearly ready.'

Pip dropped his school bag in the hall and shuffled into the kitchen, clearly reluctant to follow this instruction. It was soon obvious why.

'Bless me,' Rita exclaimed at the sight of him. She dropped the fork she'd been using to mash the potatoes, dragged the boy forward and tilted his face towards the window. 'Who on earth gave you that shiner?'

Surprised, Mary realised the boy was indeed sporting a black eye. He didn't seem like the kind of boy who would start a fight.

'Turn your head towards me,' Mary told him more gently, and Pip obeyed, looking sullen. The bruising was extensive, but she couldn't see any bumps on his head, and apart from a few grazes, there was nothing else the matter with him. Not visibly, at any rate.

Rita was upset, her breathing coming fast. 'Which of them blooming little hooligans thumped you? Give me a name, I'll come to the school with you tomorrow and sort it out myself.'

'Don't matter,' Pip muttered, looking away.

Mary peered into his pale face. 'Come on, Pip. You heard my mother. Tell us who did it.'

'I … I can't,' Pip told them wretchedly, twisting his school cap in his hands. 'It'll only make things worse.'

At that moment, Harold came into the kitchen in search of his dinner. Rita told him what had happened, and he too turned to study Pip's black eye while she finished mashing the potatoes. Mary helped by straining the greens and placing them in a bowl.

'Well, I hope you gave the other chap what for,' was all Harold said, ruffling the boy's hair. 'You'll live.'

'Dining room,' Rita said shortly, her back to them. 'Pip, wash your hands first.'

Mary followed her father into the dining room, carrying the gravy and the sausages, and Pip hurried after them once his hands were clean.

Rita appeared a moment later, juggling bowls of steaming veg. 'Best eat it while it's hot,' she said, but cast a quick glance at Harold as she began to serve. 'Have you managed to get a name out of him yet?'

'I didn't try,' Harold admitted. 'The lad's right. The other boys would only call him a snitch, and nobody likes a snitch.'

Rita glared but said nothing, depositing two skinny-looking sausages, some boiled veg and a large dollop of mash onto his plate before slamming it down in front of her husband. Nervously, Harold helped himself to gravy and a sliver of yellow mustard from the jar.

'Nobody likes a bully either, Dad,' Mary pointed out as Pip sat down opposite her, in the place her brother Stephen had always occupied when they were kids, 'and that black eye strikes me as bullying. I mean, look at the size of him.'

Pip hung his head, clearly embarrassed to have his lack of height mentioned as a factor.

'Boys fight. Not much else to be said, love.' Her father got up to pull down the blackout curtain, as the sun was beginning to dip and it would be dusk within another half hour. 'Let it go.'

But Mary fretted, picking at her greens without much appetite, unable to follow his advice. She thought of all the young men at the convalescent home, wounded in the war, and wished that boys could be taught better ways to resolve differences than beating seven kinds of hell out of each other.

'The teacher should be told at least,' she muttered at last.

Perversely, her mother shot her a quelling glance. 'Your father says to leave it, so let's talk about something else, if you please.'

Mary held her breath at this reprimand and then expelled it slowly, focusing on her sausage instead, which didn't taste like any kind of meat she had ever eaten. Perhaps it wasn't meat, she decided, but chewed on it dutifully. It was better than no sausage at all, she told herself, not really believing a word of that guff.

'So, Mum,' she said brightly after a long silence, 'is there anything you'd like for your sixtieth birthday?' She winked at her dad, who had discussed it with her a month ago, suggesting various ways they could mark such a special occasion. 'It's coming up soon, in case you'd forgotten.'

'I don't keep birthdays anymore,' her mother said flatly, reaching for the gravy jug. 'And I'll thank you not to mention my age at the dinner table. It's not polite.'

Fork poised halfway to her mouth, Mary stared from her mum to her dad in dismay. Was she serious?

Dad gave her a frown, indicating they would talk about it later when Mum wasn't within earshot, and then hurriedly changed the subject, discussing improvements he was making to their vegetable garden this spring, and how he'd stolen a march on Mr Blythe next door, who hadn't even turned over his soil yet.

Mary listened to his anecdotes with a smile but inwardly she felt quite downcast. She returned to her heap of gravy-slicked greens with a sigh, trying to be grateful even for such plain fare. She loved her mum and still wanted her sixtieth birthday year to be extra-special, war or no war. But it might prove difficult to say thank you to somebody who didn't want to be thanked.

CHAPTER FOUR

Sonya collected the textbooks and stacked them in the cupboard at the back of the orphanage 'classroom' at Symmonds Hall, pleased at how well the children under her charge were progressing in their language skills. The school-age children walked into St Ives every day for their schooling, but Rose Lanyon, now in charge of the orphanage and wishing to improve their chances in life, had asked Sonya to give a few extra lessons out of school time to any children struggling with their letters and arithmetic.

Since she had been taught French at school, and had practised it frequently while travelling with Lady Symmonds, Sonya had also volunteered – without realising what a daunting task it would be – to instruct some of the children in that language. A few of them had already learned a smattering of French at school, while the younger ones knew little more than 'Bonjour' and 'Au revoir'. Since their small numbers – only six children wished to take extra lessons after school – made dividing the classes impractical, it had been a struggle to work out a curriculum that would suit all of them together. But, after the first few lessons, the younger ones had almost caught up with their elders, and she was now feeling more confident as a teacher.

A sound from the doorway made her turn, and she was surprised to see Rose Lanyon standing there, a glow in her cheeks as though she'd been out in the spring sunshine.

'Ah, Miss Thorpe,' she said

'Hello, Mrs Lanyon,' Sonya said, suddenly nervous. Closing the cupboard door, she found herself hoping that none of the children had complained her lessons were too difficult for them. There was no payment involved, of course – her work at the orphanage was entirely voluntary – but she had begun to enjoy looking at all those smiling faces and knowing her French lessons might improve their chances of gaining future employment. 'Is everything all right?'

'Perfectly,' Rose said in her usual forthright way, coming to look out of the window at the children, now playing in the courtyard outside as they waited for the dinner bell to ring. The orphanage director was of a diminutive build, and Sonya, who was five foot eight inches, couldn't help but look down on her. But that didn't make her any the less nervous.

With flaming red hair and a direct stare that had terrified patients and staff alike when she'd been Sister Rose at the convalescent home next door, she was not the easiest person to talk to. But Sonya had noted, since volunteering at the orphanage, that Rose was very different with the children under her care. Almost another person, in fact – kind and gentle, always ready to tend to a grazed knee or read a story out loud before bedtime.

'I was wondering,' Rose said, still looking out of the window, 'how you've been getting on with teaching the children French.'

'They seem to enjoy the subject,' Sonya said defensively.

'I'm sure they do. But are you happy teaching them? Spending time in their company?'

'Of course.'

'Good. Because I hoped you might spend even more time with the children in future.'

'I could do that, yes.' Sonya was bewildered. 'But why?'

'I need to cut back on my hours,' Rose said, turning to face her. 'Doctor's orders, you might say.'

This was an in-joke, for her husband was Dr Lewis Lanyon, who worked at the convalescent home next door as well as at the local hospital and as a General Practitioner.

'Oh dear.' Sonya was at once sympathetic. She knew how ill health could take its toll, for she had nursed Lady Symmonds through many bouts of rheumatism and sciatica. 'Are you unwell, Mrs Lanyon?'

'Please, call me Rose when we're alone together,' Mrs Lanyon insisted. 'Why don't we sit down for a moment?'

Sitting behind one of the children's tiny work desks, Rose crossed one leg over the other and smoothed her smart blue skirt over her knees. Sonya pulled out a child's seat opposite, lowering herself with difficulty to the miniature chair.

'What I need to tell you is of a personal nature,' Rose said, 'and I trust you'll keep it to yourself for now.'

'I won't breathe a word.'

'Thank you. You see, I'm expecting a child in the autumn.'

'Oh!'

'It's knocked me about a little, I'm afraid.' Rose checked the door, which was still ajar, and lowered her voice conspiratorially. 'Morning sickness.'

Sonya was still gathering her thoughts. 'Congratulations,' she said quickly, 'that's wonderful news.'

That explained Rose's look of glowing health recently, Sonya thought. But she also knew exactly what was meant by 'morning sickness,' for she herself had suffered dreadfully as a young girl, carrying a dead man's child and barely able to keep a morsel down for months. 'This is God's punishment for your wickedness,' her father had raged over her. It had been one of the worst times of her life.

But Rose was a married woman and no doubt she and Dr Lewis were ecstatic to be expecting their first child together. Her bouts of morning sickness must be marring what ought to be a time of joy for the poor woman.

'Have … have you tried eating a plain biscuit before getting out of bed?' she asked cautiously, also in a low voice, for this was not a conversation she wished any of the children to overhear. 'Or a cup of ginger tea?'

Rose gave a wry half-smile. 'I've tried both, at Lewis's suggestion. And they do help. But only marginally.' She blinked, giving Sonya a curious look. 'How did you know about that? Plain biscuits and ginger?'

Sonya felt transfixed, squirming under that penetrating gaze. 'I … I don't recall. Lady Symmonds mentioned it once. She had nausea too, with her own son.'

'They do say it's worse with boys,' Rose agreed, laughing.

'Oh, not necessarily,' Sonya said, and could have bitten her tongue out when Rose gave her that funny look again.

Goodness, she told herself crossly, do be quiet. An unmarried woman in her forties shouldn't know anything about babies and pregnancy. 'But how marvellous for you and Dr Lanyon,' she babbled. 'You must both be over the moon.'

'We are, yes. Completely moonstruck and still taking it in.' Rose smiled, her whole face softening for an instant. Then she got straight back to business. 'But since I'm not on top form first thing in the morning, I can't fulfil all my duties as orphanage director. I can shift some of my administration jobs to the afternoon instead, but that will make it difficult for me also to instruct the children in extra-curricular activities. And, as you know, I've been trying hard to improve their education, so I don't want to let their special lessons slide.' She sighed, looking up at Sonya with a speculative expression. 'It's a bit of a dilemma, as you can see.'

'I'd be happy to take over those extra classes for you,' Sonya said at once, even though it would mean a great deal more work, particularly when it came to preparing lessons beforehand. 'If that's what you'd like.'

It was a gamble, and Sonya knew it. Teaching poetry or a short Shakespeare extract – as she knew Rose had done with some of the more academically inclined children – or studying world maps and discussing major historical events like the French Revolution or the English Civil War, would require her to study those topics herself in advance. And while she had been taught them at school, and read a few books and articles about such things as an adult, it was not the same as being knowledgeable enough to convey information to a group aged roughly nine to fourteen. But the alternative was disappointing the children, and that she couldn't bear to do.

'Would you?' Rose stood, looking as though a weight had been lifted from her shoulders. 'That's very kind of you, Sonya. Thank you.'

Sonya stood too, following her to the door before a thought struck her. 'Erm, Mrs Lanyon ... I mean, Rose,' she said tentatively, 'what are your plans for later on? I mean, for when you...' She tailed off, not sure how to put it delicately enough.

'When I'm so huge I can't move about the place very easily,' Rose finished for her, chuckling a little, 'or when I've had the baby and have no thought in my head for anything else?' She nodded. 'I'm not sure yet. For now, I'm just shuffling my duties about and hoping for the best.' She studied Sonya thoughtfully. 'But yes, it may be that I'll have to resign as orphanage director and allow someone else to replace me.'

'I'm sorry,' Sonya said, feeling distraught for the poor woman. 'You love your work so much. I can't imagine you'd ever want to leave it.'

'Well, many women leave their jobs once they marry, and especially once they have children to take care of,' Rose pointed out, ever the pragmatist. 'You're right, I won't be happy to go. But the baby must be my reward, mustn't it?'

And with a smile, Rose nodded and whisked away to check the dinner table had been laid for the children, leaving Sonya to make her lonely way back to the apartments she used to share with Lady Symmonds.

The baby must be my reward...

For some reason, those words had brought tears to

Sonya's eyes, and once she was on her own again, with the door to her apartment firmly shut, she sank down onto the sofa, took out a hanky, and gave way to a fit of weeping that lasted nearly an hour and left her eyes red and her nose sore.

Lady Symmonds was right, she thought afterwards, staring at herself dolefully in the mirror. She was in her forties now, no longer a young girl to be frightened of gossip and what it might do to her standing in the community. There was a gaping hole in her heart, a baby-shaped hole, and after years of suffering in silence, it was surely time to do something about it.

Going to the table, she picked up the reply her mother had sent to her recent letter, agreeing that she could visit them in Truro, and read through it again, trying to find some kindness or emotion behind the cold words of duty and restraint.

Sonya dried her eyes, feeling lost and hopeless, even though she now had an opportunity to discuss her adopted baby with her parents. Some women seemed born to be mothers, embracing parenthood with joy and delight, and others turned away from it as soon as possible, pushing their offspring out of the nest at the very first opportunity.

If she had kept in touch with her child, is this the kind of letter she would have sent? She hoped not. But how could she tell?

Someone knocked at the main door to the apartment.

Startled, Sonya jumped up to put away the letter. The orphans would have finished their dinner by now and be on their way up to bed. Who on earth could be calling at this hour?

Warily, she checked her reflection again before hurrying to open the door, praying it was not obvious she had been crying.

To her surprise, it was Nurse Stannard from the convalescent home, still in her uniform, her curly dark hair barely restrained under her nurse's cap. 'Oh, Sonya, I'm so glad you're in,' she said, looking flustered. 'I've got a problem, and I think you might be able to help me with it.'

CHAPTER FIVE

'One more big push,' Lily urged Mrs Gilbert, who lay red-faced and panting, nearly falling off the narrow little bed the hospital seemed to think appropriate for women in labour. 'I can see the baby's head. That's it, excellent. And again, when you feel the urge ... a nice big push.'

'You said ... one more ... push...' Mrs Gilbert gasped, gripping the sides of the bed for leverage. 'That's ... two more.'

'Sorry.' Lily grabbed a cool cloth to mop the woman's brow. 'I thought one more would do the trick.' She pulled a face, checking Mrs Gilbert's pulse with her watch. It was racing and she didn't like the look of her patient's livid colour either. 'But trust me, Baby's nearly here.'

'You said that ... an hour ago.'

Lily gave her a quick smile. 'Well, this is your fifth, Mrs Gilbert. You ought to be telling me how to do it. Not the other way around.'

Mrs Gilbert hummed under her breath at that, muttering, 'They're all different, love. This one obviously had other plans for today.'

The door to the labour room opened and a dark head popped round. It was Katie, the other hospital midwife, a tall, slender brunette in her twenties with huge green eyes that reminded Lily of a cat.

'You done yet?' she asked, rather indiscreetly.

'Not far off,' Lily told her, and spoke a few soothing words to her patient before hurrying across the room. 'Why, what's the matter?' She caught a flicker of something in Katie's face and was struck by a horrible foreboding. It was the end of her shift in less than an hour, but she couldn't hand over if Mrs Gilbert was still in labour by then. Not when they already had three ladies and their newborns on the tiny maternity ward. The midwifery team would be too stretched if there was an emergency. 'Don't tell me we've got *another* baby on the way?'

Katie's smile was short-lived. 'No, it's just… Well, there's someone at the ward door who wants to speak to you. Says it's urgent.'

Her patient gave a yelp and bore down, gritting her teeth and straining every sinew. Lily eyed her with alarm, afraid the poor woman might burst a blood vessel if this stubborn baby didn't arrive. It was possible she would need to summon a doctor soon, which was something she was loath to do. Doctors tended to sweep in like Napoleon and take over the birth, and although the welfare of the mother was paramount, she often found the presence of a doctor in the labour room made the women more nervous, not less.

'More urgent than Mrs Gilbert?' she hissed.

'I know, I know… But it's a middle-aged woman, not a

44

patient. I told her you were in the labour room. She said she still had to speak to you.'

Lily shook her head. 'Take a message for me, would you? Sorry, but I can't leave Mrs Gilbert, not even for five minutes. She's about to pop.'

'I can step in. Just give me a minute to wash my hands and put on a clean apron.'

'Thanks, but she's been with me for hours now. It would be wrong to change midwives on her at this late stage.'

'All right.' Katie hesitated, glancing at the woman on the bed. 'Are you ready for Bertha to pop back in and check how things are going?'

Bertha Whitely was the senior midwife for St Ives and the surrounding countryside, and the expert who was called in whenever a birth was not going according to plan. Lily had only attended at three births without constant supervision, but they had all been women like Mrs Gilbert, who had birthed multiple healthy babies in the past and had no record of problems during labour. She was worried that Bertha would think she couldn't handle making decisions under pressure if she asked for a second opinion, and then she would never be allowed out to preside over home births, which was her greatest wish.

'Yes, if she's ready.'

Bertha came in five minutes later, sporting the blue hat of a fully qualified midwife; a large woman in her forties, with greying brown hair and a practical manner, she greeted Mrs Gilbert cheerfully before giving her a quick examination.

'Nearly there,' she murmured, agreeing with Lily's estimate, and then stayed for the actual birth, supervising Lily in the final stages. 'Good steady pushing, lots of puff on the exhale,' she called out as she turned to ready the weighing scales. 'We'll soon have Baby out of there.'

Lily gripped Mrs Gilbert's hand and urged her on with a smile and plenty of loud encouragement.

Thirty minutes later, a red-faced Baby Gilbert was nestled in his mother's arms, having been weighed and tightly swaddled, a tiny cotton cap on his head.

'Congratulations, Mrs Gilbert,' Lily told her patient, tired but satisfied at the outcome of what had become a surprisingly difficult birth. But she was already learning that there was no such thing as a predictable labour. Even the easy-looking births could turn complicated in the blink of an eye. 'You'll be moved to the ward soon. Is your husband in the waiting room? If so, I can let him know to come in.'

In most cases, husbands preferred not to be present at hospital births, something Lily didn't personally approve of, but sadly seemed to be the usual way of doing things. The midwife who had trained her at Penzance had been keen to stress how useful a woman's husband could be during birth, and that a home birth made it more likely he would be present and able to lend his wife support. But maybe there was something about a hospital that put these gentlemen off sitting with their wives during labour. Or perhaps they were too squeamish to watch their babies being born, Lily often thought secretly.

During the war, however, it had become normal for husbands not to be present during a birth, as most were on active service.

'He's away with his regiment, love,' Mrs Gilbert told her, and sighed with pleasure as she studied her little boy's face. 'Somewhere in the Home Counties last time I heard. I'll write Ronald a letter when I get home from hospital. He'll be thrilled. Four girls, and at last, he's got a son!'

Having checked that Mrs Gilbert was comfortable and healthy, and the baby was a good colour and breathing well, Bertha took Lily aside for a quick but brutal assessment of the things she had done well, and what could have been done better.

'It will all be in my report. Overall though, that was excellent work, so well done,' Bertha finished with a wink. 'You can clock off now. And tomorrow's your day off, isn't it?' When Lily nodded, she smiled. 'Then I'll see you in two days' time.'

'Thanks for your help,' Lily said gratefully.

With a sense of relief, she handed mother and baby over to Katie's care, and slipped out of the labour room.

She exchanged her soiled apron for a clean one, washed her hands, checked her cap was on straight, and headed for the waiting area. One day, once she had completed her training and was fully qualified as a midwife, she would be allowed the blue cap and uniform that Bertha wore. That would be the happiest day of her life, for she could hardly wait to have those letters after her name and be a State Registered Midwife. But it was less than a year since she'd decided to leaving nursing and retrain, and she wasn't there yet.

To her astonishment, she found Sonya Thorpe in the waiting room, looking worried and impatient. She glanced down at the watch attached to her uniform. It was nearly eight o'clock in the evening and would soon be quite dark. What on earth was Lady Symmonds' former companion doing here at the hospital, asking for her by name?

'Hello,' Lily said, smiling but confused.

'Oh, my dear.' Sonya stood, clasping her hands together, her face rather pale. 'I have a message from Mary Stannard.'

'Mary?'

'She couldn't get away from the hall. On a late shift, she said. So she asked me to come and give you some urgent news.' There were tears in her eyes. 'It's not very nice, I'm afraid.'

'Blimey.' Lily was frightened now. 'Better spit it out, then,' she urged her, tensed for bad news.

'Mary says they've had a new patient admitted at the hall with very bad burns, and she thinks you may know him.' Sonya bit her lip, her tone apologetic. 'His name is Private Tristan Minear.'

'Tristan?' Lily clenched her fists and held her breath, staring in utter consternation at Sonya as she battled to stay calm. 'God help us.' She went suddenly cold and light-headed, and realised she might be about to faint. 'I … I need to sit down.'

Sonya helped her to one of the wooden chairs in the waiting room and advised her to lean forward and take slow, deep breaths. 'Her ladyship often has funny turns when it gets too hot in the summer,' she said quickly, crouching beside her. 'This helps steady her breathing.'

'I know,' Lily managed to say, bending over her knees and snatching at the air as though she'd been running, 'I … I'm a nurse, remember.'

'I'm sorry, I didn't mean to be condescending.' Sonya

pulled up a chair and sat, watching her sympathetically. 'You and this soldier, Tristan Minear. You were going steady, were you?'

'We never got to that stage. But we were – still are, in fact – good friends. We often exchange letters.' Lily took a deep breath and sat up, pushing aside her fears and reminding herself to remain professional. Until she knew exactly what had happened to Tristan, it was pointless torturing herself about his condition. 'He's badly burnt, you said?'

'Yes, but that's all I know.'

'When was he admitted?'

'A few days ago, I think. Apparently, Mary didn't realise who he was at first. Then, this evening, he asked if she knew Lily Fisher. By the sound of it, he recognised her name from your letters.'

Lily tried to hope for the best. 'So, Tristan can talk, then. He's not … unconscious?'

'I haven't seen him myself but I don't think so, no.' Sonya gave her a falsely cheerful smile that was clearly meant to reassure her. 'Mary said you should go and visit him. That you could see him straightaway if you like. She'll let you onto the ward, whatever the hour.'

'That's very kind of her.' Lily stood, back in control. 'And it was good of you to let me know. Thank you, Sonya.'

'You're welcome.' But the older woman still looked anxious. 'Do you intend to visit him this evening? Because, if so, we could walk back to the hall together. I'm afraid we've missed the last bus, but it's not too far.'

'That would be marvellous.' Lily was not thinking, only reacting, planning, considering what must happen next. She knew that thinking too much would only make

49

her break down in hysterics, and that wouldn't help anyone. 'I'm sorry but could you wait a little longer? I need to change out of my uniform and grab my coat and hat.'

'Of course.' Sonya's steady gaze met hers. 'You know, I'm sure he'll be all right. Dr Lewis is very good with burns.'

'Yes.' Lily tried to smile but couldn't quite manage it. 'I'll be as quick as I can,' she added falteringly, and left the room before a flood of tears could burst out and betray her.

In the darkened ward, lit only by the light from the nurse's station now that the blackout curtains were in place, Lily stood at the foot of the bed and clasped her hands at her waist, staring. She sucked in an unsteady breath and let it out slowly to avoid crying aloud in agony.

The man in the bed in front of her could not be Tristan Minear. It was simply unthinkable. And yet she knew it to be him.

In her mind's eye, she compared this slumped figure to her last sighting of Tristan as he headed off to join the other enlisted men on their way to basic training. Straight-backed and as handsome as ever, a young farmer until he joined up, Tristan had glanced back at them with a cheerful wave, no doubt as much for his weepy sister's benefit as her own. His aunt and father had not come to see him off, too busy on their farm above Penzance to spare the time, but his sister Demelza had been there, along with her sweetheart Robert, a vast giant of a man who worked as an ambulance driver, and Lily herself, of course.

'We're only friends,' she had told Tristan last summer,

warning him off getting too involved with her. She'd had her nursing career to think of back then and hadn't felt ready at the time to commit to a serious relationship.

Tristan had understood, yet still asked permission to write to her while he was away on his basic training, and then later too, once he received his first posting. She had agreed, of course, knowing how much letters from home had always buoyed up the soldiers she'd once cared for as a nurse. But she'd made it plain they would not be exchanging *love* letters. All the same, their friendship had rather blossomed over the months, growing warmer and more affectionate as they wrote to each other more frequently and at greater length, Lily's handwriting tiny and cramped as she struggled to convey everything she wished despite the restrictions of paper rationing.

Now he lay crumpled in this hospital bed at the Convalescent Home for Wounded Servicemen, his bright ginger curls and half his face obscured by heavy bandaging.

'Tris?' she whispered, for it was late evening and most of the patients in the ward were asleep. When he didn't stir, she ventured closer, bending over him. 'Tristan? It's Lily.'

At last, he stirred, turning his head on the pillow. 'Lily?' His voice was low and hoarse. His one unbandaged eye stared up at her, brimming with tears. 'Oh, Lily... Thank you for coming. Though I wish you didn't have to see me like this.'

'Nonsense,' she said briskly, pulling up a chair. Her chest was tight and she badly wanted to weep, yet somehow suppressed it, her training as a nurse coming back to her in a flash. 'Don't you worry your head about that. The doctors and nurses here are bloody brilliant. They'll have you right as rain and back on your feet in no time, see if they don't.'

But Tristan shook his head sadly. 'You're a lovely girl, Lily Fisher, I've always thought so, and I know you mean well. But I'm done for and there's no point pretending otherwise.' The fire-damaged rasp of his voice hissed through the sleeping ward. 'If you don't believe me, take a look for yourself.' Lily began to protest but Tristan had already dragged a corner of his facial bandages to one side, grimacing with pain as he did so.

Shocked into silence, she stared down at him, hands clenched into fists, unable to take her eyes off the coarse red flesh with its thick-gouged, blackened streaks that now made up half his face. As he turned that side of his head fully towards her, Lily heard herself gasp and cursed herself for a coward. She had come here tonight to see her dear friend Tristan Minear. But there was no trace left of the handsome young man who had once proposed to her on a bright summer's day in Penzance. Only this absolute horror…

CHAPTER SIX

Mary had spent most of her afternoon off wandering in and out of the shops in St Ives, hunting for something suitable for her mother's birthday present, but all to no avail. Nothing seemed right for her very picky mother, whom she loved to bits but who could not even on a good day be considered an 'easy' woman to please. By half past three, she was footsore and frustrated and, she realised, catching her reflection in a shop window, a little windswept. Although it was a bright, sunny day, the sea winds had become brisk after lunch, whisking up and down the narrow, cobbled lanes of the Atlantic-facing town.

Removing her hat, she struggled to repin her curly, wayward hair into some semblance of order, then replaced her hat. As she did so, grimacing at herself in the murky glass, she caught sight of a familiar face opposite.

It was Pip, the young evacuee lodging with her parents, presumably on his way home from school. Intending to say hello, Mary straightened and turned with a smile.

Only he was not alone.

A group of five lads in school uniform were behind him, catching up fast. 'Hey, Lunnon,' the tallest one called after him in snarling tones, his accent Cornish. 'You deaf or rude? I'm talking to you, Lunnon.'

He meant London, of course. Which was where Pip came from.

Pip paid no attention.

'Go back where you came from, Lunnon,' another boy yelled, and the others laughed and made noises of agreement. As she watched, one of them stooped to grab a small stone lying in the road and pitched it at Pip, striking him squarely on his shoulder.

Pip gave a yelp and turned, backing away. 'Stop it,' he told them, his voice high and shaking. 'Or I … I …'

'What you going to do, Lunnon? Run crying for Mummy?' The tallest lad made a mocking impersonation of someone rubbing their eyes and blubbing, and again his friends laughed and jeered at Pip. 'Oh, hang on, she's dead, isn't she? I s'pose you'll just have to put up with it. Or throw yourself in the sea.'

'Throw yourself i'the sea,' the other boys began to chant in sing-song voices, grinning as they came level with Pip and surrounded him. 'Throw yourself i'the sea!'

Mary had heard enough. 'What on earth do you lads think you're up to?' She stormed across the road in front of a lumbering milk truck, her face hot with indignation. 'Get along with you! Go on, take yourselves home!'

The boys scattered, though the tallest one hesitated long enough to get a cold and steely look from Mary, used to recalcitrant patients on the ward, and fled before it.

When they'd gone, she turned to Pip, who was red-cheeked and trembling. 'You all right?' she asked a little breathlessly. She gestured to his shoulder. 'That stone must have hurt though. What a rotten lot. I can walk you home and take a look at it, if you like.'

'It's fine.' Pip cast her an unhappy look. 'Only they won't like it. You shouting at 'em like that, Miss. They'll be back, and worse next time.'

'Then you need to tell the teacher.'

His face grew shuttered. 'I ain't no snitch.'

'They're bullies,' she told him. 'It's not snitching to tell on a bully.'

Pip merely shook his head, his expression mulish.

'Very well, have it your own way,' Mary said with a shrug, but made a mental note that she might need to go to the school and speak to his teacher herself. 'Here, how about I buy you a bag of sweets? I've my ration book here, you can have my share for this week.' She indicated the store she had just passed, which sold assorted sweets from large, colourful glass jars kept behind the counter. 'To put a smile back on your face.'

Sure enough, the young boy perked up at once. 'I wouldn't say no, Miss,' he said shyly.

'It's not Miss. You must call me Mary. We're practically family, aren't we?'

His smile faded a little, and she recalled with a pang of anguish that he had lost his family in the Blitz. But he merely nodded. 'Thank you, Miss… I mean, Mary.'

She led him back to the store, where he chose a small selection of sweets, and seemed happier once he had an aniseed ball tucked in his cheek.

'I'll walk you home,' she said, and insisted when he tried to refuse. 'I'm going that way anyway,' she lied.

On their way through town, Mary kept up a steady stream of comments and questions until she felt he had forgotten that unpleasant attack. But at the back of her mind, she was memorising those boys' faces, in case she ever needed to describe them to a teacher or to point them out in the playground. It wasn't right for Cornish kids to be throwing stones and insults at evacuees like Pip, come down from London to escape the German bombardment only to be taunted and tormented here. She was heartily ashamed of the local boys and wished they had not run away so fast, so she could have given them a piece of her mind.

As they headed past the lending library, which she eyed with regret, having previously intended to pay it a quick visit, a high-pitched wail drove all thought of those nasty boys from her mind.

'An air raid!' She gasped, looking about herself. 'Oh blow… We haven't had one in weeks. And now I'm caught out of doors. I wonder where the nearest shelter is?'

Old Mr Landry in his striped apron, hurriedly dragging down the shades of his butcher's shop, must have spotted her dithering on the pavement, for he waved a hand. 'This way, Miss,' he called across the street.

Accompanied by the piercing wail of the siren, they followed him along a side alley to a dark doorway marked PUBLIC SHELTER, where steps led down into the shop cellar. Others had already congregated at the top of the steps, forming an orderly queue.

'Everyone's welcome here,' Mr Landry told them in a

husky voice, untying his apron with a friendly smile. 'It's a nice big space. Belongs to the shop but I'm happy to do my bit, especially now them blasted Jerries keep sending their bombers down Cornwall.'

In the cellar below, Mary was relieved to find various chairs and mattresses spread about the space. Some shelters were not terribly comfortable, especially when full or over capacity, and everyone had to squeeze in together like sardines in a tin. She found a quiet corner for her and Pip, settled the boy on a mattress with his schoolbag and pulled up a low chair beside him. Gradually, the shelter began to fill with townsfolk, several of them shopkeepers from the town centre, others shoppers laden with baskets and bags.

Nodding cheerily to those she knew, Mary wondered how they would be coping up at the convalescent home, which stood on a steep climb out of the town, its raised site overlooking Carbis Bay. There had been a few near misses at the home lately, and Matron had instructed staff to act double-quick when the sirens went off in the town. Not all patients were fit to be moved, of course, and government advice was laughably for such unfortunate individuals to be helped to shelter under their own beds. 'Fat lot of good that'll do,' Harriet, one of the other nurses at Symmonds Hall, had muttered only the other day, and then blushed when she was overheard. But it wasn't their place to make the rules, as Matron had frostily pointed out, only to *follow* them.

In his school jacket and grey short trousers, Pip drew bare knees up to his chin and stared glumly at an old lady seated opposite in a deckchair, who was reading a book.

He looked pale and scared at being down in the air raid shelter, which surprised her. Daytime raids had been far more frequent in the London area, and more destructive too. This kind of thing should be old hat to him now. But maybe it all still felt strange to him, being here in Cornwall instead of back home.

The high-pitched whine of German planes could now be heard overheard; the sound sent a chill down her spine.

Mary settled her shopping basket on her lap. 'So,' she said to Pip, hoping to take both their minds off the enemy planes homing in on St Ives, 'how are you settling in with my parents?' When he said nothing, she added cheerily, 'Dad's bark is worse than his bite, you know, and Mum could fuss for Britain. But I expect you've noticed all that.'

The boy didn't smile but nodded, his freckled face serious. 'They're nice people,' he mumbled, head still down. 'Very kind of 'em to take me in.' It sounded to Mary as though he was being polite rather than entirely truthful. 'And your mum's dinners are bang on.'

'Ah, now I know *that*'s a fib.' He didn't laugh but his shoulders relaxed. She hesitated before asking about the bullies, afraid she might make him clam up again. 'Those boys in the street earlier... Do they act like that in school too? Call you names, I mean.'

'Sometimes.'

'And do you ever tell the teachers?'

'Course not.' Lifting his head at last, Pip shot her a scornful look. 'What d'you take me for?'

'But what they're doing is wrong,' she reminded him softly. 'It's mean and unkind. You're an evacuee, that's all. You've done nothing to deserve that kind of treatment.'

He merely shrugged.

Mary sighed, thinking hard while she watched him. It was clearly pointless trying to get through to the boy. The only thing she could do to help was to visit the school herself. It was too late today as all the staff would have left by now. But maybe another time.

She tried another tack. 'Do you enjoy your school work, Pip?' When he nodded, she asked, 'Which subjects are you best at?'

'Reading and writing, I s'pose.' Pip scowled, pulling up his loose grey socks. 'I'm not much good at arithmetic though. Can't do sums for toffee.'

'Same here,' she agreed fervently. 'What does your teacher say about that? Mine used to punish me for mistakes in long division.'

'Oh, Mr Jeffries ain't too bad.' He seemed to cheer up, a brief grin touching his face. 'Sir likes to make a joke of it, see?' When she looked puzzled, he explained, 'Mr Jeffries says, if I don't watch out, I'll be paying double for my lemon sherbets, and not know it. He says sums is useful, and I've to work harder or else.'

Or else...

Mary thought that sounded like bullying too. Perhaps Mr Jeffries even gave naughty boys the rod. Her lips pursed in disapproval. It was true that most schoolteachers were strict, especially with boys. She supposed they had to keep the rowdier lads in check or nobody would learn anything. But that didn't mean it was right to control the class with threats.

Still, Pip seemed to hero-worship this teacher, so it was probably best not to criticise him.

'Sounds like your Mr Jeffries has his head screwed on. Maybe next time I'm home, I can help you with your arithmetic. How's that?'

'You, Miss?' Pip peered at her sideways. 'I thought you said you was rubbish wiv sums?' He gave a little chuckle when she bit her lip. 'I can get me own sums wrong, thanks. Though I could show you my new library book. It's in my satchel and it's got some lovely pictures.' He glanced up at the sound of planes overhead, his face drained of all colour, but bravely went on, 'Your mum says you like books and reading.'

'That's right.' Mary nodded enthusiastically. 'Mum used to call me her "bookworm" when I was growing up, because I chomped my way through so many of them. I left some of my old books at the house, in fact. Maybe you've seen them.'

'Yeah, I seen 'em...' He pulled a face, unbuckling his school satchel. 'Bloomin' stories for girls. Kittens and flowers and what not. No offence, Miss, but I prefer the boys' annual.' He drew out a library hardback. 'War stories, adventure, all that.'

'No offence taken. Of course you prefer boys' stories. And it's Mary, remember. Not Miss.'

He handed her his library book, which was a story book for boys, and she flicked through a few pages. It seemed harmless enough, though some of the scenes she came across were a little bloodthirsty. Still, if it kept him out of trouble and his head occupied during the air raid...

He kept looking up from his book later though and shivered once or twice. 'I don't like being underground,' he said, seeing her watching him. 'It ain't natural.'

A lady came to offer him a biscuit, and Mary watched with amusement as he accepted politely, saying 'Thank you, Missus,' despite his obvious discomfort at being in the shelter.

He's a good lad, she thought, and felt again that stab of anger at the bullies who'd insulted him in the street, throwing a stone at the poor boy. It simply wasn't right that those Cornish lads should be allowed to behave so badly and get away with it.

The name 'Mr Jeffries' rang a vague bell. She rather thought Sister Rose from the hall – Mrs Lanyon, now that she'd married Dr Lewis – might have mentioned that name a few times. Yes, the two of them had been to school together in St Ives, she recalled, and judging by Rose's smile when talking of him, he'd been a favourite of hers back in the day. Now he was back teaching at the same school he'd attended as a boy. Though he must have been there a few years before Mary's own time at the school because she didn't remember him.

Well, Mr Jeffries was going to meet her now. And he'd better listen to what she had to say about Pip and these bullies, *or else*!

CHAPTER SEVEN

Truro, Cornwall, early April 1943

Sonya's mother Eloise brought out tea and biscuits, served on her second-best china service, to her daughter waiting in the front parlour. 'Remind me, dear, do you take sugar?' Eloise asked, pouring weak golden liquid from the pot with an embarrassed grimace. 'I'm sorry it's not stronger, but rationing, you know...'

It felt as though they were strangers, Sonya thought, but smiled. 'I don't mind. I'm used to it.' Then added hurriedly, 'No sugar for me, thanks.'

'Oh, good.' Her mother handed her the pretty china cup, decorated with rosebuds but with a small chip opposite the handle. 'We're running low.'

Sonya nibbled on a ginger biscuit, studying the parlour. It had not changed much since she had come to see her parents last year, after her father had fallen sick with pneumonia, and her mother had reluctantly asked her to visit, just in case... The straight-backed armchairs and red woollen rug looked a little faded, but a cheerful spring sunshine was filtering through lacy net curtains, lending a cool, airy feel to the room. Outside she heard the constant rumble of traffic in busy Truro, for her parents' terraced house was close to the city centre, only a few streets from the beautiful three-spired cathedral, built around the turn of the century.

Her parents had moved here from a parish just outside Truro when her vicar father retired five years ago. After the outbreak of war, he had been asked to help out occasionally in the local diocese or group of parishes, but his memory was no longer what it had once been, and a few muddled services had left him wary of taking on too much.

'Where's Father?' Sonya asked, after they had been through the inevitable chit-chat about her orphanage work and Lady Symmonds' recent marriage. She was not unhappy to find him out during her visit. But it would have been odd for her not to query his absence. 'Not unwell again, I hope?'

'He's gone out for a walk. A long walk.'

'I see.' She was sure her mother was lying but decided not to comment.

'So,' Eloise with a brief smile, 'why have you come to see us? I know there must be a reason.' She paused. 'Not that you're unwelcome. It's just…' Her voice tailed off but Sonya guessed what she was thinking. Since she'd been packed off to live with the widowed Lady Symmonds, more than two decades ago and mere weeks after the birth of her illegitimate child, she had only visited her parents twice, despite the easy distance between them.

'Lady Symmonds suggested I ought to come to see you.'

It was a bit of a fudge to draw Babs into it. But her mother held her sponsor in awe, and Sonya suspected she might get more cooperation by mentioning her.

'Oh yes?' Her mother's eyes had widened. A tall woman, like Sonya herself, her waist had thickened in recent years, but her grey hair was still thick and springing, set in waves brushed back from a high forehead. Her dress was grey cotton with a narrow white stripe at the hem. Even though she was no longer technically a vicar's wife, she was still dressing the part, Sonya thought. Everything about her mother gave the impression of something strong being subdued, forcibly held down. But her smile gave nothing away, careful and polite. 'How kind of her ladyship to think of you at a time like this. Newly-wed, I mean. I hope you expressed your gratitude before she left for Scotland. All these years, all the things she'd done for you.' Her voice dropped. 'Taking you in after your disgrace like that, with no questions or conditions. Such a generous lady.'

As she now knew, Sonya's grandmother had worked as lady's maid to Lady Symmonds back in the day, before leaving to get married. That family connection had prompted her parents to reach out to her ladyship after Sonya's 'disgrace', as her mother had put it.

Sonya felt herself stiffen in anger and fought an impulse to stand and walk out for good, to turn her back on her parents forever. She'd hoped to find her mother mellowed, now she no longer needed to fear losing face with her husband's congregation. But it seemed the past had not been forgotten, not even now, when the war with Germany had made so many previously shocking things seem trivial and unimportant.

Leaning forward, she set her teacup down rather more abruptly than intended. 'Lady Symmonds thought you might be able to help me trace my daughter.' It was difficult to keep the long years of pain and hurt out of her voice. 'The child you made me give up for adoption, though I begged you to let me keep her.'

Her mother had paled at her first mention of a daughter. Now she made a frightened noise of distress, shaking her head wordlessly.

Pressing on, Sonya said, 'I've decided to find out if she's still alive and well, what she looks like, whether she might want to … to meet me.' There was heat in her cheeks, but she was determined to finish what she had come here to say. 'She may not want to, of course. But I won't know for sure unless I ask.'

'Sonya, no, that's not a good idea,' her mother burst out at last, her voice low and urgent.

'Why not?'

'Because… Well, it's just not.' Her mother was staring at her in consternation. 'Think about it for a moment. She may hate you.'

'I don't care.'

'You say that now, but it's a hard thing, for a mother to know her daughter hates her…' Eloise looked away, her voice faltering. 'And what about your father? Consider what it would do to him to dredge up the past like this. The shock might kill him.'

Sonya's lips tightened. 'Piffle!'

At this vulgarity, her mother sat up straight, colour flooding her cheeks. She put down her own teacup, which she had been holding defensively against her chest. 'Sonya

65

Thorpe,' she exclaimed, 'how dare you use such language in this house?'

Sonya ignored this. 'Lady Symmonds insisted that I visit you, and I'm beginning to think there was a specific reason for that.' Sonya's eyes narrowed at her mother's instinctive recoil. 'What do you know?'

'Nothing, nothing.' But her mother's voice lacked conviction, and abruptly she got up and paced the room, wringing her hands. 'If I had known the purpose of your visit, I would never have agreed to let you come.' There was a wild look in her face. 'I ... I think you should go now, before your father comes back.'

Sonya stood but did not move to the door. 'Mother, tell me the truth. Do you know where my daughter is?'

'Please don't ask me that. You mustn't.' Her mother clasped her hands to her cheeks, stopping dead in the centre of the room. 'I can't say ... I dare not.' Her eyes sought Sonya's. 'He would never forgive me,' she finished in a terrified whisper.

Her body turning ice-cold, Sonya understood at last. She strode out into the hall and to the bottom of the stairs, looking up into gloom. 'Father?'

Her mother stood in the doorway to the parlour, watching in silence, her eyes wide with fright.

A floorboard creaked upstairs. Then a figure came to the top of the stairs, staring down at her.

'Hello, Sonya,' her father said, without a hint of apology for having hidden from her, as he slowly began to descend the stairs in trousers and snowy white shirt, pulling up his braces with a familiar snap. 'How are you, girl?'

Girl, she thought fiercely, everything in her jarring at

the sound of his deep voice. *Girl*. As though she were still a child, not a woman in her forties.

'Where is my daughter?' she demanded, not mincing her words.

'Now, you be quiet and listen to me.' His tone, as ever, was unyielding. 'You're not thinking straight. You've got yourself a respectable position at Symmonds Hall. Nobody there knows what you did, thanks to her ladyship. Why jeopardise all that for some idiotic flight of fancy?' Coming to the bottom of the stairs, he faced her with his habitual stern expression, though his shoulders were stooped now he was heading for seventy. 'You're not that child's mother. You never were.'

Sonya stared into her father's face and knew nothing had changed. Not since that awful day when she'd broken down in tears and admitted she was pregnant, and he had taken his belt to her and called her a whore. Never mind that Bobby, all of nineteen at the time, had faithfully promised to marry her before he left for the front, and had written back as soon as he received her anguished letter informing him of the pregnancy, insisting he would get leave as soon as he could. Never mind too that Bobby had been killed within days of writing that letter, destroying her world and leaving her unmarried with a child on the way. No, her father had not cared about the circumstances then, and still didn't care. All he was concerned about was whether people might *talk* and put him, the Reverend Thorpe, to shame.

His daughter, his only child, had committed the unspeakable sin of falling in love and acting on it, and for that mistake, she was forever condemned and cast out.

'How it must have tortured you, Father,' she said, her heart thumping, 'to stand in the pulpit every Sunday, preaching chastity and proper Christian living, while all the time your unmarried daughter was about to give birth to a bastard.'

He slapped her face.

The blow was weak, no strength behind it. He had slapped her that day too, sending her flying. But now he was older. She gasped but didn't yield any ground, turning her head deliberately.

'Better try that again,' she told him, 'only this time on the other cheek. Because I don't think I've learned my lesson yet.'

'You always were a stubborn little…' Her mother made a protest, and her father didn't finish, his chest heaving with fury and indignation. 'Get out of my house. And never come back.'

'No, no,' her mother cried, running to intercept her as Sonya turned blindly to fetch her handbag and coat, 'We have to tell her, Stanley. It's time.'

'Tell me what?' Sonya demanded.

But Eloise only looked pleadingly at her husband.

Her father stared stonily at them both, and then shrugged. 'Do as you like. I wash my hands of the business.' His voice was brusque as he headed up the stairs, leaning heavily on the banister, his breathing unsteady. 'I'm going back to bed.'

Sonya watched him go, her eyes widening. 'Back to bed?' she echoed, but he didn't respond, disappearing into the gloom above.

'It's his chest, that's all,' her mother said hurriedly. 'He's been wheezing again. The doctor recommended a few days' bed rest. I didn't like lying to you, but your father... You know what he's like. Too proud to admit when there's something wrong.' Tentatively, her mother touched her sleeve. 'Come back into the parlour, Sonya, and finish your tea. I've something to show you.'

While Sonya sat anxiously, hands knitted together in her lap, her mother freshened the pot with hot water, and cut them two thin slices of dry-looking fruit cake without much fruit in it. 'I don't have any other cake in the house, I'm afraid.'

'It looks delicious,' Sonya lied, but devoured the meagre slice nonetheless, trying not to compare it to pre-war fruit cakes she had enjoyed at Symmonds Hall. She was hungry enough not to care about the taste, and besides, eating it took her mind off that awful scene with her father. She wondered how sick he was, and if it was more serious than her mother had let on. 'What was it you had to show me?'

Her mother reached behind the armchair cushion and drew out a crumpled envelope she must have been concealing there. It had been opened. Slowly, Eloise drew a single sheet of thin, folded paper out of the envelope.

'This arrived about six years ago,' she said, her troubled gaze on Sonya's face. 'I wanted to send it to you at Symmonds Hall straightaway. But Stanley expressly forbade it, and I...' Her mother hesitated, and then handed Sonya the letter with a reluctant air. 'In the end, I decided maybe he was right and it was for the best. We were worried, you see, that you might lose your position with her ladyship if things came out about ... well, about your past.'

Trembling and filled with sudden trepidation, Sonya unfolded the creased letter, not sure what to expect, and began to read.

Dear Reverend Thorpe,

I hope you don't mind my writing to you in this manner. My name is Mrs Yvonne Fairweather, and I have reason to believe I may be your granddaughter. A few years ago, when I was married, I obtained my birth certificate and saw that my mother's name was noted as a Miss Sonya Thorpe of Back Lane, St Clement, Cornwall. My father's column was left blank. I made a few discreet enquiries and the church adoption service gave me your name and address; they seemed to think you might be related to this lady, but refused to confirm this.

Having recently become a mother myself, I would very much like to make contact with my birth mother. If Miss Sonya Thorpe is indeed your daughter, I hope you would pass this letter onto her with my best wishes.

Yours sincerely,

Mrs Yvonne Fairweather

The address at the top of the letter was Kenwyn Hill, a district on the northern outskirts of Truro.

The date was June 1937.

'You received this years ago,' Sonya whispered, distraught, 'while you were still at the vicarage in St Clement.'

'Yes.'

'But you chose not to tell me?'

Her mother bit her lip. 'It was before the war. A different world. Things are so topsy-turvy now, maybe it wouldn't have seemed so important to conceal the truth, but in those days...' She leant forward earnestly. 'As I said before, your father thought you might lose your position with Lady Symmonds if it was all dredged up again. Her ladyship was more than understanding about your past, but I can't believe she would have welcomed a visit from your ... your illegitimate daughter.'

'That was for me to decide, not you. You and Father had no right to interfere.' Sonya's voice shook, and her eyes blurred with tears. 'Did you even reply to her?'

Her mother shook her head. 'We thought it best—' she began to repeat, but Sonya interrupted her in bitter tones.

'Best for whom? Me or you?'

'I swear, we were only thinking of you, dear. Though it's true your father was still a vicar in those days,' she said unhappily. 'Stanley might have lost everything if the archdeacon had learned of it. Besides, we couldn't believe this girl's husband would wish to involve himself with his unmarried mother-in-law,' she added, shaking her head. 'Least said, soonest mended.'

Having recently become a mother myself, I would very much like to make contact with my birth mother.

She was a grandmother, Sonya realised with a jolt.

Standing, she took the envelope from her mother's hands and folded the letter into it. 'This is mine,' she said decisively, and bent to kiss her mother on the cheek. 'Goodbye, Mother.' It was hard not to feel a deep burning resentment towards her parents for keeping this precious letter from her. But what good would it do? 'Say goodbye to Father for me.'

Her mother followed her to the front door, apprehension in her face. 'Oh dear… What are you planning, Sonya?'

'Something I ought to have done years ago, of course,' she said, with more confidence than she felt inside. For how welcome would she really be after all these years?

She had been forced to abandon her baby, and 'Yvonne' as she had been named would not know the circumstances, only that she had not been wanted by her mother. This letter held out some hope. But it was already six years old. Anything might have happened in the intervening time. Yvonne might even have changed her mind about wanting to meet her birth mother. But she had to try.

'I'm going to find my daughter.'

CHAPTER EIGHT

St Ives, Cornwall, April 1943

After a long shift on the labour ward, Lily had a quick wash, pulled on fresh civvies, and stood buttoning her blouse in the cool, shadowy light of her bedroom. As a midwife, she had been allotted a cottage on the outskirts of St Ives, where her predecessor had also lived. Her front windows looked down over the town to the turbulent blue of the Atlantic Ocean, a view she could never tire of admiring, and although the mid-terrace cottage was tiny – basically one up, one down – she loved having a home of her own. The main room downstairs had been skilfully divided into two, leaving a snug sitting room with a fire-place for winter heating, and a separate kitchen, albeit not much bigger than a pantry. But it was perfect for her needs, and the road outside her door led straight down into the town, with easy access to the hospital, a mere quarter of an hour's walk away.

She was trying hard not to fret about Tristan's horrifying

burns. His skin would soon heal, wouldn't it? All the same, it was with a sense of trepidation that she checked her smooth blonde waves, fixed a fashionable beret on her head, and set off across town for Symmonds Hall. She had enough experience as a nurse to know that not every burns patient would fully recover, and with some, the wounds could become infected and cause further pain and mutilation or even death. It all depended on how deeply the flames had damaged the skin and what kind of fire had been involved. Since she didn't know the answer to either of those questions, she must simply be patient and hope for the best.

On Carbis Ward, Lily was thrown to discover that Tristan already had visitors. Three visitors, in fact. Two men and a woman. Suddenly shy, she hung back, unsure what to do. But the woman turned at that moment and spotted her, raising her hand in greeting.

It was Demelza Minear, Tristan's older sister. She too had the family's trademark ginger curls, though hers hung bountifully past her shoulders, framing a sweet, freckled face that smiled at Lily with open friendliness.

'Hello, Lily,' Demelza said warmly, and came across to kiss her cheek. 'How wonderful to see you again. Have you come to see Tristan? But of course you have. How are you?'

'I'm very well, thank you, and how are you?' As they chatted, her gaze stole across to Tristan's bedside. She recognised both men standing there. Tristan's father, Farmer Minear, and Robert Day, an ambulance driver well-known to most people in Penzance. He and Demelza had been walking out since last summer, but apparently

74

Robert was a Quaker and didn't believe in 'engagements', only marriage. 'I see Robert came with you,' she added teasingly. 'Are you two married yet?'

Demelza shook her head, grinning back at her. 'Soon though,' she whispered in her ear. 'We've pencilled in a date for late May. Mum's the word though.' The redhead glanced back at the grim-faced farmer now seated by the bed, surveying his son's injuries. 'Father's not keen on us marrying, as I've told him we'll be joining the ambulance service at the front once we're man and wife.' Her smile faded. 'He doesn't want me to leave Penzance, you see.'

Lily gave her a quick hug, sad for her friend. 'It's difficult for him, I expect,' she whispered in return. 'What with his son enlisting, and then his daughter planning to marry... Now Tris coming back in such bad shape. Your dad must feel his world's been turned upside down. But I'm sure he'll come around.'

'I hope you're right. Because I'm determined to marry Robert and apply for the frontline ancillary services.' Demelza's chin rose bravely. 'Whatever he has to say about it.'

They approached the bed together, and Lily shook Robert's hand. 'Hello again,' she said cheerfully. 'I hope you're well. And you too, Mr Minear.' She held out a hand to Tristan's father, who ignored it.

'I know you. You're his fancy blonde piece, that Dagenham girl he used to dote on.' Mr Minear looked her up and down without disguising his contempt. 'I hoped we'd seen the last of you when Tris up and left.' He pointed to his son, still swathed in bandages. 'See what you've done, girl? This is what comes of encouraging a child to join up.

75

A mere boy, he was, barely knew his left from right. Now look at him.'

Lily felt her heart sink under his accusing stare. He was wrong, of course; she had never encouraged his son to join up. Tristan had made that decision on his own after they'd broken up.

But his father had worked out they'd been seeing each other, and had kicked up a fuss, even trying to get Lily the sack from her job at Penzance Hospital. She'd hoped his heart attack shortly afterwards might have changed his view of life and mellowed his irascible personality as Tristan had told her that his father was 'much kinder' since then. Maybe that kindness was only extended to his family though. Because his cold stare made it clear he didn't consider her worthy to speak to her son.

'Mr Minear,' Lily said, anxious not to upset Tristan further, who was already grimacing and making hoarse noises. 'This is hardly the time or place to—'

But Mr Minear paid no attention, raising his voice above hers. 'My boy never needed to enlist. It's a protected profession, farming. Then he met you, and all he could think about was leaving home. Doing his bit,' he spat out. 'And all to impress *you*, I daresay.'

'Honestly, no,' she began again, hot-cheeked, trying to stem his flow of malice, but the farmer continued as though she hadn't spoken.

'Doctor says he'll need specialist care for three months at least, maybe longer. Aye, and surgery later, perhaps.' His thick finger jabbed towards Tristan's prone figure. 'Not in hospital though… They want to send him home soon, free up his bed for other wounded servicemen.'

'Please, not so loud, Mr Minear,' Lily said urgently, glancing about the ward in embarrassment.

'Seems I'm supposed to look after him,' the farmer thundered on, regardless. 'Or his aunt Sarah, who's never been the same since her stroke. I thought maybe his own sister could have lent a hand. But no, she's to be wed soon, she says, and off to foreign climes. So, who's going to look after my sick boy, eh? Answer me that, Miss Clever-Clogs. Because it won't be me. I've got the farm to tend to, I can't be playing nursemaid to a grown man.'

Robert Day, who'd been standing quietly all this time, a frown on his face, put a hand on Mr Minear's shoulder. 'Perhaps we should take this outside,' he said, and indeed most of the patients in the ward were sitting up in bed, listening to this exchange with curious faces. 'For the boy's sake.'

'It's none of your damned business either, *conchie*,' Mr Minear roared at him, and then saw Dr Lewis approaching and pulled a face, hurriedly backing off. 'Well, I've said my piece.'

Conchie.

He was referring to Robert's stance on war work, Lily realised with a quick shudder. Being a Quaker, Robert was a pacifist and had refused to take up arms when war broke out. However, he had volunteered for the ambulance service instead, and made it plain he wanted to serve on the front line as soon as he could.

Mr Minear took a few steps away, settling his flat cap back on his head, and then paused. He glanced back at Tristan, barely making eye contact as he added, 'I'm sorry for you, lad. You look right poorly. But there's no place on a working farm for an invalid who can't pull their weight, as well you know. So you'll need to find some other place to stay until you can get back on your feet.'

Dr Lewis had come to a halt beside the bed, staring from Tristan to Mr Minear. 'What on earth's going on? I'll not have raised voices on the ward, is that clear?'

'I'll wait for you outside,' Mr Minear told his daughter, and headed for the ward door without even a glance at the doctor. 'Don't be long, mind. We need to get home before dark.'

Dr Lewis watched him go, frowning in disapproval, and then turned to Lily, blinking as he recognised her. 'Hello, Lily. Everything all right here?'

'Mr Minear is upset, that's all,' she said, carefully explaining the situation. 'He was shocked to discover how much care his son is going to need.'

'Of course, I see. Perfectly understandable. No excuse for yelling on the ward though. Hopefully he'll calm down once he's outside.' Dr Lewis stooped to check Tristan's pulse. Tristan's face was unnaturally flushed, his eyes furious and glittering. 'Now, my dear chap, this will never do. Your pulse is racing like a greyhound. Deep, slow breaths. In through the nose, out through the mouth.' He replaced Tristan's hand gently on the covers. 'No, don't try to speak. You need to rest those vocal cords. Smoke damage, remember?'

Tristan expelled his breath in a frustrated sigh but nodded. His gaze shifted to Lily, and then hurriedly away. He was embarrassed, she realised, and felt so sorry for him, tears filling her eyes. His own father had just rejected him, and openly too, in front of friends and family, and all these other servicemen in the beds around them. Small wonder his pulse was racing and he was struggling not to vent his anger.

As Dr Lewis took himself off to speak to another patient further up the ward, Lily caught Robert and Demelza exchanging a worried look.

'Perhaps we should delay the wedding,' Demelza whispered to her sweetheart, but Tristan made a sound of protest.

'Oh no, you don't,' he insisted, his voice croaking. 'Not on my account, Dem. I'd rather sleep in the streets.'

'I'll speak to Father, get him to see sense,' Demelza assured her brother, though he didn't look convinced. 'There's no question of you not having somewhere to go. Hill View Farm is your home, Tris. You were born there, it's where you belong.' With a bright smile, she turned to hug Lily. 'It's been lovely to see you again, Lily. And I'm so glad you're enjoying your new career as a midwife. I'm sure you'll be brilliant.'

'I hope you're right,' Lily said fervently.

'Write to me at the farm and let me have your new address. I'll send you an invitation to the wedding once all the details have been finalised. Though it won't be like other weddings, Robert says. Quakers do things differently. No church, for instance.' When her husband-to-be put his arm about her waist, smiling enigmatically, Demelza blushed, her cheeks almost as fiery as her hair. 'You … you do still want to come, don't you, Lily?'

'I wouldn't miss it for the world.'

'Thank goodness. I'll be inviting quite a few nurses, plus all the Fire Guard Service, so you'll know plenty of people at the wedding reception.'

When Lily had been working in Penzance, she and some of the other nurses had been given temporary lodging in the women's auxiliary fire service building after the nurses' home was partly demolished by a bomb, so they'd all mucked in together and got to know each other famously.

'By the way, it was very kind of you to drop by to see Tris,' Demelza added under her breath. 'He's been feeling a bit lonely, poor thing.'

'Dem,' Tristan groaned, clearly able to hear her whisper. 'For goodness' sake…'

'Sorry, little brother,' Demelza told him airily, looking far from apologetic. 'But if ever you needed a friend, it's now.'

Demelza and Robert left, with promises to come and see Tristan again soon, and Lily pulled up a chair to Tristan's bedside.

His colour looked rather better today, Lily thought, examining Tristan with a nurse's eye, though he was still trussed up in bandages like an Egyptian mummy. She wondered whether the surgery his father had mentioned was facial, and what that would mean for the handsome, smiling face she remembered. But she steeled her heart against such questions. Tristan was alive; that was all that mattered. The rest could wait.

'Don't fret,' she said briskly, 'I know you must be exhausted, so I'll be on my way soon. I just wanted to check how you were doing.'

She had automatically adopted the no-nonsense tone she had constantly used when working here, she realised, and felt a stab of irritation. Tristan wasn't her patient but one of her dearest friends. More than that, perhaps.

'Feeling rotten,' he mumbled.

'You must be in a fair bit of pain, so that's hardly surprising.' She imagined he must be on pain relief though, which would no doubt be suppressing his other functions. She couldn't expect much sense from him until he no longer needed such a large dose. 'You'll feel better in another week or so, mark my words.'

She leant forward to check his pulse. His unbandaged wrist was cool and clammy, but his fingers curled inwards at her touch and his pulse began to rocket, his gaze drawn back to her face.

'What … what are you doing?' he demanded indistinctly. 'You're not my nurse. There's no need to fuss.'

Lily restored his hand to the starched white coverlet and sat back, her eyes steady on his face. 'All right, I won't fuss then. But more to the point, Tristan, what are *you* going to do?'

His gaze warred with hers. 'I don't know what you mean,' he said in his hoarse voice, the words almost inaudible.

'Your dad won't look after you on the farm at Penzance, that's obvious, and your sister's hoping to go abroad with Robert as soon as they've tied the knot. That don't leave you many options, I'm afraid.'

'Dad will change his mind.'

She shook her head, sorrow welling up inside her at the forlorn look on his face. 'He won't, Tris. We both know what kind of man your dad is, I'm sorry to say. Even if he could be persuaded to take you in, which I doubt, what kind of nursing would you receive on the farm? None at all, I'd guess. Your aunt's not a well woman herself, and your father's got his hands full managing the farm and them new Land Girls he's taken on. Besides which, the farm's too far out of town for a nurse to visit every day, even if he could afford to pay for one.' She shook her head when he looked away, his face turbulent. 'Come on, you know I'm right. You won't find shelter in Penzance.'

He said nothing for a while, then his hand clenched into a fist and he gasped hoarsely, 'I … I can't stay here.'

'No, you certainly can't,' she agreed, and sat a moment, thinking back to how horrified she'd been to see his facial burns beneath the bandages. Considering her long experience as a nurse, that knee-jerk response had been both shocking and unprofessional. If Tristan hadn't been such a sturdy soul, her reaction might have set his recovery back weeks. Perhaps this was her chance to make up for it. 'But you could come and stay with me.' She saw his stunned look and continued briskly, 'As a local midwife, I was given a small cottage for my use here in St Ives. It's nothing grand but there's room for two. When I'm not at work, I could nurse you. And if I have to be out a long while, I could ask one of the community nurses to check on you.'

Everything she'd ever done had been leading up to this moment, she realised, joy dancing with surprise in her heart. All them long, back-breaking hours as a nurse, her almost obsessive desire to care for others, to make a real difference in someone's life… What had it all been for if she couldn't hold out a hand to this man who badly needed a friend? More than a friend, in fact. Tristan needed a *soul-mate*, someone he could turn to and depend on in times of trouble, and who would never judge him or think worse of him for not being like other men, for not being perfect.

Tristan was staring at her. 'You and me? Share a cottage?' He blinked. 'But my burns… They're all down my body. You'd have to change the dressings,' he managed with difficulty, his face troubled, 'and bathe me. You'd see me without … without…'

'Without your clothes on. I know.'

His jaw worked silently for a moment, his colour shifting from livid pallor to a hot blush, then Tristan shook his head and whispered, 'Lily, no. We couldn't. What … what would folk say?'

'They wouldn't say anything,' Lily told him calmly, her mind made up. 'Because we'd be married.'

CHAPTER NINE

Before Mary could put her plan into action to visit the school on Pip's behalf, she received a note from her mother, letting her know that Pip had been expelled. He'd been caught fighting in the playground after school, and when the teacher tried to intervene, Pip had accidentally broken the man's nose. All this had happened a few days ago and the poor boy had been stuck at home ever since, looking 'as bruised and battered as a prize fighter', and constantly getting into mischief because he was so bored.

Her mum's urgently scrawled note ended, *Please come and see us as soon as you can. I'm at my wits' end with the boy, and I need your advice. With love, Your Mother*

Pip had broken his teacher's nose? That scrawny little boy?

Mary could barely contain her impatience until the end of her afternoon shift, then excused herself from supper in the hall dining room and headed straight home instead. She had to be back on the wards by lunch-time the next day. But it was clear that her mother expected her back home at once, even if it could only be a flying visit.

Back home, she found Pip playing jacks in the sunny front yard. He had a new shiner and bruises on his shin, as though someone had given him a kicking too.

'Hello, Pip.' The sun was behind her, and the boy looked up awkwardly, shielding his eyes. 'I hear you're in a spot of bother.'

'It weren't my fault. Honest.'

'I believe you.' Mary crouched to watch him finish his game of jacks. 'Who were you fighting with?'

'Tom, mostly, and Jacob, and a couple of the other lads.' He didn't look up, bouncing the ball and scooping up a handful of metal jacks with an expert hand. 'It was just after school. The bell rang and we all went outside in the yard. Tom pushed me first. So I pushed him back. The others pushed me too. They was all yellin', callin' me bad names. Then…' His voice tailed off.

'Then Mr Jeffries got in the way?'

Pip didn't smile. 'I didn't mean it, I swear. My arm flew out and … and Sir was bent over between me and Tom, like he wanted to talk to us. There was this bloomin' awful crack, like a twig snappin'… Then Mr Jeffries, he had blood on his face. He was so angry.' His voice shook. 'The other boys scarpered, double quick. But I just stood there. I didn't know what to do.'

'So you got the blame.'

Pip shrugged, looking helpless. 'It weren't my fault,' he repeatedly stubbornly. 'If someone pushes me, I push back. That's what your dad told me to do, anyway.'

'My dad?' Mary was puzzled.

85

'That interfering man... I knew it!'

They both looked up, and there was Mary's mum in the doorway, hands on her hips, a dark frown on her face.

'Knew what, Mum?' Mary stood to give her mother a hug, perplexed and concerned. 'Who are you talking about?'

'Your father.' Rita's face was screwed up in lines of annoyance, but Mary could see her concern beneath the scowl. 'He's been egging the boy on, telling him to stand up for himself, to fight back, and look what's happened. All this fighting talk has got him expelled from school, and now he's on my hands, every day of the week.'

'Mum, come on... I'm sure it's not Dad's fault.'

Her mother pursed her lips. 'Whose fault is it, then?'

'Well,' Mary said consideringly, 'Pip shouldn't have been fighting in the first place, it's true. But it sounds as though the teacher stepped into the fight, and this expulsion is more to do with his broken nose than Pip's bad behaviour.' She hesitated. 'I've been thinking, you know.'

'Oh aye? Sounds dangerous,' her mother quipped.

Mary ignored her sarcastic tone. 'Perhaps if I were to go up to the school and talk to this Mr Jeffries myself, I could explain about the bullying. Then maybe he'll relent and let Pip come back to school.'

'I don't want that,' Pip said in a strained voice.

Mary looked down at him sympathetically. 'I know you don't, Pip.' She bent down, peering into his worried face. 'But sometimes we have to do things we don't like, in order to fix something that's broken.'

'What, like his teacher's nose?' Her mother gave a shout of laughter at her own joke.

Pip glared up at Rita accusingly. Then he scrambled to

his feet, ducked under Mary's arm, and ran off down the street.

'Hey,' Mary shouted after the boy. But her mother caught her arm.

'No, let him go. He's been driving me crackers today, constantly going on about being "bored". And it's a nice day. It'll do the lad good to get some proper fresh air.' Rita jerked her head towards the house, her expression softening. 'Come on, love. I'll put the kettle on and tell you all about it.'

Pip glanced back once before disappearing around the street corner, and Mary gave up, reluctantly following her mum inside.

When several hours passed and Pip still didn't return, Mary began to feel serious concern for the boy. To her dismay though, her parents shrugged off his absence as mere horseplay. Her father came back from meeting some old friends down by the harbour and asked when supper would be ready, so Rita briskly pulled on her apron and set about peeling spuds. 'Lay the table for me, would you?' she asked her daughter.

Mary obeyed, conscientiously setting out knives and forks for four people. But her insides were churning. Where was Pip? What could have happened to him?

'Let me go and look for the boy,' she pleaded with her mother after she'd finished her chore. 'What if he's bumped into those bullies again? He could be in real trouble.'

Her father put a hand on her shoulder. 'Calm down, Mary. Boys aren't like girls, you know. They like to run free. I'm sure he'll be safe enough.'

But Pip still hadn't returned by the time they were sitting down to a rather lacklustre fish pie with more potato in it than fish, though with plenty of greens on the side. Even Mary's mother was starting to glance at the clock with a furrowed brow.

A loud knock at the front door startled them.

Mary's father got up, looking grave. 'Something must have happened. You know Pip never uses the front door. And he wouldn't knock.'

Mary crept into the hall, watching as her father opened the front door. She gasped to see Pip on the step, looking dirty and dishevelled, and behind him a large man with unkempt fair hair, spectacles, a sticking plaster across his nose, and a decidedly lazy eye that gazed off to one side while he was looking directly ahead.

Mary was relieved, at least, that their visitor wasn't a policeman, which was what she'd feared on first hearing that authoritative knock. But she was also intrigued. This had to be the teacher behind Pip's expulsion from school, she realised, studying him closely. Why else would there be a large sticking plaster across his nose, and dark bruises around his eyes, unless it had recently been broken?

'Mr Stannard?' The fair-haired man extended a hand, and Harold shook it, his face bemused. 'I hope you don't mind, but I found this young man wandering in the streets, rather the worse for wear, and thought I'd better accompany him home.' His smile was frank and friendly, which surprised Mary, after the account both Pip and her parents had given of him. 'We have met once or twice, but you may have forgotten. I'm Dick Jeffries, one of Pip's teachers at the school.'

'Thank you for bringing him home,' her dad told the teacher rather gruffly. She could tell he wasn't pleased at this interruption to his supper. 'As for you, Pip... Get yourself washed up and ready for your tea. Mrs Stannard's been keeping it warm for you. Not that you deserve it,' he added, 'leading us such a merry dance lately.'

'Yes, sir,' Pip muttered, and ran to the kitchen to wash his hands and face, barely glancing at Mary on his way past.

Mr Stannard was about to close the door rudely in the teacher's face, but Mary caught it. 'I'd just like a quick word with Mr Jeffries, Dad,' she said without further explanation, and slipped outside, following the man down the garden path. 'Excuse me?'

Mr Jeffries turned, closing the garden gate after himself. He looked surprised. 'Yes?'

She held out a hand. 'Hello, I'm Mary Stannard. Thank you for looking out for Pip tonight. We were all very worried about him.' She paused, feeling oddly shy, which was ridiculous. 'I ... I wonder if I could talk to you for a few minutes?'

'Of course,' he said, looking her up and down with interest. His eyes held a merry twinkle, even though the one was slightly awry. She guessed his eye was why he had not joined up. Any minor defect like that could put a man out of the running to be a soldier. 'I'm Dick Jeffries, in case you didn't catch my name,' he said, and shook her hand, pumping it up and down.

'Yes, Pip's told us all about you,' she admitted.

He gave a self-conscious laugh. 'Nothing good, I expect.'

Mary grinned, liking his self-effacing sense of humour.

'To be honest, it's because of Pip that I wanted to talk to you.'

'All right, Miss Stannard, so what would you like to know?'

Releasing the wooden gate, Pip's teacher thrust both hands into his trouser pockets, watching her with a smile in his eyes.

She thought he seemed a little shy. But perhaps he was worried she might be about to make a complaint. That sort of thing always put her on edge too, whenever a troublesome patient suggested she hadn't seen to his needs promptly enough and threatened to tell Matron or one of the doctors. Even when there was nothing behind it, it still made her nervous.

Though she had been planning to make a complaint, hadn't she? About his treatment of young Pip.

'The thing is,' she began awkwardly, 'I was hoping you might reconsider Pip's expulsion from school.'

'Oh.' His hands dug deeper into his pockets and he pulled a face.

'You see, I know it was awful, what happened to your nose.' She glanced at his bruised face with its prominent sticking-plaster and then looked hurriedly away. 'But it was an accident and Pip is very sorry, trust me.'

'I'm sure he is. But the fact remains that he was fighting,' he pointed out apologetically, 'and fighting is not condoned on school premises.' He paused, a quirky smile on his lips. 'We don't condone it anywhere, of course. But certainly not in the playground.'

'But he didn't start the fight.'

'Is that so?' He sounded unconvinced.

'Yes, it is,' she told him hotly. 'The fact is, those same boys have been bullying him ever since he started at the school, Mr Jeffries. Don't tell me you've failed to notice what's been going on right under your nose?'

'Ah, I wondered when my nose was going to come into it,' he joked, and gently tapped the tip of his plaster-covered nose. Then he caught her disapproving glare and his smile vanished. 'It's true that Pip gets more than his fair share of name-calling. And he's turned up to class with a few unexplained bruises too. But boys, you know—'

'Yes, yes,' she interrupted him impatiently, 'I've heard it all before. Only you listen to me. Pip's a quiet, well-behaved boy who lost his whole family in the Blitz, and those brutish lads have been making his life a misery for weeks. It's high time somebody put a stop to it.'

'*Somebody*?'

'That's correct, Mr Jeffries,' she agreed, crossing her arms and fixing him with a stern eye. 'Somebody.' She pursed her lips. 'So, what are you going to do about it?'

'Oh, right, *I'm* the somebody, am I?' When she didn't respond, merely continuing to glare at him, he said more hesitantly, 'Well, I … erm…'

Pip's teacher scratched his head, cocked an eyebrow at her, and then remarked, half-joking, half-serious, 'I imagine I'm going to do whatever you suggest, Miss Stannard.'

CHAPTER TEN

Truro, Cornwall, April 1943

Sonya could not quite believe her own bravado. She checked the new address on her daughter's letter for about the fifteenth time, and then raised a hand boldly to knock at the front door. Then she stepped back, the letter still clutched in her hand, and studied her reflection in the net-covered window beside her. Thankfully, her hair seemed to be under control, her hat and summer coat looked smart, and no nervousness was evident in her face.

Her daughter Yvonne, she had discovered, was now living with her in-laws in Truro. While her husband was away serving his country, it had seemed like a good idea for the young mother to move in with his family, according to her letter. Looking up at the place, Sonya could perfectly understand that decision. It was a large, double-fronted detached house with a well-maintained garden and a gravel path. The house number was engraved on a shiny golden plaque beside the blue door. The area was very genteel too, far from the poorer districts of Truro.

It had taken several days for Sonya to write to her daughter, using the address on the old letter her mother had given her. Not because she didn't want to meet Yvonne but because she couldn't seem to get the wording right. She had started the letter several times, and then screwed up the sheet and thrown it aside, hating herself for wasting precious paper in this time of war but also aware that this was the most important letter she would ever write in her life.

About a week after sending it, she'd received a reply, inviting her to meet Yvonne and her six-year-old son, Walter. The letter had been short but friendly. Still, Sonya had felt some trepidation, wondering if she should back out before it was too late.

She was about to turn away, fearing her daughter must have changed her mind about the meeting, when she heard a hurried click of heels inside and the front door jerked open.

Sonya found herself looking back at a young woman with charming, chocolate-brown eyes and an anxious smile. Her wavy dark hair was as thick and glossy as her own had been in her early twenties. She wore a knee-length summer dress, immaculate white with red cherries and short-capped sleeves, and rather swish black heels that matched the narrow black belt at her waist.

'Hello,' the young woman said breathlessly, her gaze darting nervously up and down Sonya's hesitant figure, 'I'm sorry it took so long to open the door but I was trying to persuade Walter to come down and meet you. Only he's six and rather stubborn, I'm afraid.' Mrs Yvonne Fairweather – for that had to be who she was, Sonya had decided – glanced over her shoulder, and sighed. 'I don't think he's coming down. He's been a little difficult all morning, in fact. Ordinarily, he would be at school. But I kept him off especially so he could meet you, and now…' She bit her lip. 'But here I am, stupidly rambling on about Walter instead of…'

Sonya did not know what to say or how to react, dazed by this eager torrent of words.

Yvonne blinked and shook her head. 'Oh goodness. Let's start again, shall we? You must be Sonya, and I… Well, you know who I am.' They shook hands. Her daughter's grip was brief and uncertain. 'Please, come in.'

Sonya was enchanted, both by her daughter's shy candour and the thought of a young grandson she might soon be meeting. But her nerves were still jangling fiercely.

'Thank you, you're very kind.' She stepped into the cool, elegantly decorated hallway, sliding off her hat and coat when Yvonne asked for them and watching as her daughter hung them on the coat stand. 'Please don't worry about your son,' she added, trying to fill an awkward silence. 'I work with orphans in St Ives. We have one rather stubborn six-year-old in the orphanage, so I perfectly…' She caught a flash of something in Yvonne's face and clamped her lips shut. Dear God, how insensitive of her, going on about orphans when she herself had given this beautiful girl up for adoption. 'I'm sorry,' she finished huskily.

Yvonne said nothing, looking away. With a strained smile, she led Sonya through into a bright, airy front parlour with net curtains drawn across large bay windows, stopping sunlight from fading the lavish blue carpet. It held a deep-seated blue sofa and two sturdy, matching armchairs, all three covered with intricately embroidered, floral antimacassars. The small hearth had a shiny front rail and decorative tiling to each side of the grate, each dainty tile depicting a different Cornish landmark.

'Please, take a seat. I'll fetch some tea.' Yvonne tightened her belt with a fidgety gesture that struck Sonya as nervousness. 'Would you like a slice of cake?'

'Yes, thank you.'

Left alone, Sonya's curious gaze darted about the room, taking everything in. Above the hearth, a large oval mirror dominated the wall, while below it on the mantelpiece stood a variety of holiday curios and sepia photographs of Victorian relatives. There was also a framed photograph of her daughter on her wedding day, which Sonya studied with avid interest. Yvonne looked radiant beside her handsome husband, both smiling into the camera. She hoped their marriage was a happy one.

Hearing footsteps, Sonya hurriedly sank into an armchair and took off her hat. Seconds later, her daughter appeared in the doorway with a tea tray, and a smell of fresh-made lemon cake. Yvonne slid the heavy tray onto the table and began to pour the tea into china cups, the silence awkward.

'So this is your husband's parents' home, have I got that right?' Sonya asked delicately.

'Yes, they've been very good to me and Walter.' Yvonne hesitated, adding, 'They didn't like me living alone after Patrick had gone off to do his bit, so they asked us to move in with them.'

'They sound very like nice people.'

'Oh, quite.' Handing her a cup and saucer with a not quite steady hand, Yvonne asked, 'Have you been enjoying this lovely weather? It's been so warm lately.' She was smiling again but her eyes concealed some private fear. Sonya felt sure she had changed the subject deliberately to avoid discussing her in-laws. 'It's hard to believe we're at war when the sun is shining, don't you think?'

With polite agreement, Sonya eased into the familiar topics of weather and the current situation with the war. Yvonne spoke quietly but with well-informed opinion on their ongoing struggle against Herr Hitler while Sonya nodded, making appropriate noises whenever a response was required and devouring every word and gesture with deep joy and fascination.

This is my daughter, she kept thinking, and almost had to pinch herself at the strangeness of the idea. *My grown-up daughter.*

'Lemon cake?'

Sonya nodded, murmuring, 'Thank you,' and they ate the dainty slices of cake without further conversation, both stealing glances at the other before looking swiftly away. 'What pretty tiles those are,' she said in the end, nodding to the hearth. 'Cornish scenes... Such a lovely idea. Is that Land's End?'

'Yes.' Yvonne put down her plate, having picked at only half her thin slice of cake. 'And, on the other side, the three spires of Truro's cathedral.'

'Marvellous.'

There was a short, high-pitched cry from upstairs, and Yvonne jumped up at once, her cup rattling in its china saucer, her worried gaze cast upwards as though she could see through the ceiling.

'Walter,' she said, unnecessarily. 'Though I'm sure he'll be fine. My mother is sitting with him upstairs.' She faltered, and her eyes shot to Sonya's face in abrupt consternation. 'I mean, my adopted mother...'

'Please... Don't.' Sonya stood too. They were the same height, she realised with a start, smiling reassuringly at her daughter. 'She is your mother. She brought you up. I merely gave birth to you.' She flushed. 'How strange that sounds. I'm sorry ... I ought to have been better prepared for this. You must have so many questions.'

Yvonne swallowed, looking directly at her. 'Only one, really.' She paused, seeing that Sonya was waiting to hear it, and asked simply, 'Why?'

Shock flooded through Sonya, though of course the question was perfectly natural. 'Why did I give you up?'

Yvonne sucked in her breath and nodded.

Sonya wished she could lie. She had even prepared some ridiculous story about being too ill to look after a child... But now, faced with her daughter's clear need for the truth, she could only say, 'Because they made me, and I was too scared of them to say no.' At once, she felt sick inside and could not hold Yvonne's surprised stare. 'There, now you know all about me,' she added in a rush. 'I'm a coward. And because of that, you grew up in another woman's household.'

'Who are "they"?' Yvonne probed softly.

'My ... my parents.' Sonya wrung her hands, her chest heaving with difficult breaths. She was struggling to get the words out. 'My father, mostly. But Mother always goes

97

along with whatever he decides. And he decided that I was bringing disgrace on the family, and the only way to save us all was for me to give up the baby – you, that is – and to leave home immediately. So, after it was all over, I took up a position as companion to Lady Symmonds at Symmonds Hall in St Ives, and the whole thing was hushed up. I even gave birth under a false name, at a discreet clinic on the south coast. All very cloak-and-dagger.' Her laugh was hollow. 'They whisked you away almost the second you were born, and I … I didn't even get to hold you, or give you a name.' She paused, forcing a smile though she felt more like weeping. 'Though Yvonne is a lovely name. So chic and elegant.'

'Thank you.' Yvonne took her hands in her own, which were shaking. Her eyes were kind but her voice was stilted. 'Please don't cry.'

'I … I didn't know I was.' Sonya managed a tremulous smile.

'I was happy as a child. You have nothing to be sorry about.' Her daughter turned to some papers on a side table. From among these, she drew a photograph and handed it hesitantly to Sonya. 'This was taken when I was about six months old. That's my late great-grandmother holding me.'

Sonya took the photograph, tears in her eyes as she studied a large, solemn-eyed baby in a charming white bonnet and frilly dress, being cradled by a starchy-looking woman in her seventies. Yvonne had been strikingly similar to herself as a baby, though Sonya had been younger in her own baby photograph and wearing a grim woollen cap instead of a bonnet.

'Oh, all the years I missed,' Sonya whispered, tracing the baby's face with a trembling fingertip. 'If only...'

Words failed her and she choked into silence, handing back the photograph. It was useless to think what might have happened if she had not agreed to give up her baby. For she had done so, after all, and there was no changing the past. Only dealing with the present.

Before Yvonne could reply, there was a sound of thundering feet on the stairs, and a small, dark-haired figure burst into the room like a cannonball. 'Mother, Mother,' he was shouting indistinctly, 'Granny won't let me play outside. She says I'll get dirty.' He stopped dead, staring at Sonya, a lock of dark hair flopping over one eye. 'Oh, hello.' He studied her with only passing interest, then turned to his mother. 'Mother, I want to take my football in the street for a kick-about. Please say yes.'

'Walter, do lower your voice, there's a good boy.' Yvonne caught the restless boy by the shoulders and turned him to face their visitor. She seemed hesitant again now, her eyes downcast, not meeting Sonya's. 'Walter, I want to introduce you to someone very special. This is your ... your grandmother.'

He looked puzzled. 'You can't have three grannies, silly, and Granny Truro and Granny Exeter are upstairs.'

Granny Truro and Granny Exeter.

Granny Exeter had to be Yvonne's adopted mother, Sonya thought anxiously, watching the boy's face, while Granny Truro was obviously her mother-in-law, Mrs Fairweather. With a shock, she realised she'd barely asked about Yvonne's husband during their chat and felt awful at this *faux pas*. Her daughter must think her awfully rude.

All she knew about him was that Mr Fairweather was away doing his bit for King and country.

'In some families, you can have an extra granny,' Yvonne explained awkwardly to her son. 'I'll explain later, shall I? For now, I'd like you to meet Miss … erm … Mrs Thorpe.' She stumbled over the title, blushing and with her eyes finally lifting to Sonya's in acute embarrassment. 'That is to say, Granny Thorpe.'

'But you can call me Granny St Ives,' Sonya said diplomatically, bending to shake his small hand, which was rather sticky, 'because that's where I live.'

He looked her over dismissively. 'You don't look much like a granny.'

'I'm not used to being one, I suppose,' Sonya said, looking back at him every bit as frankly. 'What a handsome boy you are. And so tall for your age.' She straightened, smiling shyly at her daughter. 'He'll be a real heartbreaker when he grows up.'

'I'm already grown up,' he told her, sounding aggrieved. 'I'm six, and Granny Truro says that's grown up.'

'Oh, then I'm sure she must be right.' Sonya drew breath to ask if she could accompany him into the garden, but he had turned his back on her and was complaining loudly to his mother that he didn't want another granny and she didn't look right, anyway.

'Grannies are old, and she's not that old,' he was saying. 'She doesn't have silver hair. Maybe you made a mistake and she's an aunty instead, like Aunty Val.' He ran to the door. 'I like Aunty Val, she's fun. When's she coming back?'

Aunty Val was presumably his father's sister, Sonya guessed. And he must have missed the few silver strands in her hair. But she blushed, burningly aware that she had been a naïve sixteen-year-old on giving birth to Yvonne, while these other 'grannies' had more likely been well into their twenties before they married.

'Not for ages, I'm afraid,' his mother said in a conciliatory tone. 'But now you've got three grandmothers, you won't need an aunt to play with. Listen,' she said cheerily, patting her knee, 'why not come and tell Granny St Ives how good you are at football?'

Walter turned, stared at Sonya again, and then blew a very loud and very deliberate raspberry at her before ducking out of the room.

'Walter, don't be so rude,' Yvonne called after him in a horrified tone, but when he didn't return, she shot Sonya an embarrassed look. 'I'm so sorry. He's not usually naughty. I'll get him back.'

'No, better not,' Sonya said, not overly anxious to speak to the boy again, given his boisterous mood. 'He's just high-spirited, I expect. There's no harm done.'

Sonya sat down again and picked up her tea, but it had gone cold. She felt a little shaken, not simply by having met her daughter at last but by how poorly behaved her grandson had been. But he had every right to be suspicious, she decided on longer reflection; most families only had two grandmothers, and to be presented with a third one, without any explanation, had no doubt thrown him into confusion. Perhaps next time, once his mother had found a way to set his young mind at peace over this vexed question of three 'grannies', he would be more friendly.

'I'm sorry,' Yvonne repeated, sitting opposite. She smoothed down her pretty white dress with its pattern of bright red cherries, the automatic gesture somehow nervous. 'He's still upset over Valerie leaving. But she got her papers, you see. And she chose to go to Manchester, to work in one of the factories up there.'

'Is she your husband's sister?' Sonya asked without thinking, and then wished she'd kept quiet, seeing Yvonne's stricken look. 'Oh my dear, I do apologise.' She knew only too well what it was like to have someone ask about a husband that didn't exist. Perhaps poor Yvonne had been widowed recently and hadn't felt able to admit this in her letter. 'Have I put my foot in it?'

'No,' Yvonne faltered. 'It's just…' She sat straighter, taking a deep breath. 'Yes, Valerie is Patrick's younger sister. A lovely girl, and I miss her terribly. My mother-in-law has been very generous, letting us live with her during the war. But Granny Truro can be a bit…' With a brave smile, Yvonne cut that sentence off before it could be finished. 'Well, we all have to make sacrifices, don't we? I'm really very lucky that we have so much support, and such a nice house to live in.'

'And your own mother is living here too?' Sonya found it hard to ask about the woman who had adopted her baby girl. But she was determined to like her and be polite to her when they eventually met. She had clearly done an excellent job with Yvonne's upbringing; nobody could want for a lovelier daughter, in fact.

'No, Mother's only here on a brief visit, more's the pity,' Yvonne explained, her tone wistful. 'Granny Truro was kind enough to invite her to stay with us for a few days but she goes home tomorrow. She and my father live in Exeter, but their house is very small and there isn't much room for Walter.' She looked embarrassed again. 'He does like to run about quite a bit and make a noise, and my father's not a well man.'

'I'm sorry to hear that.'

'I've been sustaining myself by thinking of the future. About what we'll do when the war's over and Patrick comes home…' Again, her voice cracked. 'My husband is a fighter pilot with the RAF, you see, based near London. He comes home on leave sometimes but we haven't seen him in more than three months.'

'A fighter pilot?' Sonya was impressed. 'That's marvellous. You must be very proud of him.'

'I am, I truly am. Patrick's so dashing and brave and I love him madly.' Yvonne's voice cracked and tears began to roll down her cheeks. 'But the thing is… We got an official letter yesterday.' Her face had turned very pale. 'They don't seem to know where he is.'

Sonya was horrified, suddenly realising what the problem was. 'Oh my goodness, how awful.'

'His plane was shot down in enemy territory, they told us, though the Ministry didn't say where. Only that he's m-m-missing.' Her daughter's anguished, tearful gaze rose to Sonya's face. 'And I don't have a clue what I'm going to do if he never comes home. You see, I haven't told anyone else yet, but … I'm in the family way again. I'm going to have another baby.'

CHAPTER ELEVEN

St Ives, Cornwall, April 1943

Lily was copying notes from her pocketbook into her official maternity records file when there was a knock at the door, and someone walked into the examination room. She looked up with a smile, ready to greet her next patient, and stared dumbstruck, dropping her pen.

'Rose?' She jumped up to hug her friend, whom she still thought of as Sister Rose Grey, though she had retired from nursing after her marriage and was now plain Mrs Lanyon. ''Ere, what on earth are you doing at the maternity clinic? Blimey, don't tell me...' Her incredulous gaze dropped to Rose's figure, carefully concealed under a loose, beltless dress. 'Are you expecting?'

'I am,' Rose admitted, and took a seat as Lily looked her over with an expert eye. Her friend looked healthy enough, cheeks glowing, her smooth red hair set into waves above a freckled forehead. But there was a hesitancy about her, a slight frown in her eyes, that told a different story.

'Well, congratulations,' Lily exclaimed, grinning. 'You must be thrilled. You've kept that quiet too, I didn't have a clue.' She paused. 'How did Lewis take the news?'

'He's over the moon.' Rose rolled her eyes. 'Fussing around me like a mother hen too, more's the pity. I can barely get out of bed without him watching me like I'm about to faint or collapse.'

'Oh, some fathers-to-be are like that. And doctors are probably the worst.' So, Lily thought, it wasn't Dr Lewis who had caused that furrowed brow. 'Is this your first visit? Sorry, it's usually Katie who sees day clinic patients but she's off for a few days with a sprained ankle. Managed to take a fall while out walking, poor thing.' She turned to the ante-natal records file. 'Will I find you in here?'

'No, this is my first visit. Lewis examined me himself when I first realised my monthlies were late, but once he was sure, we decided to keep the news between ourselves.' Rose paused. 'But I thought it was probably time for a proper check-up.'

There was definitely something on her mind, Lily thought, catching an odd inflexion in her voice. But she knew there was no point being too heavy-handed. Whatever it was, Rose would mention it in her own good time, and probably only once she felt safe and relaxed.

'I'd better examine you, then,' Lily said, getting up, and then paused. She was suddenly aware of an awkwardness she hadn't anticipated. At Symmonds Hall, Sister Rose Grey had been a stern taskmaster with an eagle eye for errors and omissions; all the nurses had been a little scared of her, even Lily. But now the tables were turned and she was in charge, which felt odd and unsettling. 'Do you mind?'

'Of course not, that's why I'm here,' Rose said calmly, and swung herself up onto the examination table.

During the examination, Lily tried to be as gentle as possible, keeping up a cheery flow of conversation while she took Rose's vitals and checked the height of the fundus against the chart in her book, and then asked a few careful questions, such as the date of Rose's last monthly bleed and any symptoms she might have experienced.

'Well,' Rose said, biting her lip when it came to discussing her symptoms, no longer as confident-looking, 'I have been feeling rather sick.'

'Morning sickness? That's perfectly normal in the early months.' Lily helped her to sit up, and then supported her off the examination table. 'There you go, all finished.'

'Thank you.' Rose's anxious gaze followed Lily as she put away her equipment and washed her hands. 'Perhaps I'm worrying too much, but shouldn't the nausea have stopped by now? I'm into my fourth month now and it's still pretty horrid.'

'Morning sickness can last a little longer in some cases. But you'd better give me a bit more detail for my records. That way, it'll be easier to chart your progress at your next appointment.' Lily sat next to her, pencil poised above the 'Additional Notes' section. 'Describe "pretty horrid",' she prompted her friend.

Rose gave a detailed and highly specific description of her symptoms, in her usual frank fashion. But then, as nurses, they had both discussed far more symptoms than nausea and sickness in the past. Lily took more notes, and then got up to check one of her reference books on the shelf above her desk. As she was still not fully qualified, she would need to mention Rose's case to her supervisor, Bertha Whitely, and pass on her advice at a later date. But she could give some reassurance now, at least.

'It sounds as though you're able to eat enough to stay healthy,' Lily concluded, closing her pocketbook. 'So I wouldn't worry too much. The usual advice is to eat a dry biscuit before rising in the morning.'

'Yes, I know. And drink ginger tea.' Rose grimaced. 'Lewis has been giving me advice and monitoring my symptoms day and night. Lord only knows what he'll be like when I go into labour.'

Lily grinned. 'Well, you've a good while to go yet. I agree with a delivery date in late October, and make you about thirteen weeks gone, give or take a few days.'

'A long way to go.' Rose sighed.

'I know it's hard when you feel queasy and you're struggling even with everyday things.' She reached forward to squeeze Rose's hand. 'But it's only for another few weeks, I'm sure, and then it'll be plain sailing until Baby arrives.'

Rose gave her a wan smile. 'Promise?'

'Cross my heart and hope to die.'

Rose got up, looking rather happier than when she'd walked in. Her mouth quirked. 'I must say, Nurse Fisher, you make a rather excellent midwife.'

'Just as I'm sure you'll make a smashin' mum, Sister Rose.'

They both laughed, and then hugged again.

'Come back in a month,' Lily told her, and walked her friend to the door. 'But if you have any niggles or worries before then, come and see me anytime. And not just here at the clinic. Come and see me at home, if you prefer to keep it informal.'

Rose gave her an odd look. 'If you're sure you won't be too busy.'

Lily stared at her, puzzled. 'Sorry?'

'I shouldn't have said anything, really, but Lewis heard a rumour on the wards…'

'Go on.'

'It's probably nonsense, you know what gossip's like up at the hall, but… Did you really ask Tristan Minear to marry you?'

Lily felt her cheeks fill with heat but didn't look away. St Ives was a small community; everyone would know all about her and Tristan soon enough, so there was no point pretending.

'Yes, I did,' she admitted.

Rose's green eyes widened. 'Goodness me.' She blinked. 'And? What did he say?'

Lily bit her lip, stupidly tearful, though she was sure there was no reason to cry about it, then blurted out, 'He said yes.'

'Oh, Lily!'

'We haven't set a date yet. But it'll be as soon as he's able to leave the convalescent home, I suppose. We'll marry here in St Ives rather than his home parish of Penzance, but we won't bother with a honeymoon. Not while he's still so poorly.'

'That's wonderful news, congratulations! I can't wait to tell Lewis his suspicions were right, though he'll roast me for it, I expect, because I refused to believe it when he first told me.' Rose took her hands but then looked more closely at her flushed face when Lily didn't respond. 'You are happy, I take it?'

'Yes, of course.' Lily brushed aside her worries, not willing to discuss them yet even with Rose, at least not until she'd fully decided how she was feeling. Briefly, she explained how Tristan's father had refused to take responsibility for him at their farm in Penzance, leaving his injured son homeless and with nobody to care for him. 'Marrying me will be a practical solution to his problems, you see.'

'Well, yes, but… You love each other too, don't you?'

There was a tentative knock at the door, saving her from answering that complicated question, and Lily opened it to find several women waiting to be seen. In a flash of guilt, she realised they had hugely overshot the usual appointment time by chatting so long.

'Oops,' she muttered, turning to her friend with a quick apology. 'Let's talk more when you visit me at home, shall we? It was lovely to see you again. Take care.'

As Rose left, her face alive with curiosity, Lily's gaze turned in relief to her next patient, who was nearly nine months gone and had to walk with a hand supporting her lower back. 'Mrs Leadbetter, how are you? Blimey, you look ready to pop.'

After work, Lily trudged up the hill to Symmonds Hall. As the large, stately building loomed in the distance, its Atlantic-facing windows lit up by the late afternoon sun, she thought the hall itself looked like it could do with a lick of paint. The orphanage, just beyond the hall, had always been a little ramshackle, but with the deprivations of the war, Lady Symmonds had clearly let the hall go too. She recalled how smart everything had looked back in the autumn of 1941 when she had first arrived in St Ives, fresh-faced and eager to train as a nurse. Her friend Eva had suggested nursing as a possible career, and Lily had fallen in love with the job and St Ives too. Then she'd been forced into a hospital transfer to Penzance, which was where she'd met Tristan and his sister Demelza.

Looking back at her time in Penzance, Lily was embarrassed to recall how innocent and impressionable she'd been in those days. But Tris had seemed so handsome, with such a charming smile, she had been entranced. Misunderstandings had driven them apart for a spell, but after Tristan left for his basic training, she'd felt genuinely bereft. Which was stupid, given she was the one who had rejected his offer of marriage. But when that long hard winter set in, with frequent bombing raids over Penzance and nights spent in freezing underground shelters, Lily had begun to realise what she'd lost in saying goodbye to him.

Not that she blamed herself for that decision. Breaking up with Tristan had seemed like the sensible thing to do, unsure how she felt about him or even whether his passion for her would last. Now, she wondered if she'd been a coward. The war kept dragging on, with no end in sight. Perhaps it would never end, she thought desperately. Or Germany would win and they would all end up prisoners in their own country, living under occupation like much of Europe. Life felt so precarious these days. Surely if there was even a small chance of happiness with Tristan, she should seize it, not shy away out of fear of what might lie ahead?

But although she knew Tristan had felt fond enough of her to propose marriage back in Penzance, and had reluctantly agreed they should marry, she still had no real idea how he felt now. After all, hurt as he was, perhaps his emotions towards her had changed.

She knew she ought to ask him outright. So why did the thought terrify her so much?

To her surprise, Tristan's bed was empty when she arrived on Carbis Ward. She asked a young blonde nurse hurrying past, whom she didn't know, where he had gone, and was directed outside into the grounds. Knowing the way like the back of her hand, she followed the path around the lawn, looking about for him. Hesitating between two paths, she decided against the woodlands where she had once kissed Private Daniel Orde – and then run away because she'd found kissing so disturbing in those days – and headed towards the cliffs instead.

She found Tristan seated in a wheelchair beside a sea-facing bench, still in pyjamas and dressing gown, staring out over the blue Atlantic. The bandaging to his face and head had been readjusted, she noticed, and more of his face was showing. His exposed cheek looked red-raw and inflamed, and she winced at the puckered, pinkish skin about his burnt eye. But it seemed he still had his eye, at least.

Knowing he could not have got there alone, she glanced about and soon spotted two nurses deep in conversation, a little way off, and guessed that Tristan must have asked for some time alone, as patients often did when brought outside for an hour of fresh air.

However, the way he was staring out across the cliffs, stiff-backed and motionless, worried her. As she came level with him, she caught something desolate in his face. She had seen that expression before on the faces of men who had been given a death sentence or feared to be.

'Hello,' she said shyly, for it still felt as though they were strangers. They had courted so briefly last summer and, since his return, Tristan had barely spoken a dozen words to her.

His head turned at her voice, a troubled look on his face. 'Lily.' His good hand gripped the arm of the wheel-chair. 'I wasn't sure I'd ever see you again.'

'What?' Her worst fears realised, Lily sank onto the bench. A cold, creeping sensation came over her despite the spring sunshine. She had been so full of hopes for the future when she got up this morning… Now she felt lost. Had he changed his mind already? Hurt built in her chest as she hesitated, searching his face for clues. 'I don't under-stand. I thought it was all decided. You and me, getting wed, moving into the cottage together… Weren't it?' She bit her lip, feeling shaky inside. 'Or was you just pulling my leg when you said yes?'

'I know what we arranged,' he said hoarsely. 'I haven't been able to sleep for thinking about it. It's been driving me crazy. The thing is,' he added, 'I can't believe you mean it, Lily. Marry me? Care for me?' His hands clenched into fists. 'Let's face it, even my own father doesn't want me.'

'That's only because your dad's a fool,' she burst out, and saw the shock in his face. 'There, I've said it, and I'm not sorry. You're worth a hundred of him, Tris, even stuck in that bloomin' chair like you are. And you'll be back on your feet in no time, I promise.' Lily held his gaze fiercely, her heart thumping. 'Do … do you like me?'

'Of course.' He seemed startled by the question, even a little embarrassed.

She didn't know how she had the nerve, yet somehow she pushed on, demanding, 'How much?'

Tristan blinked, hesitating. 'I already told you how I felt,' he said slowly, 'back in Penzance.'

It wasn't exactly the glowing reassurance she'd been looking for. But it would have to do for now, Lily decided, folding her arms tightly across her chest as she stared him down. Everyone knew that men found it hard to talk about their feelings, and Tristan was clearly no exception.

'So you still want to marry me?'

He flushed, looking uncomfortable. 'I've said so, haven't I?'

'Then you'd better buck up your ideas, Tristan Minear, and stop making a great fuss over nothing. Or I might just change my mind about marrying you.'

Tristan seemed to relax at last, running a hand over his bandaged face. 'Well,' he said on a long sigh, and gave a little grin. 'That's me told.'

CHAPTER TWELVE

Mary had never seen the sky look so blue nor known the vasefuls of flowers on the ward to smell quite so gorgeous. Her uniform was crisply starched, her step was light, and she found herself smiling at every patient. Even the annoying ones. She didn't know why but today she felt absolutely … joyful.

Yes, 'joyful' was the word, she decided, hurrying to open the conservatory door for a patient being wheeled back in from the gardens. She was filled with the joy of life. Which was perfectly ludicrous, considering they were at war with Germany, everything nice was impossible to get or rationed to the hilt, and the whole world was sliding down the pan. She knew all that, and yet still couldn't wipe the silly grin off her face.

'Better watch out, Mary,' Harriet warned her in a low voice, stopping as they passed each other in the corridor between wards. She was a shy young woman of about twenty-three, with big blue eyes and a slight stammer. 'M-Matron's on the warpath.'

Mary laughed. 'Oh, it must be a day with a "y" in it.'

'You feeling all right?' Harriet peered at her dubiously.

'Tip-top, thank you,' Mary replied, grinning at her friend over the stack of clean linen she'd been carrying. 'Why do you ask?'

'Well, you're not usually quite so...' Harriet pulled an apologetic face. 'Cheerful.'

'Nonsense, I'm always in a good mood.'

'If you say so.'

Mary forgave her. Perhaps she did tend to look on the gloomy side of life at times. Nursing could be tough, and she was no longer as convinced as she once had been that it was the best job for her. But any gloominess was all in the past, she decided. From now on, she was going to be as jolly as Father Christmas. Though without the beard. 'So, what's the latest bee in Matron's bonnet?' she asked airily.

'Something about a window having been left open on C-Carbis Ward and a bird getting in? It's done its business all over the floor. Caused quite a to-do.' Harriet gave Mary a wink, adding in a conspiratorial whisper, 'Apparently, one of the p-patients joked it was a pity the bird hadn't done it on Matron, and the old girl heard him. First, she tore a strip off the patient, then off that new girl, Nurse Carrington, for giggling, and now Matron's looking for you. I think she's decided you're to b-blame.'

'Yes, I left the window open,' Mary admitted. 'I'd better go and see her, then.'

Harriet's eyes widened at this carefree response. No doubt she had expected Mary to be terrified and run in the opposite direction. Matron did have a reputation for

115

being starchy and unpleasant, after all. But nothing could dampen Mary's spirits today, it seemed.

'Are you sure you're not coming down with something?'

'I'm as healthy as a horse.' Mary continued down the corridor. 'Have a lovely day, Harriet,' she said over her shoulder. 'Try to get outside if you can. The weather is *glorious*.'

She found Matron in her office and knocked on the partly open door, still laden with a heavy armful of bedsheets. Hearing a terse order to come in, she popped her head round the door. 'You asked to see me, Matron?'

'Ah yes, Nurse Stannard. Where are you going with that linen?'

'Atlantic Ward.'

'I see.' Matron stood from behind her desk, her face stern. 'Well, I won't keep you long. An alarming situation has arisen on Carbis Ward.' She drew breath, ready to launch into an offensive, but was interrupted.

'Yes, I'm sorry about the bird, Matron,' Mary told her candidly. 'It wasn't deliberate. One of the patients was complaining about the heat, so I threw open a window. I did mean to close it before I left the ward but... Well, I forgot.'

'*Forgot*?' Matron's eyes bulged, glaring at her. 'You seem astonishingly off-hand about it.'

'Not at all, I'm really sorry,' Mary said, but then spoiled the effect by adding, 'Though it was awfully stuffy.'

'Nurse Stannard,' Matron thundered, rising to her full height, which was a good three inches taller than Mary. 'You allowed a wild creature to penetrate the ward. You endangered the health of your patients. Further, you dese-crated the sanitary conditions of this convalescent home and wilfully lowered your colleagues' working conditions to those of a back-alley slum. And all you can say in your defence is, *it was awfully stuffy*?'

Defiantly, Mary looked away, waiting to be released.

'Tell me, Nurse Stannard,' Matron continued more softly, 'what made you choose this profession?'

Mary blinked. 'I wanted to help people. To make their lives better.'

'And were you fulfilling that desire by permitting a bird to...' Matron shuddered. 'To do its business,' she hissed, 'all over the ward?'

'No, Matron.'

'You came in here with a jaunty step and a foolish grin, Nurse Stannard. You will leave it with a serious question to answer.' Matron opened the door and pointed her out into the corridor, her face a cold mask of dislike. 'If you think so little of your patients' welfare that you can laugh at this appalling incident, perhaps you should be asking yourself whether this is an appropriate career for you. Not everyone is cut out to be a nurse, Mary.'

Mary swallowed, clutching the linen like a lifeline in rough seas. *Not everyone is cut out to be a nurse.* That stung. Though it was no more than she had been thinking privately in recent months, she had to admit. It was just a shock to hear it said out loud. And by Matron herself, no less.

'You will finish your tasks in Atlantic Ward and afterwards return to Carbis, where you will apologise to every patient personally for having caused such an upset this morning,' Matron ordered her. 'Is that understood?'

'Yes, Matron.'

'Good. And do not abuse my trust again. I had hoped

117

you might rise to Sister in time. But after today's debacle…' Matron gave a curt shake of her head and closed the door in her face.

Mary stared at the shut door in dismay before heading for Atlantic Ward, head down and hurrying now, her insides churning.

Not everyone is cut out to be a nurse.

Once upon a time, she had loved the idea of nursing. Mum and Dad had given her a nurse's uniform for an eighth birthday present. In reality, it had only been a white apron and cap, with a little red cross on the cap. Wearing it though, she had truly believed she was a nurse, carefully bandaging up all of her dolls' and teddies' supposedly broken arms and legs, afterwards giving them 'injections' with a pencil stub, then conscientiously rubbing the injection site better.

After that, she'd grown up wanting to be a nurse, realised her dream by signing up to a local training course as soon as war had broken out, and had never really questioned her choice of career until this year, the long hours and sheer drudgery of nursing gradually wearing her down.

Now though, she was genuinely beginning to wonder… If even Matron, who was always moaning about how short-staffed they were at the hall, was telling her to reconsider whether she wanted to be a nurse… Perhaps it really was time to ask herself that question.

Just before Easter break, which fell in late April that year, Mary decided to visit the school on her afternoon off. Dick Jeffries had kindly agreed to have Pip back in the classroom after their discussion at the house, on the strict understanding that he should go directly to a teacher if any further bullying occurred. But her mum had written Mary another anxious note a few days back, complaining that Pip was falling behind with his work and she couldn't get him to talk about it. It was clear that she expected Mary to step in and somehow make the boy's problems go away again, presumably because she'd been so successful in getting his expulsion reversed.

Her feet and legs ached after a full morning on the wards, but Mary didn't mind more walking when it was for a good cause. It was a bright and breezy spring afternoon, the sky was cloudless blue to the horizon, and the Atlantic Ocean sparkled and glittered below the town, gladdening her heart.

Soon they would be in May, with all the traditional May Day celebrations to look forward to, and not too many noisy strangers in the streets yet to spoil everything. Most summers, the picturesque seaside town still became overrun with summer visitors, despite the war, especially artistic types who liked to set up their easels along the harbourside and paint pretty pictures of fishing boats and the sea.

Also, she admitted to herself, it was no hardship for her to walk into St Ives to visit the school and see for herself how young Pip was getting along with the local boys. Not when it afforded a chance to speak to that teacher again, Mr Jeffries, who had rather caught her eye when he brought Pip home.

Dick Jeffries wasn't much of a looker, she conceded, but then neither was she. He was an educated man and she respected that, not having had much of an education herself, though she'd become an avid reader after she left school, all the same. And there was something about him… She didn't rightly know what it was. But she liked it.

Once again, she had that feeling of being joyful, stepping more lightly now as she turned through the school gates. Maybe it was simply the change of season, everything warming up at last after a particularly gruelling winter…

To her shock, Dick Jeffries was suddenly there, in front of her, striding out of the school entrance with an easel under one arm and fistfuls of paintbrushes in both hands. The teacher was wearing an old misshapen smock, its front stained with paint, his fair hair flopping over his face, not looking where he was going until he had almost bumped into her. But since he wasn't wearing his spectacles this time, Mary noted, that might explain it.

'What on earth…?' he exclaimed, coming to a halt. Perplexed, his gaze settled on her face. 'Oh, it's you.' A curious smile hovered on his lips as he recognised her. 'I should have known.'

Behind him came a small group of children walking in pairs and armed with miniature easels, palettes and pots of paint. They all stopped too, staring at her.

'I'm sorry,' she told the teacher, a flush in her cheeks. 'I was coming to speak to you, Mr Jeffries. But you look busy. I'll come back after Easter break.'

'Not at all.' He waved the children forward, calling out, 'Find somewhere to set up your easels and begin sketching the outline of the building and playground. Once you have that, you can start painting.' He leant forward, handing his bristling handfuls of brushes to a young girl with huge eyes and a solemn stare. 'Nancy, could you do the honours and hand these out for me? Thank you.'

Mary could feel all the curious glances being thrown in her direction and felt flustered. 'I'm in the way. I'll come back.'

'No, don't go. I'm just treating my seniors to a painting class. A bit of fun before examination work starts in earnest. Hang on a tick.' He walked across the yard and set up his own easel a few feet away, then returned with a courteous smile. 'Now, let's see. This will be about young Pip. Am I right?'

'Yes.' Hurriedly, she explained the situation as her mother had described it in her most recent note. 'We don't know what the trouble is. But his last few marks have been very poor, especially in arithmetic, and we're worried about him. My mother is afraid he's being bullied again.'

He looked concerned. 'And what does Pip say?'

'Nothing. Tight-lipped as ever, according to my mum.'

'You haven't asked him yourself?'

'I don't live with my parents,' she explained, feeling awkward. 'I'm a nurse. I live up at Symmonds Hall. But I try to go home every few weeks.'

'A nurse?' He nodded slowly. 'That makes sense.'

'Sorry?'

'The natural air of authority.'

Her gaze rose to his face, full of dignity. 'Are you making fun of me, Mr Jeffries?'

'Only a little.' He grinned, but quickly became serious again. 'Listen, I'll have a chat with Pip before school breaks up for Easter. See what I can find out. But it's not unusual for boys to have difficult patches where their marks slide. Especially boys in Pip's position.'

'What do you mean?'

'As an evacuee. The poor lad's a long way from home. He's an orphan too, from what I've been able to discover. Plus, there's a war on. Hardly ideal conditions for kids to knuckle down to their school work. So, it may be nothing. Or it may be bullies again.' He gave her a wink. 'Let's put on our sleuthing caps and see what we can discover. Eh, Dr Watson?'

Her face glowed as she realised he was referring to the Victorian detective Sherlock Holmes, the fictional creation of one of her favourite writers, Arthur Conan Doyle. Or rather, his trusty side-kick, Dr Watson.

'Oh, I'm Dr Watson, am I?' she asked, raising her eyebrows. 'I suppose that makes you Sherlock Holmes.'

'Of course.' Dick gave a chuckle. 'You're the medically-minded one, after all. And, as you can see, I'm the chaotic genius,' he added, indicating his messy artist's smock.

Her heart began to thud and she felt almost faint. The late April sunshine burnt behind his head, dazzling her as she stared upwards, and she lowered her gaze again, trying to catch her breath. Goodness, anyone would think she'd been running, she realised with a shock. What on earth was wrong with her?

'If you say so,' she said, and gave him a prim, no-nonsense smile, developed over her years as a nurse. 'Well, thank you. In that case, I'll come back after Easter to find out what you discovered.' And with that she turned, making for the school gate again, almost tripping in her hurry.

'Just a minute.'

Reluctantly, Mary pivoted on one heel, looking back at him. She was keen to get away, for she had suddenly real-ised she was in danger of making a fool of herself over the man. 'Yes, Mr Jeffries?'

'We could meet a little sooner, if you like,' he said hesitantly, coming closer. His hazel eyes had flecks of tawny orange and hints of green, she realised, staring into them. Fascinating depths, she thought, and took an instinctive step back. 'How about a drink one evening? Not too late, of course. I know you nurses often have early starts.'

'Where?'

The teacher suggested a pub she knew down on the harbourside, and she heard herself agree to meet him there soon after seven o'clock on Thursday, the eve of Good Friday. Then he nodded and went back to his flock of happy painters.

Mary turned out of the school, heading for her mum's house before she realised she had work early the next day and wouldn't be expected at home. Sighing, she reversed direction and trudged back up to Symmonds Hall, her brain in a daze.

Had she just agreed to a drink with Pip's teacher, of all people? She must have windmills in her head.

All right, Mary decided firmly, she would meet Dick Jeffries as agreed, because that was the polite thing to do. But she would not see him a second time. Whatever this was, it must be nipped in the bud. Matron had just made it clear she would be out of a job if she put so much as a foot wrong.

No, she had no time for silly frivolities like dating.

Yet the sky was so blue, it took her breath clean away, and she had never felt lighter. She might almost have been flying...

CHAPTER THIRTEEN

For the third day running, Sonya helped the younger
orphans wash and get ready for school in Rose's absence.
It was noisy and chaotic, but she didn't mind one jot. Not
only was the job taking her mind off her daughter's
worrying situation but she enjoyed performing these
simple, homely tasks for the children. It made her feel
maternal, something she had never experienced before
and which filled her heart with gladness. She had spent
years watching other women with their children and
wondering what it would be like to spend even a day with
her own child, to hold her and care for her as a mother
should, while feeling hollow inside, her arms empty, her
heart aching for the daughter she had lost.

At a quarter past eight, the crocodile of children began
its daily trek downhill to the school, headed by the most
senior boy at the orphanage, aged thirteen and nearly at
the end of his schooling.

Sonya waved the children off with a smile and turned
back towards her apartments, for the very youngest

children were cared for by Rose's other assistant, Teresa, and her help would not be required again until this afternoon, when school closed for the Easter break.

But Teresa came running, a tiny tot balanced on her hip, holding out an envelope.

'Miss Thorpe,' she said breathlessly, 'the postie saw you weren't in, so she left this with me to give to you.' Their postman was now a postwoman, the previous one having joined up early on in the war. 'The postmark is Truro.'

Sonya took the envelope without any change of expression, aware of Teresa's curious gaze on her face. 'Thank you,' she said calmly, and hurried back to the apartment to read her letter in private.

As she'd suspected from the handwriting and postmark, the letter was from her daughter. Safely back in the apartment, Sonya spread out the sheet with trembling fingers, barely able to contain her shock as she read what it contained.

I'm in a fix, I'm afraid, and wonder if you would be willing to help me. I've fallen out with my in-laws over Walter's behaviour. They don't seem to understand that he is simply upset over his father's disappearance. I wanted to keep the truth from him a while longer but my mother-in-law insisted on telling him. Walter became quite hysterical when he learned that his father was missing in action, and things have been rather beastly ever since.

I'm sorry to impose on you but would it be possible for me and Walter to stay with you for a few weeks instead? It would only be until his behaviour has improved and things can be patched up with his grandmother. I recall you saying there was a spare room if we ever wanted to visit St Ives and stay over, and I hope you will say yes. It would be lovely for us to get to know each other better too.

Your daughter, Yvonne Fairweather

Sonya jumped up, tears in her eyes. She knew at once, with no question in her heart, that she must say yes. To have her daughter and grandson here to stay would be wonderful, and with her ladyship still in Scotland until at least the end of the year, there should be plenty of room for them all.

Darting to the escritoire desk where her ladyship always kept her best writing paper and ink, she was in the middle of drafting a reply when there was a tentative knock on the door to the apartment.

Mystified, Sonya got up and opened the door to find her daughter standing there, looking harassed and holding Walter by the hand. There was a small suitcase beside them.

'Yvonne?' Stunned, she stared at them both in bewilderment. Her daughter bit her lip deeply, her cheeks cherry red, while Walter looked up sulkily, his eyes red-rimmed as though he had recently been crying. 'Goodness me. You're here already... But I only just received your letter.'

'Yes, I'm awfully sorry for crashing in like this. Is it a bad time?'

'Not at all.' Sonya stood back and gestured them inside. 'Though nothing is ready,' she added, a little flustered by this unexpected development. 'I'm delighted to see you, and you must absolutely stay with me until all this with Granny Truro is sorted out. But I will need to air your room and put sheets on the guest bed before it's habitable. And then there's the question of where little Walter will sleep. We only have one guest room, and I'm afraid I don't have her ladyship's permission to use her room while she's gone.'

'Oh, never mind about that, Walter will sleep in my room. He always does.' Yvonne was unpinning her hat, looking around the elegant apartment with an interested eye. 'And please, leave all the domestic arrangements to me. If you show me where the linen is kept, I'll make up the bed myself. There's no question of you doing it.' She released Walter and turned to Sonya, giving her a hug. 'I'm sorry to be imposing myself on you without any decent warning, but I had the most awful bust-up with Granny Truro yesterday. She screamed in my face and threw a coffee pot, and my father-in-law said nothing whatsoever, just walked away. It was unspeakably horrid. And she said such cruel things about Walter, I couldn't bear it. There was nothing for it but to pack our bags and jump on the first train west with Walter this morning. I know you hadn't said yes, but I was hopeful that—'

'My dear, I've told you, of course you must stay with me.' Sonya gave her a reassuring smile. 'I'm delighted to see you. And little Walter too.' She hesitated. 'Are you hungry? Did you lunch yet? I usually take my meals in the canteen where the hall staff eat, but I can speak to Cook and have things brought up here on a tray instead, if you prefer to eat in the apartment.'

Yvonne shook her head, smiling. 'I don't want to put anyone out. We'll fall in with your usual routine and eat in the canteen too. If that's all right with you.' She hunted through her handbag and produced two ration books. 'You must give these to Cook to cover the extra food. Or I could do it, whichever is best.' She had a pretty flush in her cheeks. 'Thank you so much. You don't know how much this has relieved my mind. All the way here on the train, I was frantic in case you were unable to accommodate us and I would have to return to Truro.'

'But what about your ... your other mother?' Sonja asked awkwardly. 'Granny Exeter, that is. Your adopted parents.'

'There's no chance of her and my father putting us up in Exeter. As I said, they simply don't have the room.' Yvonne spotted her son idly picking at the wallpaper and raised her voice. 'Walter Fairweather, stop that this instant. Come over here and say thank you to Granny St Ives for putting us up.' She grimaced. 'Or maybe I should say, for putting up with us, if you intend to behave as badly here as you did as in Truro. Which I sincerely hope you won't.' She peered down into her son's sullen face. 'Will you?'

'No, Mummy,' the little boy muttered, rubbing his shoe restlessly against the sofa leg. 'Is there a garden? May I go play?'

Yvonne looked at Sonya helplessly. 'Is there anywhere he can run about? It's what he most likes to do.'

'There isn't a garden. Just a yard. But he can certainly run about there. It's where the orphans play.' Sonya took Walter to the window and pointed. He stared down with interest, though the yard was empty. 'The children won't be back from school until this afternoon, I'm afraid. But I'm sure there'll be a ball down in the yard. In fine weather, the bigger boys leave it out for a game of football at the end of each school day. Would you like to kick it around for a while?'

'Yes, please,' Walter said eagerly.

'I'll take him down,' Yvonne said promptly, grabbing her son before he could dash out the door and throwing Sonya a grateful look, 'and then maybe you and I could sit down for a chat? There's a great deal to be discussed,' she said, adding hesitantly, 'though I don't want to intrude on your privacy.'

'Of course you're not intruding,' Sonya insisted. 'Goodness, I'm thrilled to have you and Walter here. You go, I'll put the kettle on.'

Once they had gone back downstairs, Walter chattering noisily all the way, Sonya stood in the middle of the empty apartment and willed her heart to stop beating so fast and her hands to stop trembling. But it was hard not to feel overwhelmed by emotion.

Yvonne had turned to her in a moment of great need, as any daughter would, trusting her to say yes. On top of that, the two of them would be living together for some weeks, by the sound of things. She felt some uneasiness over Walter's boisterous nature, it was true. But no doubt his behaviour was only to be expected from a six-year-old boy, especially one who had been rather over-indulged.

After years of aching to know her lost daughter, this opportunity was a dream come true and Sonya was determined to make sure nothing would spoil it.

Sonya brought in the tea tray and found Yvonne peering with interest at the ornaments and framed photographs on the mantel, exactly as she herself had done in Truro. But that was hardly surprising. Her daughter knew next to nothing about her life and was no doubt curious. But Yvonne would glean no information from studying any of the objects in this room, for they all belonged to the Symmonds family. What few possessions Sonya owned were kept in her private room, and they were mainly books and a few embroidery projects, nothing terribly exciting.

'Who are all these people?' Yvonne asked, indicating the photographs.

'Members of Lady Symmonds' family… That was her husband, Christopher,' she said, nodding to one of her ladyship's wedding photographs, 'and that was her son George, and this one,' she said more fondly, picking up a smaller cameo photograph, 'was Francis, her grandson. Such a handsome boy. All gone now, sadly. Her son and Francis were both killed in the service of our country. I don't think her ladyship ever really recovered from losing them. Especially Francis, perhaps. He was a shining boy, so full of life.'

'How awful. Poor woman.'

'Yes, it was a particularly hard loss to bear.' Sonya lingered over the poignant cameo of Francis, photographed in his smart naval uniform on the eve of war, then replaced it reverently on the mantelpiece. She pointed to the large group photograph of Lady Symmonds' wedding. 'She has many cousins, of course, to sustain her, and friends of the family. But a close blood tie… It means so much, perhaps especially as we get older.'

Yvonne nodded, watching her face. 'And you've been with her ladyship ever since…'

'Since you were born, yes,' Sonya agreed, hearing a slight tremble in her voice, and worked up a brisk smile. 'Shall we have tea?'

Yvonne checked out of the window first, clearly fretting about her son's safety, and then came and sat down on the sofa. 'You think me overprotective, no doubt,' she said, though Sonya had said nothing, 'but he's only six, and this is a new place. Also,' she admitted, 'Walter has an alarming tendency to dash off without permission. He had to be watched when playing outside in Truro, for he often ran off as soon as one's back was turned.'

Sonya felt uneasy about this admission but smiled politely. 'A boy with spirit,' she said with more generosity than she really felt. She poured the tea and offered a cup to Yvonne but couldn't help noting how uncomfortable her daughter seemed. 'Is something wrong?'

'Oh, it's only… All these lovely *objets d'art*,' Yvonne murmured, gesturing about the expensively decorated apartment. 'I'm terrified in case Walter breaks something precious in here. Those two Chinese vases, for instance,' she whispered, nodding to the large twin porcelain vases that always stood on either side of the hearth during the summer months, decorated with entwined flower stems and leaves in delicate blue paint. 'Are they worth a great deal?'

131

'Priceless, I believe.'

'Oh Lord… And that figurine? Meissen, isn't it?'

'Yes.' Sonya turned to study the pretty figurine of a rosy-cheeked boy climbing an apple tree. 'You know much about art?'

'My husband's father collects porcelain, that's all. Though I'd like to know more. That piece is very pretty.'

Sonya nodded her agreement. 'His lordship bought it for her ladyship as a gift shortly before he passed away. I expect it's worth at least fifty pounds, maybe more. But the sentimental value would be far higher…'

'I'm not sure I dare allow Walter to set foot in here again. He's like the proverbial bull in a china shop. My father-in-law had to put away his most prized pieces when we moved in with them. And it doesn't seem to matter how often I tell Walter not to touch, he can't seem to help himself.'

With an inward sigh, Sonya said calmly, 'Then we'll do the same here. Her ladyship won't mind, I'm sure, if anything breakable is put safely away for the duration of your stay.'

'I'll help, of course,' Yvonne said hurriedly. 'I'm so sorry to be causing such a nuisance. And we've barely walked in the door.'

'No, it's perfectly all right.' Sonya put a brave face on. 'They all need a good dusting anyway. This gives me a reason to see it done properly.' She perused the room, mentally noting which items would need to be removed. 'I'll store them in her ladyship's bedroom. It's quite a large room, thankfully. Then I'll lock the door and keep the key safe, so there's no danger of him getting in there by accident.'

'Thank you.' Yvonne nibbled meekly on a biscuit. 'You're very kind. I can't thank you enough for taking us in like this.'

'There's really no need. I'm sure we'll all get along brilliantly.'

At that moment, there was a loud knock at the front door. Before Sonya could even get up, she heard swift footsteps in the hall, and then the parlour door opened and Teresa stood there, her face flushed.

'Oh, hello,' Sonya said, embarrassed by this rude intrusion, and got to her feet. 'Yvonne, this is Teresa. She works with me at the orphanage.' But before she could introduce her daughter, still struggling with what to say for the best, their unexpected visitor interrupted her, directing an angry gaze at Yvonne.

'Is that little boy with you, then?' Teresa demanded. 'The one who's been playing in the yard?'

Yvonne jumped up, looking stricken. 'Yes,' she gasped. 'Why? What's happened? Is he hurt?'

'No, *he* isn't hurt,' Teresa said with heavy emphasis, 'but one of the orphanage windows certainly is and will need to be repaired. He kept kicking his football straight at it, even after I asked him to stop. He's cracked the pane.'

'Oh no.' Yvonne rushed out and down the stairs.

On the verge of following, Teresa threw a sharp look back at Sonya. 'Friend of yours, is she?'

'She's my … my…' But her nerve failed her, for everyone at Symmonds Hall knew her as Miss Thorpe and would be shocked to learn she had a grown-up daughter. 'My guest,' she finished lamely. 'A friend of mine, yes.'

'Well, that son of hers is a tearaway.' Teresa shook her

head. 'I took him to task for breaking the window, and all the boy did was stare and say nothing. Needs to learn a few manners, that one.'

'I'm so sorry. I'll help you clear away the broken glass and make the window secure, and we'll use her ladyship's telephone first thing in the morning to call a glazier.'

'We'll never get one to come out this close to Easter.'

'Oh dear.' Sonya managed a thin smile. 'After the Easter holiday, then. I'll see to it myself. Please don't worry.'

Teresa stomped back down the stairs without saying another word, and Sonya followed, her stomach in knots. But her upset was more to do with how she had introduced her daughter than with Walter's continuing naughty behaviour.

Her *guest*? A *friend*? Sonya clasped her cheeks in anguish. Oh, why could she not simply have said, *this is my daughter*? Yet even as she attacked herself for being such a coward, she knew she could not have admitted their true relationship so freely. She hated lying and would much rather be honest. But this was not merely about her own shame as an unmarried mother. The thought of being greeted with a shocked stare and cold silence was almost too much to bear, and any disrespect directed towards her might reflect badly on her ladyship too, and even on poor Yvonne herself, an even more upsetting thought.

And any chance of her daughter's stay at Symmonds Hall remaining low-key and unnoticed was fading by the minute, with Yvonne choosing to eat with her in the staff canteen and now a broken window...

This reunion with her long-lost daughter was turning out to be far more complicated than she'd imagined.

134

CHAPTER FOURTEEN

Lily did not know what to expect as Dr Lewis slowly and gingerly unpeeled the bandages from Tristan's lower leg and thigh. To her relief, Tristan had agreed to some sedation during this process, although he claimed the pain was greatly lessened since he was first admitted to hospital.

He lay with the good side of his face turned away into the pillow, staring at nothing with a set expression. Every now and then he gave a muffled groan and bit his lip.

Anxiously, she studied his skin as it was revealed in sections. Not knowing how his leg had looked immediately after suffering the burns, she guessed from its swollen, discoloured state that it had been bad. Really bad. Even now, the skin was dark red and leathery, with patches of ashen-white like the remains of a charred log. At least there was no bone showing, so far as she could tell. She had seen a few severe burn victims during her time as a nurse and remembered one particular case where the poor man's arm had been burnt right down to the bone. It had been amputated in the end. She had feared this might be

135

the case with Tristan's leg, but from what she could see, and judging by Dr Lewis's relieved expression, the burn damage had not gone deep enough to warrant amputation.

'How do you feel?' she asked Tristan, seeing that he was still conscious though drifting slightly.

Tristan murmured something inaudible, lifted his good hand an inch or two off the covers, and then let it drop.

Doctor Lewis straightened from his examination. 'Well, the good news is, it all seems to be healing nicely.' He looked from Lily to Tristan, a smile hovering on his lips. 'And I believe congratulations are in order. I've heard on the St Ives grapevine that you two are to be married.'

Lily blushed. 'Thank you.'

Tristan made no comment on his congratulations but moved his head round to stare at the doctor. 'Let me have it straight,' he mumbled. 'That was the good news. Now, what's the bad news?'

'There's some swelling, which isn't a good sign. But it's nothing a simple exercise regime won't help.'

'Exercise?' Tristan looked baffled.

'I know it seems impossible right now. But the sooner you get moving again, the better. Gently does it at first, though.'

'I can hardly bear to move my leg, let alone stand on it.'

'I perfectly understand, young man,' Dr Lewis said, nodding. 'You've done amazingly well. But you can't expect miracles. Try one or two steps every day with the aid of a nurse and let's see how you are in another week or so, shall we?' He put a reassuring hand on Tristan's shoulder. 'Listen, when you first came in, I didn't give much for your chances of saving that leg. But you've beaten the odds, and if we can keep any infection from setting in, you'll leave here a whole man, even if it hurts to put weight on that leg. How's that for a promise?'

Tristan's mouth quirked in a reluctant smile. 'Thank you, Doctor.'

'Not at all,' Dr Lewis replied cheerfully. 'Now, finish up your chat with Lily here, and then try to get some sleep.' He shot Lily a significant look, adding in a lower voice, 'Come and see me before you leave, would you? I'd like to go over his treatment regime with you.'

When the doctor had gone, Lily turned to find Tristan watching her.

'Why does he need to speak to you alone?' he asked suspiciously.

'I imagine he thinks you'd be bored, listening to him rattling off a list of treatment instructions as long as your arm.'

Lily had tried to sound matter-of-fact, but it was still very new to her, this idea of marrying Tristan and looking after him as a wife, not merely a nurse. She had not changed her mind, of course. But the nearer it drew to becoming a reality, the more nervous she felt inside. And she guessed from his expression that she wasn't doing a good job of disguising her nerves.

'You can still drop out, you know,' he said roughly.

'I've no intention of dropping out, thank you.' Lily handed him the newspaper she had brought for him to read. 'Here, take this, I would have brought a book but I wasn't sure what kind of thing you like to read.'

He stared at the newspaper on his lap and then grimaced.

'It's too hard, reading with one eye. I can't focus on the print.'

'Oh,' she said blankly. 'I hadn't thought of that. I'm sorry. Would you like me to take the newspaper away?'

'No, I'll manage.' He shot her a smile. 'I'll see you later.'

Dr Lewis sent the young nurse away for five minutes while he spoke to Lily about how often dressings would need to be changed, and how to handle issues around shaving and bathing, and even the type of clothing Tristan would need to wear, to avoid rubbing at his scars. He also suggested the use of a wheelchair for a short while after Tristan had left the convalescent home, though he felt confident he should be able to walk with a stick in time, given the best outcome.

'Indeed, he must get back on his feet as soon as possible,' he added, 'and try to resume normal daily function, for swelling and infection are more likely if he just keeps lying there in bed.'

'I'll bear that in mind,' Lily muttered, wondering how she could cajole an already reluctant Tristan to take some daily exercise.

'Of course, it would only be a few steps a day at first. So I can arrange for you to borrow a wheelchair for as long as you need,' the doctor assured her, and then caught her troubled gaze, misinterpreting it. 'The only medicaments you'll need will be to prevent infection, and I can make sure there'll be no charge for the wheelchair use. Any expense will be minimal.'

'It's not the cost what's on my mind, Doc.' Lily hesitated.

'Will Tris be able to stand beside me at the altar? For the wedding ceremony, I mean.'

She didn't mind if he had to use a wheelchair in the church. It made no difference to her. But she was convinced that Tristan himself would be unhappy about it, and that might ruin their big day.

'I'm sorry, Lily. I can't say for certain.'

She appreciated his honesty. 'Well,' she said, 'at least he's not going to lose his leg.'

'No, he's been spared that horror. Though it's important not to let infection set in or that situation could change rapidly.'

'Right you are,' she agreed, gripping her handbag tightly as she considered that alarming possibility.

Hygiene would need to be her main priority, she decided. Keeping Tristan's burns and scars clean and dry, and free of infection. Thankfully, she knew how to do that, always assuming her new husband would allow her to care for him so intimately. But she'd cross that particular bridge another day...

Shyly, she murmured, 'By the way, I saw Rose the other day. Congratulations.' She was careful to keep her voice down, for she suspected the happy couple had not told anyone else yet about the baby.

He beamed, turning slightly red. 'Thank you. I'm very grateful to you for setting Rose's mind at rest. She came home from the clinic a much happier woman.'

'My pleasure.'

Doctor Lewis checked the wall clock and grimaced. 'Damn, it's nearly the hour. I have to get on with my rounds or I'll never hear the end of it.' He nodded behind her, his look significant, and Lily turned to find Matron bearing down on them.

'Oh blimey.' Lily gave a stifled groan. 'I don't miss seeing her face in my dreams every night.'

He suppressed a grin. 'You're still friends with Mary though, aren't you?'

'Of course. We're thick as thieves.'

'In that case, I'll ask Mary if she can call in and help you with Tristan. In the early days, at least,' he added, seeing her discomfort. 'Just until you have a routine established at home.'

'Thank you,' she said, reminding herself that she would need all the help she could get once she was coping with Tristan's care alone. 'That's a smashing idea. I just hope she won't mind giving up her spare time for it.'

'I can always ask for it to be considered overtime for her,' he suggested, 'though if there's one thing I've learned about you nurses since marrying Rose, it's how loyal you are to each other and how you always stick together, come hell or high water.' Doctor Lewis lowered his voice as Matron came within earshot. 'Talking of which…'

With a chuckle, Lily escaped before Matron could nobble her for loitering on the ward outside permitted visiting hours.

Matron had never liked her much, probably because she found her Dagenham accent too common. But Lily had to admit the old girl was good at her job, always keeping the nursing staff – and even the doctors too, sometimes – in line.

Doctor Lewis had given her much to think about, not least all the daily care Tristan would need once he was living in the cottage. But what he'd said about Mary had warmed her heart and put fresh courage in her. Because he was right when he said nurses stick together, come what may. She knew she could rely on Mary and even Rose to help her out if things got tough, just as she would always be there for them too.

Walking down from Symmonds Hall, Lily caught the bus to Porthcurno, a small village on the west coast of Cornwall where her aunt Violet lived with Joe on his farm. Her gran and her younger sister Alice lived with them too, though Lily couldn't imagine Alice staying there much longer. Alice had been working at a school in Penzance since leaving her cleaning job at the listening station in tiny Porthcurno, and seemed much happier in a busy school environment, for she had a natural love of books and learning, and a disdain for skivvying. But there was a restlessness about the girl too. Ever since Alice turned eighteen back in February, Lily had suspected her sister would soon grow tired of rural life in Cornwall and find a way to escape.

When the bus finally reached Porthcurno, after meandering through narrow lanes thick with hedgerows, Lily jumped off with a call of thanks to the driver and began the slow trek uphill to Joe's farm.

As she walked through the quiet, bee-rich countryside, a loud thrumming filled the air, and she turned, eyes wide, to see three Lancaster bombers flying overhead, the deep vibrating hum of their engines so loud as they passed that she could feel it in her bones.

Lily stopped and waved, watching until the Lancasters

were out of sight, her heart gladdened by the sight of those huge metal beasts.

She recalled the Messerschmitt plane that had peppered the beach at Penzance last summer, severely wounding a man, and how scared they had been, fleeing from the gunfire. To see those majestic Lancasters filling the Cornish skies, perhaps on a training mission, made her feel proud and confident in her country's ability to defeat the military might of Germany and its allies.

About a quarter of a mile before she reached the farm gate, she was overtaken by an ancient tractor dragging a roller behind it, and stared, hearing shouts and laughter from the tractor cab. There was a large, rosy-cheeked girl behind the wheel, and another leaning out of the open window, waving. Lily recognised them at once as Caroline and Penny, two of the Land Girls who worked on Joe's farm.

'Hey there, stranger, fancy a lift?' Penny called out to her, grinning as the lumbering farm vehicle slowed to a halt.

Lily climbed up thankfully into the warm cab, squeezing in beside the two girls. There wasn't really room for two passengers, let alone three, but her feet were hurting.

'You've come to see the family for Easter, is that it?' Caroline asked her, slamming the tractor into its lowest gear to get it chugging up the hill again. 'I don't think Violet's expecting you,' she added dubiously.

'Though I'm sure you'll be welcome,' Penny threw in cheerfully, chewing on a long stalk of grass. 'The more the merrier. Especially if you're any good at cooking.'

'Which none of us are,' Caroline added, chuckling.

Up at the farm, Lily found her Aunt Violet and Gran in the kitchen, covered in flour as they toiled together on a massive pie.

Gran saw her first, exclaiming, 'Well, I never. Look who the cat dragged in.'

Violet turned in amazement. 'Lily?' She wiped her floury hands on her apron before hugging her with a cry of delight. 'This is a surprise.'

'Hello, Aunty Vi, Gran.' Lily grinned. 'How is everyone?'

'Don't worry about us, we're all fine,' Violet insisted. 'But what on earth are you doing here? Blimey, you could have knocked me down with a feather, seeing you walk in just now.' Violet held her niece at arm's length, scanning her face. 'Is everything all right, love?'

'I'm fine, honestly,' Lily reassured her.

Gran hugged her too, covering her liberally with flour. 'Gawd, I swear you've grown again. At least another inch since her ladyship's wedding. Ain't she grown, Vi?'

'Pay no attention to your gran,' Violet said, whipping off her floury apron with a laugh. 'Truth is, she's shrinking. It's not everyone else getting taller.'

'You're not too old to go over my knee, Violet Postbridge,' Gran said, threatening her daughter with a pastry brush.

Lily grinned.

'It's smashin' to see you, Lily,' Violet said, ignoring her mother's wrath. 'A real treat. But I know you ain't come all this way just for a cuppa and a chinwag.' All the same, she filled the kettle and swung it over the hot range. 'So, come on, what's up? You not enjoying that new job in St Ives? We won't think any the less of you if you've changed your mind about being a midwife. It's not for everyone.'

She pulled out a chair for her niece and Lily sat down at the kitchen table, watching in fascination as Gran put the finishing touches to the pie, decorating the top crust and sides with dainty, thin-rolled pastry leaves.

'No, honest,' Lily told her aunt. 'I love midwifery. There's nothing more satisfying than bringing a new soul into the world.' She hesitated, picking nervously at the edge of her cardigan. 'But you're right, Aunty Vi, I do have a special reason for coming to see you.'

'I knew it.' Her aunt pulled up a chair next to her, her mobile face beaming and expectant, eyebrows raised. 'Go on, love, spill the beans.'

'I … I'm getting married.'

All the laughter vanished from Violet's face and she stared at Lily in consternation, then shot a hurried glance at her mother.

'*Married*?'

Gran came shuffling round the table to stand before her, still rolling a piece of pastry between floured fingers. 'What's this? Getting wed? At your age?' There was disbelief in her face. 'You're pulling my leg?'

'No, it's true. I'm marrying Tristan Minear.'

'The farmer's son?' Violet sat back, her gaze fixed on Lily's face. 'Well, he's a nice enough lad, and I know you were courting before he went away, but… Didn't he get hurt? You said in your last letter that he was at the convalescent home.' She was frowning. 'Nasty burns, all over his body.'

'Not all over, just his right side. But yes, he's still at Symmonds Hall.'

Gran was staring. 'What, you going to marry this boy while he's still in his hospital bed? Whatever for?'

144

'Of c-course not, Gran,' Lily stammered, floundering as her much-practised announcement failed to go to plan. 'We're going to wait until he's been discharged.'

Violet was still frowning. 'So, he's on the mend, then?'

'Yes.' Lily hesitated. 'More or less.'

Gran groaned and shook her head. 'No, no, no. You can't go throwing yourself away on this boy.'

'Gran, for goodness' sake, I'm not throwing myself away.' Lily had to count to ten in her head, not wanting to snap at her grandmother. 'I ... I love Tristan.'

'You don't sound very certain about that,' Gran said.

Violet was eyeing her suspiciously. 'Hang on, what does that "more or less" mean?'

'Tristan will need looking after for a while once we're married and living together, that's all. You see, the damage to his leg was quite deep and extensive, so he's not able to walk yet.' Lily saw the horror in their faces and stumbled on, her voice rising as she tried to explain, 'But Dr Lewis says he should make a good recovery, if infection doesn't set in. He's told me what to watch for and how to manage his treatments. I know it's not ideal but... Oh blimey, I thought you'd be pleased for me. And I've made my mind up, so don't bother telling me to forget it, all right?'

Then she burst into tears.

CHAPTER FIFTEEN

Near the harbourside in St Ives, Mary sat on a low wall outside the pub where she had agreed to meet Dick Jeffries, staring at the Atlantic as it shimmered gently in the sunshine. Every now and then, clouds would skim the face of the sun, and the rippling ocean below darkened like the skin on a burnt rice pudding, flipping back to silver as soon as the sun beamed down again.

'Here's your beer,' Dick said, emerging from the pub doorway with their two drinks. His appreciative gaze shifted to the ocean. 'Ah now, look at that. What a lovely day.' He lifted his pint, half in a salute to her and half to the view. 'Cheers.'

'Cheers.' She took three good swallows of her beer, feeling hot and thirsty. 'So, like me, you were born and bred in St Ives, and you went to the same school where you teach, so I expect we know a lot of the same people.'

He took a moment to reply again. 'I was always happy here in St Ives, so I stayed.'

He sounded gruff and on his dignity, as though he

thought she had been mocking him for being dull or attached to his mother's apron strings.

'I just meant…' She hesitated. 'It's odd we've never met before. It's not that big a town.'

'I've seen *you* a few times before. But you probably didn't notice me.' His voice was still gruff.

'Where do you live?'

He swallowed almost half the remaining beer in his glass before saying defensively, 'Near the gas works with my mum and dad. Not exactly the poshest part of town. But we like it.'

Mary nodded, understanding why he was uncomfortable. 'Nothing wrong with living with your parents. I'd still be at home too if it wasn't for work. Symmonds Hall offers its nurses free bed and board on the premises.'

He whistled. 'Not bad.'

A small fishing boat was sailing into the bay and they watched it in silence for a while. Mary could hear the faint voices of the fishermen on board as they called to each other, see the dappled sunlight on the red-painted stern of the boat and its name plate: 'Sweet Breeze'. Fishermen were such romantics, she thought, smiling to herself.

'But what made you become a teacher?' she asked.

'It was either teach or work on the herring boats.'

He had to be joking, surely? But his face was serious, so she went along with it. 'Do you ever wish you'd chosen differently? Gone to sea?'

'Like I said, I'm happy where I am.' Dick finished his pint and peered into the bottom of the glass, watching the dregs slide down its sides. 'Though I wouldn't have minded signing up and doing my bit. But with this lazy eye… The recruiting office wouldn't take me. Besides, the kids here need a teacher. An experienced teacher, someone who can help them achieve their potential.'

'Achieve their potential?' She was secretly impressed but said, with a grin to soften her words, 'You sound like a government pamphlet.'

Dick laughed, cradling his empty glass. 'All right, maybe that was a bit over the top, but … I like my job. And I think I'm good at it, for what that's worth.'

'Helping kids achieve their potential? That's worth a great deal in my book, especially at the moment, when nobody knows what's going to happen with the world and everything is going to rack and ruin. I can't think of a more worthwhile profession right now than teaching.'

'How about nursing?' Dick grinned, giving her a wink, and they both chuckled. His gaze warmed on her face, and for a moment it felt as though the sun was shining more brightly.

'Are there any particular qualities you need to be a good teacher?' she asked impulsively.

He considered that question carefully. 'A desire to help people, I would say. To bring out the best in someone.' He grinned. 'Being able to keep order in a classroom is useful too, though. Can't teach a rabble.'

'No, I imagine not.'

'Think back to your own school days,' he urged her. 'Which teachers do you remember best and why? The ones who let you get away with making very little effort, or the ones who taught you something valuable? The ones who made you see the world a different way, perhaps.'

Mary hadn't done terribly well at school, except when

it came to story time. 'I won the Reading Prize,' she said, and then felt ludicrous for boasting about something she'd done as a child. That had been years ago, for goodness' sake. He must think her an idiot.

But he didn't laugh. 'And have you kept up your reading since school days? Do you still love stories, books and so on?'

'Yes,' she admitted, feeling shy as she met his eyes.

'Then that teacher, the one who helped you develop a love of books, did a good job.' He smiled. 'Sometimes I meet former pupils in the street, and they stop to tell me how they're getting on. And when they tell me they landed a job or made an important decision in life because of something they learned in my classroom...' His voice choked and she was amazed to see tears in his eyes. 'That's what you hope for as a teacher. To give a youngster skills they can use later in life. And that's not always going to be reading, writing and arithmetic.'

They looked at each other in silence for a moment, then Dick cleared his throat. 'But enough about me. Tell me about you.'

'Not much to tell,' she confessed. 'I'm a nurse, I've always been a nurse, and I'll probably never be anything else.'

'Well, if you love your work.' He shrugged.

'I'm not sure I do.'

'Oh.' He grimaced. 'That's not so good. But you're young. There's plenty of time to find something you enjoy more.'

'Is there?' After his stirring speech about how wonderful he found being a teacher, Mary was feeling a little despondent. 'Right now, with the war and everything, I'm finding it hard to see the good things in life.' She pulled a face. 'I can't even decide what to get my mother for her sixtieth birthday. That's how useless I am.'

'You're not useless, Mary. You're just tired.' Dick rubbed his chin, staring out at the sea again. 'We're all tired. Tired of the war, tired of rationing, tired of air raids, tired of newspapers reporting dreadful news every day. Tired of life.'

'Yes,' she whispered.

He drew a deep breath, looking back at her. 'But at least with your mother's birthday, that's something positive to think about. Something to celebrate.' He gave her an encouraging smile. 'Have you had any ideas yet?'

'My mind's a blank.'

'I see.' He sat down on the wall beside her. 'Our parents must be about the same age, you know. My mother just celebrated her sixtieth. I bought her a cut-glass decanter. It's not my taste, but Mum loves that sort of thing.'

'So does mine,' Mary admitted, 'but she already has a cut-glass decanter. For sherry, in case we ever have guests round. Which we don't, mainly because of rationing and the blackout. Though I know Mum would love people to come round the house more.'

He thought for a moment, and then suggested lightly. 'How about a surprise party, then?'

Mary stared at him. 'That's a fabulous idea. Not sure how I'd organise it though. She'd soon spot me sneaking in extra food for a party.'

'Several of the pubs round here would host a small get-together, if you ask nicely, and probably wouldn't charge too much if you brought your own food.'

'Dick, you're a genius.' Mary beamed at him.

'How about another drink?'

'Oh, why not?' Mary handed him her empty glass, though she probably shouldn't have another beer. She was already feeling giddy enough without adding the demon drink to the equation. 'If you're sure you can afford it.'

'I told you,' he said, with a wry shrug. 'I live with my parents.' And he disappeared back into the pub.

While he was gone, Mary thought back over what he'd said about teaching, and knew it had made a deep impression on her. No wonder he was proud of his profession. It seemed to her a marvellous thing to be a teacher. Not the ones who rapped your knuckles with a ruler and gave you lines to copy out but the teachers like Dick Jeffries who put their heart and soul into each lesson.

Dick insisted on walking her home after the pub. She was staying at her parents' home for the Easter weekend, but he didn't seem to mind traipsing halfway across town with her. They talked endlessly, mostly about the war, but also about St Ives and the weather and their favourite authors, and she couldn't remember when she had felt so happy nor enjoyed a Saturday afternoon quite so much.

At her front door, they said goodbye, and although Dick didn't suggest another date, he did invite her to come into the school after Easter and look at the little library of classics that he reserved for his top readers – Jane Austen, Charles Dickens, Thomas Hardy, and so on. Eagerly, she agreed.

Then he did something extraordinary. Without any warning, he bent his head and kissed her.

Mary, who had only ever been kissed by relatives before,

and then only on the cheek, felt blood rush into her face, and stood staring at him, shocked and speechless.

Dick grinned, nodded, and set off back down the road into town with his hands in his pockets whistling like a schoolboy.

Before he was even out of sight, the door behind her jerked open, and her mother glared out at her. 'Mary Stannard, get inside here this instant.' As soon as Mary had been dragged unceremoniously indoors, the door was slammed shut and her mother faced her, chest heaving with outrage. 'I saw you out the window. You let that man kiss you.'

'Yes, I did.' Still in a daze, Mary didn't even consider denying it. Why should she? They were both adults and there was no law against it. 'It was only a kiss, Mum. Calm down.'

'Was that Pip's teacher?' her mother demanded, suspicion dark in her face.

Mary clamped her lips shut, not willing to get either Dick or Pip into trouble if her mum was going to be difficult, but her father, who had been peering out through the net curtains after Dick, gave her away.

'That was definitely the Jeffries boy,' he confirmed. 'Pip's teacher, who brought him round to the house the other day.'

'Jeffries?' Her mother gave a dreadful shriek and tore at her hair. 'I knew it. As soon as I realised he was Pip's teacher, I knew there'd be trouble…'

'Rita, you'll wake the boy.'

'He's not asleep,' Rita told her husband in scathing tones. 'And anyway, let him hear. He deserves to know.' Rita

152

turned her attention to her daughter. 'I can't believe you let That Man kiss you.'

'Well, he did it before I knew what was happening. But if he offers to do it again, I expect I'll let him, yes.' Mary pressed both hands over her ears as her mother shrieked again, moaning about the decadent youth of today and how the world was falling down around their ears, or some such nonsense. 'For goodness' sake, Mum, keep it down. What will the neighbours think?'

'Best make yourself scarce, love.' Her dad put a hand on Mary's arm, anxiously trying to steer her away. 'Your mother's upset,' he added, unnecessarily.

'Thanks, I'd worked that out for myself. But why is she upset? That's what I don't understand.' Mary was aware of a slow anger rising inside her. Her very first boyfriend. And apparently she was being warned off him after only one date. 'Is a schoolteacher not good enough for you now?'

Rita folded her arms and raised her chin, fixing Mary with a bitter look. 'It's not what he is, my girl, but who he is.'

Mary stared at her, perplexed. 'And who is he?'

'Best not ask,' her father muttered.

'He's Mrs Jeffries' *son*,' her mother hissed, as if this simple fact explained everything.

'Well, I can safely say I was expecting that, at least,' Mary said, repressing an urge to roll her eyes. 'But who is Mrs Jeffries to you and why do you disapprove of her so much?'

Her mother's face was highly flushed and agitated. 'Because ... because she's a thief.'

Shocked by this accusation, Mary gasped, 'A *thief*?'

'Now, Rita, don't go saying something you might regret later,' her father began but her mother ignored him.

'Yes, a *thief*,' she repeated with bitter emphasis, her mouth pinched and furious. 'That Cynthia Jeffries is a no-good, man-stealing tramp, and I won't have her or her son within a stone's throw of this house.' She was shouting now. 'Do you hear me?'

'I should imagine the whole street can hear you.' Mary shook her head in disbelief. 'But … a man-stealing tramp? What on earth are you going on about?' Her eyes narrowed on her mother's face as a terrible new suspicion began to form in her head. 'Which man did she steal and who did she steal him from?'

'She stole *Mr Jeffries*, of course,' her mother snapped, and then stabbed a finger at her own chest. 'And she stole him from me.'

Silence followed this stunning admission, except for Mary's dad, who groaned and sank his balding head in his hands.

CHAPTER SIXTEEN

'I'm not sure about this,' Yvonne whispered to Sonya, her face anxious as she watched Walter, seated at their feet, flick through the pages of a board book. 'I'm only used to seeing my own doctor. This all feels rather awkward.'

Sonya patted her daughter's hand. 'There's nothing to worry about, I assure you. I've known Lily Fisher a good while now, and she's the best person for you to see in your condition.'

It was difficult to know what to say to her daughter, for this business of motherhood was still very new to her. Yet she seemed to be muddling through so far, simply by trusting her instincts. Besides, there was no doubt in her mind that Yvonne ought to be examined by Lily if she was planning a stay of several weeks' duration. For a start, her daughter didn't know exactly when this baby would arrive, and that was surely the first thing an expectant mother ought to ascertain.

Lily emerged from her office, smiling in welcome. A

pretty young blonde, she looked reassuringly capable in her smart uniform and cap. 'Hello, Sonya,' she said in her cheery East End accent, though Sonya couldn't quite recall exactly where the Fisher family came from in that part of London. 'How are you? I was so surprised to get your note.' Her curious gaze transferred to Yvonne. 'This must be your friend, the one who's staying with you. How do you do, Mrs Fairweather?' She shook hands with Yvonne, before glancing down at Walter. 'Oh, you already have a kid. And how old are you, young man?'

Walter studied her suspiciously. 'I'm six.'

'My goodness. I could have sworn you was ten, at least.'

'You talk funny,' he accused her.

'Walter!' Sonya exclaimed, horrified, but thankfully Lily didn't seem offended.

'I suppose I do, if you're not used to it. I'm from Dagenham, which is east of London. We all talk funny there. Don't you like it?'

Walter considered this question seriously, then shrugged. 'It's all right.' He looked at her through narrowed eyes though. 'Are you going to take my mummy away?'

'Only for half an hour,' Lily promised him. 'Can you cope?'

'Granny St Ives is taking me for a walk,' he said darkly, throwing a sceptical look at Sonya, who blanched.

'Granny St Ives?' Lily repeated blankly, then looked from Yvonne to Sonya in dawning realisation. 'Oh, I see. But...' She stopped short and gave them all a bright smile. 'In that case, we'd better get on with it. Follow me, Mrs Fairweather, if you would.'

Leaning down to her son, Yvonne whispered, 'Behave

yourself, do you hear?' before kissing him on the forehead and handing him over to Sonya. 'Good luck.'

Sonya had originally planned to take her grandson down to the sea, but it was a blustery day and she feared losing her hat. Instead, she took his hand and they walked together through the narrow, cobbled lanes of St Ives, stopping every now and then to peer into shop windows. She had a story prepared should any of her acquaintances happen to pass by, but after Walter's *faux pas* in the hospital clinic, she decided to tackle him on the subject ahead of time.

'Now, Walter, dear,' she began hesitantly as he studied an old toy train in the boarded-up window of an antique shop. 'I have something important to tell you.'

The shopkeeper came out and stood in the doorway, nodding to her. 'Miss Thorpe.'

'How do you, Mr Rafferty,' she said politely, but was careful not to introduce Walter.

Lady Symmonds had often frequented Mr Rafferty's antique shop over the years, invariably with Sonya in tow. But since her departure, Sonya had barely been into town at all, and had no spare money for spending on anything that was not an everyday essential.

She was dismayed but not surprised by the large rectangle of chipboard fixed over one of the front windows to protect the goods inside. There had been several bombing raids over St Ives since the war began, mostly in the past year as Mr Hitler grew ever more desperate to win, and some of the shops and buildings had become casualties. Luckily, very few people had been killed in these abominable attacks. But Sonya was acutely aware that very few was not none, and she had known one of the dead, at least by sight. But it still made her rather furious whenever she thought of it or heard the sirens go off above the town, her fists clenching automatically. She would never describe herself as a violent person. But this war had brought out an aggressive streak that embarrassed her at times, for all that it was aimed entirely at the enemy.

With another nod, Mr Rafferty went back inside and closed the shop door, and Sonya cleared her throat.

'Train,' Walter said before she could speak. 'I like trains.'

'Yes, it's a very nice train. But I need you to pay attention to Grandma now. Are you listening, Walter?'

Clearly he was not, for the little boy ignored her, counting the windows in the toy train carriage instead.

'Walter, I know your mother asked you to call me Granny St Ives,' she went on doggedly. 'And that's lovely. But I'd much rather you only called me that when we're not in company. That is to say, when it's only you and I together … and your mother, of course.' She peered down at him anxiously. 'Do you understand what Granny … I mean, what I'm saying?'

A middle-aged gentleman she vaguely knew from church tipped his hat to her in passing and stopped to inquire after Lady Symmonds and how she was getting on with her new husband in Scotland. 'Mrs Golightly, as she is now,' he added with a smile.

'Granny St Ives, Granny St Ives,' Walter chanted loudly and deliberately, grinning as he looked from the man's astonished expression to hers. 'Granny St Ives, Granny St Ives.'

'I don't understand,' the gentleman said, looking puzzled.

'I beg your pardon,' Sonya babbled, already beginning to drag Walter away down the street. 'Um, dear little boy. The son of a friend of mine, you know. He wants his … his grandmother. Please excuse us.'

Without waiting to hear his reply, she hurried around the next corner into a side-street, and then stopped to glare at her grandson.

'That was very naughty of you, Walter,' she exclaimed, quite exasperated with the boy. 'Very naughty indeed. Whatever will your mother say when I tell her?'

'Silly old bag!' Walter shouted and, tugging his hand free from hers, ran off.

Sonya, shocked by this outburst, did not immediately respond. But the sight of her little grandson disappearing around the next bend in the sunny street galvanised her into action. Clutching her hat as another fierce gust of wind blew down the road, she set off after him at an undignified trot, blinking and breathless as she struggled to negotiate the uneven paving stones.

'Walter Fairweather,' she called after him, 'come back here this minute, or else!'

By the time she had finally caught up with Walter, read him the Riot Act, and then half-dragged, half-cajoled him back to the hospital, Yvonne's examination was long since over. They met his mother waiting anxiously in the hospital entrance, peering up and down the street for them, looking as pale and vulnerable as the day she had first arrived in St Ives, Sonya thought guiltily.

'I'm so sorry to have kept you waiting, Yvonne,' she told her daughter in a gasp, aware that her own cheeks were flushed and her hat askew, 'but Walter was very poorly behaved, I'm afraid. He disobeyed me, called me something so rude I cannot possibly repeat it, and then ran away. It took me a full ten minutes to find him again, and even then, I had to enlist the help of a shopkeeper to catch him.'

To her astonishment, Yvonne barely seemed to hear her. 'Come here, Walter,' she said, holding out to her hand. The boy went to her side immediately, triumph in his face. 'What have you been up to with Granny St Ives?'

'Nothing,' he said mendaciously, and then chanted, his expression almost malicious, 'Granny St Ives, Granny St Ives,' and chuckled at Sonya's bewilderment.

'But aren't you going to call him to task for behaving like that?' she demanded.

Her daughter seemed almost as surprised as she was. 'Boys are always like that. Of course he misbehaved,' she said in an absentminded tone as they set off uphill towards Symmonds Hall. 'He knew he could get away with it, that's all. It's only because you don't know how to handle a child his age.'

'I beg your pardon?' Sonya's heart was beating so fast it felt like it would burst. 'I work in an orphanage. I oversee many young children. None of them have ever led me such a merry dance as your son.'

'That's not the same,' Yvonne said dismissively. 'What I mean is, you've never been a mother. Not the same way I have.'

Sonya felt as though she'd been slapped across the face. She did not know what to say without being intolerably rude to her own daughter, so kept her lips tightly sealed.

* * *

Soon, they were back at the apartment, sitting down to some bread and luncheon meat, which Cook had kindly brought up on a tray, given that they had missed the official lunch hour at Symmonds Hall.

Once she was a little calmer, Sonya ventured to start a more neutral conversation. 'Forgive me, I forgot to ask, but how did your examination go with Lily Fisher? She confirmed the, erm, situation, I suppose?' As she asked this, she kept one wary eye on Walter, for so far he knew nothing of his mother's interesting condition.

'Yes, she confirmed it,' Yvonne said with a sigh, also glancing cautiously in her son's direction. 'The thing is, she wasn't able to give me a firm date.'

'How extraordinary.'

Her daughter hesitated. 'Walter, dearest,' she said with a bright smile, 'would you run and fetch Mummy a glass of water? I have such a dry throat. Thank you, that's a good boy.'

As soon as her son had scampered away, Yvonne leant forward, whispering, 'Lily said the bump is bigger than it ought to be. My dates are fairly certain, you see. From when...' She coloured delicately. 'From when Patrick was home on leave.'

'Of course,' Sonya needed no interpretation of that oblique statement. 'But what did Lily say that means?'

'She couldn't be sure. But she did suggest... Only the merest possibility, you understand, that it could be twins.'

Twins?

That would certainly explain why Yvonne had been looking so pale after her hospital visit and why she had barely listened to Sonya's description of her son's escapades.

161

'Goodness me,' Sonya said, shocked. 'Lily is very new to midwifery, of course. Perhaps she's mistaken.'

'She said much the same herself,' Yvonne agreed in a whisper. 'And also that we might not know for sure that it's twins until the birth. It's quite unsettling, but what can one do except wait?' Walter was already hurrying back with a full glass of water, going too fast as usual and spilling it as he went. Her daughter turned to him with a grateful smile. 'Thank you, darling. What would Mummy do without you?'

The day after their difficult trip to the hospital clinic, they took lunch in the hall canteen with the nursing staff, opting for the second sitting as Yvonne had been for a walk with Walter earlier that morning and was feeling tired.

Walter always excited interest at mealtimes in the canteen, several of the nurses having taken a shine to his cheeky smile and dark curls. And Cook was no different.

'Will the boy be starting school here in St Ives?' Mrs Penhallow asked a little breathlessly, stopping to check their meals were to their liking, both fists resting on her generous hips. Sonya had previously told her and the other staff that Yvonne was a friend of hers who would be staying at the hall while she recovered from the shock of her husband being listed as missing in action, and to her relief, nobody had questioned this tale. The truth might have placed them all in an embarrassing situation.

'I certainly hope so,' Yvonne told her, pausing in her meal to flash an indulgent smile at young Walter. 'That reminds me, I need to walk down there and speak to the head teacher. I imagine school must have started again now after the Easter break.'

Cook winked at Walter, who had finished his stew in double-quick time. 'Want to come and lay out some jellies for tonight's dessert? My assistant Piotr is busy washing pots and I could do with another helper.'

'Rather!' Walter exclaimed and trotted into the kitchen after Mrs Penhallow without even asking permission.

When he'd gone, Sonya said quickly, 'It's an excellent idea to enrol him at the school. I'm sure Walter must be missing a school environment. Friends, things to do all day, and plenty of running about.'

'You think I spoil him,' Yvonne said, not looking at her. 'You think Walter spends too much time with me, that he's tied to my apron strings.'

Sonya flushed with embarrassment, though she could hardly deny it outright. 'A boy that age needs to be at school,' she replied in the end, stammering a little. 'I hope you haven't taken offence.'

'No,' Yvonne said, much to her relief. 'You're probably right. But he's been unhappy ever since Granny Truro blurted out that his father is … missing.' She did not use the 'd' word, so Sonya presumed she was still living in hope that her husband was alive. All the same, tears sprang to her eyes. 'It's no surprise he's been playing up, is it? Poor boy.'

A tap on Sonya's shoulder made her jump. She turned to find Matron there, looking as starchy as ever. Hurriedly getting up, Sonya greeted her, asking, 'Can I help you, Matron?'

But Matron was looking past her at Yvonne. 'Is this the friend who's been staying with you, Miss Thorpe?'

'Yes, Matron. May I introduce Mrs Yvonne Fairweather?' Sonya wished she had never agreed to them taking meals in the canteen, for this was exactly the kind of awkward situation she had envisaged. 'Yvonne, this is Matron, who rules the convalescent home with a rod of iron.' She meant it for a joke, but nobody laughed.

'How do you do?' Yvonne said politely.

'This came to my office a short while ago, since the orderly who received it at the front door didn't know what else to do with it,' Matron said mysteriously, and handed over a small buff envelope. 'Telegram for Mrs Fairweather.'

'Oh my God,' Yvonne said faintly, staring at it in horror. 'No, no.' She shook her head, and then covered her face with her hands. 'No.'

'We'll take it up to the apartment to read it,' Sonya said firmly, and took the envelope for her. 'Thank you, Matron. You've been very kind.' If Matron heard the irony in her voice, the woman gave no sign of it, merely turning with a nod and striding away in her usual abrupt manner. 'Yvonne, shall we leave all this and go back to the apartment? We can be private there.'

'Walter...' Yvonne whimpered, her face still hidden.

'Don't worry, I'll fetch him for you.' She put the envelope in front of Yvonne. 'I won't be a moment.'

Hurrying into the kitchen, Sonya found the boy helping Cook spoon jelly portions into bowls. 'I'm sorry, Walter, but I need you to come with me. Your mother's not feeling well and she wants to go back to her room.'

'Not something she ate, I hope?' Cook looked worried.

'No, of course not.' Sonya touched the boy's arm, for he was not listening. 'Walter, dear, I need you to stop that and—'

'I don't want to stop! I'm helping Cook.' With a furious roar, Walter spun with a spoonful of quivering red jelly and flung it towards her. Strawberry jelly spattered Sonya's face and dress. Gasping in shock, she groped for him, but the boy dodged past her in search of his mother, shrieking, 'Mummy, Mummy? It's not my fault. Granny St Ives made me do it!'

Granny St Ives.

'Dearie me.' Cook's eyes were wide with speculation, but she merely tutted and dabbed at Sonya's face with a tea towel. 'Lively little thing, ain't he?'

'Excuse me, I must go and see if...' Hot with embarrassment, Sonya dashed out of the kitchen but found Yvonne and her son already gone, the others in the canteen looking round at her, eyes bright with curiosity.

By the time Sonya had hurried through the convalescent home, across the outside yard and up the steep stairs back to the apartment, breathless and out of her mind with worry, Walter was nowhere to be seen and Yvonne was sitting with her head in her hands, her shoulders shaking.

Full of dread, Sonya crept into the room, wishing she knew what to say. 'My dear, I'm so sorry,' she said tentatively. 'Was it *very* bad news?'

But Yvonne stood and came to embrace her, and although she had been crying, a handkerchief clutched in her hand, she was smiling too.

'Patrick's alive,' she gushed, with a tremble in her voice.

165

'Isn't that just the most marvellous thing?' She held out the telegram for Sonya to read. 'He's a Prisoner of War though. In a German camp. It's all rather beastly. But he's not dead, and he could have been. I could have been a widow and I'm not. So that's something, isn't it?'

'That's something indeed,' Sonya agreed, hugging her daughter. Her heart flooding with joy, she raised her face to heaven with a silent prayer of thanks. 'Something very wonderful and to be celebrated.'

CHAPTER SEVENTEEN

Penzance, Cornwall, May 1943

Lily couldn't believe she was back in Penzance so soon. It felt like only yesterday she'd been working as a nurse at the hospital here and rooming above the Fire Guard Headquarters after the nurses' quarters got bombed out. In the back of Joe's van, she leant forward over the front seat, staring eagerly at all the familiar landmarks passing them by. It was strange how a place could so rapidly feel like home. Dagenham – her birthplace – was another world away.

And now she was starting to feel at home in St Ives, and indeed she wondered if she would ever leave Cornwall. She had fallen in love with the south-west coast and felt sure it would be her home for evermore. But part of that certainty lay in her feelings for Tristan. Without that tie, perhaps it would not feel so much like home.

Joe drove through the centre of Penzance at a slow and majestic pace, whistling under his breath.

'It's very kind of you to put yourself out like this, Uncle Joe,' Lily said for about the fifth time. 'Especially with fuel rationing cut to the bone now.'

'I don't mind sparing a bit of fuel from the farm's rations for a good cause,' the Cornishman said in his slow, deep, humorous voice. 'Besides, I didn't have no choice in the matter. Your aunt can be very determined when she wants.'

Aunt Violet, seated in the front of the van, must have heard her name, because she stirred from her nap and yawned. 'Are we there yet?'

'We're in Penzance,' Joe told her. 'The wedding's in Marazion. East side of the bay. Another ten minutes.'

Violet sat up, rubbing her eyes. 'Blimey, I'm starving. I could eat a horse. Lily, do you reckon they put on sarnies at a Quaker do?'

'I should imagine so,' Lily said, and then caught sight of St Michael's Mount again, the beautiful fairy-tale castle built out in the bay with its long causeway that got submerged at high tide, and fell silent, so happy that she couldn't speak for several minutes.

'Quakers eat food, just like everybody else,' Joe pointed out. 'Stands to reason they'd have sandwiches. Or a big pie, maybe.' He followed the road to Marazion at the same slow pace, with the sea sparkling to their right the whole way.

'Do they drink alcohol though? That's the question.' Violet sounded dubious. 'I hope so, or this is going to be a very long day.'

Lily turned to her charge in the back of the van. Tristan was lying on a makeshift bed in the back, wearing a smart jacket with pyjama trousers, as ordinary trousers would not fit over his bandages. They had also managed to tuck the wheelchair that Dr Lewis had so generously provided for them into the back of the van, folded up out of the way.

'Comfortable, Tristan?' Lily was aware that he had not slept during the long journey from St Ives to Penzance but had lain there in silence most of the way, gritting his teeth whenever Joe went over a pothole. 'Is the pain very bad?'

'Hardly any pain at all,' Tristan insisted but she felt sure he was lying. 'I'm looking forward to seeing my sister married. Thank you for arranging this. You must let me pay Joe back for the fuel somehow.'

'Don't you worry about that,' Joe insisted from the front of the van. 'Now listen, I don't know much about this fellow she's marrying. Except that he's a Quaker and I don't know much about them neither. How about you, Tristan?'

'All I know is, they're crazy about each other.'

Aunty Violet turned around in her seat. 'I thought Quakers couldn't get married,' she said. 'I mean, they're not allowed to swear oaths, and a wedding is a kind of oath, isn't it?'

'Demelza explained it to me in a letter,' Tristan admitted, his voice still a little husky from the smoke he must have inhaled during the fire. 'Quakers make a kind of commitment to each other, rather than swearing an oath. It's a sort of informal arrangement, with the congregation – if it's called that – as witnesses. But it's treated the same as a proper marriage.'

'I call that shabby,' Violet exclaimed, looking shocked. 'Informal arrangement? How can your sister be sure this fellow won't go off with somebody else, if they ain't properly married?' She shook her head. 'It don't seem right.'

Lily was embarrassed, seeing Tristan's surprised expression. 'I know Robert and he's a lovely man, and very brave too. I'm sure he'd never do anything like that to Demelza.' She smiled, thinking of when she'd last seen the couple together; pretty, soft-faced Demelza with her rugged, well-built Robert. 'I think it's romantic.'

'Hush,' Violet said, pointing ahead up the hill. 'Isn't that the place?'

'Aye,' Joe agreed, and slowed to a halt, finding a place to park his van as close as possible to the building, though there were already a number of people gathered outside, chatting in the sunshine.

They got Tristan into the wheelchair and looking smart in his jacket and hat, with a blanket draped discreetly over his pyjama-clad legs.

'How are you feeling?' Lily whispered, leaning close as she helped him tuck the blanket over his knees.

'Bloody stupid,' he grumbled, and then caught her expression and pulled a face. 'I'm sorry, I'm behaving like an idiot.' His face softened. 'Thank you for doing this.'

Lily felt a glow of warmth inside. Taking a deep breath, she said, 'You're welcome.'

'The thing is, my father will be here, and I'm stuck in this chair. No doubt he'll see me like this and be congratulating himself that he didn't agree to take me back at the farm.'

Lily felt her cheeks grow hot with fury on his behalf, but she merely said, 'Then he's the idiot, Tris, not you.'

Lily pushed him up the last few feet to the stone-built

Quaker meeting house, with Violet and Joe following slowly behind.

She was surprised to see Demelza in front of the meeting house, standing shoulder to shoulder with Robert. In traditional church weddings, the groom would ordinarily arrive before the bride, though sometimes she had heard of rural weddings in Cornwall where a young couple would walk together to church. But it seemed Quaker ceremonies were very different.

Demelza was wearing a pale lemon summer frock with capped sleeves and a slight frill to the hem. She wore no jewellery and carried no flowers, but a corsage of white rosebuds, nestling on fern, was pinned to her frock. Her cheeks were glowing, and her bright ginger curls clustered merrily about her face. The merest hint of lipstick and powder set off her healthy good looks, and her smile, trembling and widening every time she glanced at her husband-to-be, suggested pure joy.

Robert too had made an effort with his usual careless appearance. A huge man, the kind who filled doorways and loomed over people, he had somehow managed to find a jacket that fitted his broad chest and shoulders, and his springing fair hair had been cut and brushed back from his temple. He was listening to Demelza talk in her cheerful, forthright way and smiling down at her, a tender look in his striking blue eyes.

Spotting Tristan and Lily approaching, Demelza gave a cry and excused herself, plunging through the assembled people to shake Lily's hand and kiss her brother's cheek.

'You made it,' Demelza said in her rolling Cornish burr.

'I'm so glad.' There were tears in her eyes. 'Oh, Tris, it's the happiest day of my life. I'm over the moon that you're here to share it with me.'

'Wouldn't have missed it for the world, Sis.' Tristan grinned self-consciously. 'I'd rather be on my feet, but … there it is.'

'I'll hear none of that self-pity, thank you.' She threw a dazzling smile at Lily. 'And when are you two tying the knot? I hope I'll be invited. No secret weddings down in St Ives, you hear?'

Lily blushed, aware of her aunt's gaze on her face, for she knew Violet didn't approve of their impending marriage. 'I'll be sending out invitations soon, don't worry.'

Tristan leant forward and caught at his sister's hand. 'Is Father here?' he asked in a low voice.

'No,' Demelza told him, and her disappointment was clear in the sudden downturned look, her lips compressing. 'Father agreed to come but then changed his mind at the last minute. Said he wasn't sitting down with a roomful of Quakers.' She pulled a face. 'Aunt Sarah's here though. One of Robert's friends was kind enough to pick her up from the farm, and he'll take her back again after the do.'

'There is a do, then?' Violet asked hopefully.

'Of course, and you're all very welcome to…' Demelza's voice trailed off as everyone began heading into the meeting house. Gulping for breath, she put a hand to her tummy, her chest heaving. 'Oh goodness, it's time. I've got butterflies.'

Robert took his intended's hand. 'You'll be fine,' he murmured, and Demelza blushed as she looked up at him.

The couple headed inside the meeting house, hand in

hand, and Lily watched them almost enviously. To be so much in love...

'Here we go,' she said with a sigh, and pushed Tristan through the door and into the main room, which was set out with benches. The meeting house was solid and snug, a quaint old stone structure that must have stood there for centuries. Deep voices echoed in the rafters as she entered. Someone was speaking to Robert and Demelza, showing them a place specially prepared for them at the front of the meeting.

Lily found a place for Tristan at the end of one bench, then sat down beside him, while Violet and Joe tucked in on the bench behind them. The Quakers did not stare at them for being strangers, as Lily had feared they might, but smiled in an amiable way, and one woman even said, 'Welcome, friends,' which made her feel less out of place.

Robert and Demelza sat down at the front. People shuffled their feet, cleared their throats, and then silence fell.

After what felt like a very long time, during which Lily became a little uncomfortable, wondering if anything would ever happen, Robert got to his feet and began to speak.

'In the fear of the Lord and in the presence of this assembly, I take this my friend, Demelza Minear,' he said deeply, 'to be my spouse.' He paused, studying her with a smile. 'Demelza, I love you and I promise to be true to you and to you alone, and to be your helpmate in sickness and in health until death parts us. May our friends witness this promise today as God joins us in marriage.'

Then Robert sat down again.

Demelza did not immediately speak but bent her head,

her hands clasped in her lap, a mass of ginger curls hiding her face. What was she thinking? Had she changed her mind?

Lily began to feel anxious and shot a glance at Tristan. But he seemed unperturbed by the silence, even winking at her. His faith in his sister was inspiring.

At last, Demelza stood and repeated, quite firmly, looking at Robert, the same formal words he had used to her, adding, 'I love you and I promise to be a faithful wife and to care for you and any children we may have, no matter what. You are the light in my life, and I will always be grateful for having found you. I call on our friends to witness my promise and ask God to join us today as man and wife.' Her voice shook with emotion on those last words, then she sat down again too.

Robert touched her hand gently, and their eyes met. Lily saw him mouth, 'I love you,' and felt tears roll down her cheeks quite unexpectedly. She began to rummage in her bag for a hanky but Violet, sniffing loudly, tapped her on the shoulder and passed one across.

There was silence for a long while after that. At last, an elderly woman in an old-fashioned hat spoke without standing up. 'Marriage,' she announced, 'requires a great deal of hard work and vigilance from both men and women. But God will always help us in that work if we look to him for guidance.'

The meeting continued with lengthy silences and occasional comments from a few of those gathered in the hall, while Lily tried to stem the flow of joyful tears, thinking of all the promises she would like to make to Tristan. She listened with interest when others stood to speak about love and marriage, and on other matters too, such as the war with Germany and how friends should help each other in times of need. She could see how Demelza had fallen so deeply in love with her steady, dependable Quaker, and began to understand why those who followed this way of life preferred not to fight but chose other ways to serve Britain in the war effort.

After an hour or so, the meeting seemed to come to an end quite spontaneously. People simply got up, shook hands, and began to talk quietly among themselves.

Robert said loudly, 'Would all those present come and sign their names on a sheet as witnesses to our wedding, please?'

A little touched by this request, Lily pushed Tristan forward to add his name to the sheet, and then signed her name too, followed by Violet and Joe. She hugged Demelza and shook Robert's hand.

'That was lovely,' Violet told Demelza, her voice thickened by tears. 'You make a beautiful couple. Good luck to you both.'

The wedding reception was held in the meeting house too. A tea urn was produced along with plates of sandwiches, and people stood about, chatting and laughing. The elderly lady in the funny hat turned out to be Robert's eccentric and amusing mother. His father had sadly passed away over the winter, and his mother had moved in with another elderly Quaker couple in Penzance, allowing Robert and Demelza to serve abroad without worrying about leaving her alone. There was no music or dancing, but Lily still enjoyed herself thoroughly, chatting to several of the Quakers about Demelza and Robert, and about nothing in particular too. But even as she was nodding and smiling, she found her gaze constantly returning to Tristan, as she considered the position they were in, getting married for practical rather than romantic reasons.

After the food was finished and the meeting house began to empty, Tristan held his sister's hand and spoke to her alone for a few minutes.

Lily waited discreetly out of earshot, exchanging a few words with Robert, who was taking Demelza to London in a few days' time. They had secured somewhere to live while Demelza underwent training for the Ambulance Service and both seemed tremendously excited about a new life in the city.

'Give my love to the big smoke,' Lily told the happy couple, grinning broadly as she took in their glowing faces and linked hands. 'I can't say as how I miss it all that much. But good luck to you both.'

She pushed Tristan back outside into the sunshine, a stiff breeze whipping at frocks and threatening to blow off all the ladies' hats. As they stood waiting for Violet and Joe to fetch the van a bit closer, Lily felt oddly calm and at peace, and realised why with a shock.

'All right, I'll bite.' Tristan looked up at her, smiling but with one eyebrow cocked. 'Why are you grinning like that?'

'I've realised something important,' she told him.

'Why am I worried?'

'No, it's nothing bad. Quite the opposite.' Lily drew in a breath and let it out slowly, trying to get the words right in her head, then looked at him shyly. 'I've been thinking all this time that if you and me were truly meant to be together, things would be easier all round. That everything would just fall into place.' She shook her head, laughing at her own idiocy. 'But listening to them in that meeting house, I've realised it don't always work like that.' She smiled at him, holding onto her hat as the sea breeze snatched at it. 'That's what marriage is all about, ain't it? Getting through the hard times *together*.'

Tristan had listened to her in silence, curiously intent. Now he stirred. 'Yes,' he agreed, holding her gaze. 'Together.'

CHAPTER EIGHTEEN

St Ives, Cornwall, May 1943

Mary knocked at the door to Rose's office in the orphanage, then popped her head round the door on hearing her call, 'Come in.'

'Mary?' Rose put down her pen and got up from behind her desk. 'How lovely to see you. No, don't worry, I was only organising the menus for next week's meals for the children. Dreary stuff and I'm glad of an interruption. Just finished your shift?' she asked, for Mary was still in her nursing uniform.

'Yes, and I hoped you might be free for a chat.'

'Glad to. But will you mind if we talk while taking a walk along the cliffs?' Rose stretched, looking a little fatigued, though it was only early afternoon. 'I seize up if I sit too long, and with all this paperwork, I seem to be constantly sitting these days.'

Mary readily agreed, for she loved walking by the sea, and they headed out together into the breezy spring afternoon, not bothering with hats or coats, for it would only be a short walk. It had been raining earlier that day, but only a passing shower, and all the colours of heather and grassland towards the cliffs looked newly bright. They followed one of the winding paths that led seaward from the back of the convalescent home, soon reaching the rugged cliff-path that overlooked Carbis Bay. Here, it was more blustery but the sun was strong enough to ward off any chill.

'That's better,' Rose said with a sigh, looking out across the choppy waters of the Atlantic.

Mary had been intending to ask her friend's advice but instead found herself concerned by the troubled look on her face. 'Rose, is everything all right?'

Rose turned to Mary, her green eyes serious. 'I'd like to tell you something,' she said earnestly, 'but you need to keep it a secret. You know how much I dislike people talking about me behind my back.'

'Goodness, you know you can trust me. Mum's the word.' Mary put a hand on her arm, seeing her friend flinch. 'Hey, you're worrying me now. Whatever's wrong?'

Rose pulled a face. 'I'm expecting a baby. Only it's a little harder going than I'd expected, being pregnant.'

'Oh my Lord.' Mary's jaw dropped at this unexpected news. 'I mean … congratulations!' She peered at her friend. 'But you're having difficulties? Have you seen a doctor?'

'Lily examined me. She says I'm fine and there's nothing to worry about. But I can hardly keep anything down and my morning sickness simply isn't going away.'

'It's not my area of expertise but I'm sure Lily is right

and there's nothing to worry about. You're strong, Rose.' She chuckled. 'Strongest person I know, in fact. You'll get through this.'

'Yes, I'll just have to cope, won't I? There are women out there having a much tougher time in this war. I think I can stick it through a few months of sickness.' Rose thrust her chin in the air and forced a smile. 'How about you? You wanted a chat.'

'No, it can wait.' She didn't want to give Rose any more problems to think about.

Rose's lips thinned, and her hands dropped to her hips. Now *that* was the tough old Rose she remembered from the wards, Mary thought. 'Nurse Stannard, you tell me what's up, or I swear I'll pitch you over this cliff faster than you can blink.'

'All right, keep your hair on,' Mary quipped, and they both laughed. 'It's a bit of a mess, I'm afraid. I've been walking out with this fellow, Dick Jeffries.'

'Oh, I know him. He teaches at the school.'

'That's right. Well, we've had one proper date, but it feels like it might be serious between us. Only it turns out my mum's at daggers drawn with his mum, and she's basically forbidden me to see him again.'

'What on earth?'

Briefly, Mary repeated what her mother had told her about Cynthia Jeffries, how she'd wickedly stolen her mum's boyfriend, Charles, when they were both fresh out of school, and married him.

'When Mum saw me with Dick,' she concluded, 'she lost her temper and yelled. She said no child of hers was going to be seen with a Jeffries. I'm afraid we exchanged a few cross words about it. Now I feel wretched and don't know what to do.'

'First of all, you should tell your mother to mind her own business,' Rose said, a snap in her voice, and then checked herself, seeing Mary's expression. 'Easier said than done when it's your mother though, I suppose.' She looked away, her face troubled once more. 'I've never had that problem.'

Rose was an orphan who'd lived at the Symmonds Hall orphanage as a child, along with her sister. That experience had made her all the more determined to uncover the truth when the Treverricks had been running the place so badly last year. Now Rose was in charge there, Mary felt sure the children were in a safe and sympathetic pair of hands.

'It has been rather tricky.' Mary gave a sigh. 'Mum was barely speaking to me when I left to come back here.'

Rose was chewing her lip, staring thoughtfully out to sea. Bright sunshine gleamed on her red hair, set in smooth rolls above her forehead. But she did look alarmingly pale, Mary thought, studying her averted face. It was such a shame she was suffering with this pregnancy, as she was sure Rose and Dr Lewis must be over the moon about having a little one on the way.

'Dick thinks I should organise a surprise party for my mother's sixtieth birthday next month,' Mary added. 'I thought maybe it would help soften her up if I make it really special. A birthday she'll never forget. What do you think?'

'It can't hurt.'

'Thing is, I don't know many good places to eat out in

town. We've never been the sort of family who bother with restaurants.'

'I haven't eaten out in ages either. Too busy. And there can't be many places still open, what with rationing.'

'Dick said I should arrange a pub do. But I'm worried Mum will think it's common, going to a pub for her birthday bash.'

Rose gave her a speculative look. 'Will Dick be at this party?'

'I hope so. But will it spoil everything, do you think? It would be too awful if Mum stormed out of her own birthday party rather than sit down to a drink with him.'

'Maybe you could sneak him in halfway through.' Rose gave a sly smile. 'Or he could burst out of a birthday cake. Like in the movies.'

They both chuckled at that ludicrous image.

Mary gave her a quick hug. 'Thank you for listening, Rose. And I hope you feel better soon.' She looked out to sea too, admiring the churn of waves at the base of the cliffs and the blue glitter of water as the Atlantic stretched away into haze, a sight that always lifted her heart. 'I've been going round in circles on this. But I've made my mind up. I'm going to book a pub and send out secret invitations to all my mother's old friends.'

'Not *all* of her old friends, I hope,' Rose said delicately.

'Oh Lord,' Mary said, laughing despite herself at the idea of Cynthia Jeffries walking in on her mum's birthday party. 'Can you imagine?'

That evening, there was a knock at the door to Mary's bedroom in Symmonds Hall. Mary was seated in her armchair, darning an old pair of socks, for there wasn't much to do in the evenings when she was off-duty.

'Visitor for you, Mary,' Harriet breathed, peering around the partly open door. '*A man.*'

Mary blushed at her amazed tone. 'Thank you, Harriet.' Flustered, she put away her darning needle and checked her reflection in the mirror.

'I d-didn't know you were seeing anyone,' Harriet stammered, watching her with curious blue eyes.

'It's all very new.' Mary didn't want to give the gossips anything to talk about, so shrugged carelessly. 'Probably won't last.'

'He's waiting out on the front steps. I couldn't risk asking him to wait inside in case M-Matron spotted him. She'd have fifty fits if she thought you were inviting men into the convalescent home.'

'Matron and her rules... She drives me crazy.' Mary flashed her a grateful smile. 'I'll see you later, Harriet.' Then she dashed downstairs, taking care not to make too much noise as she opened the front door and sneaked outside, closing it softly behind her.

Sure enough, Dick Jeffries was waiting for her in a smart jacket and what she suspected was a new hat. He looked rather handsome, she thought, and felt her heart beat faster as he turned towards her with a smile.

'Mary,' he said warmly, and took her hands. 'Thank you for coming out to speak to me. I was afraid you might not.'

'We have to be quiet,' she told him, smiling shyly in return, 'in case Matron comes out to see what's going on.'

'Matron doesn't sound like much fun.'

'She'd have my guts for garters if she knew I was meeting a man out here.' When he raised his eyebrows, she added in a low voice, 'Rose nearly got busted for kissing Dr Lewis before they were married. She was only saved from being thrown out on her ear because Matron was afraid what old Dr Edmund would say about it. He's Dr Lewis's granddad and very fond of Rose, and Matron is very fond of *him*. So, you see, it was a complicated situation.'

Dick, listening to all this, threw back his head and laughed. 'What a life of intrigue you nurses lead up here at Symmonds Hall. Things are far more relaxed at the board school.' He looked her up and down. She was wearing a knee-length skirt and blouse with a cardigan over the top. 'Will you be warm enough if we go for a walk?'

It was quite breezy that evening, and although dusk was still a way off, there were clouds over the sun and the air was a little chilly.

'Perhaps I should go back up to my room for a coat and hat,' Mary said, glancing uncertainly at the sky.

'Oh no,' Dick said at once. 'I wouldn't want to risk Matron giving you a black mark. Let's just stay here and talk, in that case.' His smile dazzled her. 'I could hold you close so you don't get cold, if you like.'

Mary giggled. He could be charming when he wanted to be, she thought. 'You're a bad man, Dick Jeffries.' She turned her face away, pretending to be shocked. 'I'm a respectable girl, I'll have you know.'

'That's what I like about you.' Dick slipped his arm about her waist. 'Mary, would you mind terribly if I kiss you?'

'Oh!' she exclaimed, torn between laughter and amazement. 'You really *are* a bad man.' She didn't say yes but, in truth, she couldn't wait for him to kiss her again. Their lips met and her heart began to sing.

Mary probably ought to have been shocked rigid by his behaviour and told him off. Then she recalled all the gossip around Sister Rose and Lewis being discovered in a passionate clinch by Matron, and gave an inner shrug, wrapping her arms around his broad shoulders. If Rose could get away with it…

She gasped when at last they came up for air. 'My goodness! I'll give you this, Dick Jeffries, you're a good kisser.'

'Thank you, I do my best.' He grinned. 'I say,' he added, 'have you ever considered teaching?'

Mary clung to him, her brain in a flat spin. 'I … I beg your pardon?'

'You'd make a smashing teacher. The way you are with Pip… I've seen how you speak to him, you're a natural.'

She stared at him, baffled by the sudden change in topic. 'What?'

'One of our teachers in the lower school, Tim Broadbent, has volunteered for the auxiliary services and will be leaving us next week. Off to Africa, he says. So we'll be a teacher short. We can shuffle our duties around and double up on classes until the end of term, but what about next academic year?' He sounded in deadly earnest, she realised, blinking up at him. 'It's desperately hard to recruit new teachers at the moment. Everyone qualified seems to have enlisted. And I don't want to get lumped with another well-meaning but ancient do-gooder with antiquated notions of how to teach. I swear, the last retired teacher who came back to help was in his eighties.'

'You're serious,' she exclaimed, taking a step back.

'Of course, or I wouldn't have asked.'

'I can't leave nursing.' Mary was astonished. 'For starters, it comes with bed and board. Where would I live?'

He considered that. 'With your parents?'

Mary didn't much like the sound of that, having grown used to her precious independence since coming to live at Symmonds Hall.

'I'm sorry,' she began cautiously, 'but I don't know the first thing about teaching. I like kids, but that's not enough, is it?'

'We offer all our new recruits full training.' He gave her a reassuring smile. 'And we'd start you off with the youngest set. You can read, I take it?' The question had been ironic but she nodded warily. 'Then you can teach a child to read. Some of these kids come to us barely literate.'

Despite her surprise, she did rather like the idea of helping children to read. And while she had once felt great satisfaction as a nurse, it no longer felt like something she could do forever. But the sheer enormity of the decision made her nervous.

'We can talk about this another time if you prefer,' he added. 'Right now, you're getting cold in this wind, so I won't keep you.'

'Yes, I ought to go back in.'

But neither of them moved.

Abruptly, Dick gave an exasperated groan under his breath and bent his head again. This time as they kissed her toes curled with delight and she hung on to him like a limpet, heat rising in her cheeks, kissing him back until she was gasping.

'Nurse Stannard!' The furious bark of Matron's voice

186

behind her on the porch broke the two of them apart like a dash of cold water. 'What on earth do you think you are doing? Get back inside,' she commanded in her strictest, most horrified tone. 'And as for you, sir,' she said, glaring at Dick, 'please leave these premises at once.'

'Now hang on,' Dick began but Mary shook her head.

'I … I'll see you soon,' she stammered, and fled back inside the convalescent home. Golly, she was in hot water now. Up to her neck in it and no mistake. Yet, even mortified as she was, it was hard not to feel a little giddy too.

She had fallen in love with Dick Jeffries, and after tonight, she was convinced the feeling was mutual.

Her mum was going to be livid.

CHAPTER NINETEEN

Truro, Cornwall, June 1943

Sonya was helping her daughter collect clothes and toys she'd left behind at her in-laws' house, while Walter talked in an excited rush to Granny Truro, explaining all about his new home in St Ives. Sonya had one ear for Yvonne's quiet comments as they packed a suitcase with the last of her possessions and one ear for her grandson, amused by his glowing descriptions of the orphanage and the other children he'd met since leaving Truro. His other grand-mother listened in a restrained silence, with occasional exclamations when Walter explained about football and the broken window, and then talked of Lady Symmonds' priceless ornaments, which had all now been moved beyond his reach.

'Coz I mustn't break them or I'll be for the high jump, Granny St Ives says,' Walter told her, and then rushed off to stare out of the window at a passing fire engine, loudly imitating its jangling bell.

Finally, the suitcase was packed, and anything that couldn't easily be carried had been stored for a future visit.

'Thank you for lunch,' Yvonne told her mother-in-law, still a little stiff after their disagreement. 'I know it's not what you wanted to hear, discovering that Patrick is a prisoner of war. But at least he's still alive.'

She had finally told Walter about his father's captivity in Germany, though much to her surprise the boy had seemed more excited than upset. He seemed to think it a rare distinction to have a father who was being held prisoner by the Hun and had been cheerfully boasting about it to the orphans at Symmonds Hall. But then, Sonya reflected, the boy was too young to have any real idea what it meant to be a POW in this desperate war against the Nazis. And thank goodness for that.

'For now,' Granny Truro said unhappily.

'I'm sure Patrick would want us to stay hopeful and not let this bring us down,' Yvonne told her with dignity, and took her son's hand. 'Time to go, I think. Say goodbye to Granny Truro, Walt.'

'Why can't we stay another hour?' Walter demanded, tugging on her hand. 'I want to listen to the wireless.'

'Because we have another visit to make today,' Sonya told him with an awkward smile. 'To some very special people.'

'Who? Who?'

'Yes, I'd like to know that too,' Mrs Fairweather agreed sharply. 'Whom are you taking Walter to visit now?'

'My parents,' Sonya said, uncomfortable under Granny Truro's disapproving stare, not least because she knew the other woman suspected her of being 'no better than she ought to be,' as the saying went. 'That is to say, Walter's great-grandparents. They also live in Truro, not far from here.' Picking up Yvonne's suitcase, she added tartly, more for his other grandmother's benefit than his own, 'My father is the Reverend Thorpe, retired. And I'm sure he will be very happy to make your acquaintance, Walter.' This wasn't exactly true but her father's status as a retired vicar was an undeniable badge of respectability, and she was not afraid to use it to silence further criticism.

In fact, on sending her mother a brief note to explain that she had met Yvonne and Walter, and they were now staying with her in St Ives, her mother had written to invite them to call next time they were in Truro. Her letter had been apologetic and friendly, and Sonya had good reason to hope there might be a reconciliation there, even if there'd been no mention of her father's attitude in the letter. But she was willing to give it another try. After all, they were still her parents, despite the harsh words that had passed between them, and today seemed as good a time as any to call at the house.

'Hmm,' was all Granny Truro said. Her lips were pursed as she registered that Sonya still went by her maiden name, but she waved them off at the door without further questions.

Yvonne was quiet as they walked downhill and through Truro's narrow, winding streets, past the handsome three-spired cathedral, on their way to Sonya's parents' house. But eventually she said, 'That went well, I thought, considering how unpleasantly we parted. Don't you agree?'

'Oh, quite.' Sonya secretly thought Granny Truro would never look with anything but disdain on her own connection to the family, which must inevitably rub off on poor Yvonne. But this was hardly the time to voice such concerns. Her daughter needed comforting words, not more worries to contend with. 'I'm sorry you argued with your husband's parents though. Perhaps after the war, when Patrick returns, you'll be able to patch things up more easily.'

Yvonne smiled. 'Yes,' she agreed quietly, 'when Patrick gets home, everything will be put to rights.'

'When will Daddy come home?' Walter asked his mother, not for the first time since being told of his father's whereabouts.

'Not for a while yet, I'm afraid,' Yvonne said, a slight wobble to her voice as she gave her son's hand a reassuring squeeze. 'But if we pray very hard, and keep our fingers crossed, maybe it will hurry things up.'

His face solemn, Walter tried crossing the fingers of his free hand, but gave up in frustration. 'Can't do it,' he burst out.

'I'll show you how to do it later,' Sonya promised him. 'Granny is forever crossing her fingers,' she added, and grinned at her daughter, who laughed.

'Aren't we all these days?' Yvonne said wryly.

It was mid-afternoon by the time they reached her parents' house and knocked at the front door with its gleaming, well-scrubbed step. Sonya only hoped that her mother's letter, inviting them to call, had been written with her father's knowledge. Otherwise this could become an awkward visit. But it was important to try, at least. Her parents would not only be meeting their granddaughter for the first time but also their great-grandchild. This might be the very thing she needed to bring about a reconciliation with her father, something she had always desired but had thought impossible. His personal convictions about the evils of unmarried mothers were so strong, he had resisted all attempts to see his daughter as anything but a fallen woman who must be shunned. But perhaps this would show the Reverend Thorpe that time, at least, could heal this wound, in the form of a respectable, grown-up granddaughter and her son.

Unfortunately, it seemed the 'sins of the fathers' were to be visited upon the children too, she thought bitterly, sitting in her parents' front room with a sense of growing dread. Or the sins of the mothers, in her case.

Despite her apologetic letter, Eloise did not seem overjoyed to see them and sat like a waxwork figure with a cup of tea poised on a saucer before her. Sonya's father stood in front of the unlit hearth, hands clasped behind his back, frowning heavily at Walter, who kept running in and out of the room, churning his arms like train wheels and shouting, 'Choo-choo!' at the top of his voice.

As for poor Yvonne, she looked pale and delicate, occasionally begging Walter to stop with a despairing expression.

'Walter,' Sonya said loudly, holding out a biscuit. 'Would you like this nice biscuit?'

Walter stopped dead and studied it, then gave a decisive nod. 'Choo-choo,' he repeated, clearly intending this for an affirmative.

'Then you may have it,' she said calmly, aware of her father's censorious gaze on her face. 'But only if you agree to stop making that infernal racket and sit down with the jigsaw puzzle Great-Grandma looked out for you.'

'Blackmail,' her father muttered.

'Oh yes,' her mother said, smiling hurriedly as she opened the jigsaw puzzle box and set the pieces on the coffee table for him to sort out. 'What an excellent idea. Do come and sit down, Walter, dear. You see, it's a picture of kittens in a basket.'

'Kittens are for girls,' Walter said rebelliously.

'Oh, but they grow up to be cats,' Eloise told the boy. 'And cats have very sharp, dangerous claws. They catch and eat mice and rats, you know, and even rabbits sometimes.' She lowered her voice. 'Heads and all.'

Looking suitably impressed by this grisly fact, Walter knelt at the table to begin fitting the large puzzle pieces together.

'Thank you,' Yvonne mouthed at her grandmother, even giving her grandfather a tentative, apologetic smile, though it was clear she found his brooding presence intimidating. 'Walter can be a little excitable at times. But once I've spoken to the headteacher, I hope he'll soon be starting at the school in St Ives, and Mother thinks that will calm him down.'

'*Mother*?' Eloise repeated, looking bewildered.

Sonya stared at her daughter, and then caught her breath with a little inward whoop of joy. Yvonne had called her Mother for the very first time. And in front of her parents too. 'She means *me*,' she explained, and tilted her chin to look up at her father, a growing note of defiance in her voice. 'I'm Yvonne's *mother*, in case you'd forgotten.'

'Well, of course you are, dear,' Eloise stuttered. 'Only I

thought… I'm sorry, but do you call the lady who brought you up "Mother" too?' When Yvonne nodded her agreement, she sat back with a sigh. 'How confusing that must be. Especially for the boy.'

'We advised Sonya against seeking you out,' Stanley interrupted in stern tones. 'I know you meant well, sending us that letter. But your mother gave you up as a baby, and that's how it should have been left. No good can come of this … *reunion*.'

'I disagree,' Yvonne said clearly, throwing a grateful smile at Sonya. 'I was in a terrible spot when Mother contacted me, and she was so generous, offering me and Walter a place to stay. She's been my saviour, frankly.'

'Your *saviour*?' Stanley glared at her.

'Gosh, I'm sorry,' Yvonne said, quick colour in her cheeks. 'I'd forgotten you were a vicar, Grandfather. I'm sorry if I caused any offence.'

'Oh, Stanley,' Eloise said, clasping her hands together as she gazed up at her husband, 'please don't take on so. It was just a turn of phrase and I'm sure Yvonne didn't mean anything by it.' Politely, she offered her granddaughter a plate of tiny cakes. 'Are you hungry, my dear?'

'A little, yes.' Yvonne took a cake and then handed the plate to Sonya. 'Cake, Mother?' she said, placing a deliberate emphasis on the word 'Mother' this time.

Her heart swelling with joy at this show of solidarity, Sonya accepted a small cake and thanked her. 'I'm so glad you were both able to be home today,' she said to her parents, hoping her father's heart in particular had been softened by meeting Yvonne and Walter. 'Not only because you've been able to meet my daughter and grandson, but also hear these glad tidings that Walter's father is not dead, as we had feared, but a prisoner of war. And we have every hope that Patrick will be safely returned to us in time.'

'I shall pray for him,' Eloise said devoutly, and glanced up at her husband. 'We shall both pray for him. Shall we not, dear?'

'Naturally,' he said, though his air was one of restraint.

Sonya wished he would unbend for once and simply enjoy the pleasure of being a family. But perhaps, after years of careful self-control as a vicar, her father no longer had it in him to let down his guard.

'It means a great deal to me that we're all together in the same room,' she said, giving her parents a hopeful smile. 'Four generations… That's a very special thing, don't you agree? A happy ending, of sorts.'

'Only where there is complete honesty,' Sonya's father ground out, 'can there be a happy ending.'

An uncomfortable silence fell over the room, with only little Walter unaffected by it, bent busily over his jigsaw puzzle.

Yvonne glanced from him to Sonya, beginning to frown as she finished a mouthful of cake. 'I'm sorry, Grandfather, you must think me rather foolish but I don't entirely understand what you mean by that.'

'I am talking of your mother's disgrace,' he said flatly.

'Stanley, no,' Eloise cried, sitting up straight with a haunted look on her face.

But Sonya's father ignored her, addressing himself directly to Yvonne. 'In case you are unaware of the shameful circumstances of your birth and adoption, I must tell you that, as a young woman, barely out of school, your mother allowed herself to be seduced by a man not much older than herself. Her seducer then met his end in the Great War, before they could be respectably married, leaving our daughter in an unfortunate condition. As you can imagine,' he added grimly, 'my position as vicar was thrown into jeopardy by her promiscuous behaviour, which the Archdeacon himself described as being "better suited to a woman of low repute than a cleric's daughter".'

Sonya, who had heard it all before, barely flinched at this damning indictment of her character. But her gaze flew in trepidation to her daughter's face.

'Naturally, we wished to distance ourselves from Sonya's predicament,' her father continued. 'The Archdeacon recommended sending her away before her condition became too obvious, and then putting the child up for adoption via church channels. Afterwards, knowing awkward questions might be asked about her long absence, we found Sonya a position on the other side of Cornwall.' He paused, his brows tugging together. 'Please know, I strongly cautioned her against ever seeking you out. It's my opinion that this reunion can only harm your reputation as a respectable woman.'

Yvonne heard him out without comment, her face half-turned away, her intent gaze fixed on her son as he played with the puzzle. But when he finished, she looked up, and Sonya was amazed to see a flushed face and tears sparkling on the ends of her eyelashes.

'Grandfather,' Yvonne began unsteadily, her chest heaving as she took several deep breaths before continuing, 'most of what you've told me I already knew. You mentioned honesty earlier. I assure you, my mother has been completely honest about my birth and the reasons why I was given up for adoption. Having heard your account though, I believe she was too generous about your role in the situation. She did not tell me how small-minded and old-fashioned you are, and how happy you were to sacrifice your daughter's happiness to save your own wretched skin.'

'I beg your pardon?' He looked astonished.

'You should beg my mother's pardon instead,' Yvonne snapped at him. 'She is the one you've wronged. Though you wronged me too, by wilfully depriving me of my natural mother from birth.'

Sonya stared, wide-eyed, from her daughter to her father, and didn't know whether to laugh or cry. She didn't imagine that the Reverend Stanley Thorpe had ever been spoken to with such candid disapproval in his entire life. But she was deeply pleased that it had happened at last, and that her own brave daughter had been the one to deliver his comeuppance.

'I think you should both leave.' Sonya's father sounded furious now, his mouth compressed, eyes narrowed.

'Frankly, I couldn't agree more.' Yvonne stooped for her handbag and rose to her feet. She held out a hand to her son. 'Come, Walter, it's time to leave.'

Walter left the puzzle and came to her at once, staring up at his mother's over-bright eyes and flushed cheeks, his mouth open with surprise.

'My adopted parents have been very kind,' Yvonne added, waiting while Sonya herself got to her feet, 'but they never let me forget I was not their own flesh and blood. That uncomfortable upbringing was all your doing,' she told Stanley bluntly, 'and I hold you responsible, for I

197

know you must have brought terrible pressure to bear on my mother or she would never have relinquished me. I am also convinced she gave me up to increase my chances of a happy life. However, I'm determined my son will come to know his natural grandmother as well as he knows his other grandparents, and that he will respect her as I do.'

Sonya's father stood dumbfounded by this impassioned speech, his sallow cheeks blotched with spots of red.

'Oh, my dear, please don't go,' Eloise said, tears in her eyes as she stretched out a hand to Yvonne. 'I so wanted to meet you and Walter. That's why I wrote to Sonya to ask if she would bring you here. But I'm very sorry indeed if you had an unhappy childhood. Please don't think too poorly of us for insisting that she gave you up. Your mother was so very young, barely more than a child herself. We only thought to spare you – to spare both of you – from unpleasant gossip.'

'I expect you did what you felt was right at the time,' Yvonne agreed, a little stiffly, but smiled at her grandmother. 'Thank you for your hospitality. You may write to me in St Ives if you wish. And if you visit us on your own, you would be more than welcome. However, I'm afraid I will not agree to see my grandfather again. Not until he can bring himself to speak to my mother in a polite and civilised manner.'

With this, Yvonne swept out to the front door, bearing Walter away with her, and Sonya followed, trembling with a mixture of apprehension and joy that Yvonne had – against all the odds – defended her in the face of her father's habitual cruelty and unkindness.

* * *

'Thank you,' she told her daughter as they stood together in the sunlit Truro street, and felt a tear roll down her cheek.

'You're my mother,' Yvonne said simply, 'of course I'd defend you.' She smiled. 'Come on, let's get home.'

Walking to the train station beside her daughter, Sonya felt the weight of years of shame being gradually lifted from her shoulders. Her step became lighter as she walked, and she felt younger, almost youthful, despite being in her forties now.

I know you must have brought terrible pressure to bear on my mother or she would never have relinquished me to anyone else. I am also convinced she gave me up to increase my chances of a happy life.

Her daughter did not blame her for what had happened. On the contrary, she seemed to understand the overwhelming powerlessness of Sonya's position, a young woman under her father's iron control, facing the censure of society and a life of grinding poverty for both her and the child if she didn't make the 'right' choice.

And she'd called her 'Mother' at last.

Sonya could have shouted to the rooftops for joy. But she didn't, of course, for people would have thought her mad. Instead, she gave a dazzling smile to every passer-by, and even allowed Walter to behave abominably at the train station without a single cross word to him.

Sometimes, Sonya thought happily, watching her small grandson run up and down the platform making his loudest 'choo-choo' noise and flailing his arms about, the universe could surprise you with a blessing.

CHAPTER TWENTY

St Ives, Cornwall, late June 1943

It was the happiest day of Lily's life, which had to be the most unexpected thing about it. She'd been planning her wedding for weeks, approaching it with a cool, pragmatic spirit, as though an extension of her work. Often, she had taken herself to task for not being more romantic about it. But this was largely a marriage of convenience for Tristan, after all. She was under no illusions that he loved her, for he was only ever affectionate towards her, while her own feelings for him had become so muddled, she could barely express them. So why go all misty-eyed over a wedding that was purely practical in nature?

Now the day was finally at hand, however, Lily found herself weeping uncontrollably at every tiny detail. The sweet heady fragrance of her bridal bouquet of white roses, clutched now in her hand. The sight of all of her dearest friends and family gathered outside the old church at St Ives, smiling and chatting together. Warm sunshine glittering on the water in the harbour, only a few clouds reflected in its blue ripples. It was all so perfect, she was glad to have Aunty Violet at her side, with a seemingly endless supply of handkerchiefs.

'You all right, love?' Gran asked, peering at her in alarm.

'Oh, Gran… Aunty Vi… I'm fine, I'm just … so blooming happy!' Lily blew her nose, sniffing loudly. She gazed across the harbour at luggers and rowboats bobbing on the water, smelt the tang of salt on the air, and heard the cheery back-and-forth of Cornish fishermen as they dragged lobster pots along the wharf. It was all so different from the grim, terraced streets of Dagenham where she had grown up, and she loved it. 'In less than an hour, I'm going to be Mrs Tristan Minear. Isn't that the most amazing thing?'

'It's wonderful, Lily,' her aunt agreed, also with red-rimmed eyes, and gave her a tearful hug, whispering in her ear, 'I only wish your dad could be here to see you looking so beautiful. Our little Lily … about to be wed.' Violet pressed a hanky to her mouth. 'Ain't she a sight for sore eyes, Mum?'

'She is, indeed,' Gran agreed, beaming. 'Don't you think so, Alice?'

Lily's sister, who had been adjusting the belt on her own dress, looked up quickly. Little white flowers decorated her fair waves of hair and she looked really quite pretty. 'It's true,' Alice said, with a frank grin that spoiled her elegant appearance. 'I barely recognised you this morning. You scrub up well, I'll give you that.'

Lily laughed, and then the two sisters hugged. They had been through so much together. It would be strange, Lily thought wistfully, to be a married woman while her sister was still single. It felt like the end of an era. But the beginning of something marvellous and new.

'I wish Mum and Dad were both here,' Alice added in a low voice, meant only for her.

Lily's tears began afresh as she thought of their mum, killed in the Blitz. But at least she held out some hope of seeing their dad again in the future. It was all hush hush, of course, since everyone had been told he was missing, presumed dead. But in fact, Ernest Fisher was somewhere overseas, serving Britain as an undercover agent, and she and Alice were madly proud of him.

'There you are,' Demelza cried, dragging her new husband out of the crowd of well-wishers milling about the church entrance. Lily was glad that they had managed to make it back to St Ives for the wedding, for Demelza and Robert had been in London, preparing to serve overseas. But apparently Demelza had managed to wangle two free days from her training in order to see her little brother married. 'Come on,' she said breathlessly. 'It's time. Tris is already inside, waiting for you.'

Lily was instantly worried for her husband-to-be, knowing that it was only a few days since he'd finally been able to walk with the aid of a stick instead of being pushed everywhere in a wheelchair.

'How's he coping?'

'Brilliantly. And Mary's sitting with him, just in case.'

'Oh, thank goodness.' Lily sighed, her tensed limbs relaxing at these words. An even more experienced nurse than herself, if anyone would know what to do if Tristan got into difficulties, it was Mary. 'What a lovely soul she is.' But her grip on her bouquet of white roses tightened as another worry nagged at her. 'And … your dad?' she asked, wondering if the elder Mr Minear had got over his aversion to Tristan's burns and decided to attend. 'Is he here? We sent him an invitation.'

Demelza bit her lip. 'Sorry, no,' she admitted. 'But Aunt Sarah came with us, and the Land Girls too. We'll be dropping them back after the do, on our way back to London.' She hesitated, her gaze sympathetic. 'Look, don't worry. I'm sure Dad will come around in the end. He's a stubborn brute but he does love our Tristan.'

Lily realised she would just have to be satisfied with that. But she did wish Tristan's dad could have managed to show up for his son's big day.

With a bear hug, Robert congratulated her. 'You look stunning,' he said in his deep, gravelly voice, looking her up and down.

'Thank you,' Lily whispered, though she felt far from stunning. Her stomach was turning somersaults as she checked that her headdress of flowers was on straight, and her pale cream, knee-length dress wasn't creased. 'I'm ready… I think,' she told Violet, and felt her aunt squeeze her hand.

'Who's giving you away?' Demelza asked gently, aware that Lily's dad was reputed to be dead.

'My uncle Joe,' Lily told her, and glanced at her aunt. 'Where is he, by the way?'

Aunt Violet's eyes grew round and horrified. 'I'd forgotten about Joe. He dropped us off, but I've not seen him since.' Looking frantically around, she called out, 'Joe? Joe? Where have you got to? Lily's ready and you're nowhere to be seen.' When there was no answer, she put a hand to her flushed forehead. 'Oh, my Lord, that man… I swear, he'll be the death of me.'

Demelza giggled at her panic, as did Alice.

Lily's heart began to thud as she realised there was nobody to walk her down the aisle. What would she do?

At last, Gran threw out an arm, pointing along the harbourside. 'There he is,' she said in her husky voice. 'Stop fussing, for gawd's sake. You're upsetting Lily.'

Joe came limping across to them, looking harassed. 'I'm sorry I'm late,' he told his wife, and tugged at his crumpled jacket. 'I couldn't find anywhere to park the van. The town's packed.'

'Blimey, don't worry about that now,' Violet told him in exasperation, pushing him and Lily towards the church door. A woman was waiting at the door; as they approached, she gave a nod inside and the organist began to play. Lily suddenly found it hard to breathe, hearing that music… 'Give us a few seconds to get to our seats,' her aunt was saying, 'and then come in behind us. Listen, the music's already starting.'

'Good luck,' Demelza mouthed at Lily, and dashed after Violet into the softly lit church interior.

Alice, who was her bridesmaid, gave Lily a final reassuring wink before falling in behind her and Joe.

'You good?' Joe rumbled in her ear.

Lily was sick with nerves as she stopped to stare down the aisle, her hand trembling as she gripped his arm. What if Tristan had changed his mind? Worse yet, what if she was making the biggest mistake of her life, marrying a man who probably only wanted a nursemaid, not a wife?

But she managed a jerky nod, forcing a smile to her face. She had chosen this path and there was no turning back. Besides, once they were man and wife, perhaps Tristan would begin to feel something for her again, as he had done in the early days of their courtship.

'Yes, Uncle Joe,' she said firmly.

They walked slowly down the aisle together, music playing, summer sun pouring through stained-glass to leave glowing patches of colour on the stone flags. The people in the pews turned to smile, with little coos of pleasure from some of the older ladies in the congregation, who always loved to see a bride. She had invited her old nursing friend, Eva, with her husband Max Carmichael, but they hadn't been able to come, sending their apologies with an expensive wedding gift of pure Irish bedlinen that had left Violet quite speechless. But some local nurses had come, girls she used to work with up at Symmonds Hall, Rose and Dr Lewis among them. Her fellow midwives were there too, plus a few nurses from the hospital, and a couple of neighbours from the street where she lived. She even spotted Sonya, old Lady Symmonds' companion, sitting with Mrs Yvonne Fairweather, the lady who had come to her clinic recently, and young Walter.

Almost everyone she knew had come to witness her marriage to Tristan, and the happiness brought a tremulous smile to her face. Though she felt a repeated pang at the absence of her spy father, and a flicker of fear too, the terror of not knowing if he was still safe. After all, anything could have happened since she'd received that top-secret message from her dad last summer, letting her know he was still alive and thinking of her and Alice. And perhaps she ought to have told Tristan the truth about him. But somehow it had never felt like the right time…

Near the front of the church, she spotted the three young evacuees who lived with Violet and Joe in Porthcurno dressed up in their Sunday best and with faces freshly scrubbed. The two boys, Eustace and young Timothy, gave her a thumbs-up, their smiles mischievous. Their older sister, Janice, grinned as Lily passed; she had lived briefly at the Minears' farm but had returned to Porthcurno when Demelza got married and left home for good.

Gran, seated at the end of their aisle, watched Lily over the embroidered edge of a large hanky, sniffing and giving little whimpers of joy. 'Oh, my sweet, darlin' Lily,' she sobbed, while the evacuee kids giggled, glancing at each other in amusement.

Clutching her white roses, Lily looked ahead and felt her breath suck in with a gasp, her heart thumping so loudly under her ribs she was convinced everyone must be able to hear it. But the whole world faded away as she realised the handsomest man in the world was waiting at the altar for her. Tristan was on his feet, leaning on a stick, yes, but with both feet planted determinedly on the ground, despite the pain he must be suffering. He had removed his cap, now tucked under one arm, and his military uniform had been adapted by Gran's clever needle skills to fit more loosely over his burns, but his highly polished boots and buttons gleamed bright as stars and she thought he had never looked more dashing.

Tears dazzled through her eyelashes, blurring her vision as Lily caught what seemed like the misty gold of a halo about Tristan's ginger curls, and then saw the uninjured side of his face turn towards her, his slow smile only for her...

'Oh, Tristan,' she breathed, and met his eyes at last.

They had decided against a honeymoon, with the war still raging and Tristan's injuries preventing him from walking far. But Lily had managed to beg three days off work and was looking forward to spending that time alone with her new husband in their cosy little cottage. After the wedding celebrations, when most of the guests had gone and only their family and friends still remained at the Star Inn, drinking to their health, Lily said her tearful goodbyes to her closest friends and family.

"Thank you for helping out today,' she told Mary, who had accompanied Tristan to the church, and stayed on hand throughout the do afterwards in case he needed any care.

But Mary shook her head with her usual modesty, insisting, 'Oh, it was nothing, honest.' With a kiss for Lily and a merry shake of Tristan's hand, she said her goodbyes before heading back to Symmonds Hall.

Mary had come to the wedding with a man, Lily had noted, a heavy-set man with a constant grin and untidy fair hair, and the couple had spent some time in conversation with Rose and Dr Lewis, both of whom seemed to know him too.

Had Mary – quiet, mousey, permanently worried Mary – caught herself a *boyfriend* at last? Lily had not dared ask in front of everyone, not wanting to embarrass her friend, but resolved to wheedle the gossip out of Rose at her next clinic appointment.

Lily hugged her aunt Violet, thanking her for all of her help and support since her mum had died, and shook hands with Joe. 'You did my dad proud today,' she told him, 'giving me away.' The tips of Joe's ears turned pink and he mumbled something, grinning. Gran was still weeping, but they hugged each other in silence.

Family was so important, Lily thought, her heart near bursting.

'Good luck, Lily,' Janice called out, and the other two evacuees echoed her, young Timothy adding cheekily, 'Let us know when you're ready to buy a pram.'

Lily ruffled his hair, laughing awkwardly.

Turning to her sister Alice last, she whispered a few words of advice in her ear, and then waved them all off in Joe's van.

To her relief, Demelza and Robert were still there, chatting to Tristan, who had not been able to stand throughout the whole afternoon, but was back in his wheelchair.

'Fancy a hand?' Robert asked, reading Lily's expression correctly, as she eyed the wheelchair uncertainly. 'Bit hilly, St Ives.'

Lily smiled. 'Thank you, yes.'

Tristan looked uncomfortable at this offer of help but also thanked him. 'I barely need the wheelchair anymore,' he insisted. 'It's just been a long day, that's all.'

'Of course.' Robert gave Lily a wink. 'Now, don't you tire him out during this honeymoon, you hear? The poor boy's still on the mend.'

'Oh.' Lily's cheeks blushed fierily. 'I…' She did not know what to say or where to look, but heard Tristan growl something under his breath, also unamused.

'Robert, be quiet, you naughty man,' Demelza cried in mock horror. 'Pay no attention, either of you.' She grabbed Lily's arm, whispering in her ear, 'I'm so sorry about my husband. I'll take him to task for it later, I promise.'

Embarrassed though she was, Lily watched with gratitude as huge, grinning Robert – now her brother-in-law, she realised – pushed Tristan's wheelchair with ease through the winding, cobbled streets of St Ives, not even sweating at the steep ones, until they reached the pretty terraced cottage with its window box full of bright summer flowers.

At the cottage door, Tristan said grimly, 'Thanks, but I'll take it from here,' and grabbed his stick, struggling out of the wheelchair. His damaged leg and hip were still paining him, that was obvious from his grimaces, but he seemed determined not to let that stop him moving about under his own power.

'I'll miss you, Tris,' Demelza told her brother, giving him a fond kiss on the cheek. 'My training with the Ambulance Service is nearly done. I'll write and let you know once we get a posting abroad.'

Tristan said, 'I hope you'll be careful, Sis.' He glanced at Robert. 'Try to stop her taking too many risks, won't you? I know what she's like once she's got the bit between her teeth.'

'He can try,' Demelza said with a laugh.

Once they'd gone, Tristan turned his gaze on Lily. 'I would carry you over the threshold,' he said quietly, 'but I don't think—'

'I don't need to be carried over the threshold,' Lily interrupted him. 'Come on, home sweet home.'

She shut the door while Tristan made his way down the shadowy hallway, following him into the cosy back kitchen of her – their – tiny cottage. He sat at the table and stretched out his bad leg with a low groan, clearly in pain. Hurriedly, she lit the gas ring and swung the kettle over it.

'More tea, is it?' he asked.

'I thought you might want a nice cuppa after the day we've had. Or there's beer in the crate there.' Lily hesitated, seeing his frown and unsure what it meant. 'I'm sorry, I wasn't sure what you'd like.'

'I'd like some peace and quiet,' he said tightly.

She felt cold and hollow inside, a statue rather than a real woman. 'Peace and quiet,' she repeated, turning away so he couldn't see the hurt in her eyes. 'Yes, well, I need to put that lovely new linen on the bed. Our wedding gift from Eva and Max.'

'Lily, wait.' Tristan reached out, catching her arm as she passed. He looked so handsome in his uniform, her heart thumped as his gaze searched her face. 'I'm the one who should be sorry. You must be hoping for... Well, what every bride hopes for on her wedding night.' He pulled a face, his voice strained. 'But look, I don't know if I'll be able to... That is, can you give me a little time?'

'Of course,' she said, and gave him a reassuring smile.

Upstairs, Lily stripped and remade the bed in double-quick time, glad of her nurse's training that made it a simple, automatic task. She plumped up pillows and smoothed out the top sheet with brisk, forceful gestures, busying herself with housewifely chores.

She had never expected him to be capable of a normal honeymoon. But she had at least hoped they might spend time together in these precious first few days of their marriage, getting to know each other as friends if not lovers. Besides, Tristan was capable of a kiss and a cuddle, so long as they were careful not to disturb his bandaged side. Instead, he had asked for *peace and quiet*, to be left alone on their wedding night.

Gran had often told her and Alice that men couldn't be fixed. 'You either take them as they are, or you keep walking.'

How could she have been so blind to think that advice would never apply to her and Tristan? She had gone ahead and married him, thinking his hesitancy towards her was simply due to his difficult condition, but he had just put her right on that score. She had suggested herself as his nurse, someone who would care for him, and it was clear that was all he wanted from the relationship.

Was it too much to hope they could become friends in time?

They ate a simple cold supper in the kitchen that evening, as she was too weary to cook, and then Lily helped him slowly up the stairs.

Tristan refused to let her help him undress, even though she had seen his scars before, waiting until she was tucked up in bed in her nightdress before pulling off his uniform and climbing into bed beside her. The mattress creaked and dipped under the unaccustomed extra weight, and the bedside lamp cast long, sombre shadows on the wall.

Not yet ten o'clock, it was still light outside, a quiet summer's evening. But she'd pinned up the blackout curtains, so as soon as Tristan clicked the lamp off, the room was plunged into darkness.

Her lumpy bed had never seemed so tiny, she thought, barely daring to move as Tristan adjusted the pillows and settled himself down.

'Goodnight, Mrs Minear,' he said softly, close to her ear.

She waited, hoping for a kiss and a cuddle. But Tristan turned his back to her with a sigh and, within minutes, his breathing had slowed and he seemed to be asleep.

So much for her bloomin' wedding night, Lily thought miserably. Maybe her new husband couldn't do everything that was expected, but that didn't mean he couldn't show her some affection, or at least hold her tight as they fell asleep on their first night together...

CHAPTER TWENTY-ONE

'You ready yet, Pip?' Mary called up the stairs.

Her mum wandered out of the front room, pinny on, feather duster in her hand. 'Where are you two going, then?'

'I promised Pip I'd take him over to play with Benjamin and Joshua,' Mary explained, adding when her mother looked at her blankly, 'You remember... The two evacuee boys that old Dr Lanyon took in.'

'Oh, Dr Edmund, you mean.' Her mother relaxed, smiling. 'He's a dear, that one. And so distinguished looking. It was a sad day for St Ives when they forced him into retirement.'

'Mum, he had a heart attack.'

'So they say.' Her mum checked her reflection in the hall mirror, patting her hair. 'He may be a bit long in the tooth, but he looked fit enough to me last time I saw him. Anyway, you can't trust doctors these days. All these young chaps... None of them know what they're talking about. Though his grandson Lewis is a good doctor. A chip off the old block, I hear.'

Mary hid her smile. 'I'll tell Dr Edmund you were asking after him, shall I?'

But to Mary's dismay, her mother turned to fetch her hat. 'No, I'll come with you and say hello to him myself. It's a nice day and I could do with a walk.'

Mary stared at her in consternation. 'Erm, I'd rather you didn't.'

'Excuse me?'

'You see, I'm not going in with Pip at Dr Lanyon's. I'm just walking him there and picking him up again afterwards.' Mary fidgeted, uncomfortable under her mother's glare. 'The thing is, the three boys are going to play chess together, while I...' Her voice tailed off.

'While you what?'

Mary swallowed, and then blurted out, 'If you must know, I'm going window shopping with Dick.'

Her mother's eyes bulged in horror. 'With Dick? Dick Jeffries?' Her chest heaved and her lips compressed. 'I thought I told you never to meet that horrid man again.'

Mary felt awful, struggling to say the right thing. She really did love her mum, but sometimes it was hard to remember that...

'I never agreed not to see him, Mum. I've just been keeping quiet about it, that's all. Like Dad says, what the eye doesn't see the heart can't grieve over.'

Her mother gasped. 'Why, you little—'

'Oh, please don't get on your high horse,' Mary interrupted her, feeling nettled, 'whom I date is my own business. Besides, it's serious between me and Dick. So you'll just have to get used to it.' Pip came clumping down the stairs in his heavy shoes and Mary flashed the boy a bright smile, thankful to be able to bring this difficult conversation to an end. 'Ready, Pip? Then off we go.'

Left speechless, her mother stood watching with folded arms and flushed cheeks as they hurried out into the afternoon sunshine.

That's torn it, Mary thought. Her mum would be in a right stew by the time she got home. But what else was she supposed to do? She really liked Dick and she wasn't going to chuck him over just because her mum didn't like the idea of them dating.

'What was all that about?' Pip asked once they'd safely turned the corner into the next street. He looked worried. 'Don't your mum like me playing chess with them other evacuees?'

'She doesn't mind about the chess, Pip,' Mary told him firmly. 'It's me she was moaning about, not you. And she's glad you're making friends at last. We all are, so don't fret yourself.'

Pip smiled, pausing to kick a stone along the pavement. 'That's good,' he said, looking relieved, 'coz I like chess, and Josh and Benji too. I don't know Dr Lanyon though.' He scratched his head. 'He ain't one of them bad-tempered old codgers who shouts at boys, is he?

'Dr Edmund Lanyon is a lovely gent, and I'm sure he never shouts at anyone. He's also very well-respected in St Ives. So you behave yourself in his house, is that clear?'

Pip nodded, looking earnest. 'I'll mind my p's and q's,' he promised. 'I want to play chess.'

Mary knocked at the door to Dr Lanyon's imposing, detached residence set in neatly maintained gardens, and was amazed when her old friend Rose answered the door instead of Mrs Delaney, his housekeeper. Then she recalled that Rose was Doctor Lanyon's granddaughter-in-law.

'Hullo, Mary,' Rose said cheerfully, a headscarf knotted about her startling red hair, her face made paler by bold scarlet lipstick. But Mary remembered what she'd said about the pregnancy not being an easy one. 'Please, come in. And you must be Pip. I'm Mrs Lanyon.' She bent to shake the boy's hand. 'It's Mrs Delaney's day off, but never fear, I'm all up to speed in the kitchen. I've made biscuits and orange squash for you boys, so I hope you're feeling peckish.'

'Blimey, course I am,' Pip exclaimed, his eyes shining.

'Off you go, then. Josh and Benjamin are waiting for you in the back room, and the chess board's all set up. Jimmy's going to join you later, once he's finished playing football, so you'll have plenty of chances for a game.' Jimmy was Rose and Lewis's adopted son, an orphan they'd befriended at Symmonds Hall last summer.

'Thanks, Missus,' Pip cried and ran off to find his chums.

Rose grinned. 'There's tea for the grown-ups,' she told Mary, 'unless you'd prefer something stronger. Do come in. Lewis is still at the hospital, but he'll be home soon.'

'I can't stay, I'm sorry. Do you mind terribly? I've arranged to meet someone in town.'

'You're meeting someone?' Rose shot her a teasing smile. 'Would that be Dick Jeffries, by any chance? When I saw you two together at Lily's wedding, it was obvious there was more than just friendship between you.' She winked. 'Better not keep him waiting, then. But be back by six, if you can. That's the boys' suppertime and I'm not very good at keeping food warm for long.'

'Back by six,' Mary agreed, and then asked curiously, 'Are you and Lewis living with Dr Edmund now?'

'Off and on,' Rose admitted, pulling a face. 'Officially, we still live at the orphanage. But now that I'm expecting, it's likely I'll be giving up my work at the orphanage soon. So, moving in here with Lewis's grandfather seems like a good idea.'

'If you need any help packing, just holler.'

'Don't worry, I will.'

At that moment, Dr Edmund wandered out into the hall. He was looking quite old and tired, Mary thought, but his eyes were as sharp as ever. 'Hello, my dear,' he said, recognising her at once and shaking her hand. 'Nurse Stannard, isn't it? How are you? But no need to tell me, I can see you're in perfect health.' He tapped the side of his patrician nose. 'Now, leave Pip with us and go enjoy your date.' A mischievous look popped into his face. 'I apologise for having eavesdropped on your conversation with Rose. I didn't mean to, but the door was open.'

Mary blushed, but the retired doctor had already given her a wave and gone off to see how the boys were getting on with their games.

Once Dr Edmund had gone, Rose gave her an arch smile, saying, 'Dick and I were quite close at school, you know.'

'Is that so?' Mary laughed, knowing her friend was only joking. 'Then I'm glad Lewis has already snatched you up. Though if my mum has her way, I won't be seeing Dick for much longer, anyway.'

'Your mother can't still be causing trouble between you, surely?'

'I'm afraid so.' Briefly, Mary outlined what her mother had said as she left the house.

'How ridiculous.' Rose shook her head in disapproval. 'I hope you won't let any of that nonsense put you off Dick. He's a nice chap and he deserves someone like you in his life.'

Hugging those words to herself, Mary hurried into town to meet Dick near the Scala Cinema on the High Street as arranged. Rose was better known for her sharp and searing honesty than kindness, so it meant all the more to hear her praise Dick so highly.

She found Dick waiting for her outside the picture house, hands in his trouser pockets, studying a movie poster. He turned as she hurried towards him, smiling at her from under the wide brim of his hat, and her heart lifted.

'Hullo,' he said, his eyes crinkling.

She'd never met anyone before who made her happy just by looking at her. How could that be a bad thing?

'Hullo,' she replied, grinning at him like an idiot.

Rose was right, she thought with a sudden flash of insight. Dick was a decent chap, and her mum had no business warning her to steer clear of him, just because of something his mother had done before he was even born. Mum had barely even spoken to him, for goodness' sake, and only knew him as Pip's teacher.

For a moment, Mary toyed with the idea of asking Dick to supper at their house so he could meet her parents properly. But she quickly changed her mind, imagining her mum's cross expression on finding the son of her arch-enemy seated at the dining table, knife and fork in hand, waiting for her to serve him supper.

'Ready for your secret mission?' Dick asked with a wink.

'Absolutely.'

She had fibbed to her mum earlier, claiming that she and Dick would be window shopping in town. In fact, she was going to book her surprise party. And perhaps that was where she could arrange for the two of them to meet properly... At her mum's birthday bash.

They called into the pub and spoke to the landlord, a jolly old Cornishman with a twinkle in his eye.

'Mum's the word,' the landlord agreed, tapping the side of his nose when Mary asked him not to mention the party to anyone, for fear of it getting back to her parents. St Ives was a small town, after all, and people had a tendency to gossip. 'You leave it all to me and the wife. It'll be your mother's best birthday party ever.'

'And should we bring our own food?'

'The wife can do sandwiches and scones with a little jam and Cornish cream.' After some wrangling, they agreed on a price that Mary felt she could afford. Though it would mean using up most of her meagre savings. 'But if you'd like to bring a birthday cake,' he added kindly, seeing her expression, 'I'm sure that would be acceptable.'

'Oh yes, thank you.'

After it was all arranged, Mary and Dick wandered down to the seafront, shyly holding hands in the afternoon sun. An elderly lady walked past, glancing at them through narrowed eyes, and Mary hurriedly dropped his hand and took a step away, biting her lip.

'Don't let her scare you,' Dick said, laughing softly. 'There's no law against holding hands.'

'But people talk,' Mary muttered. 'I don't want it getting back to Matron.'

'I'm sorry about the other night. It was all my fault, as I told that old dragon. But she wouldn't listen, of course. Just sent me off with a flea in my ear.' He heaved a sigh when she looked away. 'Oh dear, did she tear a strip off you for kissing me?'

Tight-lipped, leaving out the cruellest things Matron had said to her, she gave him a quick summary of her telling-off, ending with, 'Apparently, I have no sense of morality, and instead of setting an example to the younger nurses, I've been behaving like a trollop.'

His gaze grew serious. 'She called you that? A trollop?'

'And worse.' Mary clapped both hands to her cheeks, wishing she didn't have an unfortunate tendency to blush so readily. 'Oh, let's change the subject. It was awful. I wanted to die.'

He came after her as she turned away. 'Hey, love,' he said, and she stared round at him, wondering what he meant by that word, *love*, her heart thudding wildly, 'I'm so sorry you had to put up with that. I would never have left you to face her wrath if I'd realised.'

She searched his face. 'What, you would have intervened?'

'I'm not that brave,' he admitted, a smile hovering on his lips, 'but I would certainly have scooped you up in my arms and carried you home. Saved you from the dragon by running away, rather than doing battle.'

She chortled, staring into his humorous blue eyes, and then realised how close they were standing, and in public too.

'I should be getting back to Dr Lanyon's house,' she told him. 'I promised Rose I wouldn't be late.'

'One more minute,' he insisted, his gaze turning serious again. 'I meant it about coming to teach at the school, if you're interested. Teacher training has become a bit chaotic since the start of the war, but I'm sure the headmaster will arrange a training course for you in time. Either way, we'd only let you loose on the little ones at first, like I said. Let you build up steam gradually.'

'I do rather like the idea,' she admitted. 'But I couldn't possibly... They need nurses so urgently up at the hall.'

'Your friend Rose left though, didn't she? And your other friend, what was her name?'

'Eva.'

'That's right. You told me Rose and Eva both left nursing, and that pretty, fair-haired pal of yours too. The girl who just got married.'

'Lily.'

'So, three of your friends left nursing, and you think that's all well and dandy. But when it comes to you, that's different.' He scratched his head. 'I'm trying to work that one out.'

'It's not the same. That is, it would be lovely to work with children. But you have to understand, it's not a simple decision. Not when there are wounded men coming in every week.'

'Mary, you can't fix the world's problems on your own,' he pointed out, 'and nobody expects you to. If you leave the convalescent home, someone else will nurse those men. Just as they did when your three friends left.'

'Rose and Eva left because they got married,' she said

simply, 'and married women can't be nurses. And Lily didn't exactly leave nursing. She became a midwife, which is a related field.'

'Oh, in that case,' he said, and dropped to one knee before her. 'Will you make me the happiest of men by agreeing to be my wife, Mary Stannard?'

She gawped at him, bemused.

A couple walking along the seafront glanced at them both and smiled before continuing on their way.

'For goodness' sake,' she whispered, her cheeks fiery now, 'please get up before someone else sees you.'

'Only if you say yes,' Dick said. 'Or that you'll consider my proposal, at least.'

'I, erm...'

Mary opened and closed her mouth, and knitted her fingers together, her mind in turmoil. He couldn't possibly be serious. Could he?

'Obviously, I wouldn't dream of hurrying your decision. But this kneeling lark is rather harder than I'd anticipated.'

'Are you joking?'

'No, the ground is really quite uncomfortable,' Dick said plaintively, grimacing as he adjusted his position. 'But for you, anything.'

'Please don't muck about. You know perfectly well what I mean. Are you joking about *this*,' she asked hotly, 'about asking me to marry you? Because if so—'

'I was never more serious in my whole life.'

'Oh.' She swallowed.

Dick waited a little longer, then sighed and got up, brushing down the dusty knees of his trousers. 'I take it you're turning me down?'

'I'm not sure what I'm doing.'

'So there's hope?'

'I had no idea you felt so strongly. I have to admit, you've taken me by surprise.' Mary found she was stammering. 'I need time to think.'

'Your wish is my command,' he said with a smile. 'Take as long as you need. It's an open offer.'

They walked back to Dr Lanyon's house, arm in arm, and Mary tried not to worry what her mother would say. Goodness though, she hadn't expected a proposal of marriage. Surely he must have been kidding about? Yet he'd seemed serious.

'Goodness, I can't imagine what Mum would say if I told her we were getting married,' she remarked.

Dick threw back his head in laughter. 'Worth doing just to see her expression, I'd say.'

'People don't get married just to see their mum's expression,' she said sternly, but her mouth twitched at the thought of it. It was more than tempting to consider a change of career too. Her love of nursing had been slowly deteriorating over the past year and falling foul of Matron had not helped make life on the wards any easier. But it felt like such a huge step and she didn't quite see herself making that shift. Not until she'd had time to consider it more carefully, at least.

They collected Pip, who was full of animated tales of how he'd won his first-ever game of chess and what moves he'd learned, and although Dick escorted them both to the end of her street, he left them there on Mary's insistence.

'Best not push our luck,' she said, but allowed him to

give her a quick peck on the cheek, aware of Pip's interested gaze.

'Will you come to the school next time you're free?' he asked, out of Pip's hearing. 'I'll give you a tour, let you see what kind of things you'd be doing if you choose to up sticks and begin teaching.'

'I'll let you know.'

They had to leave it at that, for it was getting late and poor Pip's tummy was rumbling. Mary waved Dick goodbye and then hurried home. But her mum glared at her throughout their evening meal, and finally cornered her over the tea tray once Pip had gone up to bed.

'I told your father what you told me earlier,' her mother snapped. 'That you're still seeing that Dick Jeffries and how you told me it was none of my business.'

'Well, it isn't,' Mary retorted, stirring her tea.

'Harold, tell her.'

They both looked across at her father, who reluctantly lowered the local paper he'd been reading, cleared his throat, and said, 'You heard your mother. She doesn't like it. Best knock it on the head, there's a good girl.'

'I'm not ten, Dad.'

'I know that,' he began, frowning, and then shrugged, returning to the sporting pages. 'Well, I've said my piece, Rita. If she isn't willing to give this chap up, that's all there is to it.'

Her mother glared at him too, fulminating. But when she opened her mouth, clearly about to hold forth on the topic again, Mary jumped in first.

'No point going on about it, Mum,' she said, 'because I'm going to be seeing a great deal more of him in future.'

'Is that so?'

'Yes,' Mary told her, with a sudden burst of energy. 'I'm going to give up nursing and train to be a schoolteacher instead, just like him.' Her mother gave a shriek, which she ignored. 'And we're going to be married.'

Her mother's jaw dropped.

Her dad peered over the top of his newspaper. 'Well, Mary Stannard,' he said into the silence that followed this announcement, 'you're a dark horse, and no mistake.'

And he gave her a wink.

CHAPTER TWENTY-TWO

St Ives, Cornwall, early July 1943

It was a sunny afternoon but Yvonne had a headache and was lying down in her bedroom with a lace hanky, sprinkled with lavender water, draped across her eyes. Walter, who had no interest in headaches, continued to run up and down the apartment, blowing a pretend trumpet, and once even flinging open his mother's door and charging into the bedroom to show her his scribblings, for Sonya had been helping him with his letters that afternoon. Sonya hurried after him in dismay, shooing the boy away from his suffering mother. But Walter was having none of it.

'Too dark in here,' Walter announced, and ran to drag the curtains open, garish sunlight pouring into the room so that her daughter winced and put a hand to her head.

'No, Walter. Your mother needs the room kept dark. She has a bad head today.' Quickly, Sonya closed the curtains again to shut out the light. 'I'm so sorry,' she whispered to Yvonne. 'I did ask him not to disturb you. But he pays no attention to me.'

'That's coz I want Mummy to see my W's,' Walter said, a stubborn light in his eyes, and waved his workbook in the air. 'See, Mummy, I can do W's proper now.'

'Properly, darling,' Yvonne corrected him, removing the hanky over her eyes, and sat up dutifully to admire his wobbly W's. 'Well done, those are excellent W's. But maybe you could try a row of M's now.' Her smile was fragile and appealing. 'M for Mummy?'

'M for Mummy,' Walter repeated, dashing out to begin fulfilling her wishes. 'M for Mummy, M for Mummy.'

'How are you feeling now, dear?' Sonya asked her daughter. 'Any better?'

'I'm afraid not. If anything, it's getting worse. I may be out of commission all afternoon. Can you cope alone with Walter that long?'

'Of course. Though I'd better take him out for a walk, in that case. If he stays cooped up here, he'll be constantly disturbing you.' Sonya sighed. 'I'm not terribly good at getting him to do what I ask, I'm afraid. He's a very ... determined child.' She had been planning to say 'wilful' but decided at the last second not to risk offending her daughter. Yvonne and Walter were very close, as was only to be expected, both worrying about his father so far away and in such a perilous situation. 'But a nice long walk will chase away his fidgets, I daresay.'

'Oh, could you? Thank you, Mother. You're a treasure.' And with a groan, Yvonne lay down again, replacing the hanky over her eyes. 'I'm so sorry I haven't been to see the headteacher at the school about him yet,' she added indistinctly. 'I'll go tomorrow, I promise.'

Sonya said nothing. But since the school holidays were due to start soon, it hardly seemed worth the bother of enrolling him.

Once Walter had finished his page of M's, Sonya wrangled him into his shoes and a cardigan, in case of a strong sea breeze, and led him by the hand down the steep steps into the cobbled backyard of Symmonds Hall. The boy protested the whole way, wanting his mummy to come with them and not caring, it seemed, that she was too ill to leave the apartment.

'Let's leave Mummy to sleep, shall we? I expect she'll be much better once she's rested, and then you can play with her after supper.'

Walter, easily distracted, pointed up at a group of seagulls, wheeling and screaming overhead. 'Look at the big birds! What are they? Vultures?' He had been flicking through a book on African wildlife that he'd found in a dusty corner of the apartment and asking Sonya to read out the captions under each bold pen-and-ink sketch.

'Seagulls, dear.'

He blinked, pulling a face. 'Vultures,' he repeated firmly. 'From Afica.'

'Africa.'

'That's what I said.'

She did not bother arguing with him, just led him out through the back of the hall, across the rambling grounds and onto the cliff-path that overlooked Carbis Bay. Walter ran ahead some of the way, or wheeled around her with his arms wide, in imitation of the 'vultures' at one stage, swiftly changing this to a Spitfire impersonation when they spotted a plane in the distance, a shining speck in the deep blue sky.

Sonya watched the plane with a stab of apprehension but it came no nearer, flying steadily east along the Cornish coast, and besides, it did seem to be one of theirs.

St Ives had not suffered too badly with bombing raids this summer, she realised, though she'd seen in the local papers that Penzance had suffered a few bad hits, and there was some suggestion that the enemy might soon turn their attention further west and north. Dratted Germans, she thought, but smiled for the boy's sake as he glanced back at her. He must be in enough turmoil over his father's imprisonment without adding her own worries to his.

She pointed out some of the more attractive wildflowers that grew along the coast path – cow parsley, mesembry-anthemums, trefoil, pink thrift – and even allowed him to pick a few flowerheads to be pressed carefully between the pages of a book for safe-keeping. That was something she had done once with her own mother, on a family holiday to Wales, and she remembered with bitter-sweet nostalgia how much pleasure it had afforded her to find those flattened flowers years later, between the pages of a poetry book awarded to her as a school prize. That was the kind of simple joy she had missed out on by giving up Yvonne, and she was determined to share it with Walter at least, even if he clearly found her an inferior companion compared to his beloved mother.

Once they had completed the cliff-path circuit and headed back inland to Symmonds Hall, she suggested he could kick his football in the backyard for a short spell.

'Just mind you avoid kicking the ball too hard,' she said hurriedly, remembering the broken window, 'and not at any doors or windows.'

Walter ran off busily to find the football, which he'd left in a corner of the yard, and began to kick it about, but she could see he looked a little bored, just kicking his ball against a plain wall.

'The other children will be back from school soon,' she reminded him, 'and then you can play with them. You'd like that, wouldn't you?'

'Not much,' Walter said dismissively. 'They're only orphans.'

She stared at the boy, disconcerted. *Only orphans?* But before she could take him to task for his rude attitude, she heard raised voices in the convalescent home and turned in surprise, seeking the source.

Matron's voice was instantly recognisable, though she had never heard her sound so furious before. Usually such a stately, dignified woman, Matron was not the type to get her feathers easily ruffled.

Sonya struggled to identify the other voice at first, gradually realising with a shock that it was Mary Stannard. Quiet, well-behaved Nurse Stannard, whose big dark solemn eyes always seemed so worried in case she had done something wrong, yet whose abrupt grins and giggles suited the chaos of her naturally curly brown hair.

'I knew you weren't cut out for a career in nursing,' Matron was saying in an angry, high-pitched voice. 'As for marriage… I suppose you must have got yourself in the family way.'

Sonya's eyes widened at this. What on earth?

'How dare you!' Unsurprisingly, Mary sounded furious. 'There's no call for that kind of talk. Mr Jeffries is a very respectable man.'

'Oh yes, I saw how respectable he was, kissing you on the porch where anyone could see, without a care in the world. He seems to think he's Rudolph Valentino.'

Biting back a gasp, Sonya threw a quick glance towards Walter, who was kicking his football at the other end of the yard. The boy didn't appear to have heard the two women arguing, which was just as well, considering what was being discussed.

Assured that her grandson was safe enough for the moment, Sonya crept along the wall and a few steps through the open double doors into the convalescent home. There was nobody about, so she took another three or four steps along the corridor, wondering if she ought to interfere or leave well alone.

It was none of her business. But she liked Mary Stannard and couldn't bear to think of her being bullied by Matron.

The door to Matron's office was flung open just then and Mary herself stormed out. She charged along the corridor with her head down, not looking where she was going, and almost ran into Sonya.

'Are you all right?' Sonya asked, jumping out of the way before they collided. Mary looked up, turmoil in her face. There was a spot of red burning in each cheek and her eyes were no longer solemn but flashing with fury.

'Oh, it's you,' she muttered, meeting Sonya's curious gaze. 'I'm sorry, I didn't see you there. Excuse me.' And she stamped on, and then stopped, turning around in a confused manner. 'I'm going the wrong way.'

'Where are you supposed to be?' Sonya asked tentatively, not wanting to get her head bitten off.

'I was supposed to be doing the rounds on Carbis Ward,' Mary said unevenly, her chest heaving. Her hands dropped to her hips and she sucked in a deep breath, as though trying to calm down. 'Except I don't work here anymore. I just gave my notice. With immediate effect.'

'Oh dear,' Sonya said sympathetically. 'You don't look terribly happy. Would you like to talk about it?'

'Not really,' Mary said with a gasp, then put both hands to her cheeks, looking horrified. 'Oh, what have I done? I lost my temper with the nasty old dragon. I told myself I would be calm and give a month's notice but she made me so cross.' Her face flushed cherry-red, her eyes narrowing as she looked along the corridor to where Matron's door still stood partly ajar. 'The horrid things she said… I just saw red. There was nothing for it but to say I would leave immediately.'

'You could always go back and apologise,' Sonya suggested, 'and see if that makes any difference.'

'Apologise? To Herr Matron? Not flipping likely.' Mary shook her head with a defiant air, though tears were rolling down her cheeks. 'I've got a better idea. I'll go upstairs and start packing my bags. I'm not welcome here anymore. Not after that dust-up.'

'Are you sure I can't help?' Sonya wished there was something practical she could do to help the girl. 'I hate to see you so upset.' She paused, chewing on her lip. 'The thing is, I'm awfully sorry, but I did overhear some of your conversation with Matron.'

'Then you must know I didn't deserve to be shouted at

like that. Matron doesn't like me, that's what it is. Never has, never will. As soon as she saw an opportunity to get rid of me...' Mary scrubbed impatiently at her damp cheeks. 'Were we *very* loud?'

'I'm afraid so.'

'Oh golly.' Mary pulled a face. 'Thanks for the offer of help. But I don't have much to pack and I need to be alone for a while. You don't mind, do you?'

'I know exactly how you feel. Sometimes you need to deal with a problem on your own.'

'Yes, and it's all for the best, anyway,' Mary agreed, unpinning her nurse's cap and studying it with a look of chagrin.

Sonya wondered what she meant. Then she recalled Matron's cruel comment about Mary getting married. 'Is it true, then?' she asked softly. 'Should I be offering you my congratulations?'

'Goodness, don't ask me. I'm at sixes and sevens. I don't know whether I should be congratulated or pitied. My whole life has been turned upside down, Sonya. And yet, it's the oddest thing...' Mary gave her a tremulous smile. 'I don't think I've ever been happier.'

And with that, Mary marched off down the corridor, passing Matron's office with her head held high, and turned up the stairs towards the nurses' quarters. Watching her go, Sonya couldn't help smiling. Then she gasped, as a horrible realisation struck her.

'Oh my goodness, I left Walter on his own in the yard.'

She dashed outside, and at first was relieved to see her grandson still there but standing in the middle of a jostling group of children. At least he had not run away, she thought, or kicked his football through another window

233

while her attention was elsewhere. But she really ought not to have left him on his own. Yvonne would be furious if she knew what had happened.

She hurried over to where little Walter stood in the middle of the yard, dwarfed by the other children. But as she reached them, she heard Walter raise his voice, sounding quite cross, while the other children jeered at him, saying unpleasant things.

'What's wrong?' She recognised some of the older girls, who stood back respectfully at her approach. They were among the orphans she helped with extra lessons after school. 'Has something happened?'

'He's been calling us bad names,' one of the boys exclaimed, his face indignant.

'What kind of names?' Sonya frowned, not entirely sure she believed him. 'He's only a little boy. He doesn't know any bad language.'

'Yes, he does, Miss,' Susan insisted, one of the older girls who was taking French lessons with Sonya to improve her prospects for future employment. Her long fair hair was dressed neatly in braided plaits and she was wearing a simple grey tunic dress, which the orphanage girls used for school uniform. 'He said we were urchins and ragamuffins,' she explained, chewing on her plait with a distressed expression. 'But it's not true. We're not ragamuffins.'

Sonya was shocked by this accusation. 'Walter?'

Her grandson looked up at her, pale and defiant. Slowly, stumbling over the words, he told her, 'Grandpa Truro said it when I told him about the orphanage. He says orphans are good for nothing and I shouldn't play with them.'

'Walter Fairweather, you will apologise this instant.' She waited, but the boy merely stuck his lip out in a mulish fashion. 'I want to hear you tell these children how sorry you are for being so rude, and that you will never say such dreadful things again.'

Walter, still pulling a face, stuck his hands in the pocket of his short trousers and said nothing.

'I will have to find a punishment for you if you won't apologise,' Sonya said with a heavy heart, for she feared losing her daughter's friendship by taking a hard stance against her grandson.

'You can't punish me, you're not allowed.' Walter stuck his tongue out at her before dashing back to the staircase up to the apartment. 'I'm telling Mummy on you.'

In despair, Sonya watched Walter disappear inside before turning to the children, ready to sink with embarrassment.

'I'm so sorry, he should never have spoken to you like that. None of you are urchins or ragamuffins. I'll have stern words with the boy, believe me.' And she hurried after him.

Upstairs, she found Yvonne's door wide open and her daughter sitting up in bed, listening to Walter's tale of woe. As Sonya hesitated on the threshold, Yvonne looked round at her in anguish. 'What's all this about children being nasty to Walter? I thought you were out there with him?'

Sonya took a deep breath and held it. It was now or never, she thought. She could not let Walter's bad behaviour go uncorrected any longer, even if it meant Yvonne never spoke to her again. Briefly, she explained what had happened, and didn't spare any details.

'He admitted it himself,' she added quickly, seeing Yvonne's frown, and said he'd heard that kind of talk from his grandfather in Truro.

'Oh no.' To her relief, Yvonne did not leap to Walter's defence for once but turned to him with a horrified expression. 'That was very hurtful of you. Those poor children… How could you have done such a thing?'

Walter shrugged but didn't meet his mother's eyes.

'Darling, Mummy was a bit like an orphan once upon a time,' Yvonne said gently, with an apologetic glance at Sonya. 'I grew up not knowing who my real parents were.'

Walter was astonished. 'You? But isn't *she* your mummy?' He was pointing at Sonya.

'Don't point, dear, or say "she" like that, it's impolite.' Yvonne caught his hand in hers. 'When you're older, I'll tell you the whole story. For now, all you need to understand is that it's not a child's fault if they lose their parents. You must never treat someone badly simply because bad things have happened to them.'

'Grandpa Truro says—' Walter began hotly, but was silenced by his mother's glare.

'I don't give two hoots what Grandpa Truro says or thinks. You are my son and you will obey my rules, not his. Also, you must be polite to Grandma and not pull rude faces at her,' she added in stern tones. 'Is that clear?'

'Yes, Mummy.' Walter stared at her in trepidation, for no doubt his mother had never spoken to him like that before.

'Now, apologise to your grandmother.'

Jumping off the bed, he mumbled, 'I'm very sorry, Granny St Ives.'

'Thank you for saying so,' Sonya told him solemnly.

'Good boy.' Yvonne threw back the covers and slipped out of bed. 'I'll get dressed now and take you over to the orphanage, Walter, where you will apologise to the children too. And tomorrow I shall enrol you in school. No more delays. All this playing on your own is clearly bad for you. Now, please wait outside while Mummy gets dressed.'

Walter shuffled out, slumped and with glowing cheeks.

Yvonne came towards her. 'Not being allowed to kick his football for a full week sounds an appropriate punishment, don't you think?' Smiling shyly, she kissed Sonya on the cheek. 'I'm sorry he was such a beast to you. I've been so wrapped up in my own problems, I've let Walter run wild. His father would have torn a strip off him for speaking to those children like that. But Patrick's not here, so I need to take his place. From now on, I'm going to take proper charge of Walter, I promise.'

Sonya gave her a big hug, thrilled to know she hadn't lost her daughter by taking her little boy to task. 'You mustn't blame yourself. You are the kindest daughter any mother could hope to have, and Walter just needs a firm hand in his father's absence, that's all. Together, we'll sort him out, see if we don't.'

CHAPTER TWENTY-THREE

Lily had a chaotic start to the day, delivering a baby girl at half past five, and then tramping home in the soft early light to doze beside Tristan for a few hours before struggling out of bed again to do her weekly wash. It was a windy but sunny July day, and she had far too much laundry now to ignore such perfect drying weather. Tristan didn't stir, of course, snoring gently as she dressed and dragged a brush through her hair. She was exhausted, but her need to empty the wash basket outweighed her need for sleep, so it was with heavy lids that she carried the washtub out into the sunny front yard, energetically scrubbing each soapy item up and down the washboard before rinsing and running it through the mangle.

As she worked, she remembered the plump and pretty baby boy she'd delivered that morning and felt again the desperate pang of knowing she would never fall pregnant herself, not given Tristan's refusal to touch her beyond the odd peck on the cheek, even though she had nursed him back to almost full health.

She had no idea why her husband had set his mind on keeping their marriage celibate, despite having largely recovered from his injuries, but it was driving her crazy. And not merely because she had started longing for her own child. The more time she spent in Tristan's company, sharing her little cottage and her bed with him, the more handsome he seemed to her, and the more she wished he would pay her proper attention. It might be embarrassing, but she wanted him to be a real husband to her, Lily thought with a flush in her cheeks, and wondered feverishly how she could communicate this without risking another rejection, like his hurtful snub on their wedding night.

'Here, better watch yourself with that fiendish contraption,' a familiar voice said from behind her, the words laced with easy good humour, all with the slightest hint of a foreign accent. 'I've known women lose a finger to the mangle.'

Lily froze, her back to the man. But her hands started to tremble. 'Sorry, what?' she stammered, not daring to turn.

The man had stopped on the cobbled hill to address her but came closer now, entering the enclosed front yard.

'I wouldn't want you to hurt yourself,' he explained, standing right behind her, before adding, 'Lily,' so softly that no one else could possibly have heard her name. Then, as she began to look round, he said in the same low voice, 'Don't show surprise. Invite me into the house as though you don't know me. We can talk safely once we're inside.'

Slowly, a damp shirt still in her hands, Lily turned her head, looking full into the face of her visitor.

The first thing she noticed, staring at him in shock, was

the livid scar running from his temple across his left cheek. But for that, he would have been quite ordinary-looking. He had fair hair, cropped short to his scalp, and a broad, deeply lined forehead made coppery by long exposure to the sun. His strong nose jutted below intense blue eyes, narrowed now to observe her through light, sandy lashes. The facial scar made him look like a pirate, she thought, a little apprehensive as she wondered how and where he'd got it.

Nonetheless, scar or no scar, she would have known the man anywhere. It was her father, Ernest Fisher.

'I…' The sun was in her eyes and she felt suddenly dazzled and thrown off balance, her heart thumping violently. 'How on earth…?' Then she recollected what he'd just said about not making it obvious she'd recognised him, and went on more roughly, 'You'd best go in, then,' pointing him to the door. 'Though you'll have to wait a tick. I need to finish pegging me washing out first.'

Without a word, the man obeyed her, vanishing out of the sun haze into the cool, dim interior of the stone cottage.

Lily, no longer shaking, pinned up the last of the clothes in a wild, haphazard fashion, thoughts whirring through her brain that took precedence over whether or not she'd placed the peg straight on each seam, and then almost dashed into the cottage, basket under her arm.

He had put the kettle on, she realised with a shock, and was standing by the back window, peering out at the brick backs and slate roofs of the houses opposite. He seemed to dominate the small room, impossibly real and solid, and for a moment she felt as though she could hardly breathe, just staring with her mouth open.

He had turned as she came in, and now beckoned her towards him. She put down the basket and took his hands. 'Lily,' he said with a sigh, and shook his head, looking her up and down. 'My God, you're beautiful. An angel from heaven. I left a little girl in pigtails and here's a grown woman in her place.' Again, she caught the faintest German accent in his voice, and caught her breath, staring at him with wide eyes. His blue gaze locked with hers, and she knew he hadn't missed her shiver of apprehension. 'And you're married, too?'

It was a question. But she guessed he already knew the answer.

She nodded, her mouth almost too dry to speak. 'Recently, yes. But forget about me. How are you, Dad? Where have you been?'

'You want to know everything. Of course you do, my darling. But first, let me hold you.' Ernest Fisher pulled her into the circle of his arms, and she went willingly, feeling safe for the first time in years, laying her head on her father's broad shoulder and closing her eyes. His hand stroked her hair, slow and gentle, as he said quietly, 'I was so sorry to learn about your mother. My poor Betsy. It was the worst news.'

Her dad was silent for a long while, and then added softly, 'As soon as I heard, I wanted to come home, to see my little Lily and Alice, to comfort you both. I was desperate to let you know that you still had one parent. But it simply wasn't possible for me to leave, not right then. The mission was too important.' He sounded almost angry. 'It nearly tore me apart, having to leave you alone and grieving at such a time. But you must understand, more than my own safety was at stake.'

241

'I do understand,' she whispered, remembering those long, difficult months following her mum's death. 'That man in Penzance gave me your message. Your friend, was he?'

It was a strange, unsettling memory. Last summer, while waiting for Tristan outside the picture house in Penzance, a stranger in a trench coat and trilby had approached her, claiming to have been sent by her father and swearing her to secrecy on the grounds of national security. Ever since, Lily had half wondered if she'd imagined that meeting, it had been so brief and mysterious. And yet, here was her father, not dead as everyone thought, but very much alive and standing in the kitchen of her cottage in St Ives.

'Ah yes, Fred...' He gave a low chuckle. 'Not his real name, but we all use assumed names. I've been staying with him since I came back. In fact, Fred tried to persuade me against coming here today. He warned me it would be dangerous. But blood is thicker than water, or so my darling Betsy used to say. And I couldn't come back to England without seeing you, however briefly.'

She caught something in his voice, possibly regret or even fear, and wondered if he thought he might never come back again... That this could be his last chance to see her. The idea terrified her.

She wished she could stand there forever, eyes closed, safe in the comforting strength of his presence. But she wasn't a child anymore, and questions had begun to press inside her.

Taking a step back, Lily studied him properly. Her father had aged since he'd left them, looking about ten years older, not three ... and yet his voice was eerily the same, that hint of a German accent holding a bitter-sweet familiarity for her.

'So,' she said faintly, 'you're going back to … wherever you came from? You're not staying in England?'

'No, I have to go back next week. It's vital for the war effort.' At her questioning look, he shook his head. 'I can't tell you where; sorry.' He looked apologetic. 'The less you know, the better.'

'That's all right, I understand.' The kettle was beginning to whistle, a high, eerie noise that set the hairs stiffening on the back of her neck. Moving automatically, Lily unfastened her damp pinny and set it over the back of a chair to dry, and then turned to make the tea. 'How long are you in Cornwall?'

'A day, maybe two. If you don't mind the risk of letting me stay here at the cottage, that is.' Ernest sat at the kitchen table, watching her with the clever, thoughtful look she remembered from her childhood. 'I don't want to endanger you.'

'But, Dad, who on earth would know you was even here? And how could that be dangerous?' Lily poured hot water into the pot, blinking as she considered what he was saying. 'Oh my God, surely you're not…' She stopped short, gasping.

'Not what?'

For a few dizzying seconds, she fell silent, terrified that her beloved father was about to disclose that he'd been working for Germany. That he was one of the enemy, after everything they'd said in his defence.

'From what your chum Fred told me, I guessed you must be a … a spy.' Her voice dropped on those last words, for although the front door was firmly closed and the walls of the old fisherman's cottage many inches thick, she still felt uneasy saying them aloud. 'I assumed he meant for England. Please don't tell me you're on the other side.'

'No, I'm in British intelligence.' Her father spoke as calmly as if discussing the weather, though she noticed he threw a quick glance at the kitchen door, which stood partly ajar. 'All the same, I need to be careful. There are German spies everywhere. Even down here in Cornwall. And if I were to be spotted in your company—'

She interrupted him. 'German spies? In Cornwall?' She was aghast. 'But surely not here in St Ives?'

'Why not? I've been living in Germany, posing as a citizen sympathetic to the Nazi cause, while passing information back to the British government. But there are also Germans and German-sympathisers here at home, passing as true-blue Englishmen and women, doing exactly the same thing for Herr Hitler. And it's possible their intelligence gatherers know about me. There are always leaks, I'm sorry to say. Someone may have been instructed to keep an eye on you and your aunt in case I make contact.'

'Blimey.' Lily sank down at the table, feeling sick. German spies watching her cottage? Watching her little sister Alice and her aunt Violet? Maybe even following her old gran about the place? 'Please tell me you're pulling my leg.'

'I wish I were,' he said gently. 'Of course, they may know nothing about you. But we can't be sure, so it's important to take precautions.' His smile faded at her horrified expression. 'I can leave straightaway if you wish. I don't want to put you in danger.'

But she shook her head, dismissing that idea at once. 'Oh, Dad, come off it. The whole country's at war. Nobody is safe. I just didn't realise that Germany had any spies down here in Cornwall...' She brought the teapot to the table and fetched cups and milk. 'Now, no more talk of leaving. I'm so happy you're alive and here at last, talking to me. It feels like a miracle.' She kissed him on the cheek. 'And of course you must stay. There's only an armchair or the hearth rug, but I can find some extra blankets and a pillow. I only hope it won't be too uncomfortable for you.'

Her father grinned, his blue eyes crinkling at the corners. 'I've slept in worse places than an armchair, love.'

There was a loud thud from above their heads and they stopped speaking. She glanced up warily; Tristan must have heard voices and would soon be on his way downstairs to investigate. She knew he must have passed a troubled sleep, for he rarely got a wink while she was out at night delivering babies, so she had left him to lie in that morning.

Her father jumped up, looking startled. 'Who else is here?'

'Only my husband.'

Ernest seemed to relax a little, but stayed on his feet, watching the open door as Tristan came downstairs at his usual slow pace, the hollow 'thunk' of his stick accompanying each step.

'His name is Tristan, yes?' her father asked. 'Tristan Minear. And you're Mrs Minear.'

She wondered how he knew. But then, if he was a spy, he would have ways of finding out such things, wouldn't he? 'Yes.' She stood too, wringing her hands nervously.

'But what should I tell him? I never said a word about you before.'

'Can he keep a secret? Tell me quickly.'

Lily blinked. 'I … I don't know.' When her father threw her an odd look, she added in a whisper, 'We haven't been married long, you see, and it's complicated. We only decided to get married because…'

But her voice trailed off as Tristan pushed the kitchen door wide and stood there, leaning on his stick on the threshold, staring at her and her father in surprise.

'Hello,' Tristan said, his brows tugging together as he saw how close they were standing. No doubt he had heard them whispering too and was suspicious. 'I didn't know we were expecting a visitor today.'

Her father, who had been studying his son-in-law with an intent expression, seemed to come to a decision. He came round the table and stuck out his hand.

'Good to meet you, Tristan,' he said simply, once again the no-nonsense, plain-spoken man she remembered from her youth. 'I'm Ernest Fisher, Lily's father. How do you do?'

'I'm very well, thank you, sir.' Tristan shook his hand politely, his brows still knotted together in puzzlement. 'I'm sorry… Did you say you're Lily's dad? I don't understand. I thought…' He looked past Ernest to Lily.

'He's not dead,' Lily whispered. 'He never was. It was a story. He's a … a…'

'I work for British Intelligence,' her dad explained.

'Good God.'

'I'm only here a day or two, to see my daughter and catch up with family. But it's all hush-hush. I trust I can rely on your silence.'

'Of course, sir.'

'Thank you.' Her dad nodded to Tristan's stick. 'You had a spot of bother, I understand. Bad burn, was it? That must have been painful.'

'Rather.' Tristan grinned, suddenly looking like the boy she had fallen in love with. 'But the drugs they give you...'

'Drifting away on a cloud, were you?'

They both laughed, and then Tristan drew up a chair and sat down, his bad leg stretched out in front for ease, and after a pause, her father sat next to him, and the two men began to discuss the course of the war, low-voiced and serious again.

Ernest Fisher – or Ernst as he had been christened – could sound very British when he wished, Lily thought, watching him and her husband together.

As she moved quietly about the kitchen, pouring the tea, cutting yesterday's bread into thin slices and smearing them with a little butter, she felt the most immense pride in these two men. Her dad was half-German but had chosen to support England in the war, signing up from the earliest days, and she had no doubt his help to their government had been invaluable, able to pass as a German citizen even in the toughest spots. And Tristan had been through hell and back with his injuries and was just beginning to come out of that long dark tunnel and look ahead. She only hoped there was a future for them; that England would win this war and set all of them free from this nightmare.

'There you go, Dad,' she said, passing him a plate with bread and butter. 'In case you're hungry.'

'Thanks, love,' he said, so naturally, as though they had

never been apart, and took an absentminded bite, listening to his new son-in-law talk of how St Ives had suffered from air raids and bombings. 'Mmm, delicious.'

Lily covered her face with her hands and burst into tears.

'Hey, hey, Lily.' Her father jumped up, taking her in his arms again. 'What is it? What's the matter?'

'Nothing,' she whispered, drying her eyes with the back of her hand, and smiling at him through swimming vision. 'I'm just so happy to see you again, that's all. To know that you're safe.'

Across the room, Tristan was looking at her with a curiously intent expression, unsmiling. She wished she could see inside her husband's head and know what he was thinking. But it was pointless hungering for something he couldn't seem to give her. And maybe that was also down to this blasted war.

She could not imagine how it must feel to know you may be required to fight and kill for your country, and perhaps to die for that cause too. Small wonder some men came back wounded in mind and spirit as well as body. All she could do was watch and hope, and do her best to be there for him while he healed…

CHAPTER TWENTY-FOUR

Mary was already partly regretting her hot-headed bust-up with Matron that had meant she had to leave Symmonds Hall straightaway, rather than working her notice. Especially since the school holidays were not far off and the headmaster had been most unwilling to take her on at this stage of the term. But Dick had managed to bring him around.

Meanwhile, she was living at home with her parents, and the disappointment of being back in the room with the sloping roof where she'd slept as a child.

One big fear was whether Dick would change his mind about marrying her. His proposal had been unexpected and rather off-the-cuff after all. He might now be experiencing some regrets of his own and wondering how to break it off without hurting her feelings.

Getting washed and dressed in the early morning for her first day at the school, Mary shrugged away those fears. It didn't bear thinking about. But they continued to nag at her as she brushed her hair, fetched her smartest hat off the top of the wardrobe, and pulled on her white belted jacket, perfect for the summer. Eyeing her reflection in the mirror, she applied the tiniest smear of lipstick and then abruptly wiped it off.

Did schoolteachers wear powder and lipstick these days? She honestly didn't know. But then, the teachers she recalled from her own school days had been dour-faced old spinsters, not women in their early twenties, like her. On the other hand, nurses weren't permitted to wear make-up or jewellery on the wards. So perhaps women schoolteachers faced the same restrictions.

Mary grimaced at her mousey, uninspiring reflection. 'You'll do,' she muttered, and headed down the stairs, worried she might be late for her first day. Pip was waiting for her in the hall, as she'd agreed to walk with him the first day.

'Bye, Mum. Bye, Dad,' she called through to the kitchen as she slipped into the same sturdy black shoes she had worn as a nurse. 'Pip and I are off now.'

Her mother, in hairnet and house slippers, came shuffling to the doorstep to watch them leave, arms folded, lips pursed. 'If you hate it, don't come crying to me, Mary Stannard,' was her scathing contribution.

Mary headed uphill towards the school, eventually passing Dick's terraced house, and felt that funny little leap in her heart when the front curtains twitched. A moment later, he was on the step, waving to her and Pip.

'Good morning, Pip. Good morning, Miss Stannard,' Dick said very correctly, adding a wink and a grin that made her laugh. 'Ready for school?'

Pip merely grinned.

Mary rolled her eyes. 'Readier than you, it seems,' she said, for Dick was still wearing his carpet slippers.

'Can I run ahead?' Pip asked her, watching some boys on the other side of the road.

'Of course,' Mary said quickly. 'Don't let us hold you up.'

Pip dashed off.

While Dick disappeared to change into outdoor shoes and fetch his briefcase, Mary stood at the gate and studied the front of the house covertly, wondering what it would be like to live there once they were married. Dick's bedroom was at the back, he had told her, with a tiny view of the sea glimpsed between crowded rooftops. She almost had to pinch herself. The thought of being a married woman and sharing a bedroom with a man still felt so alien to her.

Seconds later, his mother appeared in the doorway, glaring at her in much the same way her own mum had done earlier, and Mary's brain froze, all such happy thoughts forgotten.

Cynthia Jeffries.

Dick's mum was a large, brassy looking blonde, of the kind whose hair colouring had to come out of a bottle, given that she had recently celebrated her sixtieth birthday. She was tall, with wide hips and thick ankles, and wore a knee-length patterned dress at least two sizes too small for her, so that the material clung and strained across her bosom.

'Good morning, Mrs Jeffries,' Mary said shyly from the garden gate, though her heart was thumping. Whatever her mum might think of this woman, she herself would need to rub along with Dick's mum if they were to live under the same roof in the future. 'Isn't it a fine morning? How do you do?'

Mrs Jeffries looked her up and down before turning to

Dick. 'Is this the one you want to marry?' she asked in a penetrating voice. 'Rita Stannard's daughter?'

'Yes, Mum,' Dick said calmly and kissed his mother on the cheek. 'Look, I may be back later than usual, as I'd like to walk Mary home on her first day. But I'll see you at tea-time.'

His mother made no response, merely flashed Mary another dismissive look before closing the door on them both.

'Oh dear.' Filled with trepidation, Mary set off beside him towards the school, which thankfully was only a few minutes' walk away. Her hands felt hot and clammy from where she'd been gripping her bag so tightly, as though she might suddenly be called upon to use it as a weapon. 'That didn't go terribly well. I don't think your mum likes me much.'

He grinned. 'Lucky, then, that I'm the one who's engaged to you. Not her.'

'Do be serious, Dick.' Mary felt awful and couldn't hide it. 'We can't possibly get married if your mum hates me.'

'Mum doesn't hate you. She doesn't even know you.'

She pondered this for a moment, then said stoutly, 'But what if she *does* hate me once she gets to know me? I couldn't live under the same roof as someone who hated me.'

'My dear lovely Mary, you're fretting over nonsense. Focus on today instead. Your first day as a teacher. There'll be plenty of new things to take in and to learn. You can worry about my mother's filthy looks another time.'

'So, you did notice her glaring at me, at least? I wasn't imagining it?'

'Mary, love,' he said, in that easy, offhand way that always disarmed her. 'She's just upset because of whose daughter

252

you are. But once she's got past that, she'll be sweet as pie. You'll see.'

Mary could not feel as satisfied with that answer as he appeared to be. But all thought of Mrs Jeffries faded away as they rounded the next corner and she caught the laughter and shrieks of children running about in the school yard before first bell. Whatever would the pupils think of her? New teachers always came in for a spot of mockery, if memory served from her own school days, and she dreaded being given some horrid nickname, like Miss Stammers instead of Stannard.

Dick, reading her expression correctly, said in a quick, reassuring way, 'You're going to be brilliant.'

As they turned into the school yard, a sound made them both stop and look back, while silence fell among the children, followed abruptly by fresh cries of excitement as the kids rushed to the low wall bordering the street and peered over in glee, all calling out at once.

'Soldiers, sir,' a boy shouted, seeing Dick looking around in confusion. 'On the march. I think they're coming past the school, sir.'

'Oh, I say,' Dick murmured, and turned to her with an embarrassed smile. 'Would you mind awfully if we postpone my showing you around your new classroom so we can watch the soldiers go past?'

She couldn't resist the boyish charm in his face. 'Of course not. I'd love to see them too.'

The lad had been right. Arms swinging, a group of squaddies in dusty brown uniforms were marching past in formation, singing as they went in deep, hoarse voices. One of the men nearest the wall grinned and winked at the children, which delighted them, and a cheer went up. A young boy clambered up on the wall and saluted the soldiers, his bearing ramrod-straight, head held high as he called, 'God Save The King!' after them in a thin, piping voice.

'Better get down, Tommy,' Dick warned him, though he was laughing. 'You'll catch it if the Head sees you on the wall.'

The boy jumped down, and his friends crowded around, giggling and ruffling his hair, all shouting, 'God Save The King!' in mimicry but in a good-natured way.

'Come on, into school with you,' Dick told the children, but he was still watching the dusty trail of soldiers disappearing up the road, his expression wistful.

'You wish you were marching with them,' Mary said, musing, and yet somehow it came out as a statement rather than a question.

'Sometimes,' he admitted in a low voice, so the children still milling around in the schoolyard wouldn't hear. 'Seeing them like that, a chap can't help but wish… No help for it though.' He jerked a thumb towards his face. 'This lazy eye of mine. Can't see to shoot straight. The recruitment officer explained it to me. Said I might be winging one off to the enemy and hit the Sergeant Major instead.' His burst of laughter sounded hollow. 'He offered me Auxiliary Units… Ambulance driver, cook, and so on. But that's not what I wanted to do. At least here, it feels like I'm making a difference. Teaching these kids. They're the future, not us…' His voice trailed off, and he glanced at her, an odd look in his face. 'You don't think less of me for it, do you?'

'Goodness, no.' Mary shook her head vehemently. 'Never.' She saw the doubt still in his face, and added,

'Besides, you're so marvellous with these kids. They respect you and need you, they look up to you. This is where you belong.'

Behind them, the jangle of a bell recalled them to their duties and the children to their classrooms.

'Bless you for saying so, my dear.' Dick met her eyes, and then thrust his hands into his trouser pockets, looking frustrated. 'Hell and damnation. I wish we were somewhere more private.'

'Oh, Dick.' Mary bit her lip, trying not to giggle. 'I thought you were being serious at last. Don't go and spoil it.'

'Blotting my copy book, am I?' He grinned. 'Sorry. Though I am perfectly serious. I could kiss you right now.'

Mary turned away, shocked and amused at the same time, and he followed her reluctantly.

'You're right though, I'd better go inside, get you sorted and take the register, or we'll both be for the high jump.' Dick stopped to speak to a dishevelled-looking lad with trailing shoelaces and a torn shirt hanging out of his short trousers. 'My word, Eddie. How many times do you need to be told? Re-tie that loose lace before you trip over it, boy, and tuck your shirt in.' He nodded brusquely to Mary, and she recalled how he'd warned her not to make it obvious to the kids that they were courting, for it could lead to trouble. 'I'll join you in a minute, Miss Stannard. You go ahead.'

Heading for the school entrance, Mary recognised the tall, grey-haired man energetically ringing the handbell as one of the senior teachers she had met on her last visit to the school. Mr Hardcastle, she thought his name was. She gave him a nervous smile in passing, but he was too intent on calling in late-comers and stragglers to notice.

Children streamed noisily past her as Mary stood motionless in the dim hallway, like a rock in the middle of a turbulent river, suddenly unsure which way to go or what was expected of her on this first day. She felt lost and alone, and utterly convinced she had made the wrong choice by leaving her career in nursing to become a teacher. She knew next to nothing about children and could barely remember even the most basic facts about mathematics and the English language. But Dick had been so sure, so persuasive, she had not even stopped to question it...

'Miss Stannard?' It was Mr Hardcastle, putting away the handbell in a cupboard by the entrance. He nodded her to follow him down the corridor. The children, she noticed, had all miraculously disappeared, except for one or two who had come in late and were hanging up their caps and blazers in the cloakroom. 'You're with me in Room One. The younger set.'

'Oh.' She was confused. 'I thought Dick ... I mean, Mr Jeffries was going to show me the ropes, wasn't he?'

'Sorry, no.' His smile was vaguely apologetic. 'The Head wants you to work with me for your first few weeks, Miss Stannard. I've a great deal of experience with new recruits to the profession, and Mr Jeffries has his own duties to attend to in the higher classes.' He paused before the open classroom door, looking her up and down. 'You've no experience with teaching, is that right?'

'None, I'm afraid. But I'm willing to learn.'

'Of course you are. Or you wouldn't be here, I imagine.' Mr Hardcastle gave her a slow smile. 'Let's see how you get on today, shall we? Teaching is... Well, it's not for everyone.'

She got the impression he expected her to fail. The thought was disconcerting and took her back to those first awful weeks at Symmonds Hall, when Matron and Sister Rose had both made it clear she was on probation only and they would be 'watching' for any serious errors or misdemeanours.

Down the corridor, she saw Dick walk into the school, still talking to the young lad he'd called Eddie. He glanced her way, saw her with Hardcastle, and gave her an encouraging smile. Had he known they were to be separated?

Then she was being ushered into a classroom where two dozen small children were sitting cross-legged on the floor, their curious gazes fixed on her face as she followed Mr Hardcastle to the front of the class.

'Good morning, children,' he said.

'Good morning, Mr Hardcastle,' they all replied in a sing-song way, though all of them appeared to be looking directly at her and not at him.

'Now, children,' he said, taking a chalk and writing *Miss Stannard* on the board in beautiful, clear handwriting, 'we have a new teacher with us today. Her name is Miss Stannard.' He turned to the class, nodding. 'Make her welcome, please.'

'Good morning, Miss Stannard,' they all recited in one voice, staring up at her with rapt attention.

Mary felt like a bug under a microscope, looking from one eager, wide-eyed face to another. Her cheeks felt hot with embarrassment and her heart kept banging violently under her ribs as though she'd run all the way here. Her first instinct was to apologise to Mr Hardcastle, explain that she'd made a terrible mistake and then hurriedly leave.

But she didn't want to let Dick down. She had agreed to do this and there was no way out. She was on probation all over again and would need to watch her step.

Swallowing, she managed to reply, her voice almost failing her, 'Good morning, children.'

But her heart sank. She wished Dick were there to guide and support her instead of this watchful stranger, Mr Hardcastle.

What on earth had she got herself into?

Soon after lunch, just as Mary was beginning to feel as though she could cope with the noise and the constant cries of, 'Miss, can you help me with this?' or 'Miss, I need to go, and it's urgent!' a new challenge was thrown her way. At thirteen minutes past two, when the end of the school day was finally looming, Mary heard the all too familiar wail of the air-raid siren, and Mr Hardcastle's voice saying calmly and clearly above the deafening shrieks and scrapings of chair legs, 'Line up at the door, Class One. No pushing now. And stop shouting. You know the drill.' He stopped to help a boy with a wooden leg rise from his chair, handing him a child-sized crutch. 'Let's show Miss Stannard how it's done, shall we?'

How it was done turned out to be simplicity itself. The children lined up in some mysterious order she didn't yet understand, and then marched down the corridor in relative silence, joining the other three classes and their teachers. By then, the air raid was already underway, and they could all hear the whine of approaching German aircraft.

'Down we go,' Mr Hardcastle said, waving the younger children to go first as the whole school began to file into the cellar for safety. 'Hurry up, now. On the double.' He nodded Mary down the steps with a polite smile. 'You too, Miss Stannard. Take care of the girls, would you? I'll look after the boys.'

As she ducked her head, descending into the warm, stuffy space under the school, filled with sudden trepidation, Mary felt a small hand creep into hers. She looked down and met the shyly smiling eyes of a girl with fair ringlets and a threadbare tunic.

'Don't worry, Miss,' the girl whispered. 'I'll show you what to do. I'm Lizbeth, Head Girl for Class One.'

'Thank you,' Mary said, genuinely grateful for the girl's help. She had been feeling lost again for a moment there.

Lizbeth led her haphazardly across the low-roofed space, which was already filling with noisy, chattering children. 'Girls go to the left,' she explained in a sweet, lisping voice. 'Boys on the right. Teachers sit with their classes.' She stopped at a pile of soft gym mats and gestured to the girls behind her to start distributing them to the youngest children. 'This is where we sit.'

Mary made a vague attempt to supervise the seating of children on the mats, but there really wasn't much to do. Lizbeth had it well under control.

On the other side of the room, Mr Hardcastle was instructing his boys where each mat should go, everything being arranged with military precision. But she didn't fancy the idea of barking orders at her girls. Especially not when it all seemed to be going swimmingly.

She spotted Pip sitting in a corner with his knees drawn up to his chin, looking pale and unhappy, but couldn't leave her own charges to go over and console him. Besides, the boy had a teacher with him, who seemed to be trying to explain that they were perfectly safe in the school basement.

She sank onto a mat with Lizbeth and a very small girl called Angela. The children looked up at her enquiringly.

'You're supposed to teach us something,' Lizbeth whispered helpfully. 'Maybe ask us to recite the alphabet? Or do sums in pairs?'

Looking around, Mary could see impromptu classes taking place to keep the children occupied during the air raid. Dick had his older boys singing a round. A sea shanty, by the sound of it. She caught his eye and smiled spontaneously for the first time since they'd parted that morning. Despite the noise, and the air raid, and the fear of a direct hit on the school, she was having fun at last, she realised with a start.

Now that Mr Hardcastle was no longer watching her like a hawk, Mary dared to be a little more creative.

'Who would like to hear a story about a shipwreck, a magician and a monster?' she called out to her group of girls, and several hands crept up.

For the next hour, slowly, and with plenty of stopping for questions, Mary told them the story behind Shakespeare's play *The Tempest*, though very much simplified for the youngest ones to understand, thrilled by how the children grew still with amazement and awe as she wove that magical old tale while enemy planes in the skies above threatened St Ives with death and destruction...

CHAPTER TWENTY-FIVE

The man on the wireless was reading out a long and dreary list of new ration book rules. Tired after a long day at the orphanage, helping to sweep out rooms and change the linen on over a dozen beds, Sonya was reclining in Babs' favourite armchair, knitting a yellow baby suit and only half listening to the news, her mind elsewhere. She had decided on yellow wool as a compromise, since there was no way of knowing if the babies would be boys or girls, or maybe one of each. Though she had since realised that the second baby suit would have to be white, as she didn't have enough for two, and the lady in the shop had warned her there was a shortage of coloured wool.

Her mind nagged away at the problem, for it was surely a tradition that twins should be dressed alike, and she worried that Yvonne might be upset if given one pastel yellow and one pure white woollen suit for her newborn babies.

Yvonne herself was reading a children's book aloud to her son, who was slumped on her lap in a suspiciously docile manner. Walter had been at school all day, the head teacher having accepted him earlier that week, even though it would soon be the summer holidays. But early that afternoon, enemy planes had been spotted above St Ives, and the air-raid siren had gone off, its fearful shriek driving everyone but the Fire Service into shelters. At the school too, they later learned, everyone had been herded into the basement and given entertaining tasks to do to keep them distracted.

Along with all the nurses and patients at Symmonds Hall, Sonya and Yvonne had taken refuge in the deep cellar they shared with the orphanage, helping some of the walking wounded down its steep steps to safety. There was an old cubbyhole below the apartment which Lady Symmonds had always insisted on using during an air raid, calling it her 'priest's hole' though it was really a mere peculiarity of the architecture. However, Sonya had never really felt safe there and had taken to descending to the orphanage shelter instead, which was deeper underground.

Yvonne had spent the whole air raid fretting about Walter, since this was the first raid when mother and son had been separated.

'What if they target the school?' Yvonne had whispered, pale with fear. 'All those children… It doesn't bear thinking about. They wouldn't stand a chance. I don't know what I'd do if Walter were hurt, or worse.'

'He'll be perfectly safe at the school,' Sonya had reassured her daughter, while secretly admitting to a little trepidation herself. So far this summer, they had been spared the frequent raids of the previous year and she did fear the enemy might be looking to make up for that lull in hostilities.

In the end, the raid had not lasted much above an hour and a half, and Yvonne had instantly set off to collect Walter from school, coming home with tales of a few beach strikes but nothing more serious.

A loud rap at the apartment door broke in on her thoughts. Startled, for they rarely had visitors, Sonya put down her knitting. 'Goodness.'

'Shall I get that?' Yvonne asked, looking up from Walter's book.

'No, dear, you finish the story. I'll go.' Sonya hurried down the hall, checked her reflection in the mirror, and opened the door to the apartment.

She found Mrs Lanyon outside, in a pretty summer dress and holding a buff envelope. 'Hello,' Rose said, 'how are you? I hope you don't mind but I saw the postie leave this for Mrs Fairweather in your cubbyhole and thought I'd bring it up. Save you the walk.'

The former Ward Sister was looking rather pale, Sonya thought with a pang of sympathy. The pregnancy sapping her energy, perhaps. Yet she also seemed softened around the edges, if that wasn't simply her fancy, her hair less severe and her lipstick a muted pink. Since her marriage to charming Dr Lewis, Rose's temperament did seem to have undergone a welcome improvement. No doubt impending motherhood had also made a difference.

'Of course, how kind of you,' Sonya said with a smile, opening the door wider. 'Do come in. Yvonne will be glad to see you, for we hardly ever have company and she does love to chat.' She felt sure Rose wouldn't wish to linger, for she wasn't the chatting sort, but politeness drove her to ask, 'Won't you stay for a cup of tea?'

To her surprise, Rose nodded. 'Thank you.'

Walter had come into the hall, studying their visitor. 'You look after the orphans,' he stated, and then hesitated, glancing up at Sonya. 'I like orphans,' he added awkwardly.

'I'm glad to hear it,' Rose told him, a little severely, for she had been informed of Walter's rude outburst soon after it happened.

'You need a nap before tea-time, Walter,' Yvonne announced, also appearing in the hallway. Her smile widened at the sight of Rose. 'Oh, hello.' Then her gaze fell on the envelope Rose was holding. 'That's not for me, is it?' When Rose agreed, she gave a little gasp and shrank back, shaking her head. 'I'm sorry, but I don't want to open it. It looks horribly official.' Then she fled, pulling Walter along with her and muttering something about 'Perhaps we should both have a nap.'

Frowning, Rose followed her, the envelope still in her hand, but Yvonne had vanished into the bedroom. She turned in puzzlement to Sonya. 'Is your friend expecting bad news?'

'Her husband is being held in a Prisoner of War camp in Germany,' Sonya explained in a whisper, and felt her own breathing constrict as she studied the envelope. It did look rather intimidating. 'I don't think she wants any more nasty shocks, that's all.' She bit her lip, not wanting to give away Yvonne's private business but feeling an explanation might be called for. 'She's, erm, not feeling quite the thing at the moment.'

'I know.' Rose smiled abruptly, and her whole face changed, becoming happier and friendlier. 'I saw Mrs Fairweather coming out of the clinic the other day. I perfectly understand. I'd be in bits too if my husband was in such a dangerous situation while I was expecting a baby. That's why I thought I'd better bring it up when I saw the letter arrive. It looked official, if you know what I mean.'

'I know exactly what you mean.' Feeling sombre, Sonya held out a hand for the envelope. 'Perhaps I should—'

'No,' Yvonne said, coming out of the bedroom and closing the door behind her. Her face was ashen but there was a determined tilt to her chin. 'If the letter is addressed to me, I had better open it.'

Sonya stood in tense silence while Yvonne fetched the paper knife and slit open the envelope. There were two items inside. A folded sheet of cream paper, and a small envelope that appeared to have already been opened. Yvonne unfolded the sheet and gasped, saying in a choked voice, 'It's from Patrick's parents in Truro. They received a letter from him and have sent it on to me.' Her hands began to shake and she dropped the sheet to the floor, fumbling with the other envelope instead. 'They say he … he's escaped from the POW camp.'

'Good God.' Her eyes wide, Rose took a step backwards. 'This is a private matter. I'd better leave.'

'No, please stay,' Yvonne said breathlessly, already reading the letter from her husband. 'Oh my goodness, I don't believe it.' Her voice was almost a wail. 'Oh, Patrick, why on earth would you risk your life like that?'

Quietly, Rose stooped to retrieve the note from the floor and handed it to Sonya.

Sonya didn't mean to look, but the note was so brief, it was hard not to read it at a glance.

Dear Yvonne

*We enclose a letter, received yesterday, from Patrick.
Wonderful news; he has escaped from the POW
camp and is back in England. However, it seems he
was wounded during his escape and is in hospital in
London. We have written back to give him your new
address in St Ives.*

Hoping you and little Walter are well.

Yours, etc.

Sonya folded the sheet and went quietly into the kitchen
to make a pot of tea. She did not know what to make of
the news, but if he was not too badly wounded, she
suspected he would soon be back with his wife and child.
That filled her heart with joy, for she knew how much they
had suffered in his absence. On the other hand, it did
mean they would wish to leave St Ives and return to his
parents' home in Truro. Although inevitable, the thought
of being alone again saddened her. And perhaps Patrick
would share his parents' disdain for her as an unmarried
mother. But she would just have to keep in touch with her
daughter the best she could and hope not to be forgotten.

By the time she came out with the tea tray, Rose was
seated beside Yvonne on the sofa, holding her hand, and
it was clear she had disclosed her pregnancy, for the two
young women were exchanging tales of woe and discomfort, smiling and groaning at the same time.

'Patrick's not badly wounded, Mother,' Yvonne reassured

her, looking up with a smile. 'I feared at first he might…
But it wasn't serious, he says. Shot in the shoulder.'

With a quiver of anxiety, Sonya glanced at Rose. Yvonne
had called her 'Mother', forgetting perhaps that she was
staying there under the guise of being her friend, not her
daughter. But Rose made no sign of having noticed her
mistake, and besides, Sonya felt sure the stern former Sister
was the last person to spread gossip about the hall.

'The wound was infected,' Yvonne continued blithely,
clearly unaware of her slip, 'so he's being kept in hospital
for now. But Rose says a mild infection should clear up
with the right treatment.' She gave a rapturous smile, her
face glowing. 'And Rose knows all about nursing, so she
must be right.'

'I'm a little alarmed he risked his life by escaping from
a POW camp,' Sonya admitted, 'but we should probably
be proud of him. What a daredevil he must be, dodging
all those dreadful German guards with dogs and guns.
And goodness knows how he got back to England,
wounded as he was. I expect he'll have some amazing tales
to tell us.' With a smile, she bent to kiss her daughter on
the cheek. 'I'm glad for you and Walter that he made it
out alive.'

'You should ask for him to be brought here to Symmonds
Hall,' Rose said thoughtfully. 'Better yet, I can ask my
husband to request a patient transfer. Though if he's not
in such bad shape, it might be simpler to wait for him to
be discharged.'

'But could he travel all the way to Cornwall in that state?
You're right, he is an absolute daredevil. But when he's
only just been discharged from hospital, he will hardly be

at full strength. He would have to come by train on his own.' Yvonne clutched her husband's letter to her chest, her eyes misty. 'What if he collapses on the platform in London? With nobody there to help him?'

'I suppose you could take the city train and bring him back,' Sonya said doubtfully.

Yvonne stared at her. 'What a marvellous idea. Why didn't I think of that? Of course, I could go and meet him at the hospital. We could spend a night or two in London while he rests, and then head back. Patrick has a cousin in Battersea, I'm sure we could stay with him.' Then her smile faded. 'But no, I … I can't, can I? What about Walter?' She looked downcast. 'He couldn't possibly come with me. There are so few civilian trains now, the journey would take ages, and it could be dangerous. We all know the enemy love to target the railways.'

'Plus, there's your condition to consider,' Rose reminded her softly. 'The twins.'

'Oh, I hardly notice that,' Yvonne said, dismissing her pregnancy as an unimportant consideration. 'My bump won't stop me getting on a train, not even all the way to London. I get the odd headache and need to lie down until it goes away, it's true. But I don't suffer much with morning sickness.'

Rose looked down at her hands, saying nothing, and Sonya recalled that she had been quite unwell with her own pregnancy.

'But it's no use,' her daughter added bitterly, her shoulders slumping as reality finally caught up with her. 'Walter needs to be here. He has to go to school. So that's that.'

Sonya could not bear to see that look of anguished

disappointment on her daughter's face. It cut so deep, she winced for the poor girl.

'I'll look after him for you,' Sonya announced, not stopping to think about the consequences, for she knew she might change her mind if she did. 'I'll get Walter dressed in the mornings and walk with him to school and back every day. Yes, and make sure he's properly fed and watered until you're home again.'

'Would you, really?' Her face clearing miraculously, her daughter jumped up and hugged her. 'You'd do that for me and not mind all the fuss of it? Oh, Mother, how I love you!'

After they had drunk their tea, and Yvonne, eyes sparkling with excitement, had planned her trip to retrieve her husband from London, Rose suggested they wake Walter and walk down to the hall canteen together for supper. They were halfway there when Dr Lewis caught up with them, a chirpy young lad in tow whom Sonya recognised as Jimmy.

'Hello, darling,' the doctor greeted his wife, kissing her cheek. His curious gaze flicked to Yvonne, who was reassuring her son in an animated fashion that his daddy would soon be home again, but he would have to be polite to Granny St Ives while she was away, fetching him. 'Everything all right?'

Rose whispered in his ear, while Sonya discreetly looked the other way. She turned and smiled at Jimmy instead. 'How are you getting on with your school work these days?' she asked him.

'Mr Jeffries says I'm a genius,' Jimmy told her, grinning.

'Does he?' Sonya couldn't help but smile back at the boy. 'And what are you planning to do with all your genius when you grow up?'

'Rob the Bank of England,' he said boldly.

'Jimmy.' Dr Lewis tutted, shaking his head. 'We talked about making inappropriate jokes, didn't we?'

He pulled a face. 'Yes, Dad.'

'Better answer?'

Jimmy straightened as though standing to attention. 'I'm going to get an apprenticeship and learn to be an engineer. With the army, if they'll have me.'

'That's an excellent ambition,' Sonya said seriously.

The lad blushed and turned to Walter, clearly embarrassed. "Ow about you?' he asked the younger boy. 'What you gonna do when you're older?'

Walter spread his arms and wove between them all, doing his noisy impersonation of a plane again. 'Fighter pilot,' he called back at them, 'like Daddy.'

Jimmy looked impressed. 'Is his dad really a fighter pilot?' he asked Dr Lewis.

'Yes,' his adopted father replied with a wink, 'and your mother tells me he's been wounded too. Shot while escaping from a German Prisoner of War camp. Made it home safely though. Brave fellow, I'd say.'

The lad whistled. 'Wait till they hear about that at school. Walter's going to be popular. Everyone will want to shake his hand.'

Sonya wasn't sure that would be such a good thing, given Walter's egotistical streak. But it would at least cheer him up while his mother was away.

* * *

After they had eaten a rich vegetable and bean stew followed by a rather gooey upside-down cake, and complimented Cook on her imaginative way with a ration book menu, Dr Lewis suddenly excused himself rather than enjoying a cup of tea with them.

'Terribly sorry,' he said awkwardly, 'but I have an errand to run before I clock off tonight. I'll see you later, darling,' he told his wife, nodded to Jimmy, and gave the others a charming smile. 'See you all again.'

The ladies drank their tea and chatted while the nurses and other staff finished their meals and left, until eventually Piotr, Cook's Polish assistant, began to clear the tables around them. Sonya knew they ought to say goodbye to Rose and go back to the apartment so that Walter could be put to bed. But it was a warm, still evening, and none of them had much inclination to move.

Meanwhile, Jimmy had produced a pack of cards and was patiently teaching Walter to play Snap. Sonya glanced at them occasionally, pleased that Walter had so easily made a friend of the older boy, for she knew Jimmy still had some influence with the rest of the orphans. If he took young Walter under his wing, a few bridges might be mended that had been razed to the ground with his ill-considered 'ragamuffin' comments.

Finally, Cook cleared her throat and suggested they might want to take their conversation back to their rooms. With many embarrassed apologies to Mrs Penhallow, they gathered their things and left the canteen staff to finish clearing up without them underfoot.

Outside in the yard, the sun was still shining but with that soft, sultry warmth of a Cornish evening. They stood a moment, exchanging pleasantries while the boys ran about the yard. A few fluffy white clouds could be seen rolling in from the west. Sonya glanced up at them, a gentle sea breeze lifting her hair, and wondered if the weather would soon break, ending the long dry spell.

Dr Lewis reappeared, smiling. 'Mrs Fairweather,' he said to Yvonne, 'I hope you don't mind the interference. But Rose told me what you were planning, jumping on a train to London to get your husband discharged, and I don't think it will be necessary.' He grinned at Walter, who had stopped playing to listen. 'Looks like Daddy's coming home sooner than expected. How does that sound?'

Yvonne stared at him in disbelief. 'I beg your pardon? I don't understand.'

'I made a few calls to a friend of mine,' the doctor explained. 'Chap I treated a few years ago who works in the Ministry of Defence now. He knew someone who knew someone else who was able to pull a few strings for us. And...' He paused, laughing at her stunned expression. 'Flight Lieutenant Fairweather will be heading your way fairly soon, on a military train bound for the south-west. Not the fastest form of transport, I'm afraid. But he should arrive within the next day or so.'

'But his wound...' Yvonne looked scared.

'There's a small medical unit travelling with the train, and he'll be under their care almost all the way. So please don't worry about that.'

'Well done,' Rose told him smugly.

'It was your idea, so...' Lewis waggled his eyebrows at her when she shushed him. 'Sorry, was that meant to be a secret?'

'Oh, you two,' Yvonne cried, tears in her eyes as she hugged them both in turn. 'I'll never be able to thank you enough.'

Sonya had to admit to a feeling of relief that she would not, after all, be required to look after her energetic grandson for two or three days on her own. But she smiled at Walter, whose eyes had grown huge as he listened to the doctor's explanation.

'Happy?' she asked the boy softly.

'Happy as ... as ... *this*.' Walter ran screeching about the yard with his arms spread wide, followed by his new pal, Jimmy, also imitating a fighter plane, though with rather more laughter. 'Daddy's coming home!'

CHAPTER TWENTY-SIX

Porthcurno, Cornwall, July 1943

The bus meandered through narrow, winding Cornish lanes, long feathery grasses whipping at its sides, the sea a glittering scarf that flashed bright blue and disappeared at intervals to their right. 'There, Dad,' Lily whispered to her father, pointing out a church tower in the distance. 'That's Porthcurno. Aunty Violet and Uncle Joe were married in that church. It was ever such a lovely ceremony, and the weather held up nicely. I wish you could have been there.'

'So do I,' her dad said gravely. 'Though I did hear all about it.'

Lily stared at him, puzzled. 'Sorry?'

'My friend Fred just happened to be passing Porthcurno on the day of the wedding.' He gave her a wink that told her it had *not* been a coincidence. 'He's often in the West Country, so I asked him to keep an eye on the family. Just in case anyone from the other side was watching you too.'

'Blimey, Dad.' Lily shivered. 'Is that how you knew so much about me and Tristan? That we'd got wed and where we were living?'

'Maybe.' Ernest tapped the side of his nose, then glanced over his shoulder. Tristan sat dozing comfortably in the seat behind theirs, sunlight on his upturned face. 'I hope the lad's going to be all right on this trip. You said there was some uphill walking to be done. You're sure this visit won't be too hard on him?'

'Tristan's tougher than he looks,' Lily assured him. 'In fact, he's almost recovered from his burns now.' She bit her lip. 'Though he'll probably never walk without a limp.'

'He's a survivor. That's the main thing.'

The bus slowed as it entered Porthcurno village, its engine rattling noisily. A man was leading a donkey down the hill, and the bus driver had to stop until he had turned off into a field. The narrow country lane ahead had begun to widen, with houses on one side.

'See that cottage?' Lily nudged her dad as they passed the tiny cottage where the family had lived while working at Eastern House, the top-secret communications station based at Porthcurno. 'We lived there once, me and Gran and Aunty Vi and Alice.'

'Sounds like a bit of a squeeze, love.'

'Oh, we were packed in like sardines.' She grinned. 'After I left to work in St Ives, Aunty Vi took in three evacuee children. But we had fun times there, too.'

She still looked back with nostalgia at those early years of the war, though it couldn't have been much fun at the time, or not for her aunt. It had all seemed a bit of a lark to her and Alice, travelling down to Cornwall from

Dagenham, scrounging about for work that would pay, the two girls bunking up in one room with their aunt until they got a place of their own. Now she was no longer a child, however, Lily saw things in a different light. The dread of a German invasion kept her awake at nights, living right on the Cornish coast, and her fears weren't helped by terrifying government leaflets that were handed out from time to time, telling folk what to do if Germans landed in their town or village.

'Evacuees as well? It sounds as though Violet hasn't changed. She and Betsy made a formidable pair.' There was sorrow in his voice at the mention of her late mother, but her dad cleared his throat, nodding as he continued. 'Violet was a force of nature. Your mother was a little in awe of her, I think.' His smile was wry. 'I'm only surprised Violet took three evacuees into her home, and not ten.'

'You'll probably meet the kids up at the farm. Joe has Land Girls working with him too.' She saw his frown and added in a low voice, 'Don't worry, I'll tell them you're my cousin. Besides, this is Porthcurno. Everyone knows to keep their mouth shut and their nose out of other people's business here. Loose lips sink ships, and so on.'

Her father nodded, seeming to relax, and she guessed he must know all about the secret tunnels dug into the cliffs behind Eastern House, the men who worked in them day and night, deciphering coded messages, and their vital importance to the war effort. And why not? He worked for British Intelligence, after all.

Lily gathered their belongings and got up, stooping to rouse her sleeping husband. 'We're here, Tris,' she said, touching his shoulder. 'We've reached Porthcurno.'

Tristan stirred and sat up slowly, gazing into her face. But the sleep seemed to have done him good, for there was more colour in his cheeks than when the chuntering old bus had left St Ives, and he reached for his walking stick with an air of decision.

They all piled out and stood looking across at the large white buildings of Eastern House opposite, heavily camouflaged and cordoned off from the rest of the village by rolls of barbed wire and sentry boxes at each gate. She noticed her father's interest and said quietly, 'That's Eastern House, where the transatlantic cables come in.'

'Yes,' was all he said, his hands in his pockets. But as the bus drew away, he continued to study the busy sprawling camp that now surrounded the old Victorian communications post, with soldiers, tents and army vehicles cluttering the tree-lined route that led down to the white sandy beach at Porthcurno.

'Evening.' An old man, passing them in the village street, had stopped, nodding to Lily with a look of recognition. 'You be one of Sheila's young granddaughters, unless I'm much mistaken.'

It was Arnold Newton, the old shopkeeper who was sweet on her grandmother. An ancient tweed cap had been jammed down hard on his shock of unkempt white hair, his high, sun-mottled forehead shiny with perspiration.

'Good evening, Mr Newton,' Lily said nervously. 'Yes, it's good to see you again. I hope you're well. This is my husband, Mr Minear. We're just walking up to Postbridge Farm to see Gran and the others.' She was rambling, she realised, but couldn't seem to stop. Her father was not supposed to be alive, let alone wandering Porthcurno and openly studying the secret communications base opposite. 'And this is my … my cousin,' she finished lamely, hoping to goodness he wouldn't ask for a name.

But Mr Newton merely gave them a polite nod. 'How do?' He pointed to the sky in the way of old countrymen. 'Stopped rainin'. Be a dry night now, see if it won't. Warm too.' He touched his forehead. 'Ah.'

And the old shopkeeper shuffled away, apparently suspecting nothing.

'Come on, it's a long walk.' With a rapidly beating heart, Lily turned to lead them up the steep hill to Joe's farm.

The air was cool and fresh after a shower of rain, but the late afternoon sun was out again, warming the damp roadway. Tristan walked slowly, leaning on his stick, though he showed unusual vigour, she thought, perhaps spurred on by her dad's presence. Ernest climbed the hill easily, looking around himself with interest, fitter in his forties than many men half his age. Lily, watching him secretly, imagined it must be important for him to be strong and agile, given the dangerous things he would need to do as a spy, often at a moment's notice.

The road soon narrowed to a well-worn track. Bees and tiny bright insects flitted back and forth between high hedgerows on either side. Ernest tilted back his hat to look up at the still-blue sky, no longer hiding beneath its brim.

She was fretting at not having been able to warn her family in advance about their visit. But after only one night under their roof, her dad had insisted that he wished to see Alice and stay at Joe's farm tonight before leaving Cornwall.

It was an agonisingly short time to be reunited with her

long-lost father. But Lily knew the war effort had to come before her personal feelings. Besides, she had enjoyed her brief time with him, even though she longed for him to stay a week at least. They had spent much of yesterday afternoon chatting about the old days, and then all three had eaten a hearty evening meal together, the conversation turning more naturally towards her relationship with Tristan: how they had met in Penzance, his time as a soldier, hers as a nurse, and his awful injuries. Tristan had still not explained how these had occurred, repeating the same sparse details he had given Lily, and her dad had not pressed him for more information.

But Ernest had watched the two of them closely all evening. Lily was sure he must have noted how they didn't touch hands or smile at each other like other young couples, and this distressed her, sure he must be wondering why on earth they had married. To be honest, she had begun to wonder herself.

As they came within sight of the farm, Lily saw her younger sister outside, scattering a little feed for the chickens. Still in the neat, grey linen dress she habitually wore for her work as a teacher's assistant at the school in Penzance, Alice was shod in old Wellington boots to cope with the mud and dirt of the farmyard. But her complexion looked clear and her shoulder-length hair had been styled in smooth blonde waves, no trace left of the awkward, spotty girl chewing her pigtails that Lily remembered from their childhood.

Alice had turned when the farm gate creaked, shielding her eyes against the early evening sun. Now her slender body stilled, her gaze intent on the three approaching figures. Then she dropped the feed basket and ran towards them, crying, 'Daddy!'

When they entered the farmhouse – an ecstatic, grinning Alice having been sworn to secrecy in front of the evacuees and the Land Girls – it was to find Gran at the range, wiping her hands on her apron and turning in surprise as three unexpected visitors strode into the kitchen.

Gran looked at Lily's dad blankly at first, then said, 'Ernst?' using his German name, as though sure she must be mistaken.

'Yes, Sheila, it's me.' He took her hands in his while Gran stared at him, wide-eyed. 'Listen, I'm not back for long. One night, that's all. I just have to say … I'm so sorry about Betsy. I wanted to come back as soon as I heard what had happened, but…' He choked, adding thickly, 'My heart was broken that day.'

'Oh, my poor Betsy, my gorgeous girl,' was all Gran could say before dissolving into tears.

Ernest opened his arms and hugged Sheila tight, speaking into her ear, his voice low and urgent.

Embarrassed to be witnessing what was clearly a private moment, Lily hurriedly took over stirring the soup bubbling on the range while Alice bent to tug off her muddy boots. Tristan pulled out a chair and sat down at the pine table, a thoughtful look on his face.

The two were still locked together when Joe came in from the farmyard and stopped dead, staring in astonishment at the sight of his wife's mother being fiercely embraced by a total stranger. 'Sheila?'

Fearing the three Land Girls who worked on the farm

might not be far behind, Lily closed the door to the yard and said quickly, 'Joe, this is my father.' Seeing his eyes widen, she added on a frantic note, 'But you mustn't let on that you know. He's my cousin, got it?'

'Your cousin?'

'Mum's the word, eh?' Lily was relieved when Joe nodded slowly, comprehension dawning in his face. 'Is Aunty Vi about?'

'Upstairs. I'll call her down.' He headed for the door, but Lily's dad turned to stop him, one hand outstretched.

'Wait, please. I'm Ernest.' The two men shook hands. 'You must be Violet's husband. I'm very glad to meet you, Joe.'

'Likewise,' Joe said, looking both pleased and nonplussed at the same time. 'I'll away and fetch Vi for you, shall I?' He paused, adding with a half-smile, 'Cousin Ernest.'

Ernest was the Anglicised version of his German name, Ernst. That was how Gran and her mum and aunt had always addressed him, the ones who had known him longest. Lily had never really thought much before about him using Ernest with everyone else, but she realised with a shock that her dad had always been not quite what he seemed, even before war broke out. Growing up with a German mother and English father, always having to choose between the two, he must have been primed for that double life right from the start.

'That's the ticket,' Ernest said with a laugh, watching him go. He took Alice's hand, who was still grinning wildly, looking at her father with avid eyes. 'You've sprouted, kid,' he said affectionately, and his gaze moved to Lily. 'Both of you. I have two beautiful gazelles for daughters.'

Alice blushed, clinging onto his arm. 'I work at the school in Penzance now,' she told him shyly.

'So your sister said.'

'I read books to the children at story-time. That's my favourite part of the job.'

'You always did love to read.' Their dad grinned. 'My little bookworm.'

'I'm still a big reader myself. I love adventure stories best. Spy books too.' Her voice dropped. 'They make me think of you.'

'Hush,' he said warningly, but gave her a wink. 'Chip off the old block, is it?'

Alice laughed.

Gran gave Lily a quick hug. 'Well, this is a surprise, and no mistake,' she whispered, and searched her face. 'You all right, love?'

'I'm fine. Worried about Tris, that's all. It was a long walk up from the village.'

'Joe will give you a run down in the van when you leave. You'll stay the night though? There'll be no buses back to St Ives until tomorrow.'

'Of course we'll stay. Once I can get Alice's attention, we'll go and find some extra bedding,' Lily told her, smiling broadly. 'It's so good to have him back, isn't it?'

'Your dad's a sight for sore eyes, bless him.' Gran was scratching her head though. 'Hmm, three more mouths to feed. And a celebration too. Best see what I've got in the pantry.' And with that she bustled away.

Violet came in, with Joe trailing behind. 'What's all this about visitors?' she began impatiently, and then her jaw dropped. 'Oh, my Lord. Ernst? Is that really you?' Her eyes filled with tears as she embraced her brother-in-law, her voice becoming ragged as she whispered, 'Thank God you're safe. Oh, the girls… They missed you so bad. I can't believe you're here, in Cornwall of all places. But how long are you staying?' She pulled back, wiping her damp eyes and staring at him, suddenly fearful. 'Hang on, ain't it dangerous for you to be here?'

'One question at a time,' Ernest said, laughing and shaking his head. 'So long as you all keep it quiet, I should be safe enough. Look, I was given an opportunity to come back, and I took it.' He paused, his face sobering. 'With this war, it could be my last chance to see my girls again. How could I refuse?'

Alice, hearing this, gave a sob and put a hand to her mouth. But she didn't ask him to explain or beg him not to go back. Nor did anybody else. They all knew how important his work was to England winning the war.

A tear rolling down her cheek, Lily sniffed and groped for the hanky up her sleeve. She didn't think she could bear it. And yet she had no choice, any more than her father had, or all the other brave men and women risking their lives to work against the Germans from inside their own country. It was either this or lose the war.

Gran broke the silence, carrying armfuls of tins and packets to the pine table. 'Give us a hand with the evening meal, would you, Lil? It's nearly time to eat.'

Even as she said this, the kitchen door flew open and the three Land Girls tumbled in, kicking off boots and heading straight for the sink to wash their dirty hands and faces. They checked, seeing the visitors, and then carried on after a few quick greetings, still chatting among themselves.

Lily watched the trio with interest, for the Land Girls had always been fascinating to her. Selina was no longer as slender as she'd once been, now muscular instead, made sturdy by long days of hard work on the farm and probably Gran's lard-filled cooking too. Her fair-haired friend, Caroline, by contrast, had slimmed down and lost her delicate pink hue, now nut-brown from the sun, while Penny – or 'Pickles' as they always called her – was still as comfortably round as ever, laughing at some joke as she sniffed the bubbling pot on the range.

Violet stirred. 'Where are them kids gone?' she asked huskily. 'Out in the fields, I expect, getting themselves bloomin' filthy as usual. They'll need to come in and wash up before their tea.'

'I'll go and find them,' Alice offered. 'Little pests are usually messing about in the top field at this time of day.' She laid the table quickly and expertly, and then went outside to find the evacuees.

'Come on, love. Let's have a proper chat.' Violet drew Ernest into the back room, shutting the door behind them.

Hands on hips, Lily glanced at Tris and Joe. 'You two best get out the way while we work.'

'Right you are,' Joe said mildly, and led Tristan outside with a nod. Lily poured them a mug of home brew each and carried it out. The two men sat on the bench near the back door, looking across the fields as they drank and discussed the progress of the war, their deep male voices rumbling through the door.

The three Land Girls ran upstairs to change out of their

soiled overalls. Meanwhile, Gran and Lily sorted out the grub. A thick broth, simmering on the range, had been planned for that evening's supper. But Gran was a magician when it came to making very little food go a long way, and the two of them set to, putting together a simple but filling meal. They had the broth, followed by bread and butter with cheeses and cold meats, plus two dishes of boiled veg. Pudding afterwards was a large bowl of stewed fruit each, with cream from Joe's own cows poured over the top.

When the evacuee kids rushed in, followed by Alice, they swarmed about Lily and Tristan, paying almost no attention to Lily's dad, who had been explained away as a distant cousin. Janice, who would soon be sixteen, was no longer in school but helping out around the farm instead. The girl, once a sulky tearaway, had clearly matured since Lily had spent so much time with her in Penzance last year, her air serious as she helped spoon hot stewed fruit into Gran's best china bowls. Her younger brothers, Eustace and little Timothy, were still cheeky rascals though, who set the whole table laughing as they described their antics at school during the last air raid, when apparently they had tied several boys' shoe laces together, causing mayhem when the all-clear sounded and everyone lined up to leave the shelter.

The only time Lily's father drew attention to himself during the meal was when Selina was mocked by Eustace for hurriedly concealing a letter she'd been reading between courses.

"'Ere, is that from your fancy man?' Eustace called across the table, laughing uproariously when the Land Girl blushed.

'Pipe down, you little whippersnapper,' Gran told him sternly, 'and mind your own beeswax.'

'He's not my fancy man,' Selina told them, looking awkward. 'John's my fiancé. We're hoping to be married as soon as he's able to get some leave.'

'Ooh, she's getting married,' Eustace said, still laughing.

'Love,' Lily's dad told him, 'is not a joke, young man, as you will come to understand once you're a little older. Love is what we fight for.' As the room fell silent, he glanced down the table at Lily and Tristan, his gaze somehow meaningful as he added, 'That, and the next generation.'

Love is what we fight for.

Under the table, Lily felt Tristan take her hand, and looked into his eyes, her breathing suddenly laboured as she tried to read his expression.

That, and the next generation.

Yes. She wanted to fight for love, for their relationship, for her and Tristan to be a proper married couple at last.

But could she win that war?

CHAPTER TWENTY-SEVEN

St Ives, Cornwall, late July 1943

It was still bright and sunny outside at eight o'clock, and the warm, smoky room above the pub that Mary had booked for her mother's surprise birthday party was heaving. Most of her mother's friends and neighbours had turned out for some free food and booze, and to wish Rita a happy sixtieth. Mary and Dick had been rushing about for the past fifteen minutes, checking that everyone had a glass on the go and knew to be quiet when given the signal that Rita was on her way up the stairs.

Her dad had promised faithfully that he would get her mother there by eight o'clock, so Mary popped her head behind the blackout curtains and peered down into the narrow, cobbled street.

'Come on, where are you?' she whispered under her breath, fearful lest Dad had failed in his mission.

But she needn't have worried. After a short wait, she finally spotted her mum and dad approaching, her mum in a posh blue frock and heels, her dad in his best suit. They had been for a nice meal that evening at a restaurant near the harbour, and Mary had told her dad to suggest a quick drink in the pub on their way home. They had left young Pip at home, with Clare from the next street who was keen to earn a few extra shillings from baby-sitting, since Mary had claimed she'd be out that evening too. But as soon as her parents had left for the restaurant, Mary and Dick had nipped back, thanked Clare, and taken Pip along with them to the pub. Luckily, the landlord didn't mind having the boy there, since the party was in a private room, and Mary had sat him down in a corner with a school book and a sweet drink.

Her mum, once keen on pub-going, had decided a few years back that she didn't like the smell of beer and smoke anymore, and could be heard arguing against this impromptu stop all the way along the street. But Mary's dad, sticking to his guns, ignored her complaints and guided his wife into the pub, saying loudly, 'There's a quieter room upstairs, Rita. Why don't you find a comfortable seat up there while I get the drinks in?'

Hurriedly, Mary nodded to Dick, who gave the signal, tapping a beer bottle with his metal pen, the high-pitched sound cutting through the buzz of conversation.

Hurriedly, with loud shushes, everyone in the private room fell silent. Mary laid a finger on her lips and tiptoed to the top of the stairs. Already they could hear Rita, still complaining that she didn't like pubs, clacking up the steep wooden steps in her high heels.

As Rita appeared at the top of the stairs, hanging onto the banister, Mary called out, 'Happy Birthday, Mum!' She bit her lip at her mother's shocked, wide-eyed expression, adding loudly, '*Surprise!*'

Everyone in the room raised their glasses, as pre-arranged, shouting, 'Happy Sixtieth Birthday, Rita!'

Then Dick called out, 'Three cheers for Rita Stannard. Hip hip … hooray!' and everyone joined in, laughing and cheering.

Rita directed a glare at her prospective son-in-law, for she had still refused to acknowledge their news of an engagement, simply pretending instead that it was not happening. To Mary's relief though, she didn't say anything, perhaps because there was nothing her mother could have said that would have been heard above the sound of raucous cheering and applause.

Mary's dad had surreptitiously followed Rita up the stairs, and took his wife's hand now, looking a little abashed as she turned her flushed, gaping face towards him. 'Happy Birthday, love,' he said, patting her hand. 'Our Mary arranged this party as a special surprise for you. I hope you like it.'

'I … I don't know what I think, Harold.' Rita put a hand to her mouth, her look troubled and uncertain. 'It's a surprise, that's for sure.' Pip came up to give her a hug and wish her a happy birthday, and she stared at him in amazement. 'You here too, Pip? But we left you at home. I swear, this is a conspiracy.' Then she spotted an old friend among the faces gathered around her, and exclaimed with genuine pleasure, 'Carol, is that you? My word, I've not seen you in… And you brought Jack too? Oh, my goodness. How well you both look. It must be ten years at least…'

At that point, everyone started talking at once, gathering

around Rita to shake hands or hug her, pointing out how long it was since they'd seen each other and saying how much they hoped she'd enjoy her birthday this year.

'I'm impressed, Mary Stannard,' Dick said quietly at her back.

Mary turned, grinning. 'Come on, it was your idea to have a party. You have to take some of the credit, at least.'

'If you insist,' he agreed, slipping an arm around her waist. 'In that case, I'll accept a kiss as my reward. Later on, of course.' He laughed at her embarrassed expression. 'It's all right. Nobody can hear a thing with all this hubbub going on. Besides,' he added cheekily, bending close to her ear, 'we're engaged, aren't we? Wanting to kiss you is hardly a crime.'

'You know my mum's not fully on board with the idea,' Mary reminded him, wriggling free of his grasp. 'The last thing I want is to cause a scene at her birthday bash. No more flirting, is that understood?' But she was smiling. He had a magical way of making her laugh even when she really ought to be stern with him.

'Your wish is my command,' Dick said meekly.

Seeing that her mum was looking overwhelmed, Mary steered her to a seat that had been specially set aside and where various presents from friends and family sat waiting, some wrapped in brown paper with bows. 'Happy Birthday, Mum,' she said again, and left her there to open her presents, turning to her father with a grateful look. 'Well done, Dad. Thanks for bringing her here on time.'

'I didn't think I'd even get your mother through the door, love,' her dad admitted, scratching his ear. 'She remembered halfway here that she didn't like pubs, and you know what she's like when she's got a flea in her ear.'

'Never mind, eh?' Dick handed him a pint of ale. 'Get that down you, Mr Stannard. I guarantee you'll feel better in a brace of shakes.'

'Aye, well...' Giving him a sideways glance, her dad shrugged and sipped the ale. 'Mm, that's not half bad,' he admitted after another taste, smacking his lips. 'Thank you, lad.' Her dad held up the ale to the light and studied it with the air of a connoisseur, nodding. 'Nice colour to it, as well. You've taste in ale, I'll give you that.'

Mary hid her smile. Her dad had been careful not to take her side against Mum since the shocking announcement that she and Dick were engaged. But it seemed Dad was willing to overlook the situation while he had a pint of good ale in his hand.

They all stood about chatting and having a great time, and she slowly began to relax. But before even half an hour had passed, Mary glanced idly about the room and gave a horrified gasp. She gripped Dick's arm, tugging on his sleeve with genuine terror. 'Dick, Dick,' she whispered hoarsely. 'Look!'

'All right, no need to pull my arm off. What am I looking at?'

With an unsteady hand, Mary pointed through the smoke haze across the crowded room. A tall blonde in a red dress was just emerging from the staircase in staggeringly high heels, a black pillbox set aslant on brassy locks, scarlet lipstick standing out bright against a thickly powdered complexion.

'Your blessed mother, Cynthia Jeffries,' she hissed. 'I

certainly didn't invite her. Yet there she is.' Her eyes widened, her heart nearly stopping in fright. 'And it looks like she's headed straight for my mum.'

For once, Dick seemed shaken. 'Oh Lord.'

They both watched in stunned silence as Cynthia barged her way through the gathering with little finesse, many people quickly stepping aside in surprise as she elbowed her way past them. A large, well-built man with glasses followed a few feet behind, fair hair flopping over his forehead and an anxious look on his face.

'Is that your dad?' Mary asked blankly, for she had never met the fabled Mr Jeffries in the flesh.

'I'm afraid so, yes.'

'Just to be clear,' she said slowly, 'my mum and your mum fought over him when they were younger? Is that right?'

'So I believe.'

Biting back the obvious question, Mary studied his father. He wasn't bad-looking, she supposed, and would probably have been rather better looking as a young man. But for the life of her, she couldn't see the attraction.

Catching her surprised expression, Dick said out of the corner of his mouth. 'Money.'

'I beg your pardon?'

'His family had money and a big house just out of town. That's why all the girls at school were mad for him, or so he told me.' Dick grinned. 'Unfortunately, his parents didn't much like Mum, so in the end his older brother inherited and Dad was left to fend for himself. A hollow victory for Mum, snagging him just to lose the lot.'

'Gosh, that's rather sad.'

His mother had almost reached Mary's mum, who had not yet seen her, too busy chatting to an elderly woman in a brown hat. Beside her sat Pip, munching on a sandwich and kicking his feet back and forth as he listened to the grown-ups conversing.

'Oh crikey, whatever are we going to do?' Mary whispered, tensed for the inevitable collision.

Dick grimaced. 'Run and hide?'

'That's not funny.'

'It's not a bad idea though.'

'Did you tell your mother about the party tonight?'

'Good grief, not a chance.' Dick gave her a straight look. 'She must have heard about it from one of their mutual friends.' He pulled a face. 'I expect she couldn't resist popping in to make your mother uncomfortable. Given that you and I are dating, and neither of them like it much.'

Mary could have torn her hair out in frustration. All these weeks of planning, and now this…

But perhaps it wasn't too late to prevent the two women coming to blows. Her dad was only a few feet away, listening with a resigned expression to a dreary anecdote from one of their neighbours. Mary signalled him frantically. Puzzled, Harold followed her pointing gesture and froze, his own eyes widening in similar horror as he realised what she'd seen. Then her dad downed the dregs of the pint he'd still been cradling, set the glass on a table, and headed over to where her mother sat, deep in conversation.

'Your dad's a braver man than me,' Dick said with admiration.

'Time to show everyone what you're made of, then.'

Dragging him along by the arm, Mary set off in pursuit of her father. 'Come on,' she insisted when he protested, 'Dad's going to need reinforcements.'

But it was too late.

Rita had already seen Cynthia. She broke off her conversation with the woman in the brown hat and stood, her eyes bulging with indignation.

'You,' she said in scathing tones.

'Hello, Rita Bleater.'

The conversation around them faltered, and the room gradually fell quiet. Heads turned curiously in their direction.

'This is a private party.' Mary had never seen her mother look so cross. 'So you can get out.'

'Last time I looked,' Cynthia drawled, 'this was a free country. And I often drink in here. How about you get out instead?'

Rita drew herself up, her lip curling. 'You can't bully me, Cynthia Jeffries. I'm not seventeen anymore.'

'I can see that, love. Sixtieth birthday bash? You look more like seventy, I'd say.'

'Now, ladies,' Harold began nervously, trying to step in between them, but his wife pushed him aside.

'You're hardly God's gift yourself, you mangy old trout, though I see you're still desperate to cut the mustard.' Rita looked Cynthia up and down, her eyes flashing. 'Mutton dressed as lamb, you are.'

'Well, at least my legs are straight. You're practically bow-legged, Rita. You could be a stand-in for one of these cowboys at the picture house. Best get off your high horse before I knock you off it.'

'Just you try,' Rita snarled, and dashed the remains of her sherry into Cynthia's sneering face.

Cynthia spluttered, flailing about with sherry dripping from her hair, incandescent with rage. Mr Jeffries merely looked on with a grim expression, his hands in his pockets, as though used to such scenes.

Horrified, Mary plunged forward to pull her mother aside. But at that moment, something happened that changed everything. The air-raid siren went off above the town, its fearful screech freezing everyone in the room.

'Thank heaven for small mercies.' Dick leapt to his mother's side with a hanky. 'Erm, let me help you, Mum. Stand still, we'll soon get this mess cleared up.'

There was already a queue to get down the stairs, and Mary could hear the rumble of voices from below, shouting, 'Goodnight, all,' as pub-goers dived out into the street, no doubt hoping to dash home before the planes passed overhead.

'We need to leave,' Rita was saying in a strangled voice as Harold helped her down the stairs from the private room. 'Now.'

But in the saloon bar, they found the landlord waiting by the shelter door. He'd already extinguished the lights, locked up the pub, and was ushering the last remaining drinkers into the cellar.

'Down into the shelter, please,' he told them in a big, booming voice. 'Planes overhead. You don't want to go out there, it's not safe.'

It's hardly much safer indoors, Mary thought, but said nothing. Instead, she caught Dick's eye as they headed down into the cellar together, him with his parents, Mary with her own parents and Pip in tow. Below, they found chairs and wooden benches, and a few cushions scattered on the floor.

'Oh, this is going to be fun,' Dick muttered as the two families separated, the Jeffries seated a few feet across the narrow cellar from the Stannards, both women still glaring at each other.

Pip sank onto one of the floor cushions, cradling his schoolbook and looking vaguely sick. It was only then that Mary recalled how much the boy hated being trapped underground during these air raids.

Drawing on her experience as a nurse, Mary sat beside Pip, her arm about his shaking shoulders. 'You'll be all right,' she said, trying to reassure him.

But within minutes, it was clear that Pip had a serious problem. He was gasping for air, his stiffened fingers clutching at his throat.

'What's wrong with the lad?' the landlord demanded, watching him uneasily.

'He doesn't like being underground, that's all,' Mary explained. 'Especially in such a small space. It's called claustrophobia. A fear of enclosed spaces. And all the shouting hasn't helped.'

'Come and sit with me, Pip,' her mum said encouragingly. 'I'll look after you.'

Pip paid no attention, his breathing laboured, a fine sheen of perspiration on his forehead.

'Maybe he thinks you might throw a glass of water in his face,' Cynthia remarked, her tone cutting.

'Oh, don't you start,' Rita shot back at her, tensing up.

'For goodness' sake,' Mary snapped at them both. 'Grow

up, would you? Look at the state of this poor boy. The last thing Pip needs is for you two to be scratching each other's eyes out while he's struggling to breathe.'

There was a shocked silence. But her outburst seemed to have done the trick, as both women sat shame-faced, not looking at each other.

'It's like he's suffocating,' her mum cried, watching the boy's distress. 'His lips are turning blue. What can we do to help?'

'Here, let me.' Cynthia came across to sit with Pip, easing down on the cushion at his side with a quick, reassuring smile. 'Don't fret, lad. I won't hurt you.' She nodded to Mary to release him.

'You leave him alone,' Mary's mum began hotly, but Charles Jeffries said clearly, 'Let her try, Rita. She knows what she's doing.'

Cynthia helped the boy bend forward slightly. 'Now,' she said gently, 'I need you to breathe deep and slow, following my count. In for three, out for four. You ready?' She cupped both hands around his mouth and nose and gave him a wink. 'All right, here we go... In, *one, two, three*. Out, *one two, three, four*. That's the ticket. And again.' She repeated the procedure a number of times, her voice calm and soothing, nothing like the sharp, high-pitched tone she had used with Rita earlier.

Before long, Pip's colour had returned almost to normal and he was breathing more easily. Indeed, by the time the all-clear sounded, he was sitting up again, rather sheepishly enjoying the rapt attention of everyone in that tight space.

'You feeling better, love?' Rita asked him, hands clasped tightly at her chest, her eyes anxious.

'Yeah, sorry, Mrs Stannard,' Pip agreed, rubbing his face with an embarrassed expression. 'I dunno what come over me.'

Smiling, Cynthia Jeffries left the boy to recover and crossed to collect her handbag while the others began to file out of the cellar space.

Rita stood and went after her old rival. 'Hang on, Cynthia… How did you know what to do with him?'

'My eldest boy, Percy, had the same problem when he was that age, especially on summer nights. Couldn't breathe, pains in his chest. He used to panic and make things worse.' Cynthia shrugged. 'Doctor said it was a touch of hay fever, only with a nervous complaint on top. He always was a worrier as a boy, my Percy. But if I sat with him for a while and cupped my hands for him to breathe deep, he always got better in the end.'

'Is he still like that, your son?'

'Lord, no. He grew out of it eventually.' Cynthia followed her husband to the cellar door. 'Percy's in the Navy now. Serving overseas. Like your son Stephen.'

'Well, thank you,' Rita said awkwardly.

Cynthia glanced back at her, a fierce little smile on her face. 'Consider it a birthday present,' she said, 'Rita Bleater.'

To Mary's relief, her mother laughed, turning to Pip. 'We'd best get you home, lad. It's been a more eventful birthday than I was expecting.'

'You know, I think your mum may be coming round to the idea of me as a son-in-law,' Dick whispered to Mary with a grin, waiting until everyone else had left the cellar before drawing her gently into his arms. 'Now, my lovely, any chance of a goodnight kiss?'

CHAPTER TWENTY-EIGHT

There was someone knocking at the door to the apartment, Sonya realised, swimming up through heavy sleep to consciousness. The clock on her bedroom mantel showed it to be a little after six in the morning. What on earth? Puzzled, Sonya groped for her dressing gown, pushed her bare feet into slippers, and stumbled out of her room and across the living area. The place was still in darkness, the blackout curtain still drawn across the windows from last night, and she trod inadvertently on one of Walter's toys, exclaiming in pain.

Unlocking the door, Sonya peered anxiously out into the gloom and was taken aback to find two young men confronting her.

To her relief, she recognised one of the men as Dr Lewis, though he was wearing civvies and not his habitual white coat. The other, clad in an RAF uniform, though with noticeable stubble on a strong, jutting chin, was unknown to her. His arm was in a sling and he swayed on the threshold, perhaps from fatigue, for there were dark shadows etched under his eyes and he looked exhausted.

'I apologise for disturbing you at such a barbaric hour, Mrs Thorpe,' Dr Lewis said carefully, 'but may we come in? Flight Lieutenant Fairweather has been on a medical transport all night.'

Sonya stared at the young man with his arm in a sling, abruptly wide awake. Flight Lieutenant Fairweather?

Then she realised what else the doctor had said.

Mrs Thorpe.

The children at the orphanage sometimes made that mistake, calling her Mrs instead of Miss. But never Dr Lewis.

She met his eyes, intrigued, and then opened the door wider. 'Of course.' The two men came in, the doctor supporting Yvonne's husband. 'How wonderful to meet you, Flight Lieutenant Fairweather.'

'Likewise,' the weary-looking young man told her, a twinkle in his eye. 'But please, call me Patrick.' He allowed Dr Lewis to help him to the sofa, collapsing there with a sigh. 'Thanks, old chap. Damn good of you, all this. But I'll be all right now.'

'Don't forget, I need to see you for a proper examination later today,' Dr Lewis told him, and the two men shook hands. 'Between three and five.'

'I'll be there, Doc.' The young man saluted. 'Scouts' honour.'

With a nod to Sonya, the doctor went back down the stairs, leaving her and the young man studying each other in silence.

'I'd better open the curtains,' Sonya said huskily, 'and then I'll wake Yvonne. She'll be thrilled to see you.'

'Good God, no, let sleeping wives lie. It's still infernally early. Besides, you and I ought to have a chat first, if you don't hate the idea. Get to know each other. Mother-in-law to son-in-law, like.' Patrick grinned at her surprise. 'I could murder a cup of tea, by the way.'

Astonished but flattered too, Sonya hurried off to make them both a pot of tea and buttered him two slices of bread to go with it, for she was sure he must be starving if he'd been on a medical transport all night. Patrick appeared to be sleeping when she got back but opened his eyes as she tried to tiptoe away, and pushed himself into a sitting position.

'Come and sit with me.' His gaze found the bread and butter. 'Oh, I say. You brought some grub too. Top marks, Ma.' He looked up as she sucked in a breath, and smiled again. 'You don't mind if I call you Ma, do you?'

'N-No,' she stammered, and sank down opposite him, busying herself by pouring the tea and passing him his plate of bread and butter.

'Ta, Ma,' he said informally, and demolished the two slices so rapidly she began to wish she'd doubled his ration. 'Good stuff.'

'However,' she said faintly, 'I do need to make one thing plain. Dr Lewis called me Mrs Thorpe, but in fact I have never been married. I am *Miss* Thorpe.' She searched his face for signs of disapproval, but he continued to smile. 'I felt it important to say that.'

'Get it off your chest?' He nodded. 'Quite right. Though you've no need to worry. Yvonne told me all about herself when we first met, how she was put up for adoption as a baby, and so forth. As for the rest, my mother wrote to me in hospital in London, letting me know where my wife was living … and why.' He gave a dry laugh. 'Loves to stir the muck, my mother. Unfortunately for her, I couldn't care less who begat whom, and all that. Not my cup of tea.'

Patrick scooped up his cup and saucer and took a quick slurp, nodding at her over the brim. 'Unlike this, which is excellent. I've been suffering from hospital char for days now. Like ditch water, only less flavour.' He grinned. 'This is perfect.'

She felt quite emotional, her pulse fluttering as she took in what her son-in-law – if she could call him that – had said. He was not judging her for that early mistake in falling pregnant as an unmarried woman, nor for having given in to her parents and allowing them to take Yvonne away from her as a newborn. She got the impression this was an open, friendly young man who never judged anyone. The fact that her daughter had chosen such a marvellous life partner – and such a brave man too – made her heart glad.

'Thank you,' she said, and sipped her own tea. 'You said you wanted to talk. Was it about something in particular?'

His eyes met hers keenly. 'I wondered if you wouldn't mind my staying on here a while. I know Yvonne and Walter came to you for a summer visit, rather than as permanent fixtures. But the thing is, my mother told me in her letter that she doesn't get on much with little Walter. And she wants me to "take him in hand", she says. Tell him what's what. Or she won't have us back to live with her.'

'Oh dear.'

'Problem is, I don't mind Walter kicking off now and then. Shows what he's made of. Not that I'd stand for him being rude. But a little chap like him needs to run about and make a bit of noise. Can't be forever minding his p's and q's, if you see what I mean.'

'So you want to stay here a while longer until you've explained that to your mother?'

'Wouldn't do any good. We were always having bust-ups over Walter, even before I packed my kit bag and went off to war. No, I was wondering… Since rent in Truro is a little beyond my pocket at the moment, would it be possible for us to live here instead?'

'Here?' Sonya stared at him, astonished. 'But for how long?'

'For as long as you'll have us.'

She put her hands to her cheeks. 'Oh my.' It was hard to think, especially still being in her dressing gown and slippers. She felt unprepared for such an important conversation. 'I don't see why not, except that it might be a bit cramped with four of us here.'

'Oh, we can squeeze in.'

'Well,' she said dubiously, 'I'll need to think about it. And write for permission from Lady Symmonds, of course.'

'Oh yes… Not your gaff, is it?' Patrick pulled a face. 'My mother did mention that. Yes, her ladyship will need to be asked. But you don't positively hate the idea?'

'Not at all. In fact, it sounds fun.' She smiled at him shyly. 'And Walter does seem to prefer living here rather than in Truro.'

He opened his mouth to say something, but the creak of the bedroom door brought him round in a flash.

Then he was struggling to his feet, a light in his eyes. 'Yvonne, darling… I say, I have missed you.'

Her daughter, barefoot and in her nightgown, ran forward to embrace her husband, tears in her eyes. 'Oh, my love… When did you arrive?' But he chose to kiss her ruthlessly rather than answer that question, and Sonya hurriedly put down her teacup, beginning to tiptoe away when Patrick abruptly released his wife again, and Yvonne looked round at her with flushed cheeks.

'I'm so sorry, Mother. What must you think of us?' Yvonne tidied her hair and nightgown, clearly embarrassed. 'I'd better get Walter up. He'll want to see his daddy.' But she clung on to Patrick's hand, not moving. 'It's so wonderful to have you home. Did your mother give you the news?'

'What news?'

Yvonne looked torn. 'Darling, did you receive a letter from me just before your plane went down? I wrote that I might be in an interesting condition but wasn't sure.'

'Ah,' Patrick said, with a big grin, 'so that's what my mother was trying to hint at in her letter, though she tied herself in knots trying not to be indelicate. I did get that letter, yes.' He gave her a kiss. 'Couldn't be happier. Well done, old girl.'

'Thank you, but…' Yvonne bit her lip.

His brows rose. 'Made a mistake? No bun in the oven?'

'Oh, you do say the most awful things.' Yvonne rolled her eyes. 'It may be two buns, in fact. Not one.'

He stared. 'Good God.'

'I couldn't help it.'

'I should imagine not.' He laughed, looking stunned. 'Blow me! Twins!'

'Oh, but your poor arm…' Yvonne finally seemed to notice his sling, appalled. 'How is it, darling? Are you in pain?'

'Not too bad,' he said cheerfully.

'Whatever made you escape the POW camp, though?' His wife sounded faintly accusing. 'You could have been killed.'

'Yes, sorry about that, but it's a chap's duty to escape. Got to give the enemy as much trouble as possible, don't you know?'

'No, I don't know.'

'Listen,' Sonya interrupted them firmly, 'since we're all awake now, we really ought to make ourselves presentable and go down to breakfast.' She glanced at the clock. 'The first sitting is seven o'clock. If we hurry, we should just make that. And then I'll take Walter for a nice morning walk along the cliffs,' she added with an indulgent smile, 'so you two can have a little time alone together.'

'I say, Ma, what an excellent notion,' Patrick said, winking at his wife.

At that moment, Walter stumbled out of the bedroom in his pyjamas, rubbing his eyes and demanding in a high-pitched voice to know why people were talking so loudly they'd woken him up.

He took one astonished look at his father, standing there with his good arm about Yvonne's waist, and hurtled shrieking towards him, suddenly wide awake.

'Daddy, Daddy, you're home!'

* * *

305

The canteen was buzzing with excited speculation when Patrick sauntered in with Yvonne and Walter in tow, all three as Sonya's guests. Several people turned to stare, and Sonya found herself nodding to her orphanage co-worker, Teresa, at the next table, who was tucking in to her own breakfast while watching them curiously. Teresa muttered a hello in return, but she had eyes for nobody but Patrick. The sling must make him stand out, Sonya decided, though he was also a handsome young man and rather eye-catching.

They all sat together at a table near the serving hatch, and when Mrs Penhallow and Piotr came out with an array of cutlery, teacups and pots, insisting that *they* didn't need to queue up for breakfast, Flight Lieutenant Fairweather soon introduced himself and even bandied a few words in Polish with the cook's young assistant. Mrs Penhallow cried out and clapped her hands, suitably impressed by this linguistic feat, and left Piotr to wipe down their table properly while she fetched their breakfast.

'I picked up a smattering of Polish in the POW camp,' Patrick explained to his bewildered wife. 'How d'you do, pass the salt, and all that.' His gaze fell on Walter, who was trying to saw off one of his shirt buttons with his breakfast knife. 'Here, that's enough of that, young rascal,' he instructed his son, who obediently stopped and put his knife down. 'Your poor mother's got enough to do without sewing your buttons back on, so leave 'em alone, there's a good lad.'

Sonya was aware of Teresa still listening to every word that was being said. No doubt her co-worker would have endless questions about the new arrival when Sonya went over to the orphanage later to start her shift. Thankfully, given their early start and her promise to take Walter for a long walk, she was not due at work until gone three o'clock that day, when she would be in charge of occupying the younger children after they had returned from school. She had a singing lesson lined up for that afternoon, and was rather looking forward to it, as she enjoyed singing and playing the piano.

Yvonne said rapturously, 'I'm so happy you're back, darling. Though I hope this doesn't mean we'll have to move out and get our own place. Walter's awfully fond of Granny St Ives,' she said, adding with a shy smile, 'as am I. We've had the happiest time here.'

'Don't upset yourself, my dear,' her husband said nonchalantly. 'Can't afford our own digs anyway, and your mother's agreed to put us up for the time being. If her ladyship don't object.'

'Oh, how marvellous,' Yvonne cried, and reached across the table to squeeze Sonya's hand. 'Thank you so much.' But she bit her lip. 'Though Walter will have to be on his best behaviour from now on.' Yvonne leant across the table to her husband. 'I'm afraid he's been a bit naughty in your absence. And whenever we tell him off, he pays no attention to me or his grandmother.'

'What's that?' His father shook his head at the boy in disapproval. 'You must always mind your mother, Walter. Yes, and your grandma too.'

Cook overheard this, having just come bustling back from the kitchen with a trayful of breakfast plates. 'His grandma? Is she staying with you as well, Miss Thorpe?' Mrs Penhallow asked, placing a hot plate in front of her, containing a fried egg, some black pudding, a slice of bacon, and a sliver of bread smeared thinly with butter. 'But that would make five of you in Lady Symmonds' apartment. Must be quite crowded up there.'

There was an awkward silence.

Sonya's cheeks were aflame and she could almost feel Teresa's inquisitive gaze on the back of her neck. She wished she could sink beneath the bench table and never be heard of again. But the cat was well and truly out of the bag now, and the thought of further half-truths and wary omissions had become anathema to her.

With more composure than she felt inside, Sonya picked up her knife and fork, studying her breakfast without looking up at them. 'I am the boy's grandmother, Cook.' Her heart was thudding and her lips felt oddly numb, yet somehow, she managed to add, 'Mrs Fairweather is my daughter, you see. I'm sorry I didn't make that clear before.'

To her astonishment, the sky did not fall at this shocking revelation. Now was there any outcry or censorious tut-tutting as she had expected.

'That explains it, then,' Mrs Penhallow said comfortably, and nodded to them all. 'Enjoy your food.' And, with a cheerful wave to Walter, Cook bustled back into the kitchen, followed by her assistant.

Sonya glanced towards Teresa, who had just finished eating and risen to leave the canteen. Sonya tensed, braced for some sharp remark based on what she must have over-heard. But her co-worker surprised her too.

'You kept that quiet,' Teresa said, bending towards her, her face alive with curiosity. 'A grandmother, Sonya? You must tell me all about it later.'

When the other woman had gone, Yvonne gave Sonya

a glowing look. 'Oh, well done. That was so brave, Mother,' she whispered.

'Yes, it was rather,' she agreed with a self-conscious smile. 'Goodness, whoever would have thought it?'

Sonya took a deep breath, let it out slowly, and then, with a sudden return of her appetite, applied herself to eating her breakfast.

As she walked the gusty cliff-path with Walter, looking out across the white-flecked waves of Carbis Bay, Sonya gripped her hat firmly so it wouldn't blow away and found herself smiling for no particular reason. She watched Walter skip along through the long grasses and called out occasionally to remind him not to stray from the safety of the path, all the while trying to pinpoint the source of her unexpected joy.

Finally, it struck her. She was quite simply *happy* with her life, that was all. She had been reunited with her grown-up daughter at last, and had even been welcomed into Yvonne's life, something she had never imagined would be possible. Her son-in-law was a generous and amusing young man who already held her in casual affection, as though they had known each other for years. And Walter... Well, dear little Walter might have given her a tidy helping of anguish and heartbreak so far, but she loved him very much. Besides, he was only a small child, and it was clear the boy heeded his father at least, which was promising.

Nonetheless, a tiny quiver of fear still pierced her heart as she waved to Walter, marching just ahead of her along the cliff-path.

Flight Lieutenant Fairweather had asked if they could stay here in St Ives indefinitely. But although Babs was a kind-hearted soul, her ladyship might at any point wish to return to Cornwall and take up residence there again. Indeed, she very much feared Lady Symmonds would be obliged to say no. There were limits to hospitality, after all, and giving up one's home to people who were complete strangers had to be one of them.

Walter came running back with a fistful of damp, white-flowered sea campion. 'For you, Grandma,' he cried, holding them up to her. 'Daddy says gentlemen must give flowers to their favourite ladies, and you're my favourite lady.' He paused. 'Asides Mummy, course.'

'Oh, my dear...' Sonya's eyes filled with tears. The blue sky blurred as she smiled down at him. 'We shouldn't pick wild flowers; they always look so much lovelier where they grow. But thank you, my darling boy.'

The sight and scent of those humble white flowers, mingled with a few pinkish unopened buds, gave her new resolve. She would write at once, explaining everything to Lady Symmonds, and throw herself on her ladyship's mercy. And if it proved impossible for them all to live together in the apartment at St Ives, then she would take a bold step, leave Symmonds Hall, and suggest they take a house together as a family.

The hall had been her home since Yvonne's birth and it would be a hellish wrench to leave it now. But better that than lose contact with her new and much beloved family.

CHAPTER TWENTY-NINE

Lily's little cottage felt so empty since her dad had left Cornwall, going as quietly and discreetly as he had arrived. But his unexpected visit had left her much to think about, not least her marriage. A few days after he'd gone, she came home at dawn after attending a home birth with Bertha as her supervisor, feeling weary and downcast. The woman they'd been helping was a farmer's daughter, a young wife whose husband was away with the Duke of Cornwall's Light Infantry. Christina's labour had been long and gruelling, and this being her first baby, she had also needed a great deal of support and encouragement. Her baby boy had been a healthy seven-pounder, however, and his mother had cried for joy when it was all over, nursing him in her arms after being shown how to get him to latch on.

'Thank you,' Christina had sobbed, laughing and crying at the same time. 'Isn't he just perfect? Look at those big ears though, poor love… Just like his dad!'

Lily smiled, remembering that special moment. But inside she was feeling quite down. On marrying Tristan, she had hoped for her own baby, even if they might have to wait until the war was over before making that decision. But it was clearly never meant to be, and the prospect of a life spent delivering other people's babies without ever once holding her own newborn in her arms hit her hard.

Letting herself into the cottage, Lily crept upstairs in the soft grey light, splashed herself with cold water after her exhausting night's work, and changed into a clean nightie.

Then she slipped into bed beside Tristan, trying not to wake him.

To her surprise, however, her husband turned at once to face her, his eyes open. 'Good morning,' he said quietly.

'I'm sorry, did I wake you?' Lily asked.

'No, I've hardly slept all night.' Tristan was looking moody. He brushed a finger along her cheek, watching her. 'I've been thinking...'

'Sounds ominous,' she joked, her nerves jumping at his intent expression and the unaccustomed contact between them.

But he didn't smile. 'I haven't been the best of husbands to you, Lily.' He ran a hand through his messy ginger curls. 'I thought I had it all worked out. But some of the things your dad said... I see now I've made a bit of an ass of myself.'

Lily held her breath, staring at him.

'I never told you how I got these burns,' he went on awkwardly. 'There's a reason for that. Your father's a persistent man, I'll give him that. He got the truth out of me before he left, and what he said made me realise I need to come clean about it to you too.'

312

'Go on,' she whispered.

'I wasn't injured in action,' he admitted, a bitter note in his voice. She was surprised but tried not to show it, wanting to hear the whole story. 'Quite the opposite, in fact.' He gave a groan under his breath and rolled onto his back, staring up at the whitewashed ceiling of their little bedroom. 'I was on duty with another chap, guarding a chemical store. Only it was freezing that night, so we brought a stove in and used it to keep warm, directly against orders.'

'Oh no!' Lily gasped, already able to guess what he was about to say.

He nodded slowly. 'I knocked the stove over. There was a huge explosion and I was thrown backwards and saw the other chap running to get help… To be honest, I don't remember much else from that night. I woke up in a hospital bed a day or so later, in excruciating pain and swathed in bandages, only to be told the war was over for me and I was being sent home to recuperate.' He turned to her again, his intent gaze fixed on her face as though trying to gauge her reaction. 'When I got back to Cornwall, I was too embarrassed to admit what had happened. So, I let everyone go on thinking I'd been burnt doing my duty. That I was a hero. Not an idiot.'

She had suspected it must be something like that, for he had always refused to talk about his burns in any detail. But if he thought she would now reject him just for that one silly decision, he was plain wrong.

'Tristan, love,' she began tentatively, 'everyone makes mistakes…' But he wasn't listening to her.

'I'll understand if you never want to speak to me again,' he said with evident difficulty, his face flushed.

'It would be a bit difficult never to speak to you again,' she pointed out, trying to keep her tone light, 'given that we're married.'

'But you married me under false pretences. I lied to you, and I know it. You thought I was a hero.'

'You didn't lie. You just kept what happened to yourself.'

He grimaced. 'I know you're only trying to make me feel better. But I don't deserve that. Or you.'

She shook her head and smiled, daring to touch his face as he had touched hers. 'You're still a hero to me. Goodness, Tristan, the way you've coped with the pain of those awful burns, and your bad leg... That's nothing short of heroic. And I love you for it.'

Tristan groaned. 'Lily, how can you love *this*?' He gestured to himself. 'The burns may have healed but I've never let you see the full extent of the scars they left behind. My leg and hip... They're not a pretty sight.' He groaned. 'I can't inflict that on you.'

'For goodness' sake, I'm a nurse. I've looked after men with worse burns than yours. It wouldn't be anything I haven't seen before.'

'I know, but ... I so wanted to be whole and hale for you. To be the man you remembered.'

'You're my husband,' she reminded him gently. 'We swore an oath to stick with each other, whatever happens. For better or worse, in sickness and in health, remember?'

His gaze remained locked to hers and he said nothing.

Slowly, fearing another humiliating rejection, Lily leant forward and put her lips against his.

He did not respond at first, lying still against her. Then, with a little hesitation, he kissed her back. Her heart jerked and accelerated, all the weariness of the long night abruptly falling away.

'Oh, Tristan...'

At last, his arms came around her, strong and loving, and she sighed with joy, feeling that her married life was finally about to begin.

Lily glanced up as the door opened and smiled, seeing her friend Rose on the threshold, looking smart in a green woollen skirt suit and cream blouse that perfectly complemented her bold red hair. Rose's pregnancy was finally beginning to show, and it was with some relief that Lily noted her face was beginning to fill out after that initial period of gauntness, and her colour was so much better than the last time she'd visited the clinic.

'Rose, how lovely to see you again.' Lily drew out a chair and invited her friend to sit. 'You look well. How are you feeling these days?'

Rose laced her fingers together in her lap, her face glowing with health. 'Much better,' she admitted, 'and it's all down to you.'

Lily was surprised. 'Me?'

Her friend nodded, saying emphatically, 'Your advice was spot-on. The sickness has gone and I feel marvellous. In fact, I have more energy now than I did before I fell pregnant.' She pulled a face. 'Though Lewis insists I mustn't overdo it.'

'He's quite right,' Lily said, turning to scribble down some notes in her report book. 'I'm thrilled my advice was helpful and that horrid sickness is a thing of the past. And I know how tempting it is to want to get back to normal after you've had to take everything easy for a few months. But you can't risk a relapse.'

Rose was nodding. 'That's exactly what Lewis has been telling me.' She grinned self-consciously. 'I got up this morning, saw the boys off to school, washed all the pots and pans from last night's supper, and then walked up to the orphanage and began stripping beds, before I really knew what I was doing. Teresa caught me in the act and told me off. I have to admit, I did feel rather exhausted afterwards. But a spot of fried liver for lunch soon put me right.'

Lily laughed. 'You're a very busy lady. I don't blame you at all for wanting to get on with things. But don't go exhausting yourself. I'm glad you're taking note of the diet sheet I gave you though. It's important to keep eating properly and resting, so your iron levels aren't depleted.' She stood. 'Come on, hop up on the table and I'll examine you. Let's see what's going on with this baby of yours.'

The examination went well, and Lily was soon able to reassure Rose that the pregnancy was progressing normally. 'Have you decided on any names?'

Rose began to rattle off a list of possible names, laughing as she explained each one, but they were interrupted by the wail of a siren going off in the town.

'Oh no.' Lily groaned, putting a hand to her forehead. 'That's the third time this bloomin' week. When will those ruddy Germans stop targeting the Cornish coast?'

Slipping her jacket back on and scooping up her handbag, Rose shook her head. Her expression was serious. 'Maddening, isn't it? But at least we haven't had any serious bombings... So far, anyway.'

'Yes, we mustn't tempt fate.'

They hurried out of the clinic and followed the rest of the crowd down towards the hospital shelter. It was a warm midsummer's afternoon and everyone was grumpy at the thought of spending an hour or two underground. Yet what could they do?

'I wonder how much longer this war is going to drag on?' Lily muttered to Rose as they linked arms, carefully navigating the steep steps into the shelter. 'I'm so sick of ducking into a shelter every five minutes. I shouldn't grumble though, you're right. Gawd knows I'm glad to be out of London. That was hell – air raids every night, and even in the day too. But I can't understand what the Germans are hoping to achieve, dropping bombs on a quiet seaside town like this or like Penzance. It doesn't make any sense.'

'Lewis says the enemy are softening us up.'

Lily was perplexed. 'Softening us up?' she echoed, frowning. 'Whatever for?'

'For an invasion, of course.'

'Bleedin' hell! You're not serious, Rose? I mean, there's been some talk… But I've never really believed it.' Lily felt cold inside at the thought of jack-booted Germans landing here in quiet, rural Cornwall, where so many people were simple farmers and fishermen, ill-prepared to repel an invasion force. She recalled her father discussing the possibility and wondered if he knew of plans for the enemy to land on Cornish shores. 'I've read all those awful government leaflets, of course. What to do in the event of an invasion… But pitchforks and garden spades? They won't do much against the bloomin' Hun, not when they have guns and grenades.'

317

They found a place to sit together in the hospital shelter and Lily nodded to the duty midwife, Katie, who was softly talking a lady in the early stages of labour through her contractions. Luckily, the patient was an experienced mum of three who wasn't too fazed by having to interrupt her labour by nipping down into the shelter for an hour or so. All the same, it wasn't ideal, and Lily kept a watchful eye on her colleague, aware that she might need to offer her help as well if the air raid went on too long.

'I know,' Rose agreed, knitting her fingers together in front of her swollen belly. 'Though I suppose any weapon would do in a pinch. Better than not fighting at all, just rolling over and handing them our country.' Her voice shook a little as she added, 'It doesn't bear thinking about, does it? Having Germans running the place.'

Lily glanced at Rose, worried by the note of strain in her voice. She realised too late that she ought to have been more comforting, not dwelled on the frightening idea of invasion. Rose was, after all, her patient as well as her friend.

'Oh, I'm sure it won't come to that. Our boys will soon have the enemy on the run, you see if they don't. In fact, I expect this war will be won and over long before your baby is even born.'

'Of course it will.'

Rose laughed, nodding, though it was obvious she was not convinced. Still, the two of them played along with the joke, because it was either that or give in to their fears, Lily thought, struggling to contain her own little flurry of panic.

German soldiers landing on these remote shores or

dropping out of the blue Cornish sky on parachutes, killing and maiming, and eventually taking over the whole country? It didn't bear thinking about. Lily pushed those fears aside and thought instead of her renewed happiness with Tristan, how they had finally begun to relate to each other as husband and wife, not virtual strangers, and the joy her father's surprise visit had brought them all.

When worrying brought only misery, it was better to stay optimistic and keep smiling, she thought.

The clinic was incredibly busy for the next few weeks and it was rare that Lily had much time to herself. But whenever she came home to the cottage, she would find Tristan waiting for her, a smile on his face and occasionally a simple meal warming on the stove. When she queried where he'd learned to cook, Tristan looked embarrassed and explained that his aunt Sarah had taught him a few tricks after her stroke, so he could help out in the kitchen. It gave her such joy to thank him for his efforts and see him smile because she knew how much it irked him, stuck at home while she was out at work.

One day, after a quick visit to Mrs Fairweather up at Symmonds Hall, who'd been experiencing back pain with her pregnancy, she walked into the cottage kitchen to find Tristan reading a letter from his sister. Demelza was still in London with her husband Robert but they had high hopes of being stationed abroad together very soon. His sister had finished her training with the Ambulance Service but had not yet been assigned a position overseas, while Robert himself was working as an ambulance driver for London's busiest hospitals.

London hadn't suffered as much bombing this past year, the Germans having stepped up their bombing of smaller towns and the coast instead. Still, the pace of life in the capital sounded hectic and Lily was glad to be out of it. She didn't miss Dagenham anymore, though she often thought of her old friends there and wondered what had become of them. But she had a new life here with her beloved Tristan, and she wouldn't give it up for all the tea in China.

'I know I shouldn't worry about Demelza,' Tristan admitted, a frown on his face, 'but I can't help it. If my sister goes abroad with the Ambulance Service, who knows what might happen to her?'

'But it's what Demelza wants to do.' Lily put the kettle on for a nice brew, and then sat down next to him. 'Besides, with the Germans bombing Cornwall now, even in the countryside, any of us could die at any moment. It makes me cry sometimes to think of it. The unfairness of it all.' She folded her hands in her lap, sighing. 'But what can we do except hope for the best and carry on?'

Slowly, he re-read his sister's letter and then replaced it in the envelope, setting it aside. 'You're right, of course. It's Demelza's life and she's free to do whatever she wants. But she'll always be my sister, and I'll always worry about her. That's just the way things are.' He lifted Lily's hand and kissed it, his gaze warm on her face. 'Just like I worry about you. How are you, darling? You've been so busy lately. You come home late, too exhausted to do much apart from eat and sleep, and then have to rush off again early the next morning. You need a few days off, that's what I think.'

'A holiday, you mean?' Lily laughed at the idea, incredulous. 'We don't have enough midwifery staff in the area as it is.'

'Well, it was only a thought.' He hesitated. 'The thing is, I've got some work myself. So I may not be able to help with supper and housework as much as I've been doing lately.'

'You've got a job?' She stared, unable to believe her ears.

He nodded, looking flushed.

Lily didn't know whether to be pleased or concerned. 'Are you well enough to be working?' she asked, perplexed, and then could have bitten her tongue out when she saw the downcast look in his eyes. 'I mean… With your bad leg, and all, are you really up to taking on a job?'

'It's a volunteer position. With the Fire Service.'

'The Fire Service? But that's really dangerous. Tell me you're not serious.' When his face hardened and he looked away, Lily realised she had made another mistake. 'Oh, my bloomin' tongue … I'm sorry. Look, tell me all about it. What do you have to do?'

'To be honest, it's mainly a desk job. Administration, paperwork, that kind of thing. But once I get more mobile, they've told me I'll be able to join in with attendances at fires and checking premises for compliance to fire safety regulations.'

Her tensed shoulders relaxed and Lily smiled with relief. She'd had a vision of him rushing into burning buildings and putting out fires.

'That doesn't sound too strenuous.'

'It's still important work.' He sounded defensive.

'Of course it is. Your sister was doing similar work in Penzance before she married Robert, wasn't she?' She watched him, anxious she had spoiled their happiness by making him feel awkward about his bad leg again. Hurriedly, she added, 'Though that was the Fire Guard Unit, and mostly women volunteers. Not the same thing.'

To her relief, however, Tristan didn't seem annoyed. 'Demelza was very brave, choosing to leave home and work for the Fire Guard Unit against my father's wishes. I suppose it's not surprising she now wants to serve her country abroad, even if that means putting herself in danger again. If I was healthy...' He grimaced. 'But the least I can do, having put myself out of the war by being such a chump, is to help out around St Ives. And they desperately need new volunteers for the Fire Service.'

'Then I'm very happy for you.' Lily jumped up and made the tea, and then set about frying some mackerel for their supper. But all the while she was aware of his gaze steady on her back. At last, she turned with a concerned smile. 'I didn't mean to suggest you couldn't do the job, love. I know you're getting stronger every day.'

'I am,' Tristan agreed, and to her surprise he got up and came towards her without his stick, wrapping his arms about her waist and lifting her bodily off the floor. When she shrieked with astonished laughter, he growled, 'Does this look weak to you?'

'No, it certainly doesn't,' she exclaimed, still laughing, and waved her feet in the air. 'Put me down, you crazy man!' They were both laughing by then. 'Doesn't it hurt, lifting me like that?'

'Not at all.' Gently, Tristan set her down again, his arms

still about her. He was smiling broadly, as though pleased with himself. 'Still think I can't do the job?'

'You've been keeping secrets from me, Tris, that's what I think.'

'I wanted to surprise you.'

'You managed that, all right.' Reaching up on tiptoe, Lily kissed her husband. 'You do whatever you think is right. Whatever happens, I love you very much, I hope you know that.'

'I do … and I'm beginning to realise just what a lucky man I am,' he agreed, and bent his head to kiss her.

Lily closed her eyes and sighed with pleasure.

A few minutes later, the smell of burning fish made her shriek and pull away. 'The mackerel will be ruined!'

'Damn the mackerel.' But he turned with a laugh to help her prepare supper by setting out the plates and buttering the bread, his expression indulgent. 'I love you too, Lily Minear.'

CHAPTER THIRTY

'They're here,' Mary said, and turned from the front window, letting the net curtain drop. 'Too late to change your mind now,' she told her mother.

'Who says I'm going to change my mind?' Rita stood in an unhurried fashion to check her reflection in the mirror over the mantelpiece. 'It was the only polite thing to do, asking our prospective in-laws over for dinner.' She patted her hair, tweaking one stray lock back into position. 'Though I still say Cynthia Jeffries is gutter trash.'

'Mum, please…'

'Rita?' A worried look crossed her dad's face as he lowered the newspaper he'd been reading and stared at his wife. 'I hope you don't plan on causing a scene. Mrs Jeffries did help young Pip with his breathing during the air raid, remember? We should be very grateful to her.'

Rita said nothing but pursed her lips.

Mary said soothingly, 'I'm sure Mum will be the perfect hostess,' but privately she shared her dad's concerns.

A moment later, there was a knock at the front door.

Rita, who had been reapplying her lipstick, drew a sharp breath and nodded at her own reflection. 'That'll do.' She swept past Mary, who had moved to answer the door. 'Not so fast, my girl. I invited the Jeffries over so I should be the one to welcome them.'

Mary followed her mother out into the hall and stood waiting while Rita ushered their guests into the house. Cynthia Jeffries came first, impressive as ever in a knee-length blue dress with a coordinating powder-blue hat. Her husband Charles followed her in, carrying a lidded Pyrex dish and smiling uncertainly at Mary. Behind them both came Dick in shirt and tie, hands in his trouser pockets and a self-conscious grin on his face.

'Good evening, Mrs Stannard,' he murmured to her mother before tipping a wink at Mary. School had recently broken up for the summer holidays and they had not seen each other in some days. 'Evening, Mary,' he drawled, finally taking his hands out of his pockets. 'How are you? Looking a bit peaky, I'd say.'

'Don't you start,' she whispered, but took his arm and allowed him to press a kiss on her cheek. It wasn't as though their parents didn't know about the two of them, after all. All the same, she caught a vaguely shocked expression on her mother's face and a smirk from Charles Jeffries in passing.

'Peach crumble for dessert, Rita.' Charles offered Mary's mum the Pyrex dish, then added, with the painstaking air of a man who has been made to rehearse his lines, 'Our Cynthia makes a lovely peach crumble.'

'Mmm, I daresay. Marvellous the things one can do with tinned peaches these days.' On that withering note, Rita bore the dish away to the kitchen without waiting for an answer.

'In here, please,' Mary said, showing the Jeffries into the dining room where they all shook hands with her father, now standing by the mantelpiece.

Having said a few polite things to her father, Dick turned and whispered in Mary's ear, 'Perhaps we should hope for the air-raid siren to go off again.'

Mary stifled a giggle.

Her dad poured them all a small glass of sherry and fussed about with a damp tea towel after Charles Jeffries managed to spill his on the carpet.

'How have you been enjoying life at school?' Dick asked Mary softly while the others were engaged in conversation.

'Better than expected,' she admitted, looking up at him shyly. 'Thank you for persuading me to change from nursing. It was a bit daunting at first, all those pairs of eyes staring up at me so intently... But now I've got to know most of the kids, it's rather lovely.'

'I'm glad.' Dick's smiling eyes met hers, sending a warmth through her that made Mary wish they were alone together. 'I knew you'd be happier as a teacher.'

'I've a long way to go before my training is done and I can call myself a teacher. But yes, it's what I want to do with my life.' She paused, frowning. 'Though you know married women can't be teachers. So it's all rather moot, isn't it?'

'They've relaxed that rule for the war,' Dick said reassuringly. 'Don't worry about it.'

'And after the war ends?'

Dick shrugged. 'Maybe it will never be reinstated. I

mean, everything's changed these past few years. Once all the fighting's over, how can anyone go back to the way things were before the war?' He took a deep breath, a faraway look on his face as though contemplating that misty future time. 'Always assuming our side wins, of course. Which doesn't seem very likely at the moment, going off the news reports. And I daresay they don't even tell us the worst stuff.'

'Oh, don't.' Mary shivered.

Her mother came into the dining room with a frilly white apron fastened about her waist, bearing a plate of French toast. 'Please, sit,' she said with a grand air, gesturing to the dining table, which was beautifully set with cutlery, wine glasses, napkins, and a floral centrepiece. 'Harold, put the radio on, would you?'

Mary's dad hurried to do as instructed, soft music soon playing in the background while they took their seats. With Mary's help, Rita brought out the first course of cold ox tongue in jelly, daintily sliced and served on blue-and-white willow pattern side plates, a wedding present dinner service she was rightfully proud of.

'*Bon appétit*,' Rita remarked graciously, taking her place at the head of the table. 'Help yourselves to toast.'

'Well, this is all very nice,' Charles said, nodding in approval as he tasted the cold meat. 'Very good of you to invite us over, Rita.' Catching his wife's eye, he cleared his throat and changed the subject. 'Dick's told us so much about Mary. I'm glad he's chosen such a nice young lady to settle down with.'

'He's won first prize, getting my Mary,' Rita said tartly.

'*She's* won first prize getting *him*, you mean,' Cynthia

retorted indistinctly, speaking through a mouthful of jellied tongue.

'Rita,' Mary's father said warningly.

'Mrs Jeffries,' Mary said, hoping to distract the two women from their vendetta, 'Dick was telling me you breed collie dogs. That's fascinating. Do you have any puppies at the house right now?'

'Not yet, though Jess should be dropping her third litter in a few weeks' time.' Cynthia favoured her with a careful, sideways look. 'Interested in dogs, are you?'

She wasn't interested but nodded all the same, taking a slice of toast. 'Yes, though I know nothing about breeding them. It must be very hard work.'

'Oh, I'm not afraid of hard work,' Cynthia told her, her lips thinning in disdain as she caught a muffled snort from the other end of the dining table. Her head whipped round, and she stared at her old rival. 'Did you say something, Rita?'

To Mary's surprise her mother hesitated, and then said with unexpected restraint, 'Bit of food went down the wrong way, that's all.'

Glancing at her dad, Mary caught him nodding his approval at this response, and recalled how he had asked his wife to behave herself before the Jeffries arrived. Not that Mum usually took any notice of what Dad said, she thought. But this was a special occasion.

'Dearie me.' Cynthia raised thin, pencil-drawn eyebrows. 'You ought to chew your food more carefully. I knew a woman who died like that. Choked on her dinner. Nasty way to go.'

Hastily, Dick's father turned to Harold. 'Where's that

little boy you've been looking after, then? Evacuee, isn't he? We thought he'd be eating with us tonight.'

'Pip, you mean?' Harold looked relieved at being able to discuss a neutral topic. 'He had his tea early and went over to old Dr Lanyon's house for the evening. The doctor's taken in a couple of evacuee boys himself, and the lads get together to play chess. It's company for the old doctor too, I believe. He's retired, you see, and a widower. And his grandson Dr Lewis and his wife only live there part-time at the moment. So he's often on his own.'

'Where do they live the rest of the time, then?' Charles inquired.

'Up at Symmonds Hall, in the orphanage. I believe the young doctor's wife, Rose, runs the place now.' Her dad paused, glancing at Mary. 'Friend of yours, isn't she? Used to be a nurse at the convalescent home.'

'She was a Sister on the wards, yes. Sister Rose Gray.' Mary smiled, remembering those days with a sudden flood of nostalgia. 'She kept us all in line, I can tell you. Nobody dared cross Rose when she was on the warpath. Ol' Graysides, we called her. But she's become a real sweetie since she got married, especially now she...'

Too late, Mary realised how indiscreet she was being, and clammed up, returning to her food with a bent head. But sharp-eyed Cynthia Jeffries had got the point.

'In the family way, is she?' Dick's mother asked astutely. 'Well, why not? No point keeping the old doctor hanging about for a great-grandchild. Not with this blasted war on.'

'I'd prefer not to have language at my dinner table, thank

you,' Rita said stiffly, even though she often used the word 'blasted' herself – and worse – especially when discussing politics at mealtimes.

'You don't want *language*, Rita?' Cynthia was mocking her gently. 'That's going to be tricky. What if I need someone to pass me the salt? Should I descend into dumb show, perhaps?' She demonstrated with a series of exaggerated gestures, pointing at the salt cellar and miming sprinkling salt over her food.

Rita breathed through her nostrils, audibly. 'You know perfectly well what I meant, Cynthia. *Bad* language.'

'Ladies, please,' Charles Jeffries said uneasily.

'I'd like to set a date for me and Mary to tie the knot,' Dick said calmly into the silence that followed his dad's reprimand. 'Any preferences?'

Mary stared at him in amazement, then looked at her parents, both frozen like rabbits in headlights. Well, she thought, that had certainly worked to change the subject. Though it wasn't a topic they would all agree on. Nor did she even know the answer herself.

She blushed as all eyes turned to her. 'Don't ask me. I'm happy to fall in with everyone else. Though I thought we were waiting.'

'Are we?' Dick looked surprised now.

'Because of the war. And … you know … women having to stop teaching once they're married.' She thought back over the brief conversation they had had earlier and wondered if maybe she hadn't made her feelings plain. 'You remember.'

'I thought we agreed it didn't matter.' Dick turned to her father, explaining, 'While so many men are away, most school boards are happy to take on women teachers instead, married or not.'

'Only while the war's on,' she pointed out, a little sharply. 'Then we'll all be sent back to the kitchen, same as last time.'

'That's right,' Rita muttered.

'Mary's got a point there.' Cynthia shot her son a speaking glance. 'Marriage is all well and good, Dick. And I'd like to see you happy and settled, with a family of your own. But, let's face it, getting wed is not always what's best for a woman. Not if she wants a career.'

'A career?' Harold turned to Mary, clearly perplexed. 'Is that what you want, love? A career in teaching? Not … not to get married?' He put down his knife and fork, his face troubled. 'I'll always back you, Mary, you know that. But I didn't realise you were one of them.'

'One of them?' Mary repeated, baffled.

'Women campaigners…' he mumbled, catching his wife's eye and tailing off. 'Well, anyway, it's up to you, love.'

'Doesn't sound like it,' Mary said, and crunched on her toast, abruptly depressed.

'We'll talk about it later,' Dick said lightly, but she could see her remarks had rattled him.

Guiltily, Mary took a sip of her sherry, so far untouched, and wished she knew what to do for the best. She wanted to marry Dick. He made her happy, no mistake about it, and she was convinced she'd be even happier once they were man and wife.

But she also wanted to carry on training to be a teacher, in the hope that she could make a career out of it. And if the war were to end next week – which would be amazing, but unlikely – she knew, as did all women, that as soon as the men were back in their jobs, the women who'd been doing that work so proudly and with such determination during the war years would be sent back to their homes to become housewives and mothers again. And in teaching, any woman who'd had the temerity to get married would be dismissed, and a man put in her place.

Still, she did rather love Dick Jeffries, and she didn't want to end up a starchy old maid like Matron.

It was a quandary, all right.

But at least the subject of a possible wedding had brought her mother and Cynthia together. She realised with a start that the two women had been discussing the perks of marriage compared to the disadvantages for young women today for some minutes while her own brain had been occupied elsewhere.

'I'd better clear these plates away and fetch out the meat and potato patties,' her mother said, getting up.

Unbidden, Cynthia rose too, carrying her own plate and her husband's. 'I'll join you if I may. Meat and potato patties? I heard a recipe for them on that radio cookery show the other morning. *The Kitchen Front*, that's it. Though their recipes are a bit hit-or-miss.'

'Yes,' Rita agreed, 'but this one seems to have turned out all right. Though it's made with mutton, not beef.'

'Oh well, beggars can't be choosers.'

'They'll be telling us to eat shoe leather next,' Rita said, her mouth downturned.

'Shoe leather?' Cynthia pulled a face. 'We'll be lucky to get it.'

The two women left the room still debating the merits

of the recipes on the BBC and the current crisis in food rationing.

By the end of the meal, it was clear that a tentative truce had once more been achieved between their mothers, especially when Pip returned from chess and both women were able to coo over him to their hearts' content.

Mary and Dick offered to do the washing up, using that as an excuse to leave their parents chatting and slip away to the kitchen where they could talk without being overheard.

'I say,' he said as soon as they were alone together, 'did you mean that about not wanting to get married?'

'I'm afraid so, yes,' she agreed, beginning to stack plates for washing. Feeling awkward, Mary turned on the taps and stood waiting for the deep sink to fill with water. 'Are you horribly cross? I'm only worried what it would mean for my career if I got married.'

'Not cross, no,' he said at once, leaning against the draining board, his gaze steady on her face. 'Only I thought… Well, it doesn't matter. If you'd rather be engaged forever, I suppose that will have to do.'

Mary began to wash up, placing each dripping plate on the draining board for him to dry. 'To be honest, I don't want a forever engagement,' she admitted, 'but it does seem as though I'll be giving up my ambitions if we marry. And that doesn't strike me as fair. You won't have to give up being a teacher, for instance, once we're wed.'

'I see your point.' Dick had taken up a tea towel and was drying the wet plates and stacking them on the kitchen table. 'But wouldn't you like to start a family? We've never really discussed it, but I just assumed you'd be happy to have children.' He looked at her, uncertain. 'Was I wrong?'

Mary considered the question properly for the first time and realised something that shocked her. She didn't hate the idea of motherhood at all. In fact, she rather loved it. To be a housewife would be too awful for words, stuck at home, bored out of her mind, trying out recipes and mending the household linen. But to be a mother…

'I'd love to have children,' she admitted, turning to him with glowing cheeks. 'Gosh, a baby of our own.'

Dick grinned. 'Not so dreadful, after all?'

'I suppose not. And I can always carry on teaching as a married woman, at least until…' But she shook her head, realising the futility of trying to guess what would happen when, or even if, the war ended. 'Yes, all right, let's get married.' She smiled when he kissed her on the cheek. 'But you'd better let me break the news to Mum. Just in case she's awkward about it.'

'I can tell that Rita is going to be a formidable mother-in-law,' Dick remarked.

'I love my mum,' Mary said loyally. 'She's got me through some tough times, and I won't hear a word said against her, even if she can be a bit difficult on occasion.'

'Understood.'

'Besides, I could say the same about my own future mother-in-law,' she pointed out, reaching into the depths of the soapy water to fish out the cutlery. 'Cynthia's not exactly all sweetness and light, is she? Though I'll give your mum this… She raised a good man in you, Dick Jeffries.'

His eyes warmed and he gave a low chuckle. 'I'll tell my mother you said so. Preferably *before* she finds out we've set a date for the wedding.' And they both laughed.

CHAPTER THIRTY-ONE

St Ives, Cornwall, August 1943

There was a curious echoing emptiness to the apartment. Sonya stood by the window, looking down at the yard where the orphans were playing together in the sunshine. Yvonne, Walter and Patrick had taken the train to Truro to visit his parents. She herself had decided to stay behind, even though she did not have to work today, so she could tidy up. Her grandson had left his toys and jigsaw puzzles scattered about the place, and poor Yvonne had been feeling a little queasy lately, so had not been able to pick them all up as she normally would. It was really no trouble, Sonya told herself, turning to continue with her tidying up. The mundane chore steadied her nerves and took her mind off the future.

But once the apartment was neat again, she felt that frisson of unhappiness once more, and she knew why. She was afraid they might return from Truro to say they had changed their minds and wished to live with Patrick's parents again. There was more room for a family there, after all, and a garden for Walter to stomp around in. She had to prepare herself for that possibility, she decided, yet found herself drifting back to the window to look down into the yard again, subconsciously watching for the familiar figure of the postwoman.

It was some time since she had written to Babs in Scotland. Lady Symmonds was usually such an efficient communicator, rarely leaving a letter unanswered for more than a week or two, at most. Yet it had been longer than that since Sonya had written to ask for permission for her daughter and son-in-law to live together in the apartment, along with Walter, until such time as her ladyship might decide to return from Scotland.

Perhaps Babs had been offended by the impertinence of her request. Sonya could not quite believe that, yet she couldn't rule it out either. The absence of a reply was unsettling.

It was late summer now, and the Cornish weather had settled into a bright but breezy pattern, days coming and going in much the same way, with blue skies and ruffled seas. Sonya decided to go for a walk into St Ives rather than along the cliff path as usual. She felt restless and uncertain of her fate, and could not spend another minute indoors.

Fetching a light jacket and sturdy outdoor shoes, Sonya pinned her wide-brimmed summer hat to her hair so it would not blow away. But as she made her way down the narrow stairs to the yard, the door at the bottom opened and there was the postwoman, smiling and holding out a letter.

'Good afternoon, Miss Thorpe,' the postwoman said, looking her up and down. 'On your way out? I'm glad I caught you.'

Sonya took the letter, recognising the handwriting at once. It was from Lady Symmonds. Her heart thudding with sudden trepidation, she thanked the postwoman in a shaky voice and ran back up the steps with her letter.

In the privacy of the apartment, she fetched the letter opener and slit the envelope open. It was a single sheet with her ladyship's beautiful hand on both sides in tight writing. She read through it rapidly, a hand over her mouth, gasping every now and then.

My dearest Sonya,

Thank you for your latest letter. I'm sorry it's taken so long to reply. But there was a big decision to make, and now I have made it.

I'm afraid to say it looks as though I may never come back to Cornwall. I feel so guilty, writing that, for Symmonds Hall holds so many wonderful memories, as you know. Not simply memories of my late husband and son, but my darling grandson Francis too. I miss them all terribly, more and more each year that passes. But they are in the past and I must look to the future now. I am desperately happy here in Scotland with my dearest captain. The thought of leaving Donald is impossible, and being a proud Scotsman, he would never consent to live in St Ives, so that's that.

Consequently, I have instructed my solicitors to draw up an agreement, allowing you to live at Symmonds Hall for as long as you wish, and with whomever you wish, and that my heir must respect that arrangement after my death. This is in recognition of your long years of service to me, and also because we have been – and still remain, I trust – good friends.

By the way, I received notification from Mrs Lanyon this week that she is regretfully handing in her notice at the orphanage, which leaves me short a director. Could I possibly ask you to step into the role? I can think of nobody who could take her place so well as you. It will be paid work, of course. Please let me know if you are interested.

Thank you, my dearest Sonya, and may God bless you. I wept for joy when I read of your reunion with Yvonne, and wish you both all the happiness in the world. Family is all that matters, in the end.

Yours in deepest affection, Babs

It was some time before Sonya could properly take in the contents of her ladyship's letter. She read it through three or four times, and then left it on the table under a paperweight, and went out for her walk as planned, a little dazed.

She strode down the hill into St Ives, a handbag in the crook of her elbow, holding onto her hat at times, buffeted by gusts of wind. The sunshine lay bright on the Atlantic Ocean, and the town, with its whitewashed fishermen's cottages and its narrow, winding lanes, looked more beautiful than ever in that intense light that drew so many artists to the town.

Occasionally, she saw people she recognised and stopped to exchange a few words, smiling mechanically and replying, 'Yes, I'm very well, thank you', or asking 'How do you do?' before continuing on her way.

She popped into the library to change a book, and then into a café for a pot of tea and the wicked extravagance of a cream cake. After a spot of window shopping, and the possibly unwise purchase of yet another toy locomotive for Walter, who was spoiled rotten for toys already, Sonya made her way back up the hill.

For once, she barely noticed the steep climb, her heart swelling with joy as the familiar walls of Symmonds Hall loomed before her. Home, she found herself thinking fondly, and dwelt on the importance of that word. Home. The centrality of it to her life.

She had left her first home while still essentially a child, and come to live with Babs in Symmonds Hall, and had made that place her home. And now her ladyship had granted it to her for life. *Such an act of generosity,* she thought, and had to hold back a sob. If anyone had spoken to her at that moment, they might have found a gibbering idiot, eyes brimming with tears. Luckily, she encountered nobody, and even the orphans had gone inside for their tea by the time she crossed the yard and made her slow way up the steep steps to the apartment.

The orphans…

Yes, she would take up the role of director in Rose's absence. She had struggled a little with the extra-curricular lessons she had been asked to provide at the orphanage, but she understood paperwork and organisation. She might even be good at the job. She would write back to Babs as soon as possible and accept the offer. Her friend had been right to push her into seeking out her long-lost daughter, however uncomfortable it had felt in the beginning. With a little self-belief and gumption, everything had turned out for the best. Now it was time for Sonya to stop burying herself alive and start embracing life's possibilities, despite her shaky start as an unhappy adolescent.

She let herself into the apartment, and now the silence and the emptiness seemed marvellous and no longer disturbing. This was her home, Sonya kept thinking. She walked about, touching the furniture, looking out of the windows, removing her hat and hanging it carefully, deliberately, on the hatstand.

'Home sweet home,' she whispered to her reflection in the mirror, her cheeks suffused with pink from the long, windy climb up the hill. 'This is my place, and I belong here. For ever and ever.' And her reflection smiled back at her, approving.

Now she had only to hope that Yvonne would be happy to live here too, rather than in Truro with her in-laws.

Sonya picked up the letter from Babs and re-read it, smoothing out the folded sheet with a joyful hand. She had never been so happy in all of her life, she realised. Not merely for herself and her new family, but for dear Lady Symmonds too, whose own happiness was beyond doubt. She only hoped there would be a chance for her to visit her ladyship in Scotland, and perhaps take Yvonne and her husband with her, along with Walter and even the new twins too, once they had been born and were old enough to travel such a long distance, for she longed to introduce her family to Babs, who would surely be thrilled to see how her life had blossomed.

It was late by the time Sonya heard the door below open, and the weary tramp of feet up the stairs to the apartment. She hurried off the sofa, where she had been dozing in the soft glow of evening, and tidied herself.

The door opened and Patrick came in, with a sleeping Walter slung over his shoulder, fireman-style. Smiling, he put a finger to his lips and bore the child through to the bedroom.

Yvonne came after, a look of strain in her face as she removed her hat and jacket, and greeted Sonya with a perfunctory, 'Hello, sorry we're late back. Patrick's mother kept us talking for so long.' Rubbing her back, she slumped into an armchair. 'The train was so crowded, I was lucky to find a seat. Poor Patrick had to stand with Walter. And our carriage was too close to the engine. I got a smut in my eye.'

'I'm sorry to hear that. But some hot tea should soon set you up again. Have you eaten?'

'Yes, we took sandwiches to eat on the train. But tea would be lovely, thank you, Mother.' Her daughter got up again, crossing to the bathroom. 'I need to freshen up.'

Sonya hurried to make tea, full of her exciting news, but trying to contain it. What if they were horrified by the offer, after all? She would not know where to look…

When she returned with the tea tray, it was to find Yvonne lying down on the sofa, her eyes closed as though already asleep, and Patrick intent on a new hardback he must have bought in Truro. Hands trembling, Sonya

341

poured them all a cup of tea, and having set them on the coffee table, took a deep breath and announced, 'I have received a letter from Lady Symmonds in Scotland.'

Yvonne's eyes flew open and she struggled to sit up. 'Goodness me...' Her gaze searched Sonya's face almost anxiously.

Patrick noted his page number and closed the book, looking up at her with raised eyebrows. 'Well?' he asked.

Sonya fetched the letter and read it aloud to them. They listened in intent silence to every word, and afterwards Yvonne jumped up and came to hug her.

'Oh, Mother, that's wonderful news. Will you take the job?' When Sonya nodded, she looked ecstatic. 'And you will never again have to fear leaving Symmonds Hall. I'm so thankful.'

'Indeed, congratulations.' Also getting up, Patrick pumped her hand enthusiastically. 'And timely, too.'

Sonya looked at him, alert to an odd note in his voice. 'How so?' She feared he must be about to tell her that they would be moving back to Truro, and steeled herself not to weep, for that would be most unfair on her daughter.

'My parents have asked us to come back to live with them in Truro,' he said, confirming her worst fears.

She sucked in a breath, holding herself rigid. 'I see.'

'But we said no,' Yvonne reassured her, and gave her an affectionate kiss on the cheek as Sonya sagged with relief. 'We love living here with you, dear Mother. How could we leave you?'

'And ... and Walter doesn't mind staying here?' Sonya asked faintly.

'He was the one who said no to her first,' Patrick said,

laughing at her shocked expression. 'While we were still working out a way to decline gracefully, Walter up and said, *"No thanks, Granny Truro, you're smashing, but I likes being with Granny St Ives the best."*'

Sonya stuffed a fist in her mouth to prevent herself from sobbing with joy. 'He … he did? Oh, dear little boy.' She moaned. 'But poor Granny Truro. I mean, Mrs Fairweather. How did your mother take it?'

'Not in the best humour, as you can imagine,' Patrick said frankly. 'But she hasn't been very friendly to my wife and son in my absence, so she has nobody but herself to blame. However, I said we would visit as often as possible, and also promised a long stay with them next Christmas, once the twins have been born.'

'Of course,' Sonya said, relieved that he had not parted from his parents on an argument.

'Though it seems I'll have to go on my own with Walter at Christmas,' Yvonne chipped in, looking dispirited, 'unless this horrid war is finally over by then.'

'We're doing our level best to make sure it is, darling.' Seeing Sonya's incomprehension, Patrick gave her a wry smile. 'My shoulder's almost fixed. I'm to attend a medical next week, and if I'm given the green light, it'll be back to active duty for me.'

'Oh dear.'

He shook his head at her, grinning broadly now. 'Don't want to leave Yvonne and Walter, obviously, but I'm itching to get back to HQ. Though the doc says he may have to put me down for ground work. Training new pilots, and all that. Apparently, the old shoulder joint may never be quite the thing again, and I won't be up to scratch for flight

343

duties.' He rolled his wounded shoulder with a wince, as though demonstrating what he meant. 'But at least I'll still be doing my bit.'

Sonya nodded and glanced at her daughter. 'And you, Yvonne? What about your own parents? Your … other mother, I mean?'

'Dearest Mother,' Yvonne said, hugging her again, 'you're always doing yourself down. Walter adores you, that's clear. And I'm happier than I've ever been, and it's all because of finding you again. I love my adopted mother and will write to her tomorrow and suggest a long visit next summer, always assuming they can find somewhere for us to stay nearby, for we'll be a family of five by then.' She put a hand to her back again, grimacing. 'Trust me to fall pregnant with twins.'

'Back rub, darling?' Patrick suggested gently.

Yvonne smiled at him, her expression softening. 'Oh, yes, please. How good you are to me.'

Discreetly, Sonya left the young couple to it, taking her cup of tea to her bedroom. She sat by her bedroom window and looked out over the windswept cliffs of Carbis Bay, a view so familiar and dear to her heart, it had felt like the cruellest wrench imaginable that she might have to abandon it one day in order to remain with her new family.

Now, she would never have to leave this place. She smiled and wept a little as she sipped her tea. 'God bless you, Babs,' she whispered. And the setting sun twinkled on the choppy waters of the Atlantic under a sky that seemed to go on forever.

CHAPTER THIRTY-TWO

Wandering wearily out of the hospital after work one afternoon, Lily was shocked to find Tristan waiting for her, seated on a low wall, his stick leaning against his thigh. 'What are you doing here?' she demanded, shielding her eyes against the bright August sunshine as she hurried towards him. 'Is something wrong?'

Tristan gave her a lazy smile. 'Don't be daft,' he said, beaming at her. Barely using his stick for support these days, her husband got up and gave her a kiss. 'I've just finished work myself. It's such a lovely day, I thought we could take a little walk along the harbourside.'

'What a nice idea. I'd enjoy that,' she said, linking her arm with his. 'What would you like for tea?' she asked as they walked.

'How about more of that tasty mackerel you do so well? Fried in a pan, and served with bread and butter, and maybe a little cheddar cheese, if we have any in the house.'

'All right,' she agreed cheerfully. 'We've a small block of

cheese in the pantry. And we'll stop by the fishmonger's on our way back.'

But when they reached the fishmonger's, with its impressive displays of fish with shining scales and staring eyes, Lily stopped short in the doorway, and put a hand to her mouth.

'Ugh,' she exclaimed in sudden disgust, and backed away. 'What a dreadful smell. I'm sorry, I can't bear to go in there. Perhaps you should get the fish this time.' She rummaged in her handbag for the ration book and handed it to him. 'Do you mind?'

Tristan looked at her, worried. But he nodded. 'Of course. I'll buy the fish. You wait over there,' he told her patiently, and went into the shop.

By the time he came out, a parcel of fish wrapped in paper under his arm, the feeling of queasiness had passed and Lily was feeling quite foolish. She didn't know what had come over her. She usually enjoyed the smell of the fishmonger's, even if it was quite pungent.

'I'm sorry about that,' she said apologetically. 'Maybe it's this heat. You must think me a complete idiot.'

'Not at all,' he reassured her, handing her the fish parcel. 'Here you go. Two large fillets of mackerel. That should make a tasty meal.'

Lily took the fish and again felt her stomach heave. Trembling now, and utterly baffled, she handed the parcel back to him and shook her head. 'Strewth, I don't know what's wrong with me today. I can't bear the smell.'

'You must be sickening for something.' Tristan still looked concerned. 'Perhaps you should stay home tomorrow and not work.'

'Gawd, no,' Lily said quickly, horrified. 'I'm not sick. It's just the smell of this fish… Though it's the oddest thing. Because I feel fine otherwise.' She stopped dead in the middle of the street, staring at nothing.

Tristan was frowning. 'Lily? What is it?'

Lily's mind was in a whirl. Her breathing quickened and she put a hand to her chest, feeling the deep thud of her heart. Was it possible?

'What are you thinking?' Tristan pressed her. 'Talk to me, Lily.'

But she shook her head. 'Let's get home,' she told him and began to walk again, pushing the thought aside as ridiculous. 'Honestly, I'm fine. Spouting nonsense as usual. Don't mind me.'

He wasn't satisfied but to her relief he let it go.

Back at the cottage, she asked Tristan to put the fish on the side, ready for frying. But she was fretting, for she had no idea how shc would cope with the smell of preparing it.

Upstairs, she changed out of her uniform and sat at her dressing table, brushing her hair, studying her pale complexion. She looked a little peaky, it was true. Washed-out, in fact. And she had been feeling so tired lately, as though she could sleep for a week. Reaching under her mattress, she took out her journal. Hurriedly flicking back through its pages, she counted on her fingers … and gasped, checking and re-checking before shutting the book in astonished silence. Then she looked at herself in the mirror again.

'Well, my girl,' she whispered to her own reflection, 'you've got what you wanted. Now let's hope he's as pleased as you are.'

Going downstairs, she found Tristan cleaning the mackerel while the frying pan heated gently on the stove.

Tristan laid each fillet in the spitting pan, washed his hands, and turned with a smile as he realised she had come down. Then he stopped and his smile faded, seeing her expression.

'Lily?'

'Oh, Lord…' Taking a deep breath, she went to him and laid her head on his chest. His arms came around her automatically and she felt safe in that warm circle. Safe enough to face an uncertain new future with him by her side. 'It's nothing. I just need a moment to get used to the idea, that's all.'

'What idea?' He sounded baffled.

She told him simply, 'I'm late with my monthlies. And then there's the queasy sensation… It wasn't the fish, it was me.'

'I beg your pardon?'

'Goodness, do I need to bloomin' spell it out?' With a sigh, Lily explained, 'I'm in the family way.' When he still stared down at her, his face blank, she added gently, 'I'm pregnant. You're going to be a father, Tris.' And then laughed when he picked her up and swung her again, whooping. 'Well, thank goodness you're not unhappy about it. Because it would be a bit late to put that genie back in the bottle.'

'I'm going to be a dad? For real?'

'There's no backing out now,' she agreed, smiling shyly as he kissed her. 'Though it's early days yet. So we mustn't say a word until we're sure, all right?'

'*Sure*?' he echoed, frowning.

'Early pregnancies don't always take, love. Best not count our chickens until they're hatched.'

'Understood.' Tristan drew her close. 'I love you, Lily, whatever happens. And I'm going to take extra special care of you now.' He drew out a chair and gestured to her to sit down, even though he was the one with the bad leg, not her. 'Come on, you've had a long day. You need to rest.'

Lily sat down, grinning. 'Oh, I could grow to like this. I think you'll make a fine father, Tristan Minear.' And then she grimaced at the smell and pointed behind him, gasping, 'The mackerel... They're burning! Oh, not again.'

'Oops,' he said.

'I wish I could tell my dad.' Lily thought of her father and the danger he might in, somewhere far away behind enemy lines.

Tris brought her a plate of very crispy, well-done mackerel, with two slices of bread and butter. At least they smelt less fishy like that, Lily thought with gratitude, her appetite returning as she picked up her knife and fork.

'He'll find out when he gets back,' he said firmly, and began to pour the tea for them both.

A few days later, Lily met Mary Stannard and Rose Lanyon for tea and cakes at a busy café near the waterside in St Ives. It was the first time the three of them had been off work at the same time, though it helped that Mary wasn't working during the school holidays and Rose was too heavily pregnant to do much besides knit and do the gardening. As for Lily, it was hard to swallow her queasiness at first but she soon perked up at the sight of the tasty iced sponges and cream cakes on offer from the waitress in her frilled white cap and apron. She had not been out to a café in ages and was determined to have a good time.

'I told you we'd manage to meet up one day for tea and cake, didn't I?' Lily told Mary, grinning.

'You did, indeed. Though it's taken long enough.'

'And you'd better make the most of it,' Rose chipped in, 'because who knows when we'll manage another get-together, especially with money the way it is? This jaunt of mine is breaking the bank.'

'But at least you've got an excuse,' Mary pointed out. 'It's your birthday.'

'Yes, happy birthday, Rose,' Lily said quickly.

'Thank you. Which is why I'm treating myself to *two* slices of cake today,' Rose told them, a twinkle in those usually stern eyes. 'One for me, and one for Baby.'

'Quite right too,' Mary said, chuckling. 'I believe my mum was the same when she had me. That's where she got those impressive hips.'

Lily smiled to herself, thinking of her little secret.

'What's that for, madam?' Rose demanded, having spotted her smirk. 'You think I'm being greedy, admit it. But I can tell you, eating for two is a serious business.'

Lily blushed and stammered, 'No, honestly, I—'

'You don't need to tell Lily that,' Mary interrupted, examining her reflection in the curved surface of a silver spoon. 'She is your midwife, after all.'

'I know that, silly. I was joking, wasn't I?' Rose flicked back her red hair and rubbed her conspicuously rounded tummy, her eyes narrowed on Lily's face. 'But come on, Lily, I can see you're holding back on us. What is it you're not saying?'

To Lily's immense relief, at that moment she saw Sonya Thorpe walk past the café, holding her little grandson's hand and deep in conversation with her daughter Yvonne. 'Oh, look,' she exclaimed with a gasp, jumping up so fast the cups rattled in their saucers, 'it's Yvonne … I mean, Mrs Fairweather. Excuse me a minute, I must say hello.' She hurried to the door, waving frantically. 'Coo-ee!'

Miss Thorpe and Mrs Fairweather both turned, staring at her in astonishment. The heat in Lily's cheeks deepened. But at least she had managed to avoid being put on the spot about her little secret. For the time being, anyway.

'Erm, hello,' she said to Yvonne, who was looking very pregnant these days, 'I'm having a spot of tea and cakes in the café here with some friends. You know Rose and Mary, I think. In fact, you and Rose are due only a few weeks apart.' She pointed them out through the net-hung café window, and then was suddenly struck by inspiration. 'I don't suppose you'd care to join us?'

'I'd love to,' Yvonne said promptly, and glanced at her mother. 'Do you mind?'

'Not at all,' Sonya said with a smile, and nodded to Lily. 'Hello again, good to see you. You're looking well.'

That would be her rosy cheeks, Lily thought, embarrassed, but smiled in return. 'Hello.' She bent to speak to Walter, whose big eyes were studying her frankly. 'I remember you.'

She wondered if her own baby would be a boy or a girl, and her heart missed a beat at the unfamiliar reminder that she was pregnant too. Gosh, what a thought. That one day she would be walking along this street, holding a child's hand…

They all went back inside the café, where Yvonne quickly disclosed that her husband had returned to active duty, his wound having healed. 'But he's not flying anymore, thankfully,' she admitted, looking a little guilty. 'He was dashed when they refused him his wings. But he'll be training pilots instead.'

'We're all happy he won't be flying raids against the enemy,' Sonya said. 'With Yvonne expecting twins, he'll soon be the father of three.'

'Twins means *two* babies,' Walter announced, eyeing his mother's bump uncertainly.

Sonya whispered over his head, 'He's only recently been told, poor boy. I think it's come as a shock.'

'Though it's not certain that it's twins,' Yvonne said quickly. 'Lily explained it all to me. The size makes it more likely to be twins, but we might not know for sure until… Well, until they pop out!'

'Goodness.' Mary looked intrigued. 'So it might just be…'

'Goliath,' Yvonne said with a self-conscious grin, 'yes.'

They all giggled.

But Lily soon sobered, her breath catching as she recalled Tristan's joy when she told him about the baby. She knew only too well that some pregnancies ended in tragedy in the first few months and didn't want him to be disappointed.

'There's that faraway look again,' Rose observed, watching her with that uncomfortably intent gaze she remembered from her days on the ward. 'C'mon on, Lily, spill the beans. What dark secret are you hiding under that serious frown?'

Thankfully, Lily was saved from having to answer, for at that moment Rose herself exclaimed, 'Lewis! I say, what on earth?' And they all turned to see her husband enter the café, with Jimmy beside him, a bored expression on the boy's face.

Dr Lewis came towards them apologetically. 'Happy birthday, darling,' he said, and bent to kiss Rose on the cheek. 'I'm sorry, I know I promised that I'd look after Jimmy while you got together with the ladies, but there's been an emergency. Dr Penrose has gone down with a bug, and I'm needed at the hospital sharpish.' He nodded to the boy behind him, who was staring at the cake trolley. 'I know how you feel about him running wild, so I've brought him to you.'

Rose laughed. 'No, it's fine. You go to work, Lewis. This is a good opportunity to get Jimmy measured for some new clothes for the coming term. I brought my ration book, so we might as well head off straightaway.' She held out a hand to the boy. 'Come along, Jimmy. You can have cake at home. Birthday tea tonight, remember?'

Jimmy grinned, looking happier.

Yvonne jumped up too, saying, 'Walter's legs are sprouting at a rate of knots and I could do with finding him a new pair of short trousers, maybe from the second-hand box. No point buying new when they grow so quickly, is there?' She gave Rose a look of entreaty. 'May the two of us tag along? I hope that won't be a bore for you.'

'No, I'd be glad of the company.' Rose glanced round at her husband. 'I thought you were in a hurry to get to the hospital? Why are you still standing there?'

'I have no idea,' Dr Lewis said with a laugh, and strode off, waving his hand in the air. 'Goodbye, all. See you at home, Rose, Jimmy.'

Rose watched him go, shaking her head. 'That man... He'd forget his head if it wasn't screwed on. Still, he's a good doctor and a lovely husband too,' she added with an indulgent smile.

Grabbing her handbag, Yvonne turned to Sonya. 'Shall I call back for you in half an hour, Mother? I know how bored you get hanging around when Walter and I are shopping.'

'Yes, dearest,' Sonya said, looking rather relieved that she wasn't required to tag along too. 'I'll happily wait. But do take your time.'

Rose and Yvonne gathered their things and left the café with the boys after pressing a handful of coins on Sonya to pay for their refreshments. Lily watched them go with relief in her heart, feeling sure the dangerous moment had passed. But she was wrong...

'Now, Lily,' her friend Mary pressed her, leaning forward with an eager smile, 'I know Rose is right and you have some secret you haven't told us. Don't think you'll get away with it just because Rose has left. Because I want to know too, and I'm not budging until you confess everything.'

'Oh, but not if it makes poor Lily uncomfortable,' Sonya said quickly, her dark eyes sympathetic.

With both her friends watching her so kindly, though also curiously, Lily knew she could not keep her important news to herself any longer. She was bursting with it anyway. Blushing, she admitted softly, 'Tristan and I have just found out that... Well, the fact is, I'm going to be a mother myself.'

'I knew it!' Mary clapped her hands, and heads turned in the busy café, much to Lily's embarrassment. 'How marvellous. Congratulations!'

'Hush,' Lily whispered, mortified.

Quickly, Sonya lifted a hand and summoned the waitress with a friendly smile. 'Excuse me, could we have more hot water to freshen the pot? And another toasted teacake, please? Thank you so much.'

It was a good ruse. By the time she'd finished ordering, the customers around them had lost interest. But Lily rolled her eyes at Mary. 'Don't go shouting it all over the place, for gawd's sake. Only me and Tristan know, and now you and Sonya. It's early days, anything could happen.' Even saying that made her heart thud, but she tried to smile. 'No point making an announcement. Not when there might not be anything to announce.'

'I quite understand,' Sonya said, patting her hand. 'All the same, congratulations. You must be over the moon.'

'Sorry, Lily,' Mary said, herself a little red in the face. 'I got carried away. I didn't mean to upset you. Mum's the word, of course.' Her earnest gaze searched Lily's face. 'How has Tristan taken it? Is he pleased? It barely seems any time at all since you two were married.' Then she clapped her hands to her cheeks, and said in a horrified tone, 'Oops, there I go again. Me and my big mouth. I didn't mean to suggest… Oh, I'm going to shut up now.'

Her friend was so genuinely contrite that Lily smiled and shook her head. 'It don't matter, love. Anyway, you're spot on. We did mean to wait until after the war. But things don't always work out the way you want, do they?'

Sonya nodded sagely. 'The two of you are in love. Why wait? Life is too short, anyway. You might as well try to grab whatever happiness you can…' Her voice tailing off, the older woman looked away from them, out of the café window, and Lily felt sure she must be thinking back to her own past, and her love lost in the Great War. Yvonne had let drop a few fascinating facts about her mother's past during her clinic visit, and it had all seemed rather romantic to Lily's mind. Yet it must have been awful for Sonya at the time, falling pregnant without a husband to support her. It was hard enough being in the family way as a married woman, she thought.

'Anyway, it's still a secret, so keep it under your hats for now,' Lily told them anxiously.

'I won't say a word to anyone. Cross my heart and hope to die,' Mary promised devoutly. She picked up a cream cake and began to eat it, not very daintily, and then licked her sticky fingers afterwards. 'Mmm, that was delicious.'

Lily watched her, amused. 'How did your mum enjoy her surprise birthday party? You never did tell us about it.'

'Oh, don't get me started. If Rita wasn't my mother, I would have strangled her years ago.' Mary bit her lip and then shook her head, laughing. 'No, that's not true. She's a tricky old bird, my mum. Makes me want to scream sometimes. But I love her to bits.'

'Oh dear,' Sonya said, her thin brows arched. 'It sounds as though the party didn't go terribly well.'

'In some ways, it went better than anyone could have predicted,' Mary said, rather mysteriously, but didn't elaborate. Instead, she took a noisy slurp of tea and then sighed rapturously. 'Isn't life strange? Well, you might as well know now, because I have these to hand out.' Reaching for her handbag, Mary produced two small rectangles of card, one for each of them. 'I hope you'll come. It would be wonderful to have you there.'

Baffled, Lily read the handwritten invitation she'd been given, and gave a cry of delight. 'You and Dick are getting married?'

Now it was Mary's turn to say, 'Hush!' and glance about the café in hot-cheeked embarrassment. 'We don't want a fuss. It's just family and a few friends. I'm sorry the card is handwritten. We're trying to save money. And I'd rather not make a big song and dance about it, because you know what some people are like when it comes to married women working.'

'Old-fashioned twaddle,' Sonya said dismissively. 'Congratulations. My goodness, it seems to be a day for wonderful news, doesn't it?'

'They can't sack you at the school,' Lily pointed out. 'They're desperate for teachers. They'll have to keep you on, so I wouldn't worry.' She grinned. 'And yes, congratulations. I hope you and Dick will be very happy together.'

'I'm sure we will too. We suit awfully well.' But Mary's smile faded. 'What's going to happen after the war, though? For married women who want to keep working, I mean.' She sighed. 'Always assuming our side wins.'

The three women all looked at each other in dismayed silence, for none of them had an easy answer to that question, as Lily knew only too well. Apart from a few select occupations, such as helping their husbands in a privately owned business such as a shop or on a farm, married women did not work, that was understood. Except in wartime, of course, when there were no men around to perform the jobs that kept society running.

'Apparently,' Mary added in a lowered voice, leaning forward in a conspiratorial way, 'there's a campaign afoot to allow married women to be schoolteachers. Once the war's over, I mean.'

'Good luck with that,' Lily said dryly. She knew only too

well how hostile people could be towards married women in the workplace. 'If it's anything like nursing, these school boards will be sticklers for the rules.'

Mary's face grew serious. 'I know. It's going to be an uphill battle. But Dick says things have to change, and I agree with him.'

'Quite right.' Sonya put down her cup, seeming deeply interested in this conversation. 'When I was your age, women had much more freedom because of the Great War. We all thought it was the start of a new age for women's liberation. But as soon as the war was over, all our freedoms were taken away, and life went back to how it had been before.' She shook her head, her expression grave. 'It can't be allowed to happen again.'

Lily admired her determination and Mary's fighting spirit. But she feared they were a long way from persuading men to share their jobs with women.

'Right now,' Lily said, helping herself to a cold, buttered crumpet, 'I'd be glad just to have this war over and done with, and all my family safe and sound.'

'Hear, hear,' Mary agreed.

Looking flustered, the waitress arrived with extra hot water for the teapot and a large, toasted teacake, as ordered.

Sonya smiled, replenishing the pot. 'I think we should all raise a glass to that wonderful hope. Even if it's only tea we're drinking, and not Champagne.' After pouring them all a little fresh tea, she picked up her china cup and said solemnly, 'To Britain and her allies winning this war!' And Mary and Lily drank too, echoing her toast.

CHAPTER THIRTY-THREE

St Ives, Cornwall, late August 1943

Mary could not believe her big day had come at last. The past few weeks had been an exciting and exhausting whirl of activity, making sure everything would be ready for the wedding. Her mum had baked a cake, though she'd had to ask a few neighbours to chip in some dried fruit, and there hadn't been enough sugar in the whole street to make icing, so Cynthia had donated a thick white ribbon to wrap around the cake instead. Mary had always hoped for a lovely white silk wedding dress when her time came, but rationing made that impossible, so she'd opted to wear one of her old cream dresses instead, jazzed up with lacy frills to the collar and cuffs, and the hem taken up to be more fashionable.

Besides, she thought, critically studying her reflection in the full-length mirror in her mother's bedroom on the morning of her wedding, she didn't look half bad. The frills were quite fetching, and she had borrowed a pair of posh shoes from her fellow midwife, Katie. Plus, that morning, her mum had dressed her hair for the wedding, weaving tiny paper flowers into a braided headband that now adorned her dark curls, and Mary fancied that even a professional hairdresser could not have done a more bang-up job.

The door opened after a perfunctory knock and her mum stood in the doorway, her hands clasped together as she took her first look at her daughter in her wedding dress. 'Oh love,' Rita exclaimed breathlessly, 'you are an absolute vision.'

'I don't know about that.' Mary turned to fiddle with the broad belt at her waist, suddenly unsure of herself. 'Well, it will have to do. Maybe Dick will have taken his spectacles off and won't be able to see me that well.'

'What on earth are you talking about?' Her mother was rolling her eyes. 'Don't you dare say things like that. You are the most beautiful girl in the world. Hasn't your father told you often enough?'

'Yes, Dad's a good fibber.' Mary grinned. 'Luckily, Dick is cut from much the same cloth and always very complimentary, even when I've been out in the wind and look like a scarecrow. I do love him for that.'

She glanced rather defiantly at her mother, since Rita had not been entirely happy about her choice of bridegroom in the beginning. But her mother said nothing, merely checking her own reflection in the mirror, and fussing with her smooth waves, which she had styled to fall across her forehead.

'We both look very glamorous,' Rita said firmly, and then caught her daughter's eye and laughed. 'Come on, love, it's time you were on your way. You don't want to be late to your own wedding.'

'Hang on,' Mary said, holding her back. 'Mum, I just want to say … I know we haven't always seen eye to eye, but all the things you've done for me, I really appreciate them. You're the best mum ever.'

Her mother gawped, and then blushed. 'Well…' She gave a little laugh. 'Thank you, Mary. And I'm sorry I made such a fuss over Dick. I was wrong about him. He'll make you a fine husband.'

And they hugged.

Hurrying down the stairs after her mum, Mary blinked in surprise when she saw what her father in the hall was holding out to her. 'Oh Dad, you didn't need to… That must have cost a fortune.'

Her dad handed her a gorgeous bouquet of white silk roses on green fern. 'No expense spared for my little girl. Besides, I managed to get a deal.' Harold gave her a wink, for he was good at getting stuff on the black market that you couldn't get legitimately with a ration book. He looked her up and down, his face wreathed in smiles. 'You look stunning, love. Dick's a lucky man. I hope the two of you will be very happy together.'

Struck by a flood of emotion, Mary's vision swam. 'Oh, for goodness' sake, not tears, not now…' she said in a cracked voice.

Hurriedly, Rita drew a hanky out of her bag and dabbed at Mary's make-up, soon fixing her up. 'There, darling,' she said, and gave Mary a reassuring smile. 'All perfect again. But no more crying. Now, better hurry up. Lord, look at the time!' She flung the front door open. 'Everyone will be at the church by now and wondering where you are.'

Ushering Mary out to the car, her father exclaimed, 'Don't be daft, Rita. It's a bride's prerogative to keep everyone waiting.' He climbed into the car beside her, leaving her mother and Pip, along with a few of their neighbours, to hurry down to the church on foot.

'It's only a short walk to the church. I don't know why you bothered hiring a car to take me in all this style,' Mary said, watching the elderly, dark-suited driver start the engine. 'Surely it's a waste of petrol.'

In truth though, she was impressed with the sleek lines of the black Rover that had arrived to convey her to the wedding. She knew Dick would be fascinated too, for the car would later carry them both to the wedding reception as well. 'Though I love it,' she added quickly, seeing her father's expression. 'Especially the chauffeur.'

'He's a friend of mine from work,' his dad whispered in her ear. 'It was very good of him to lend us the car. He helped us out with the petrol coupons too. Besides, you only get married once. So why not push the boat out?'

The car pulled away and began its slow drive to the church, passing in a circuitous way through the streets of St Ives, drawing everyone's attention. Mary found herself waving occasionally to people in the streets who had stopped to stare and point at the smart black car with the bride sitting inside, dressed to the nines like a princess.

'Oh, Dad, thank you.' Mary fought back tears again, clutching her father's hand. 'This is the best day of my life.'

She had never been so happy in all her born days.

* * *

The wedding ceremony passed in a blur. Afterwards, what Mary remembered most was the light pouring through the church windows, and the faces of the people watching her she walked slowly up the aisle on her father's arm, and Dick's face, his gaze locked with hers, as they exchanged vows. Then the bells pealing out as they left church together and climbed into the waiting car under a rain of rice, laughing and clutching each other. In the back of the car, Dick held her tight and whispered, 'I love you, Mrs Jeffries,' in her ear, which sounded perfectly right and yet somehow impossible.

At the reception in the popular Star Inn, Mary lost count of the number of friends who greeted her with a hug or kiss, and often a small gift too. Her mother carefully took all the wedding gifts away to a side table for safekeeping, which Mary appreciated, for she was dazed by that stage.

She was bowled over by how handsome the room looked, given how little money they'd been able to spare on the wedding arrangements. Arranged around a stunning floral centrepiece were dozens of delicate, thinly sliced, paste and cucumber sandwiches provided by the landlady, and dainty cakes made by one of Mary's cousins, plus the wedding cake decorated with a smart white bow.

Lily and Tristan were there from the start, helping Mary's mother lay out the food and plates, and welcome the wedding guests.

Mary spent some time chatting to Lily and thanking her for all of her hard work. 'You are such a good friend, Lily. Especially given how busy you are at work, and with Tristan to care for too.'

'Don't be silly,' Lily told her, beaming. 'I told you I'd help, and I meant it. It was just a question of making sure I could rearrange the rota. Besides, these days it's more Tristan looking after me, not the other way around.'

'All the same, I really appreciate it.' Mary hugged her, close to tears again, though she didn't know why. 'Everyone's been so lovely. I've had the best day of my life.'

Lily laughed. 'I know exactly what you mean. Overwhelming, isn't it? I admit, I felt the same on my wedding day. It was like being in a dream.'

'Exactly.' Mary gave a happy sigh. 'It's just marvellous. I only wish Eva could have been here. But it is rather a long way to come.'

A letter had belatedly arrived from Eva in response to the wedding invitation, apologising and blaming petrol rationing for their inability to attend. Mary had been sad not to see her old friend again, but she knew fuel rationing was vital for the war effort too. Also, there was another excellent reason Eva had not been able to attend...

'However,' she added in a whisper, for Lily's ears only, 'she did give me some rather special news in her letter, which could explain why she didn't feel able to travel down to Cornwall for the wedding.' When Lily looked at her in surprise, she blurted out, 'Eva's expecting a baby!'

'Oh, that's bloomin' marvellous!' Lily's face split in a broad grin. They hugged each other, both overjoyed by the news. 'I bet Max is over the moon about it, especially when it seemed like he'd never walk again after that awful bombing in London. Now he's going to be a father...' Lily rushed off to find Tristan and tell him the glad tidings.

A group of nurses from Symmonds Hall had also turned out for the celebration, and Sonya and Yvonne Fairweather were there too, though young Walter had apparently been left in the care of Teresa at the orphanage that evening.

Someone had arranged for Stuart Shrubsole, local fiddler, to play at the reception, and soon everyone was stamping their feet and clapping along to one of his lively tunes.

Dick, meanwhile, was standing with his mother and father, catching up on family news. His big brother Percy had sent a letter that had arrived only that morning, congratulating Dick on his wedding and letting the family know, over several sheets, how he was getting on in the fight against Germany. It was a miracle that he'd been able to write at all, Dick had explained, for being in the Navy, his brother rarely had an opportunity to post a letter.

Rose was there with young Jimmy, who was playing cards with Pip at a corner table. She had brought Mary and Dick a delightful coffee pot as a gift, something Mary had never seen before, for her mother only ever drank tea. 'I love coffee,' Rose confided in her, 'so I hope you'll soon be converted too.'

Mary doubted it but thanked her anyway. 'It looks gorgeous and I'll definitely give it a try,' she assured her friend.

Dr Lewis turned up halfway through the party, the doctor having been delayed by a gentleman having a heart attack down on the harbourside. He had stayed with him until the patient, who had thankfully survived, had been taken to the hospital by ambulance. On arriving, he came over at once to apologise, but Mary said straight out that it didn't matter and at least the gentleman sounded as though he was on the road to recovery.

After a lull in the music, Stuart Shrubsole, a bearded man with ginger hair and twinkling blue eyes, struck up again on his fiddle.

While Mary was tapping her foot to the tune, Dick appeared out of nowhere. 'Come along, Mrs Jeffries,' he called merrily, 'shake a leg.' Then he slipped an arm about her waist and drew her, protesting, into a dance.

Mary was not much of a dancer, but Dick didn't seem to mind her clumsiness, whirling her around in any old fashion. She clung to him, laughing and breathless as the two of them spun around the crowded upstairs room at the inn. Everyone was clapping and calling out to them, but she only had eyes for her new husband. After their wedding night, they would be living with her parents until they could afford a place of their own. But for tonight Dick had booked a room at a posh hotel overlooking the harbour, and she couldn't wait to be alone with him at last...

Towards the end of the reception, Mary noticed a young woman crossing the room. She was slender and fair-haired, and walked with a great deal of grace, gazing at the guests with an intent expression.

Not recognising her, Mary went up to the girl with a shy smile and said, 'Hello, I'm Mary. Are you looking for somebody in particular?' She thought perhaps the young woman was searching for a friend or relative who had come to the party.

But to her amazement, the newcomer nodded and said,

'I'm looking for Pip.' She had an East End accent. 'Do you know where I can find him?'

'Pip? Why do you want to speak to him?'

'Because I'm his sister, ain't I?' the young woman said, again astonishing Mary, and then smiled, showing bad teeth. 'His half-sister, that is. We shared a dad. Only he got blown up by the Hun, God rest his soul.'

'My goodness.' Looking hurriedly around for her mother, Mary finally located her sitting with Pip and Jimmy at the corner table. The two boys had been enjoying a feast with the leftovers from the reception meal. 'You'd better come with me.'

The young woman followed her, but said apologetically, 'Is this your wedding do? Sorry to be bargin' in like this. It's urgent, or I wouldn't have come. I had your address off the placement officer, so I went to your mum and dad's house and one of the neighbours told me where to find you.'

Mary did not know what to say to that, unsure what the young woman wanted with Pip. But she felt a sense of foreboding. 'Mum,' she said, bending to her mother to whisper in her ear, 'this girl says she's Pip's half-sister and wants to speak to him.'

'Oh, is that so?' her mother began, studying the young woman with a steely eye.

But Pip, glancing up at that moment, spotted the girl and jumped to his feet, his face cracking in a huge smile. 'Tess? What are you doing 'ere?' He threw his arms about the young woman. 'Oh, I've missed yer.'

Tess laughed, hugging him back and ruffling his hair. 'I've missed you too, you little rascal. Look, I've come to take you home with me, if you'd like that.'

At this, Rita's eyes widened in shock. She stood, coldly introducing herself. 'I'm in charge of this boy,' she pointed out, putting on her poshest voice. 'You can't just take him away. Not without proper permission. It wouldn't be legal.'

'All right, Missus,' Tess said, looking her up and up with obvious disdain, 'no need to get your knickers in a twist. I was just asking. And let's see what the boy says first, shall we?' She gave Pip a wink. 'I've married a soldier, Pip. Got meself a nice house at the barracks. It's not London, but near enough. Thought you might want to kip wiv family instead of strangers. I can take you back on the train tomorrow. I've got the money for it and everything. How about it?'

Mary looked at Pip anxiously. But she needn't have worried.

The boy was shaking his head, regret in his face. 'Sorry, Tess, that's kind of yer. But I like it 'ere. Mrs Stannard, she's...' He reddened, and then blurted out, 'She's like me mum now.'

His half-sister stared at him, crestfallen. 'But she ain't blood, like me.' She tapped herself on the chest. 'She ain't family. All the others is dead, Pip. We ain't got nobody else.'

'I know, and I said I was sorry, didn't I? But I gotta look after meself now, and Mr and Mrs Stannard are good uns.' Pip looked up at her, deeply uncomfortable, tears shining in his eyes. ''Ere, why not give us y-your address?' he stammered. 'Maybe I can visit one day.' When she began to turn away, he pulled out a chair for her, his look awkward but affectionate. 'Don't go yet, eh? I got so much to tell you.'

Tess chewed on her lip, but after a moment's indecision agreed to sit down with her brother. The two of them chatted over a plate of sandwiches while Rita and Cynthia organised the clean-up together, keeping a watchful eye on them, and Mary went to find Dick and tell him what had happened.

'Poor boy,' he said, watching the pair from across the room. 'Still, your mum must be relieved he doesn't want to leave. She's taken quite a shine to the lad.'

'We're all very fond of him.' Mary felt sorry for the girl though. 'I expect she's lonely, that's all. She's married a soldier, she says, though she barely looks old enough to be out of school. Her husband probably had to leave as soon as the ring was on her finger.'

'Yes, but it's best not to interrupt Pip's schooling by moving him again. Especially now he's started to settle down and make friends here in St Ives.'

Mary nodded, and then reached up to kiss him on the lips. Just a quick peck, since they were still in company. 'Isn't it time to leave yet?' she whispered.

'Just about,' he agreed.

'We don't want to risk being out after dark.'

'Definitely not.'

'I'll go and tell Mum and Dad, then.' She had butterflies in her tummy at the thought of their wedding night, but his lazy smile reassured her. 'Mum wants us to take some cake, by the way.'

'Good Lord,' he said blankly. 'Well, I'd better say good-night to my own mother and father. Meet you at the door.'

* * *

Ten minutes later, covered in rice all over again by Pip and Jimmy, cheered on their way by the last remaining guests, and carrying two large pieces of wedding cake wrapped in brown paper, 'just in case you get peckish,' Mary and Dick, grinning at each other, walked down the cobbled lane to the posh hotel where they would spend their wedding night.

'There'd better not be an air raid tonight,' Mary said anxiously, looking up at the softly darkening sky over St Ives.

'Even if there is, my dear,' her new husband assured her, 'I don't think we'll notice.'

EPILOGUE

St Ives, Cornwall, October 1943

'Push,' Lily urged her friend, and reached out to clutch her hand. 'That's it, love. You're doing brilliantly. One more big push, now.'

With an almighty groan, Rose pushed down hard, her face bright red despite the cool October weather. Moments later, she was lying back against the pillows, her newborn son swaddled against her chest, his lusty cries filling the air. Lily checked over mother and baby, following the hospital procedure, and found both to be in excellent health, their colour good and vital signs stable.

'He's simply gorgeous,' Rose said, touching his damp curls with a tentative finger. 'And my goodness, that noise...'

'He's got a good set of lungs on him,' Lily agreed, chuckling as she put away her instruments.

The door flew open and Dr Lewis came rushing in. He was still wearing his white coat, clearly having come straight from his duties. 'I'm so sorry, I tried to get here as fast as I could.' He bent over his wife and kissed her on the cheek, and then his gaze dropped to the baby in his arms. He looked stunned. 'Good God, you did it. I … I don't know what to say.' The usually unflappable doctor seemed lost for words.

'How about asking if it's a boy or a girl?' Rose asked tartly.

'Quite right, as usual, my darling. So, boy or girl? Not that I mind either way,' he admitted with a self-conscious laugh, stroking the baby's cheek.

'You have a son, Lewis,' his wife told him softly.

'A boy? Well, by all that's marvellous…' Dr Lewis choked up, his eyes filling with tears, and he dragged at his tie as though it was suddenly too tight. 'I really did try to get here in time. I'm ever so sorry, Rose.'

She looked up at him and smiled. 'If I'd wanted a reliable husband, I shouldn't have married a doctor,' she told him. 'Of course I forgive you, silly. Goodness, I had Lily here with me the whole time. But I'm glad you're here now. If you'd taken any longer to arrive, I might've needed to scold you.'

Lily grinned to herself as she removed her apron, washed her hands, and prepared to hand over to Bertha, the senior midwife on duty.

But before she could slip out, the doctor called her back, 'Hang on a minute, Lily. I thought you were expecting too,' he said, and rubbed his chin. 'Shouldn't you be at home, Mrs Minear, putting your feet up?' He gave her a wink at the end, as though aware his question was impertinent.

'I've a long way to go yet with this pregnancy,' Lily said

with a laugh, shaking her head. 'Though to be honest, we're too short-staffed for me to leave yet. Maybe another month or two. Besides, I'm no dainty lady who needs to put my feet up for nine months until this baby makes his or her appearance. I'm simply too busy to stop work.'

'Good job too,' Lewis agreed. 'We need all hands on deck. I didn't mean to offend you. In fact, I'm very grateful to you for helping my wife today.'

'Yes, thank you, Lily,' Rose said with a twinkling smile. 'I'll never forget it.'

'You're both very welcome,' Lily said.

But even as she turned to leave, the door opened and Bertha was there, fastening on a new apron. 'Lily, there you are,' she said hurriedly. 'Mrs Fairweather has just come in with her mother, already been in labour several hours, and she says it may be twins.' Her gaze went past Lily to Dr Lewis, and she smiled with relief. 'Ah, Dr Lewis, the very man I need. Sorry to drag you away... Oh, congratulations, and to you too, Mrs Lanyon.' As Lewis came her way, her voice dropped and Bertha said more discreetly, 'We've a multiple birth on our hands here, Doctor. Twins, almost a month premature. I could do with your advice if you're available.'

Over five hours later, Lily straightened to hand Dr Lewis a second slippery baby, draped loosely in a blanket, and announced with a flush of joy, 'And it's another little girl.' She smiled up at Yvonne, who looked utterly exhausted, poor lamb. Lily added in a reassuring tone, 'Every bit as healthy as baby number one, despite being a few weeks early. What a fantastic job you've done, Yvonne. Well done.'

Dr Lewis handed baby number two to Bertha to be examined and weighed, and then turned back to Yvonne. 'Hear hear,' he agreed heartily, 'you really were quite marvellous, my dear. And don't worry about them coming early. Twins often do.' Yvonne was cuddling baby number one in her arms, who had finally stopped shrieking and was now staring up at her mother's face with curiously dark eyes. 'Any names lined up for these two little beauties?' he asked with an indulgent smile, no doubt thinking of his own newborn son.

'I sent a list of possible names to Patrick only last week,' Yvonne admitted, giving a long sigh of pleasure as her second baby was placed in her arms. She looked from one tiny, blanket-wrapped newborn to the other with the contented smile of new motherhood. 'I shall have to write again and tell him it's two girls. He was absolutely convinced it would be boys, of course. But I don't think these two would really appreciate being called Jack and Trevor, after his two favourite uncles.'

They all laughed.

Yvonne's mother, who had been there throughout her daughter's labour, was the picture of joy. Sonya had cajoled and persuaded and nudged and reassured Yvonne during her many hours of labour. Now that it was over, however, she was rubbing her eyes, smiling wearily down at her daughter and granddaughters, still on her feet despite having lost an entire night's sleep.

'Patrick is going to be a very proud father. He won't mind a bit that they're girls instead of boys,' Sonya told her daughter firmly. 'And I daresay Walter will be over the moon too. He told me the other day that he hoped the twins wouldn't be boys, as he didn't want to share his toy trains or cars with any baby brothers.'

Lily grinned. 'When my sister, Alice, was a baby, she loved playing with trains and cars. Yes, and read mostly boys' books once she got older too. Walter may have to prepare himself for sharing anyway.'

'Would you tell Mary the good news if you get the chance?' Sonya asked her. 'I'm sure she would want to know about Yvonne and the twins. And Rose and Lewis' special delivery from the stork too.'

'Of course,' Lily said, beaming, and the doctor chuckled.

'The whole of St Ives is going to know about my son by teatime,' he prophesied, 'if I have anything to do with it.'

As she said her goodbyes, adding that she would be back next day to see how they were all getting on, Lily began to droop, feeling quite exhausted herself. But a little lost sleep was worth it to have helped three new lives into the world in such dark times. And come the spring, she thought happily, it would be her turn to be a mother and understand at last what that truly meant. And perhaps by then the war would be over too. That was her hope, at any rate.

Taking one last look at the two identical babies cradled in Yvonne's loving arms, Lily smiled contentedly and set off home, just as the sun began to rise above St Ives.

Acknowledgements

Writing a novel takes place alone, sometimes late at night with a gin at the writer's elbow, but getting it onto bookshelves and into readers' hands is nearly always a collaborative effort.

Firstly, my grateful thanks as ever go to my agent, Alison Bonomi, for her kind support and advice, and everyone at LBA for their hard work on my behalf. It's been a very difficult year for me personally, but we've got through it together. Onwards and upwards!

Heartfelt thanks also to my brilliant, insightful editor, Lucy Frederick, and also to the fab Thorne Ryan, who saw this book through edits to publication. Also a big shout-out to Becci Mansell for all her hard work, also Ella Young, Elisha Lundin, Raphaella Demetris and the whole team at Avon Books. It's been fantastic working with you all on these latest adventures of the Cornish Girls.

Also, a kiss to my husband, Steve, who after more than two decades still puts up with my odd writerly behaviour without complaint (mostly), and thanks to my youngest three, Dylan, Morris and Indigo, who have probably made me thousands of cups of tea over the years, and even occasionally bacon sandwiches (which I really shouldn't have but love all the same, especially when edits are underway). I don't know how I'll cope once you've all flown the nest…

Lastly, a hug and a resounding THANK YOU to all my readers, both old and new. A book is nothing without a reader, so my biggest thanks must go to you. I hope you've enjoyed these Cornish Girls stories. Thank you, thank you, thank you!

Betty Walker x

A Q&A with Betty Walker

What made you decide to explore the theme of mother-hood in this instalment in the Cornish Girls series?

With five children myself, first giving birth aged nineteen, motherhood has been one of the recurring themes of my life. We tend to associate the qualities of love, compassion, generosity, and nurturing with motherhood. The person who is always there for you, no matter what. But it's usually more complicated than that. Personally, I see 'mothering' as a deeply creative part of all women's lives, not only reserved for those who have children, but extended with a generous spirit to beloved pets, friends, lovers, and our most precious projects. I was lucky enough to enjoy a close relationship with my own mother, who was also a writer and whose own estranged mother had left a shadow over her from childhood. So, motherhood as an institution is not always beyond reproach, and sometimes we have to salvage something 'good' from the wreckage in order to allow ourselves to love and to nurture in our turn.

Since the first three books in the Cornish Girls series explore themes of female friendship, independence and wartime courtship, turning to motherhood – and the mother-child relationship in particular – felt like a natural progression. I wanted to focus on the term 'life-giving' in these narratives, set against the backdrop of war, and how mothers and motherhood can bring out the best in us, especially in desperate times.

What was your favourite scene to write?

There's an ongoing feud between the mothers of two courting characters in the story. At one stage, there's a celebratory meal which becomes one of these classic dinner parties from hell, with both women sniping at each other across the table, and their husbands wincing, but it's all done subtly and with smiles like fixed bayonets. The two young lovers eventually sneak away to do the washing-up and leave their mothers to it. It was a hilarious scene to write, and I still chuckle, recalling some of the one-liners as each woman vies for superiority over the other. There's one clear winner by the end of the evening but I won't spoil the story by revealing who!

Did you discover any particularly interesting or surprising history when you were doing the research for *A Mother's Hope for the Cornish Girls*?

Just as the British had secret agents working undercover in Germany and enemy-occupied territories, the Germans themselves had spies embedded in British society too.

Sometimes so deeply embedded, not even their own family and closest friends would have been aware of their true identity. It's unlikely many of these spies were native Germans though, for they would have stood out too easily in British wartime society. Many were German sympathisers, people who believed in Hitler's vision of a vast German empire, while others merely wished for peace and, given Germany's undeniable military might, had chosen the side they considered more likely to win. Personally, I find it fascinating that ordinary-seeming folk in British towns and villages were secretly acting against our interests and passing information back to the enemy. Although this idea of traitors in our midst is only briefly touched upon in *A Mother's Hope for the Cornish Girls*, I'd like to develop it further in later books.

What made you hit upon Cornwall as the perfect setting for this series?

I've lived in Cornwall for many years: I met my husband while living in Tintagel and gave birth to two of my children in Truro, so I was keen to use a Cornish setting when I first considered writing wartime sagas. Then I visited the Museum of Global Communications, PK Porthcurno, which is where the transatlantic cables come in. A beautiful, idyllic, sandy beach concealing the hub of a secret underground communications base during World War II, I instantly knew Porthcurno would be a fantastic place to set my first saga. So that's where Book 1, *Wartime for The Cornish Girls*, is set … and my characters often revisit Porthcurno in later books, although the stories now largely take place in other well-known Cornish towns, such as St. Ives, Penzance and Truro.

You've written lots of books about women during World War II. What draws you to that subject?

For most women in World War II, it was a time of terrible loss, trauma and restrictions that we can barely imagine today. Yet it was also an opportunity to move beyond the traditional domestic sphere of many women's lives, rise to difficult challenges and develop new skills. Not only did these women take on male roles within society – such as the Land Girls and the all-women fire wardens unit featured in Book 3, *Courage for The Cornish Girls* – but they dared to dream of a new life for themselves after the war, when they hoped such freedoms would continue. Sadly, as we know, in most cases they didn't continue for many decades, and we still live in a deeply unequal world today. But I'm intrigued by the ambition and self-confidence these women developed through wartime necessity, and I enjoy exploring how that led them to demand more freedom during the war, both in society and from the men in their lives. And that includes fathers, some of whom found it problematic to envisage their daughters in overalls and boilersuits!

Do you plan your books before you start writing? Or do you like to see where the story takes you?

I always plan my books. When I first started writing novels, I didn't plan; I just wrote and let the story lead me to different places. Unfortunately, as I soon discovered, that nearly always ended in disaster for me. With a trail of plotless or abandoned novels behind me, I finally decided I must plan the next one. And that was when I started writing better novels. I now plan my books in 'skeleton' form first, a 2–3-page outline to get an idea of the over-arching shape of the novel and where my characters are going to end up. Once I'm happy to start writing, I normally flesh this out with a chapter-by-chapter breakdown. But over-planning can be an issue too, so I take care to stay flexible and open to alternatives. I'm always fine with changing my mind about minor plot points or character arcs, so long as I hold true to the original structure. Some writers find planning a dead bore and get along fine without it, but I prefer to have a road map of my book in front of me from day one.

Can you give us a hint as to what your next book will be about?

My next Cornish Girls novel is set in the seaside resort of Bude, North Cornwall, a stone's throw from where I live. The beautiful but rugged coastline and sandy beaches of Bude played host to hundreds of brave American Rangers during 1943-44, who had been posted there to train in secret for the Normandy landings at Pointe Du Hoc and Omaha beaches. They more or less took over the whole town, so that even today, it's often referred to humorously as the 'American invasion' of Cornwall! Stories and anec-dotes have been handed down of how the local Cornish rubbed along with the American soldiers, and we still have many prominent landmarks in Bude today to show where they lived and trained among us, so it's a writer's dream. Plus, I'll be bringing back familiar characters from my earlier books, as their wartime stories continue…

Don't miss the first three books in the
glorious Cornish Girls series...

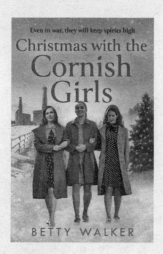

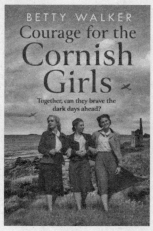

Available now in paperback, eBook
and audiobook.